The CITY
UNDERGROUND

Also by Michael Russell

The CITY UNDERGROUND

A Stefan Gillespie Novel

MICHAEL RUSSELL

CONSTABLE

CONSTABLE

First published in Great Britain in 2022 by Constable

A CIP catalogue record for this book
is available from the British Library.

ISBN: 978-1-40871-582-6 (hardback)
ISBN: 978-1-40871-583-3 (trade paperback)

Typeset in Dante by SX Composing DTP, Rayleigh, Essex
Printed and bound in Great Britain by Clays Ltd, Elcograf S.p.A.

Papers used by Constable are from well-managed forests and
other responsible sources.

Constable
An imprint of
Little, Brown Book Group
Carmelite House
50 Victoria Embankment
London EC4Y 0DZ

An Hachette UK Company
www.hachette.co.uk

www.littlebrown.co.uk

For the teachers who put whole worlds into my head:

Alf Monk
Jim De Rennes
George Worth
Christopher Tolkien

We are closed in, and the key is turned
On our uncertainty; somewhere
A man is killed, or a house burned,
Yet no clear fact to be discerned:
Come build in the empty house of the stare . . .

We had fed the heart on fantasies,
The heart's grown brutal from the fare,
More substance in our enmities
Than in our love; oh, honey bees
Come build in the empty house of the stare.

'The Stare's Nest by My Window'

W. B. Yeats

PREFACE

In the early twentieth century, after Ireland's 1916 Rising, British ruthlessness transformed a widespread, though not universal, wish for democratically achieved Home Rule into support for full independence and the violence that seemed the only way of getting it. Only in the north-east were such views in the minority among Irish people. By 1919 Republican politicians had ousted Home Rulers. The Volunteers of 1916 became the Irish Republican Army; a guerrilla war had started that would last three years. It was brutal on both sides, but nothing was more counter-productive than the brutality directed at the civilian population by British irregular forces, the Black and Tans and Auxiliaries. Despite Britain's military might, the war could not be won. The IRA could not win either; yet could not be defeated. A truce in 1921 led to a Treaty that gave twenty-six counties of Ireland a kind of independence, while six Ulster counties remained in the United Kingdom. The Irish Free State retained the British King as head of state along with other ties to Britain, many of little consequence. The Treaty was signed in London by a group of Irish leaders, including Michael Collins. The president of the would-be Irish state, Éamon de Valera, was not there. When Collins returned, de Valera rejected the Treaty. After losing the Treaty debate in Ireland's parliament, the Dáil, he and others walked out. They accepted neither partition nor ties to Britain. There were now two parties: pro-Treatyites, forming a government supported by the majority of the population, and anti-Treatyites, who refused to recognise that government. The Civil War followed.

It lasted two years and was often as nasty as the war against Britain. Michael Collins became the Free State's most prominent leader; Éamon de Valera was political leader of the anti-Treaty forces. Bloodshed on the Free State side increased when Michael Collins was ambushed and killed by the IRA. The anti-Treatyites lacked resources and support. They ended the war not by surrendering but by burying their weapons. Anti-Treaty politicians still refused to participate in government. The IRA remained a subversive organisation opposed to the Free State, sometimes violently. But times change. Éamon de Valera wearied of the wilderness. He split with his hardliners and stormed back to the political scene. By 1932 his party, Fianna Fáil, controlled the Dáil; he was leader of the country. He went on to dismantle legislative ties between Ireland and Britain and create an Irish Republic. He used the Treaty as Michael Collins said it would be used: as the freedom to achieve freedom. These events left wounds that were slow to heal. In 1941 the scars were raw, though little spoken of. They play a significant part in this story. They shape the nature of Irish neutrality in the Second World War. If most of these wounds have healed since then, not all have. The scar of partition remains, a hundred years on. The violence that this created, through much of my lifetime, has faded for the most part. But whether it is done is an open question.

PART ONE

THE SHADOW OF A GUNMAN

I watch the Red Flame fiercer glow,
The tide of War, its ebb and flow,
And see the Nations writhe and strain,
I, who my Freedom strive to gain,
The while I pray, swift fall the blow,
That lays the tyrant England low . . .
Thine aim be sure, O Germany!
This wish we send thee o'er the sea,
From Shannon fair to lordly Rhine,
The foe that fronts thee, too, is mine,
I would my troops with thine could be,
And thy Revenge, my Victory!

IRA War News, 1940

1

UPPER PEMBROKE STREET

Dublin, November 1920

The first man I killed was the easiest. I don't even know if I killed one man, or two, or maybe none. Joe Leonard was there with me, firing too. The Tommies were a long way off. But between us, one way or another, we killed two. And I wanted to do it. Perhaps I needed to. When we ran that day, we were both laughing. I remember that laughter. I remember a feeling that was close to joy.

I wasn't there in the Rising. Most of the other Volunteers I knew were. I was too young. My father wouldn't let me go into Dublin that day in 1916. And when I eventually did get into the city it was all over, bar the shooting. Hope and pride became pride and fury. I felt I had something to make up for when I finally joined the Volunteers. Nobody said I'd to be blooded, but that was in my head. I was young enough to anticipate the thrill of it. I might have said it was all about anger. I might have said it was about the war we had to fight, about what I'd give, including my life, to make Ireland a nation once again. My words were often the stuff of songs. But it was a desire. And like any desire, it gnawed at my heart.

The day we held up the mail van in Dominick Street and robbed the post for Dublin Castle was the first time I knew how excitement and fear could pump together through my veins and make my head as light as air. I wanted more. But no guns were fired that day. Back at the dugout, the Dispensary, we read the headline in the evening paper, 'Sensational Coup Robbery of Castle Mails', and congratulatory words came down from Michael Collins himself. In all my pride and elation, I only wished the gun I carried had been used, that we'd taken the lives of some peelers or Tommies along with the posts. It surprised me that the older men didn't feel the same. They had nothing to say about it. And it irked me that the Quartermaster only applauded us for doing the job and not wasting ammunition.

I was lucky to have a gun. A Mauser automatic, brought back from the war in Europe. When I joined the Volunteers, the Quartermaster tried to take it. Every weapon was needed and I was too young. I stood my ground. If anyone was going to fire the Mauser, it would be me. My temper made him laugh. But I kept the gun. I still hadn't used it, but it served me well. The fact I was armed took me into the action. The gun never left my pocket but it was a talisman. And it was because of the gun that Dick Phelan spotted me for Intelligence, and Collins himself put me in his Squad. But the itch to use the Mauser was there all the time, stronger than ever.

Wasn't I a gunman among the gunmen now? And if I was still in my teens, it wouldn't stop me being as fearless as Mick's Boys had to be. But what did I do in Intelligence? Sat in a room with a pile of newspapers and a scissors and glue. I cut out every piece and paragraph that mentioned an RIC man or soldier or Auxiliary, whatever it was. And when we intercepted letters, or got hold of bills, even tax returns, I did the same. I pasted on cards. I cross-referenced every transfer, promotion, game of rugby or soccer or cricket, every christening, wedding, funeral, concert, garden party, church fete, holiday, home address. For the higher-ups I searched *Who's Who*, for their universities and clubs. Connections, always connections. Who their friends were, who they associated with, where they lived.

But action came. A look-out here, more mail robberies, freeing prisoners – succeeding sometimes, failing more often – then look-out again, on ambush after ambush called off before a shot was fired. There was a bloody shooting war going on somewhere and I was only told not to waste ammunition. Yet the itch kept itching. Maybe to feel I was as hard as the rest. Maybe because blood mattered.

One Sunday morning I was with Joe Leonard, coming from a ceilidh at the Banba Hall, where we'd stayed because of the curfew. We called at Paddy Cullen's. There was information on two detectives from the Castle. We knew where they'd be. We were meeting more Volunteers. There'd be nine of us. Twice before an attempt on these G men had been called off. This time we'd have them.

There was a dark mood across the city. It was in the air. In Brixton Prison, Terence MacSwiney, the Mayor of Cork, was seventy days into a hunger strike. He would soon be dead. Everyone knew. And everyone knew his death would not go unmarked. If we already grieved, we were ready for what would follow. Something was changing. Killing would matter more now. We were up for that. They were, too. They were waiting, the peelers, Tommies, Auxies, Black and Tans. Two dead G men that day would let them know what they were waiting for.

We were coming to the railway bridges at Ossory Road when a lorry of Tommies passed us. They stopped at the bridge over the Royal Canal. It was an army picket. They were common enough, and you never knew where or when. We were heading straight for it. And we had guns. If you were found with a weapon, you wouldn't last long. The Tommies mightn't kill you, but they'd hand you to the Black and Tans who would. We were out of sight, but we could see the Tommies. We took Paddy's gun and sent him to the bridge. Unarmed, he could pass through and tell the others. But as we watched him, we saw more soldiers, moving towards our hiding place. Joe and I crossed the road and climbed on to the railway. As we walked the tracks we could see the Tommies on the canal bridge and more on the banks. We would not get across. If the job went ahead, it would be without us. But if it did, the soldiers were close to the ambush spot. Very close and a lot of them.

We needed to give the Tommies something else to think about. If we didn't act, the other Volunteers might walk into them. By now we were at Drumcondra Bridge, looking at the roadblock again, and people being searched as they crossed over the bridge. A bell began to strike eight in the convent along the road. The attack on the G men would happen any time. Joe's eyes followed mine to the canal and the soldiers. No words were needed. We knelt behind the parapet of the bridge. My Mauser was in my hand. Joe had his revolver. We fired. We fired until every bullet was spent. We didn't wait for results. We ran to the railway and along the tracks to come up on another road. We stopped at a Volunteer's house to drop our guns. They'd be stopping people at random now. With no weapons we were safe.

Soon afterwards, walking away from the city all the time, we were close to my home. I hadn't seen my mother for weeks. If I wasn't exactly on the run, it was better to sleep at the Dispensary or a safe house. It seemed I wasn't known yet, but you could never be sure. Sooner or later they found out. My mother asked no questions. She made breakfast. Joe and I ate in silence. Every so often we looked up and grinned, our hearts pumping blood and adrenalin like mad. I didn't think about the men we'd killed, only that we'd done it. In truth, we didn't know till later that we'd killed anyone. Yet we felt it, like an article of faith. We were blooded.

By the time the day they call Bloody Sunday came, there had been a lot more killing. I'd seen friends killed. I saw their bodies when the Auxies and the Tans had finished. We gave back what we were given. Sometimes we gave more. We knew, as they knew, that terror was the sharpest way. And I did my share. Killing not so often, but I did the work that staked men out. My scraps of lives on cards were weapons. They set the traps and loaded bait. I didn't question it. I still don't. Maybe I can't. We were an army by then, the Irish Republican Army. We fought as we had to. We fought as they made us. And *army* is a sacred word. It takes away the sin of killing. The nation gave us absolution. Every nation says it. It was true. It is true still. But you don't want the truth following you around, watching you in the darkness, snapping at your heels. I cannot leave it behind. But I need it to leave me alone. The truth should be a light, to lighten the path ahead, not a worm in my soul. Not truth with the beauty emptied out of it. Not truth that drains me of who I am.

But that was to come. That was something for time to do.

In the Squad, in the winter of 1920, we knew something big was on the way. Only the men nearest to Mick knew how big. But we felt it. Our work was behind it. All those cards, all the tittle-tattle picked from barroom conversations. We were coming for their people. Not just the RIC or the Tans, but the spies, the G men, the Castle detectives whose houses we had marked, the officers too careless about walking home. We could not guess how many. I did know one target. My target.

Then it was on. As we sat in the Dispensary with a supper of tea and hard-boiled eggs, the orders came. The next day, the Sunday, would be a killing day unlike any other. We were told just what we had to know, but the scale was clear. It would be all over the city. For some of us in the Squad the job was to go in with the Volunteers who would do the shooting and pick up what we could. Papers, notebooks, reports, names and addresses. We would meet the Volunteers at stations, on street corners, and go to our assigned locations, to hotels, homes, boarding houses. This was what Mick had planned. This would truly fuck them.

5

We greeted the orders with a murmur of excitement. Then we were quieter. Some men drifted out into the evening, to Mass, for a solitary drink. We checked our guns over and over and smoked one cigarette after another. A few half-hearted jokes came out but never found a punchline. We all had the same tightness in our chests and lungs. At the Dispensary, only a few of us slept. We sat round the fire, talking through the night, softly, quietly, about nothing that I can remember.

In the morning we hunched over tea and eggs. Guns were checked again, for something to do that didn't involve speaking. The only conversation was the repetition of orders, times, addresses, names. We were calm. It was our stock-in-trade. But there was no one not riddled with anxiety. We moved to the door. Across Dublin bells tolled the first Masses. We crossed ourselves. Someone said it was the Feast of the Presentation of Our Lady in the Temple. Whether the words were meant as a sort of prayer, I don't know, but they intensified the silence. Then someone laughed and said, 'Sure, with luck she'll be too busy to watch the sport!'

We split off as we walked into the city, each of us going to meet a group of Volunteers. I peeled away near Merrion Square to the corner of Upper Pembroke Street. Paddy Flanagan was there with half a dozen of the third battalion. I didn't know them all. The ones I didn't know were young like me, but without my experience. They were raw, excitable. The way I had been on Drumcondra Bridge. But that wasn't like this job. In minutes they would look into a man's face and put a bullet in it. No man who knew how to do that, and I did, could feel excitement.

'We have the details of their rooms,' said Paddy. 'My boys have their instructions. Quick and clean and out. And you're to get any papers in the house.'

I nodded. Two of the youngest Volunteers laughed, almost giggled.

'We're relying on your Rosie, lad.' Paddy smiled. 'Let's go, boys.'

I returned his quiet smile. He wasn't sure of some of those boys either.

I didn't find Rosie myself. I don't know who spotted her, but she was a bright, fast-talking girl from Clondalkin. Someone heard her, in a pub or at a dance or after Mass, or at some wedding or funeral with more drink taken than was good for her. She was a maid in a boarding house in Upper Pembroke Street, and she wasn't backward gossiping about the English gentlemen who stayed there. Those gents were on our cards, which made Rosie a grand girl to know. And because she had a cousin who'd been at school with my brother, and because I was only a little younger than her, I was sent to get to know her. She was a looker and it was better than clipping newspapers. I had money to take her to tea and a dance and a drink in the kind of place she'd never been. She knew I was a fierce Republican, but so was she in her common-or-garden way. And if I impressed her over cakes at Bewley's, she wanted to impress me with her knowledge of the English gentlemen at 28 and 29 Upper Pembroke Street. They had the way of military men, she said, officers, though she'd never seen one in a uniform. And they'd odd habits. They didn't go out in the day, but they were out at night, after curfew. Quiet they were, and great ones for the writing. Forever at their desks, scribbling and filling wastepaper baskets, till paper spilled on the floor. They were hard enough to clean up after.

I don't know what Rosie made of my interest in her gentlemen. She knew I wanted information, not gossip. When I asked her to bring me the papers she cleared out of their rooms, she was easy with it. She was helping the cause, in the way she saw the cause. I don't think she saw that ending with gunmen walking into the house. I don't know if she made that connection. It didn't matter to me. I got what I wanted on the men we knew were British Intelligence officers. We had their names, real and assumed. We could recognise them by sight. We knew where they went, their contacts, the layout of the house. We knew who slept where. And if on some evenings, I got something else from Rosie, that had nothing to with any of that, well, I only hoped it made her all the keener to deliver up her information.

It was exactly nine o'clock when I mounted the steps of the house in Upper Pembroke Street, with Paddy Flanagan and six Volunteers. The same thing was happening across Dublin. The front door was open. It was always open, as Rosie said. The big hall was empty. Two flights of stairs ascended to two halves of the building. Four of us took one, four the other. When my party reached the first landing, there were two doors. We divided again. A Volunteer knocked at each door. The man with me was older. Timmy Clancy, solid, reliable. No shots had been fired, barely a sound made. The door in front of us opened to show the face of a man pulled out of sleep. He had a gun in his hand, but it was there out of habit. He was expecting nothing. Timmy shot him without hesitation. The man fell back into the room. There was another shot along the landing. A scream. Shouting. Sounds of struggle. More shots, further away. More shouting. Screams of women.

I pushed the door and went in, stepping over the body. My companion looked at the man and shot him again. I stood in semi-darkness with the Mauser. I walked to the desk to pick up papers and notebooks, stuffing them in a briefcase.

'Come on, you bastard!' shouted Timmy.

'I have to see what's here. Just wait.'

'Wait be fucked! Let's get out, quick as we can.'

We came on to the landing. In front of us was the boy who had giggled with excitement in the street, staring at his hand, covered in blood. It was not his. Paddy Flanagan came through the other door. He thrust a wad of papers into my hands.

'You got him?' he said quietly. Timmy Clancy shrugged. Paddy shrugged in return, and walked on past the young Volunteer, heading downstairs into the hall.

'Move!' he called back.

The boy still gazed at his bloody hand. He was crying.

'I said, come on, you bugger!'

Paddy turned back and grabbed the boy's arm, pulling him down the stairs, down to the hall, and out through the front door. I walked down more slowly with Timmy. The shooting had stopped in the other part of the house, but there was shouting and screaming, men and women, incoherent. As we reached the hall a man staggered from an open door close to the other staircase. There was blood on his head, and blood soaked one side of his blue striped pyjamas. He slumped against the wall. As he slid down it his blood smeared the lemon flock wallpaper.

A woman rushed through the same door. She threw herself beside the man. Her dressing gown was stained with blood, though she wasn't wounded. She tried to pull him up, sobbing and shaking. More blood now, on her hands, on her chest.

'Just get up. Darling, get up. I'll get you help.'

Two more shots sounded elsewhere in the house.

'James, come on! You have to move! We can get out!'

She looked up and saw us for the first time.

'Help us! Please help us. They shot him . . . they're in the house . . .'

The man was trying to push himself up.

'They'll help us, James! You'll be all right.'

The man coughed. There was blood in his mouth. He was looking at us too. From somewhere, he had found enough strength to step forward. He shook his head slowly. He knew we wouldn't help. Timmy Clancy took out his revolver.

'Get away, Daisy! Get away from me now!'

The woman was still holding him.

9

'Do as he says,' said Timmy. 'Move away from your man.'

She stared, uncomprehending, still holding her husband. Finding another ounce of strength, he pushed her away. She fell and sprawled on the tiled floor. She had stopped sobbing. Timmy nodded at the man with a kind of respect. He fired. Nothing happened. The gun had jammed. Again. Nothing. It was enough.

'Jesus! Fuck this! Let's get out!'

'We're not done here,' I said.

'You want to wait till the Tommies arrive?'

'Mick wants it finished.'

'Then let Mick do it. We need to get away and dump the guns.'

He ran out through the front door, into the street. I could have followed. Looking back, it's unlikely the man would have survived. And I was there to collect intelligence. My instructions were to leave the shooting to the others and get out with what I could. But I didn't move. Young as I was, I wasn't just any gunman. I was in Mick Collins' Squad. If others couldn't do it right, quick and clean, I could. This man was a killer in his own way. He may not have pulled the trigger himself, but like me he was a collector of all the little things that sent men to their deaths. The woman, his wife, watched me with silent, pleading eyes. She lay on the floor where her husband had pushed her. She seemed beyond speaking, but she opened her mouth to say something. I looked back to the man. I have often wondered what it was she tried to say. It felt no more than a breath, but I think the words 'Thank you' were in that breath. She thought it was over. She thought I would go. Her husband knew better. We two understood each other in that instant.

I clutched my briefcase under one arm. My other hand took out the Mauser. I aimed. I pulled the trigger. The man was dead. I put the gun into my coat and left.

2

DINNIE O'MARA'S

Dublin, October 1941

In three years as a private detective, Emmet Warde had made many mistakes. He often felt the job itself was a mistake. The woman was certainly a mistake. He could have said no, the first time she came to see him. It was hard now. Now he would have to tell her to fuck off, in so many words. He had intended to several times. Her quiet persistence irritated him. The things she believed and never talked about irritated him too. There was that part of her, behind the careful words and the politeness, that saw him not for who he was but for who he had been. She hadn't come to him because he was a private detective with a reputation for finding missing people, sometimes the missing dead. She came because he had been on the other side; someone who mattered on the other side. Twenty years ago he had been part of what was, for her, a corrupt, canting, half-arsed gang that fought the anti-Treaty IRA, part of an Irish state she didn't even accept was her country's legitimate government. She thought the fact that he held high rank in the Free State's army during the Civil War meant he might go where she could never go.

A long time ago he would have had words for her: Republican bitch, IRA whore. Those words had gone, with everything else. But he detested what she stood for. He still had contempt for the self-righteous gunmen who claimed a sacred right to attack the fragile democracy he had defended. She was sincere, but he had no patience with that. Too much sincerity was the calling card of any fanatic, anywhere. The war beyond Ireland's shores now was a sink of sincerity.

In all that were the reasons he should have said no the day she asked him to work for her. It wouldn't have surprised her. Yet she had assumed he would help. And he was doing it. He needed the money, but it was a job he didn't want. Why take it? It wasn't sympathy. He wasn't sure it was about her at all. It was about him somewhere, about the unremarkable wreckage of his life. She couldn't know anything of that, yet instinctively she trusted him to try to find out what happened some twenty years ago, to her brother. He had been barely sixteen when he was arrested by Free State soldiers, putting up anti-Treaty posters with a friend one afternoon in 1922. He had been taken to a police station. Records insisted he had been released the same evening. However, neither boy was ever heard from again.

The woman's years of looking for the truth, born of the need to find a body to lay to rest, produced nothing. Now she had asked Emmet Warde to do what no one had done before. Perhaps he was simply one more path to a dead end. Perhaps she had been doing it too long to stop. He had said yes; now he couldn't say no. What irritated him more than almost anything else was that he did want to help her.

Emmet Warde was not a successful private detective. He wasn't sure why he did it, except that he could find nothing else to do. It made him answerable to no one and that, more than anything else, suited. And it meant that some days, when too much drinking left him indifferent to working at all, there was no one to question it. Sometimes there was a job for an insurance company, or for someone with money, that delivered over the odds for doing little more than ask questions no one had bothered to ask. More often there was hardly any income, and what there was went to the wife and family he had left behind him in Drumcondra. He could have made more chasing what kept most private detectives busy: marriage and infidelity; feckless men and women everywhere, fucking where they shouldn't fuck. But he had no stomach for it. No principles were involved, only distaste. The mess of his own marriage, born of too much drink and temper, had brought him to the two rooms above an ironmonger's in Capel Street. A desk and two chairs in one bare room; a bed and a gas ring in the other. Cataloguing the wreckage of other lives, while contemplating his own, wasn't something he could take very seriously.

Josie Kilmartin hadn't told him how she found him. She came into the office in Capel Street and recounted the story of her brother's disappearance with barely an introduction. It was a story she had told for twenty years. She told it well. There was no excess emotion, though he saw what was buried inside. She made no attempt to appeal to his sympathy. It was clear what she believed and he found no difficulty believing it himself. At some point after their arrest, Eamon Kilmartin and Brendan Davey were killed. She said she hoped they had only been shot, not tortured. She was not looking for revenge. She was past caring who did it. She wanted to see Eamon buried. Above all, her mother needed that before she died.

The idea that two teenage boys had been executed for putting up posters ought to have raised a question, even twenty years on. It raised none for Emmet Warde. The fact that the Civil War had sunk into a pit of silent invisibility in Ireland was not despite its darkest moments, but because of them. No one talked about it. There was no shortage of acts of brutality to set beside acts of bravery on both sides. They were uncounted and untold. Emmet, like many others, thought about them little but knew them better than made him comfortable. There were things he carried that were not easily filed away as the unavoidable detritus of war. He carried things not only from the war against his former brothers-in-arms, but from the war against the British before that, and from the war in the trenches he fought for Britain before that. He didn't know whether she sensed some of that when she met him. Calm as she was, quiet as she was, she had a way of looking at him and into him that was unsettling. What she wanted to know seemed reasonable enough. Didn't time make it more reasonable? But he knew no one would thank him for asking the questions that he would be asking for her. He would make no friends.

He said yes, recognising it was a mistake. He got what details Josie had; the snippets of information that had been put together at the time; the little she had gathered since. Twenty years ago the silence from the Free State had been aggressive; since then it had been passive, yet no less obstructive. For Josie, that was a statement about what Ireland was: a sham Republic, dishonest, perverted, built on lies. Emmet could see that her Republicanism was more than a political passion. She didn't say it, but she didn't hide it. She was close to the IRA. Close enough, he suspected, to hang on their coat-tails. He tackled her about the IRA only once. What he learnt surprised him. The Boys, after all that time, had little care for what happened to Eamon Kilmartin and Brendan Davey. It wasn't how she put it, but it was obvious. Maybe the Boys had too much of the present to think of; maybe they had buried too many bodies of their own. Whatever the reasons, Josie got no more help from her friends than from the state she considered her enemy.

Emmet Warde was careful what he asked and where he asked it. At first he thought he would just go through the motions, knowing it would lead nowhere, and end up telling Josie exactly that. Yet he found himself doing more. He didn't tackle it head-on. If there was anything to find, it would come from going in sideways, to look for a half-remembered conversation, half-forgotten memories. There were men in the Irish Army he still knew, more who had retired. There were Guards and Special Branch men he drank with, who had been in those jobs a long time. And once in a while Superintendent Gregory, head of Special Branch, asked him to find something or to watch someone in a pub; occasional jobs that for some reason couldn't be done inside the Branch. He was not quite an outsider. Asking a Special Branch man about Josie Kilmartin over a drink wasn't so strange. He could pretend she was a woman he was suspicious of, in terms of Republican activities that might interest Terry Gregory. But moving from that to asking about disappearances in the Civil War was different. It was stretching things to say the head of Special Branch owed him a favour, but if there were some simple facts, if there was a way to find something about how Eamon Kilmartin and Brendan Davey disappeared, maybe Superintendent Gregory would help. Maybe, at least, he wouldn't stand in the way.

He started slowly, with the neat, typed notes Josie Kilmartin gave him. Her brother Eamon had joined the Fianna, the Republican youth wing, late in 1920. The War of Independence was almost over. The truce with Britain came suddenly; then the Treaty that gave Ireland only a kind of freedom. And when another war came, between those who accepted the Treaty and those who accepted nothing less than the free Republic, Eamon and his friend Brendan, both sixteen, put their bicycles to use as scouts and runners for the IRA. They scrawled anti-Treaty slogans on walls. They shouted insults at soldiers of the new National Army. They smuggled food and drink to the Boys and scrapped with school friends whose fathers were in the new Civic Guard. And when posters rolled off secret presses, castigating the traitors who had sold out Ireland, they were draped over the crossbars of the bicycles, while pails of paste hung from the handlebars.

One afternoon, pasting anti-Treaty posters on a wall, Eamon and Brendan were seen by a National Army armoured car. They were driven into the city and the police station at Pearse Street. The soldiers wanted rid of them. They knocked them about a bit. That would do. The boys were put in a cell. That evening, Intelligence officers arrived to interrogate them. And knock them about again. Fianna boys were an irritation. They looked like kids, but they spied for the IRA. A man could die on the word of a ragged-arsed teenager. When an IRA man dumped a gun, when there was ammunition to move, the Fianna were there. Josie's pages said nothing of that, but Emmet knew what soldiers in the National Army had felt.

According to the custody sergeant, the Intelligence officers returned to Wellington Barracks. The boys were released. And then they disappeared.

Years of searching had produced no more than the fact of release, registered in the station log. There were the names of a handful of detectives and other police officers at Pearse Street that evening. The names of the Intelligence officers were unknown. Probably there were three, but no one recalled who they were. The cloak of invisibility wasn't unusual. These were Michael Collins' men. No one crossed them. No one saw them if they chose to be unseen. The senior police officers Josie had listed offered nothing at the time and offered less now. The station's chief inspector was at Garda HQ in the Phoenix Park; no man to ask for evidence of a Free State atrocity. The senior detective was a man Emmet had known during the fight against the British. He might have been worth talking to, but he was dead.

The only other name Emmet recognised in Josie's account was the commandant of the IRA battalion Eamon and Brendan were attached to. Paul Murphy fought on the opposite side in the Civil War, but it hadn't always been that way. There was an old connection. So the private detective took a train to Malahide and found Paul sitting at a bungalow window, staring at the sea. He was an old man. Emmet could still forget that. Then, they had all seemed young.

The old IRA man struggled with questions Emmet asked. Time and place seemed unsure. His wife came in with tea and biscuits and hissed in Emmet's ear.

'The stroke. It wasn't bad, but he's never been right.'

She turned to her husband.

'The words get muddled, don't they, love?'

She smiled gently at him.

He almost smiled. Then his face was blank.

Emmet thought Murphy might have some idea about the Free State Intelligence officers at Pearse Street that night. The IRA must have tried to find out something at the time. They often had one of their own in police stations or barracks. They would have assumed the boys had been killed. Wouldn't they have wanted revenge? Paul Murphy remembered the boys. He remembered them disappearing. But then, abruptly, where his slow voice had spoken with clarity, he seemed to forget them. He tried to find the names again in his head. And then the time and the place seemed to fade as well. He was somewhere else. The Tans took two friends of his in Skibbereen. They shot them and dumped the bodies at the gates of the graveyard. But the Tans had gone. All the Tans. He didn't know the names of the ones who killed his friends. But no, it wasn't in Dublin.

The IRA man stopped, frowning deeply, confused.

'I'm sorry, that's not what you want to know, is it?'

'I want to know what you remember about Eamon Kilmartin and Brendan Davey. You knew them. You were the commandant they answered to. I want to know who was there when they were arrested, at Pearse Street. Any names at all.'

'Grand lads, I'd say that of the Fianna. All of them grand lads.'

He stopped again. He looked out at the sea, then turned back.

'Something happened to them. Is that right? I don't remember now . . .'

When Emmet Warde found something, he found it, as he often found things, in an unexpected place. It took a lot of head sweat, but newspapers kept a thousand forgotten pieces of information. A piece here, a sentence there, could come together to form a trail no one had noticed. It was among short accounts of trivial crimes that Warde found Neale Bealen, a man who was in and out of jail through all the years his countrymen were fighting and dying. He was arrested at various times by the RIC, the Dublin Metropolitan Police, the Irish Republican Police, the Civic Guard and the Garda Síochána; for being drunk and disorderly, for causing affray, for stealing what hardly seemed worth stealing; sometimes it was just for his foul mouth. He served short sentences and was fined money he never paid.

Bealen had drifted into something more like ordinary life. And Emmet knew him. There were few pubs in the centre of Dublin that the private detective hadn't spent time in. He didn't pretend it was about his job. He moved from pub to pub so as not to be seen drunk in one place all the time. He knew Neale Bealen from Dinnie O'Mara's bar on Ormonde Quay. Neale had a loud mouth after a few drinks, and a grand opinion of himself he would give anyone who'd listen. He had played his part in the War of Independence, he liked to say, and he wanted people to remember. He had eyes that even Collins' boys took note of. He could spot a peeler or a G man in any Dublin pub. Many was the name he'd passed to Mick. And what thanks did he get? Fuck all! He knew gougers who got pensions from the state who never lifted a finger. He'd risked his life, his fucking life. No one cared.

Dublin's pubs were full of men who could tell, in drink, their deeds in bringing the British down. Those who really brought Britain to the edge said nothing, drunk or sober. But even in the prattle of a drunk there could be a glimmer of something. Occasionally Emmet Warde had heard a name in Bealen's barroom chatter; a man he knew was in Collins' Squad, but not well known. Wherever Bealen got it, he had known some of Collins' men. It was nothing in itself, but a report in the *Irish Times* recorded that Neale Bealen spent a night at Pearse Street police station in 1922. It was the night Eamon Kilmartin was there. Maybe not everything was invented. If Bealen knew Intelligence men, if he was at Pearse Street when they were there, if he had a memory, a few drinks would open him up.

The private detective's hopes weren't high. But when he and Neale Bealen were in a booth at Dinnie O'Mara's, with a door that shut off the rest of the pub, and after Dinnie came in with a bottle of whiskey, the small, dark man seemed to find the memory Emmet needed. He remembered that night. The cells were bursting, and he was two hours on a bench. He knew nothing about the Fianna, but there were two lads who'd been beaten up. The story of their disappearance was news. And if someone shot them, that was the way of it then. But when Emmet asked him if he recalled any Free State Intelligence men there, anyone he might have recognised from his days spotting for the Squad, the flattery brought Bealen satisfaction. It wasn't often he was taken seriously. Yes, there were a couple of those fellers. The sergeant took them to the cells with a yes-sir-no-sir and a can-I-kiss-your-arse-sir, then called them every kind of cunt when he came back up. These were real memories, and Emmet Warde knew it. It wasn't the drink. Then he pushed too hard. He asked Bealen if he knew the names. The little man filled his glass, drank it down, and shook his head. It was a long time ago. He didn't remember. Just as Emmet knew Bealen had told the truth, now he knew he was lying.

Realising he had rushed the question, the private detective asked no more. He left his informant with the rest of the whiskey. The last thing he wanted was for Bealen to think the question mattered. He avoided O'Mara's for a while. When he saw Neale Bealen again, it would need to feel like chance. He would lead him back to that conversation, but at the end of a bottle of Powers, not at the beginning.

When Emmet Warde next went to Dinnie O'Mara's, Bealen wasn't there, but he found out he had lost his job and was desperate for money; money that would only go on drink. A timely vicious circle. Emmet left a note, saying he had a bit of work to put his way, with a few quid at the end. He left his phone number. When Bealen called, he told him he was a private detective. The job would be watching someone. He thought that was another way of saying he believed the stories about spying for Ireland. Bealen would be flattered again. It wouldn't be hard to find a way back to Pearse Street and the Intelligence men. But it was not going to be a good call.

Next evening, Emmet started drinking early. He had no reason to, but some days that's how it was. When the days were empty, the bare walls in Capel Street closed in. Faced with only himself, the process of walking through the city was a necessary escape; moving from pub to pub, talking to people he almost knew, for just long enough not to know them better, exchanging only the ritual words that went with a pint and a chaser; the weather, the war, the state of the country, the bastards who ran it. Neary's, the International, Slattery's, the Oval, Davey Byrne's.

And finally to Dinnie O'Mara's, a pub you wouldn't want to spend any time in unless you'd already had too much to drink. The stench of badly kept beer met the drift of urine from toilets too close to the bar. Its only virtue was that you could sit in a booth with a door that shut out the bollocks that was barroom conversation.

Neale Bealen was waiting. Dinnie had already planted him in one of the booths with a bottle of Powers. Emmet saw his informant was already halfway down it. He poured himself a drink. He would drink slowly. He was close to the limit he tried to impose on himself. He would drink what he needed to get himself to sleep back at Capel Street. Bealen was nervous. If Emmet had been more sober, he might have noticed how nervous. Half a bottle should have put paid to nerves.

'You all right, Neale?'

'You know how it is, Mr Warde.'

Emmet didn't; he nodded as if he did.

'It's this job you want me to do.'

'Yes.'

'There's no job, is there?'

'There's money. That's close enough.'

Emmet sipped his whiskey. He had underestimated the man.

'You need cash. I want information I think you can help me with. It's very old information, Neale. And it's of no use to anyone. Except a client of mine.'

'It still worries me, Mr Warde.'

'Why? It's worthless. No one will even know where I got it.'

Bealen's eyes moved away from Emmet's gaze.

'I'd rather talk outside.'

'Whatever you want. I don't mind.'

'In the yard, Mr Warde. Dinnie won't mind. People hear things.'

As they left the booth, Bealen gave a nod to Dinnie O'Mara behind the bar. He walked down the barely lit corridor, where the smell of urine wafted more strongly from the toilets. Emmet followed, half-amused, half-irritated. But he had heard of his informant's cloak-and-dagger fantasies. If the man wanted to act them out, he'd put up with it. The little man opened the door into the yard at the back of the pub. Emmet followed him, pulling the door shut behind. It was dark. As he stepped on to the cobbles, he did not hear the bolt slide home on the back door.

The private detective pulled a packet of Player's from his pocket. He took one and held out the pack. He could feel the other man's hands tremble. He struck a match and saw the tight lines on Bealen's face. The man had problems, he knew that from Dinnie, but some of those problems were about to be solved, to the tune of three pounds. Yet there was tension, even fear, and something that almost spoke of regret. Emmet dropped the match. The troubled face was in darkness again, and so was the yard, except for a bulb behind an upstairs curtain that threw a dim light on the crates and stacked barrels that formed a gangway to a slatted door to the street.

'A name, a couple of names, Neale. Three quid. Money for nothing.'

Emmet laughed.

'Twenty years ago, Nealie. Who fucking cares?'

'I'm sorry, Mr Warde.'

'Sorry for what?'

'It's just . . . well, you know yourself, Mr Warde . . .'

Neale Bealen turned and almost ran the few yards to the gate to the street. He pulled it open and was gone, even as Emmet Warde, startled, moved after him.

'For fuck's sake. Nealie!'

Before he reached the gate, a man came from behind a stack of barrels. He pushed the gate shut. He was in shadow, but as he moved forward, a glimmer of light caught his face. It wasn't a face Emmet knew well, but he knew it. A Special Branch man, one of Terry Gregory's. MacDermott, MacDonagh, MacDonnell. He found himself going through the names, as if that mattered in some way. The fear he had seen in Bealen's frown told him it didn't matter. It didn't matter for one fucking moment. What mattered was that someone knew the questions he was asking. Someone didn't like it. The arithmetic was elementary.

'Did Terry Gregory send you?'

The detective didn't answer.

'I do the odd bit of work for Mr Gregory.' In the silence Emmet dropped his cigarette and stubbed it out. 'If he's got something to say, he knows where I am.'

Distantly, it seemed very distant, laughter from the bar.

'He knows where you are.' Finally, the Special Branch man spoke.

'Then he doesn't need to send me messages. He can pick up the phone.'

'It's not that sort of message, Emmet.'

'Well, whatever sort of fucking message, tell him to deliver it himself.'

The detective took a step closer.

'I don't think you'll have a problem understanding it.'

Emmet Warde wasn't drunk. He drank too much, too regularly, for it ever to be that simple. But he had drunk enough, he'd rarely not drunk enough, to feel that this was a mad and stupid bollox of a thing and he could stop it. If McDermott or McDonagh or McDonell, or whatever the clown's name was, wanted to threaten him, didn't he have enough about him to take the man? What was this even for?

Terry Gregory couldn't know that much about what he was doing for Josie Kilmartin. Neale Bealen was the first real connection he'd found to the night when the woman's brother disappeared. He had never looked in obvious places. He was coming in sideways. But no one came at anything sideways the way Gregory did. He should have thought harder about the toes he might tread on. He had assumed that just as he had told Neale Bealen it didn't matter, it really didn't. But why did Gregory care about this? There would be a reason. It didn't have to be much. Names might be enough. People whose names mattered. Stirring up what should be forgotten. Emmet Warde had crossed a line, not even registering it. And he had forgotten who Gregory was. Sometimes, the head of Special Branch looked lazy and fat, sitting behind a desk in clothes that were too small for him. Yet he was the one who had grown lazy, feckless, befuddled by alcohol. For an instant he knew himself, as every holy drinker does; only for an instant and always too late.

The Special Branch man was uncomfortable. Silence wasn't what he expected. Maybe argument, a fist, but not the pale, thoughtful face that seemed to be looking through him, almost smiling. There was enough light to see a smile. But then the quiet of the yard was broken. Emmet did what the detective wanted.

'I think you need to fuck off, McDermott, McDonagh, McDonnell.'

The detective didn't move. They were toe to toe and face to face.

'Superintendent Gregory can phone. Or he can fuck himself.'

Warde believed he could take the other man. Maybe he could have. He didn't find out. As he swung his fist, the detective stepped back. Emmet collapsed to the ground. The cosh that landed on the side of his head was not Garda issue, but it was less likely to crack a skull than a pistol-whipping. Sober, he might have anticipated the man behind him. Sober, he might even have heard the footsteps.

Most of what followed was kicking. Head and stomach. Emmet was dragged into a pile of crates and bottles. Fists pummelled; head and stomach again. The fists, like the feet, were hard, but the blood came from broken glass. He didn't fight back. He could have done them damage, but at a cost. There was less satisfaction in beating a man who did nothing, than one who gave something back. Unless a man wanted to kill you, it would end sooner that way. To stop it, you had to take it. They did stop, standing over him as he lay among crates and broken beer bottles.

'You know, I never did meet a private detective before, Jim. Did you ever come across Bogart, Emmet? Now there's a feller you could take a few tips from.'

They both laughed.

'Have you a fag, Mack?'

McDermott, McDonagh, McDonnell produced a packet of cigarettes. The two men lit up. The one who had coshed Emmet lit a third. He crouched down and put it between Emmet's lips. They were relaxed. The job was done, well done too.

Warde breathed in the smoke and looked up.

'Any words of wisdom from Terry, to go with the show?'

'He said you'd know what it was about.'

They knew nothing. They were used to knowing nothing.

'And if I don't?'

'It would be better if you did, Major,' said Jim. 'It was major, wasn't it?'

'Major-General, come on! Give the man his due.' Mack grinned.

The two detectives watched him for a moment longer.

'Major-General!' There was contempt in Mack's voice now. 'But the word is that you cut and run. Or maybe worse. Look at you now. A fucking piss artist.'

Then the two Special Branch men were gone.

Emmet gazed up at the night sky. The stars were clear and sharp. The yard smelled of sour beer and now of blood. Pain took a while to find its way in sometimes. Only now did he feel it. There was the noise of laughter again from the bar. It was louder. He saw the back door opening. Light from the corridor picked him out. Dinnie O'Mara peered into the darkness. He walked forward cautiously. He nodded gravely, staring at the man who lay among his beer crates. He seemed relieved.

Emmet saw it in his face. But he could feel, as the publican took in the scene, that part of the relief concerned the relatively light damage to his property.

'They've gone, then, Mr Warde?'

The private detective nodded in response.

'Ah, well,' said the publican, 'it doesn't look so bad.'

Emmet Warde started to get up, slowly and painfully. As he saw Dinnie checking the yard one more time for any extra damage he'd missed, he laughed.

'It could have been worse, couldn't it, Dinnie?'

The publican stretched out his hand and helped pull him up.

'Sure, there's always that.' He crossed himself. 'Will I call you a taxi, so?'

'Jesus, Dinnie, and isn't it some service you're offering these days!'

3

ARD-MHÚSAEM NA hÉIREANN

Stefan Gillespie had walked from the offices of Garda Special Branch, in the Carriage Yard at Dublin Castle, through the city's southside to Stephen's Green and the gates of Wesley College, the Methodist school where his son Tom was now a boarder and had been since the beginning of September. Work would take him to the National Museum of Ireland that evening, but for now he had time.

The school presented an uncoordinated array of pointed gables, irregular towers and arched windows, in grubby brick. It sat at the south end of Stephen's Green, looking out at the gardens' trees and green spaces. Behind its iron gates, the school was a hive of busyness that wasn't out of place among the other busy buildings that surrounded the Green; at the same time it had a calm and quiet that could echo the park at the heart of the great square at its emptiest. Especially after dark, when the lights were out in the dormitories, the college was a space apart.

It was an odd feeling for Stefan, the walk from the Castle to the school where his son now boarded. There had been some conflict behind the decision to take Tom from the farm at Kilranelagh, on the edge of the Wicklow Mountains, where he had spent all his life, more of it with his grandfather and

27

grandmother than with his father. It was not the kind of conflict that would normally attach itself to sending a child to a boarding school. It was not about Tom's relationship with his father, or grandparents, or the problems of being away from home at twelve years old. It was something that belonged to the Ireland the Gillespies lived in, and the fact that Tom was the child of a mixed marriage, in which his Protestant father and Catholic mother had agreed, for their marriage to take place in the sight of a Catholic God, that any children they had would be baptised as Roman Catholics.

The Catholic Church laid claim to Stefan's son's soul at the death of Maeve, his wife, when Tom was only two. The Church insisted that the boy be raised with due attention to his faith in the Gillespies' Protestant home; that he went to Mass every Sunday and to a Catholic school; that he had tuition in the catechism. The agreement that sanctioned the wedding between Stefan and Maeve, both Protestant and Catholic in little more than name, remained when she died, suddenly and unexpectedly. The promise must be kept. It was a promise the law of Ireland supported, so much so that an argument with a particularly hostile priest came close to seeing the Church try to take Tom from his father. But time had eaten at the Church's determination. And it had strengthened Stefan's resistance.

When Tom was about to leave the National School close to his home, Stefan faced down the parish priest who had arranged for him to go to the Catholic boarding school at Knockbeg. Tom had talent, he said; the Church had an investment in it. Stefan said he would decide his son's education. Tom would go to the Methodist school in Dublin, where he went himself. Nothing would stop Tom remaining a Roman Catholic, but the agreement that had shaped his life until then was done. The priest, unused to being refused, assured Stefan the matter would go further. The bishop would be told. The law was not indifferent to these issues.

For Stefan's parents, the habit all Protestants had in Holy Ireland, of keeping their heads down, was strong. Best to go the way the wind blew when it came to conflict with the Church. They were worried. Yet battle wasn't joined; to Stefan's surprise it was easier than he expected. He felt that somewhere, somehow, Superintendent Gregory, his boss in Garda Special Branch, played a part, though he had no evidence. When he asked Gregory if he had spoken to anybody, the superintendent laughed. He was happy to take on the IRA, German Intelligence, MI5, MI6, even bloody-minded politicians, in the strange neutral zone that was Ireland's war, or Emergency; but crossing the Church? He wouldn't risk his soul for an unbelieving Protestant atheist like Inspector Gillespie. But the amusement on Gregory's face was an indication that somewhere in his card index of the sins of Ireland, there were enough men in purple and red to ensure that a well-directed nod and wink could silence a recalcitrant parish priest and even an obstreperous bishop.

Now that Tom was in Dublin, where Stefan lived most of the time, there was the chance for father and son to meet sometimes at the Wesley College gates and spend half an hour on Stephen's Green. There were weekends Tom went home to Baltinglass and the farm at Kilranelagh, but they didn't always coincide with Stefan's time off. His work took up however many hours and days Special Branch demanded.

Wesley was a new life for Tom. The intimate world of Kilranelagh's fields and hills and woods had given him a few good friends but a quiet and sometimes isolated life with his grandparents. His father's presence had been erratic. Stefan had worked as a detective in Dublin even before Superintendent Gregory co-opted him at the start of the war. Special Branch was not something he chose; it was a world of secrecy, spying and unaccountable actions outside ordinary policing. The idea of giving it up and going back to the farm came and went in Stefan's head, as he came and went himself. But two truths stood in the way. The farm's acres barely supported his mother and father. The money he brought in was no longer a bonus; it was how the family survived. The other truth was that the job he often found unpalatable was too much of who he was to be abandoned. His excuse was that, for the duration of the Emergency, he was trapped in the manipulative shadow of Terry Gregory, yet he was more at ease in that shadow than he admitted.

For now, the presence of Tom in a world that had been neatly separated from the farm in West Wicklow was new; father and son were adjusting. There was a lot more for Tom to adjust to, but from what Stefan saw, it was going well. There was much Tom missed; nothing surprising about that. Initially, he had been too busy, too preoccupied to feel it. He seemed less conscious of missing his grandparents than they of missing him, but at twelve, what was at the front of his mind wasn't always what he felt. Seven weeks in it was the sheepdog, Jumble, he missed most.

On this particular evening, at around six o'clock, Tom and Stefan met, between supper at school and the time Tom had to get back to begin his prep.

'How's it going?'

Ireland's familiar, all-purpose greeting. Tom replied economically.

'Good.'

Stefan smiled. His son was not an effusive speaker. Nor was he. They both found silence comfortable. Since Tom's early days, walking Kilranelagh, and later, working with his father and his grandfather, nothing demanded unnecessary words.

'What about the Latin?'

'Yes, that's good.'

'You thought you'd enjoy it.'

'I will when I can read something. It's all lists and declensions.'

'You're sleeping all right now?'

'It's the noise.' Tom laughed. 'You realise how quiet it is at home. There's always some eejit getting up in the dorm. There's a couple of lads snore, Jesus!'

The conversation moved to what Tom thought of his teachers; ones he liked, ones he didn't, the boring ones who made him laugh. It was expressed with a reserve Stefan knew was a pale reflection of exchanges Tom would have with his friends. He seemed to have friends. And some sense of belonging. Stefan heard reticence, but nothing to worry him. Settling in was work in progress, in a new and complex world. All that struck him was that Tom wasn't reading much. Reading had been important. What he read, for his age, often surprised Stefan. Now he was reading little beyond what the curriculum demanded. But times were different. It was probably no bad thing that, for the moment, Tom's life was busy with doing.

Father and son separated at the school gates. Stefan walked through the Green to a gate that faced a more impressive Victorian pile; the red brick and chiselled stucco of the Shelbourne Hotel. Somewhere it owed a debt to Italy and the lightness of the Renaissance, but it was so buried by Victorian hands as to be almost invisible. The monotonous front was broken by stern bay windows; only in the glass entrance portico, and the Nubian torch bearers that framed it, was there anything surprising. For the most part, although the Irish tricolour flew above the Shelbourne now, at its heart there was still the remnant of the dead hand of empire.

Stefan had time to kill before the job that would take up his evening. He went into the Shelbourne and spoke to several people. The top-hatted doorman under the glass portico. The head porter in the lobby. The manager at reception. These were all people who could provide information, or the gossip and idle observation that led to information. They were the web of connections that Special Branch men kept up, not for specific purposes, but because, like any spider's web, small and insignificant vibrations in one place yielded results elsewhere.

He looked through the guest register; nothing to take away. He noted British names and wrote down passport numbers. He went to the Horseshoe Bar for a drink. The small, enclosed room was empty except for the bored barman, idly smoking. He ordered a Guinness and paid nothing. He was not a detective who took advantage of benefits that could be exercised across most of the city's hotels and bars, but it was the system. He exchanged a few words and took a seat.

He was still thinking about Tom. It was odd that his son and Dublin Castle were juxtaposed now. There had been a gap that had physical expression, in the train journey from Kingsbridge to Baltinglass. There was separation. He liked it that way. Now these places touched. For the first time, Tom sometimes asked what he had been doing, when they met after school. He wasn't looking for information. As far as his father's job went, he still had the superficial interest of a child. But Stefan realised how little he wanted to say. He had not articulated what his unease meant, yet in his head it felt harder to shut out the dark corners of what he did.

Later that evening, Stefan stood in the high, broad entrance hall of the National Museum of Ireland, along Kildare Street from the Shelbourne. The museum was one of two stone buildings that framed Leinster House, the Georgian mansion, set back in its own fountained square, that was once the home of the Dukes of Leinster and was now the Irish parliament, Oireachtas Éireann. On one side of Leinster House was the National Library of Ireland; on the other the National Museum. They made two great pillars of a particular vision of Ireland; literature and history.

It was not without irony that the vast majority of books in the library were in English; books and manuscripts in the first national language, Irish, were precious and few. It was also not without irony that Irish writers had not so much been consumed by the English language as they had reimagined it, glorying in the cadences of Tyndale and the Authorised Version, Shakespeare and Milton, but subverting and reinvigorating it. Now any library of English books, anywhere, contained disproportionately high numbers of books that were Irish by any name.

The museum presented its own ironies, especially in the gold and bronze ornaments and jewellery of its most ancient collections, stretching from the Bronze Age into the Celtic age that so acutely defined Ireland. But not a few of the most spectacular gold torcs, necklaces, bracelets, dress-fasteners and shield bosses that filled the cabinets of the Ard-Mhúsaem came out of a distant past and were not Celtic. The people who made these things were conquered by invading Celts; killed or absorbed, they disappeared. And since the Celts had to come to Ireland from somewhere, one route brought them via the larger island across the water, which they also conquered, until others arrived to take most of it from them.

Wider European connections had been in the mind of the man who planned the exhibition of treasures Inspector Gillespie was now attending. A government minister had cut a ribbon, cheerfully fudging in his speech the distinction between the art that came before the Celts and the art of the Celts themselves. Certainly, what was on show was impressive, especially as it brought to the museum items from other parts of Ireland never normally seen in that environment. But it was less ambitious than intended, when the museum's director started planning for this day, three years earlier. The director then was Adolf Mahr, a German archaeologist who had taken the Ard-Mhúsaem by the scruff of the neck and shaken it till he put Irish archaeology on the world stage. His aim for this exhibition was to bring artefacts from all over

Europe to place beside Dublin's treasures; to celebrate not only extraordinary achievements in European prehistoric art, but also cultural unity.

However, there were problems where Dr Mahr saw only opportunities. The German archaeologist combined National Museum duties with supervising the Nazi Party in Ireland. All German expatriates had to belong. For those who chose not to, his job was to collect information and send it to Germany. He felt no conflict between preserving civilisation's past and the Nazi Party's task of preserving its future against barbarism. His exhibition was to carry the message that those who came before the Celts must have been the product of Aryan stock. But as threats of war increased, Mahr's role as Nazi Gauleiter and Intelligence gatherer became more unpalatable. The outbreak of war found him in Austria, unable to return to Ireland. The Irish government expressed regret and felt relief.

Now Adolf Mahr's exhibition had opened, in a curtailed form that made a virtue of its Irishness. It had gone ahead for a number of reasons. It showed ordinary life continued in the Emergency. It reminded the people of Ireland what their neutrality was about: the singularity of their culture rather than its unity with anything beyond its shores. But those foreign shores were present. Prominent among guests at the opening were the ambassadors and press attachés of Dublin's diplomatic corps; those of other neutral nations, like America, and those of the warring nations, including Britain, Germany and Italy. It was this gathering of uneasy bedfellows that brought Special Branch to the Ard-Mhúsaem; to observe and to make it clear to the diplomats that they were, politely, under observation.

Stefan had little enough to do except glance round the hall to register who was there and who was talking to who. It was unremarkable that some politicians spent more time than was advisable in earnest conversation with the German ambassador,

34

Herr Hempel, and his press attaché, Karl Petersen. The usual suspects, with long entries in Superintendent Gregory's index. There were also those who cultivated the British more enthusiastically than was wise for a political career. And the rest, happy to talk to anyone over a glass of wine, now a rare commodity in Emergency Ireland. Hardly anyone looked at the exhibits they were there to see. Stefan, feeling his job was done, was an exception. Admiring the beaten gold of a three-thousand-year-old torc, an enthusiastic and very English voice interrupted.

'Wonderful things.'

He saw the round, beaming face of the British Press attaché, John Betjeman. He had been assigned to watch him before, mostly at functions that herded the diplomatic corps together. He had exchanged a few words with the Englishman, who was new to his job. He was unsure the man recognised him as a policeman.

'I've always wanted to say that. In the absence of any opportunity to stick my head into an ancient Egyptian tomb, this seemed like the ideal opportunity.'

They both stood for some seconds, looking at the torc.

'Gorgeous!' said Betjeman. He sipped some wine. 'Sadly, this isn't.'

'That seems to be the general opinion. Along with better than nothing.'

'It's Inspector Gillespie, isn't it?'

The Englishman knew exactly who he was. That told Stefan something about the attaché. He was good at collecting information no one had given him. Stefan had heard that Betjeman, whose name he recognised as a poet or writer, was popular in Dublin. He knew Ireland; he had friends there. He was at ease in the city. Like any press attaché from any embassy in the circus of Europe's war and Ireland's neutrality, Mr Betjeman didn't spend as much time collecting information as he did on the social round. But that was profitable too; useful information came.

'I take it you're here to keep an eye on us all, the diplomatic bunch, I mean. Or maybe some of your own bunch as well. Even bad wine makes tongues wag.'

'I'm sure you wouldn't say anything that would embarrass Britain, sir.'

'I don't know.' Betjeman laughed. 'The difference between me and my colleague Herr Petersen . . .' He glanced across at the thin, dark man who was his opposite number at the German legation. 'The difference is that I'm more than happy to see the ridiculous side of England and laugh at it, while he finds it impossible not to expose the absurdity of the Thousand Year Reich when he's at his most serious. God knows what he's saying now. Intense, wouldn't you say?'

Stefan laughed. There was no doubt about Petersen's intensity.

'I wouldn't care if he was pleasant. Do I overstep the mark, Inspector?'

Stefan laughed again. It was hard not to respond to Betjeman's grin.

'I'm glad laughter's not in short supply at least, even in Superintendent Gregory's domain.' Betjeman threw the words away, but Stefan heard them clearly; a little bit of probing, a little bit of letting him know he knew the game. 'Sometimes I wonder about my job, Inspector. I only get a sense of what it is when I'm joking. I sometimes think it's why they sent me here. There's not much else.'

'I'm sure you keep yourself busy, Mr Betjeman.'

The press attaché grinned, looking round the room.

'I try to spend some of my time telling people what it is we're fighting for. I don't mean all the moral business. That's there, of course. But it's a hard sell here. People have a considerable right to dislike us, and the empire we drag along behind us. So the fact that a country stuffed with incorrigible brutes and bastards has stumbled into a war on the side of the angels . . . well, you know yourself, as those wonderfully enigmatic words put it. It's more than the admirable Mr de Valera . . .'

The Englishman looked mischievous.

'I shouldn't comment on your dear leader.'

Stefan didn't respond. It was nothing he hadn't heard before.

'I think about different things altogether,' continued Betjeman. 'The things England stands for, for me. I occasionally prattle on about that, harmlessly I hope. Certainly with no intention of compromising your neutrality. And if it amuses people, why not? The Church of England and its half-mad incumbents, in villages so beautiful you can't quite understand how they were built at all. They seem to have come together entirely by guess and by God. Stone churches lit by oil lamps. Women's Institute bazaars. Country pubs where people still argue about whether it's right to put cow parsley on the altar. White roads lined with elms, that lead up to the chalk downs. Cathedral closes and railways that lead nowhere anyone ever goes. Church clocks that never tell the right time. And all those names that you could almost make poems out of, simply by listing. Huish Episcopi, Willingale Spain, Evenlode, Bag Enderby, South Molton, Piddletrenhide. I could go on. Doubtless there's also a list to be drawn up of what makes us such stinkers too.'

'That's not impossible,' said Stefan. 'But I'll leave that to you as well.'

'I'm only trying to liven up your report with some colour, Mr Gillespie.' The British press attaché gave a self-mocking shrug. 'Nonsense to lighten your load.'

'Thank you, sir. You might want to write those place names down.'

'And that reminds me, Inspector. I thought I'd pop in to

Dublin Castle. Something Mr Gregory might want to see. I had a letter, threatening to kill me.'

The Englishman paused for effect. 'I say threatening to kill me. They say they'd been planning my assassination, but they've changed their minds. Good to know.'

'Who was this letter from?' Stefan was unclear if this was a joke too.

'I'm sure you can imagine. Do tell Mr Gregory I'll call in.'

Stefan felt he could only nod in response. But he was aware of someone standing next to him, quite close. He turned to see Sergeant Dessie MacMahon.

'Fun's over, Stevie. The boss calls. You're wanted. We're all wanted.'

'What is it?'

'This wouldn't be the place. . .' Dessie gave a wry, knowing grin.

John Betjeman laughed.

'Something afoot, Inspector, as the Great Detective would have it. I'll leave you and accost my German colleague, dear Herr Petersen. Poetry isn't his metier, so it's what I usually talk about. It's not easy to avoid a German poet whose books haven't been burned, not that I try. He thinks he's safe with Goethe, but Goethe's like Shakespeare. You can find a weapon somewhere. "What do you think about the hatred of your neighbours, Herr Petersen? Didn't Goethe say it's most powerful at the lowest levels of civilisation?" I shall be all enthusiastic enquiry. Kunst um der Kunst willen. Childish, I know, but irritating the man is my entertainment.'

As Stefan and Dessie left, the British press attaché walked towards his German counterpart. He greeted Karl Petersen in clumsy and cheerful German.

'Wir müssen aufhören, uns so zu treffen?'

The broad smile on his face was not reciprocated.

'Sorry, old man, my grim German.' Betjeman raised his glass. 'Prost!'

Inspector Gillespie and Sergeant MacMahon walked to Kildare Street, where a small black Ford waited. The gates of the Irish Parliament were yards away. A uniformed Guard came towards the car; a policeman about to issue a reprimand.

'You're a bit slow, Jackie. I've been parked ten minutes!'

The Guard turned without even an insulting riposte. The words 'Fuck off' might have been on his lips. Dessie wasn't a bad feller; he was still Special Branch.

Sergeant McMahon started the engine.

'So, what is it?' asked Stefan.

'Couple of fellers broke out of Mountjoy.'

The Ford pulled out into Kildare Street.

'Two German agents. Your man Otto Fürst and the Dutchman, van Loon.'

'That was careless,' said Stefan. 'They only just locked them up.'

'The superintendent's at the prison now.'

'And what are we meant to do?'

'I don't know. But take a good look at any women you see on the way.'

Stefan looked puzzled. Dessie laughed.

'That's how they were dressed when they left Mountjoy.'

4

MOUNTJOY

The sound was there before Inspector Gillespie and Sergeant MacMahon entered the high well of stone and iron that was the hub of Mountjoy Prison. Off that hub, rising in layers and running out like spokes, were the galleries of cells. And tonight, the aisles were full of noise, echoing everywhere. Fists hammered on cell doors; pipes banged and clattered in sympathy. Above all, there were the voices, shouting, laughing, singing. News of the escape had filled the gaol, even though the inmates were locked up for the night. There was nothing quite like the satisfaction of that in an environment where little ever happened. Cries and songs clashed, with a cheerful intensity that would not last long. When the entertainment was done, the bleak silence of the night would be restored. For now, there was something to enjoy, all the more in response to the futile shouts of warders screaming for quiet. There was no special pleasure in the fact that two German spies had escaped. It was Mountjoy that had been screwed and everything outside the prison that made these men prisoners. The mix of chants and the snatches of song reflected no more than that. When 'Sieg Heil! Sieg Heil!' burst from one gallery, it meant no more than the 'Fuck you!' that came from others. When 'Deutschland,

40

Deutschland über alles' echoed round the galleries – repeated as no one knew the words – it had no more to do with Germany than a competing chorus of 'Hitler, has only got one ball'. As Stefan and Dessie were led into one aisle by a warder, the cacophony merged in a moment of unison. And the words of another song picked up. 'Fuck 'em all, fuck 'em all, the long and the short and the tall!'

In the cell that had been occupied by the two now-missing prisoners, Superintendent Terry Gregory, the head of Garda Special Branch, sat on one of the beds, leafing through a sheaf of papers. There were letters, some closely written foolscap pages and, incongruously, three school copybooks. He didn't look up as Stefan Gillespie and Dessie MacMahon entered. They waited in silence. Outside, the singing and shouting was dying away. All the amusement was dying with it.

Gregory stood and thrust papers and copybooks at Stefan.

'Those are in German. Your department, Inspector. Even you can be useful on occasions. There are letters, some pages of notes, or maybe letters he was writing. See what you make of them. The copybooks seem to be a diary. It's all Otto Fürst, I think. Maybe he was writing his memoirs. The letters in English seem straightforward . . . visiting, sending food and books . . . the German could say more.'

The superintendent shrugged. He wasn't expecting much from the material. He bent down to the bed and picked up some receipts. He held them up with a grin.

'But we have all the receipts for the dresses, blouses and skirts.'

Stefan and Dessie were unsure whether to laugh or not. The superintendent crossed to the other bed and they now saw the floral-patterned dress he held up.

'There are others. I particularly like this one, what do you think?'

'Well, it takes me back,' said Stefan, who had drawn his conclusions.

'Does it?'

'Isn't that how they got Dev got out of Lincoln Gaol in 1919?'

'It's one story, Stevie. I'm not sure it's true. But it is how Toad escaped from gaol in *The Wind in the Willows*.' Terry Gregory put down the dress and the receipts. 'Not with the assistance of his trusty friends Ratty, Mole and Badger, but with help from the gaoler's daughter. Something to bear in mind, would you say?'

'I don't know what that means, sir.'

'Oh, I think you do. Doesn't he, Dessie?'

The superintendent turned to the barred window at one end of the cell. Stefan Gillespie and Dessie MacMahon exchanged glances, none the wiser.

'You'll see that the bars have been sawn through. That will have taken a long time. They found a hacksaw and blades inside a mattress.' He pointed at a thin, grubby mattress, now on the floor, cut open along its length. 'The work was covered up with black boot polish during the day. Jesus, I'm sure those fellers must have been admired for how much they put into keeping their boots clean.'

Superintendent Gregory was still staring up at the window.

'Having created an exit, they were able to use a rope, a very long rope, to descend to the street.' He looked back, pointing at a coil of rope on a bed. 'Unlike boot polish, even vast quantities of boot polish, not exactly standard prisoner issue. Difficult to hide. But they did. And when they got out, they were dressed in clothes from the selection in their cell. We'll assume they walked away unremarked once they got into busier streets away from the gaol. I don't know what happened then, but since they had outside help, we can assume they were picked up quickly. They had an hour or so before the alarm was sounded here. Time to get to a safe house.'

'Is it an IRA job?' said Stefan.

'They'll be in there, Stevie. As for the rest . . .'

'Where did they get these fucking clothes?' said Dessie.

'You might well ask, Dessie. A wardrobe of women's attire wouldn't be what I'd expect in a prison cell, let alone a collection as tasteful as this seems to have been. Herr Fürst wanted to send Christmas presents to his mother and sister in Germany. Clothes are in short supply there, so the governor tells me. As Otto has friends in Dublin, who come to visit him and provide him with the occasional treat, perhaps even a lifetime's supply of boot blacking, why wouldn't you let them buy some clothes for him to parcel up for his ever-loving mammy and his dear sister?'

Neither Stefan nor Dessie could believe it was that simple.

Superintendent Gregory read their faces and laughed.

'Sure, aren't we the kind-hearted sort of fellers here in Holy Ireland?'

'And the rope?' said Stefan.

'Remember Toad, Stevie.'

'The gaoler's daughter.'

'Well, not precisely a family member, but someone or several someones. The escape was set up to look like these were clever fellers who ran rings round Mountjoy's finest, but they had help in here. The IRA may have dispatched a rat and a mole to collect them, but someone opened the door, or as near as damn it.' He glanced back at the window. 'You'd be some eejit to believe that bollocks.'

'So what now?' asked Stefan.

'I won't waste time here. Whoever helped them . . . it'll be a blind alley trying to get any information. We concentrate on the other end. They're out, so where? Whatever the IRA had to do with the escape, they'll have them now. You read through the letters and the diary. You never know. But I assume Herr Fürst hasn't left a forwarding address. Do it before we're paid a visit by Military Intelligence.'

'Do they know about the escape?'

43

'I haven't told them.' Gregory smiled, taking out a cigarette. 'But I'm sure Commandant de Paor will know by now. I'm surprised he's leaving it so long.' The superintendent lit the cigarette. 'Spies, you see. He'll want to run this show.'

'And will he?'

Stefan asked the question. Dessie didn't need to.

'He can run his bit,' said Gregory, heading for the door. 'If he thinks he's running the rest, I wouldn't want to disabuse him of that. Not until I need to.'

The offices of Garda Special Branch were in a building that took up one side of a dilapidated courtyard at Dublin Castle that was called the Carriage Yard. It sat at the edge of the castle complex, unexceptional and unimpressive alongside the grand buildings that the Irish state inherited in this place that was once the beating heart of British rule in Ireland. From here Superintendent Gregory and his men maintained their watch on Ireland, collecting information on the state's enemies and opponents, and not uncommonly on its friends and on many of the great and the good who in theory controlled the actions of the Branch. The work was often trivial, directionless and intrusive; sometimes it was of great importance; occasionally it was as brutal and unforgiving as it had been under the British Special Branch that preceded it.

In the detectives' room, Stefan Gillespie was at his desk, reading the letters and papers from the cell of the escaped prisoners. Dessie sat across from him, with nothing to do but smoke another Sweet Afton. The rest of the Branch were out in the streets and bars, looking for information, picking up IRA informants, watching the homes of known IRA men, as the Gardaí searched the city and set up roadblocks. Terry Gregory sat in his office, visible through the glass wall at one end of the room, picking the phone up at intervals to answer calls or make them.

It was ten o'clock when he walked out into the main office.

'Anything, Stevie?'

'Some names. Same ones you've got from the letters in English. Names of visitors . . . already in the prison register. A couple of letters from Fürst's sister, which mention clothes he was supposed to send. They even give the sizes. I assume that's for show. The letters are as likely to be from some Abwehr handler as his sister. There could be a code, but these must have gone through Military Intelligence before Fürst even saw them. You'll have to ask G2 if they've looked at that. And he did keep a diary, in the copybooks, but it's really just prison routine.'

'We can sound out G2 shortly. Commandant de Paor's on his way.'

The superintendent looked at his watch and walked outside. He had spoken, as he often spoke, as if he knew something no one else knew. And usually he did.

'There's something fucking odd about all this.'

The words were Dessie's. He got up and walked round the desk. He picked up the list of names Stefan had drawn up from the German letters and documents.

'Recognise any?' asked Stefan.

'A couple. He's not exactly had a trail of IRA men in to visit, but there are a couple of people who'd be close enough. Politicians, not gunmen. Water carriers. You wouldn't catch them doing the dirty work, but they'd be there for the fellers who do. What about the other one, van Loon? He's not even a German, is he?'

'Dutch, from a German-speaking area, on the border.' Stefan opened a file. 'A seaman. Came in on a ship and got stranded here when it sailed. He tried to sell information about British shipping to the German embassy. They told him to fuck off. He was arrested trying the same at the Italian embassy. Not a spy, I'd say.'

45

'But your man Fürst is?'

'Yes, he's the real thing.'

The door from the entrance hall opened. Superintendent Gregory came in with Commandant Geróid de Paor. The commandant wore civilian clothes, but he was an officer in Irish Military Intelligence, G2. He smiled, nodding a greeting.

'Stefan, Dessie. Well, this looks like a fucking mess.'

'But whose fucking mess, Gerry? That's the question,' said Gregory quietly.

De Paor continued to smile amiably. The superintendent fixed him with a smile that was more questioning and was somehow slightly less than amiable.

'I do have some information for you, Terry.'

'Is that a peace offering, Geróid?'

'Why would I need a peace offering?'

'Now there's a question, Commandant. I'll tell you when I know.'

Stefan and Dessie looked at one another. In the gaps between the vacuous words of commandant and superintendent, something unspoken was going on.

De Paor looked down at Stefan's desk.

'The governor told me you had Otto Fürst's papers. Is that right?'

The words were addressed to Stefan but included Terry Gregory.

'I've just been going through them.'

'I will need to take them. G2 material, I think.'

Stefan looked up at his boss.

'I'll have them copied.' Gregory provided the answer. 'Though if you haven't already seen the letters from Germany, I'd wonder what it is you do.'

'We need to draw some lines, that's all, Superintendent.'

The G2 officer's voice was still relaxed, but the smile had gone.

'And what lines are those, Commandant de Paor?'

'There are two escaped prisoners. One incompetent German spy and one Dutch clown. The job of the Gardaí is to find them and put them back in prison. When I say the Gardaí, that includes Special Branch. Van Loon is unimportant. Fürst is a German agent. That makes whatever he does the business of Military Intelligence. So, you do the policing, Terry, and we'll do the Intelligence work.'

Superintendent Gregory took out a cigarette. He shook his head.

'Our friend Herr Fürst didn't get out of Mountjoy without help from the IRA. I want to know what the Boys are up to. That's my fucking business, Geróid.'

Stefan and Dessie looked on in silence.

'It's also my business how these two walked out of Mountjoy. I'm not impressed by the circus act and the dressing-up box. Help came from inside, too.'

'I'm sure you're right. Over to you with that one, Terry.'

'Do you think I'll get very far?'

'You're the detective.'

'Thanks for the vote of confidence. But I've a feeling anything you leave me is going to be a dead end, and anything you don't want me to do . . . might be more promising. I've a good sense of smell. And this stinks like a barrel of rotting fish.'

'Jesus, Terry, you're a hard man to please. We are on the same side!'

Gregory finally lit the cigarette he was holding. He didn't answer.

'I did come here with information,' continued the commandant. 'A tip-off.'

'A tip-off, is it? And who's the detective now?'

'It's about van Loon.' De Paor ignored the sarcasm. 'He's somewhere north of the river at the moment, but he'll be moved to a safe house near the Grand Canal Dock, late tonight. By car. He'll be taken to Hanbury Street. I have an address.'

Geróid de Paor took a piece of paper from his pocket and handed it to the superintendent. Gregory looked at it. He walked over to Dessie and gave it to him.

'Hanbury Street? Mean anything?'

'Yes, sir, it's been used as a safe house. Not for a while.'

'I'd be interested to know where that came from, Geróid,' said Gregory.

The commandant's smile expressed amiability again.

'You give me a list of your informants and I'll give you a list of mine.'

The superintendent nodded. The batting of words was continuing.

'And if we do get the Dutchman, will G2 want to talk to him first?'

'When you've finished is grand. He's an also-ran in terms of Intelligence.'

Terry Gregory drew in some smoke. It was a statement of the obvious.

'You don't have an address for Herr Fürst, to make my job easier?'

'I don't but once you have one, maybe the rest will follow.'

De Paor's words were not accompanied by a sneer, nothing that obvious, but he wasn't a man who could hide amusement or self-satisfaction. For Gregory, it was enough to tell him a game was being played. He didn't know what it was, but he would find out. Unlike Geróid de Paor, his emotions were never obvious to anyone. When he smiled and thanked the G2 man, he was all businesslike, comradely appreciation. The commandant left as breezily as he had arrived.

Superintendent Gregory walked out with him. He returned to the detectives' room. He looked from Dessie to Stefan. He stubbed his cigarette out in an ashtray.

'What did you make of that?'

Dessie MacMahon shrugged.

Stefan Gillespie took a moment longer, then shrugged too. The head of Special Branch laughed. 'My thoughts exactly.'

He headed towards his office, briskly, purposefully. He called back.

'We'd better pick up this Dutch feller.'

'You do think he'll be at Hanbury Street, sir?' asked Stefan.

'Oh, I'd bet my fucking pension on it.'

Gregory pulled the door of his office shut and walked to the phone.

Hanbury Street was a road neither narrow nor wide, close to the Royal Canal and the back of the complex of buildings that made up the Guinness Brewery. The terraced houses were neither very large nor very small. At one end of the road there were two houses in a poorer state of repair than the others. They were empty, the lower windows boarded up. A for-sale sign was fixed to one of them. It was from an upper room in the second of these houses that Superintendent Gregory observed the street below, watching a particular house further along, number twelve. With him were Stefan and Dessie, and another Special Branch man. More officers, and two cars, were in nearby roads and at the other end of Hanbury Street.

A car pulled into the road from Bridgefoot Street and the canal. It continued until it reached number twelve and stopped. The headlights were turned on and off twice. A light went on in the front window; off, on again, then off for the last time.

'Almost military precision,' said Gregory, looking at his watch.

The driver got out of the car. A woman, tall, light-framed. There was nothing more to see except a dark bob of hair and a dark coat. She opened the back door of the car. A man emerged, heavy and broad, but again only the outline of a black figure; a dark coat, a dark hat. The front door of the house was open now. No light showed. No one was visible. The man and the woman walked to the door. The man went in. The door closed.

The woman stepped back to the car. She stood in the street, taking out a cigarette and lighting it. Her face was caught briefly in the glow of a streetlight and it was further illuminated by her lighter. She got back into the car and drove away, a little faster than she came, turning into Meath Street.

'Do we follow, sir? We've cars in Swift Alley and Pearse Street.'

'I know who she is,' said Gregory. 'Leave her. You have the number of the car. Find out who owns it when you get back. I'd doubt it's hers.' He turned to Dessie MacMahon. 'Would she be on the list of Otto Fürst's prison visitors, so?'

'Yes, sir. Josephine Kilmartin. Will we have someone at her house?'

'Yes, maybe so.' Gregory looked down at the street, drumming his fingers slowly on the windowsill. 'Have it watched, that's all. We won't be arresting her.'

'What about the Dutchman?' said Stefan.

'Haul him in.' The superintendent moved towards the landing. 'It's what we're supposed to do. I don't want a gunfight. But if he does, he's not important.'

Terry Gregory clattered down the bare stairs, followed by Stefan, Dessie and the other Special Branch officer. The arrest was as clean and quick as he wanted. No guns were produced apart from the ones Special Branch went in with. Van Loon was naked in the bathroom behind the kitchen, about to step into a bath. Oddly, the IRA man who welcomed him to the house was in the backyard, climbing over the wall, even before the front door crashed in and Special Branch entered, though he did hear the noise as he dropped into St Catherine's churchyard. Unfortunately, two detectives awaited him. A grin at one detective he knew was all the defiance offered. He had been at this game far too long not to know the rules.

*

Jan van Loon was uninspiring to interrogate. It wasn't that he didn't have anything to say because he refused to speak; he didn't know anything. He behaved as if he knew a great deal, secretly, but the act was unconvincing. His English was poor; the minimum picked up as a merchant sailor. He answered yes and no easily enough, but which of those two words came out had the quality of a dice throw. Coming from a German-speaking area near the Dutch border, he saw himself as German, whatever his nationality, and when Terry Gregory brought Stefan in to question him in German, van Loon embarked on a rambling, uninvited description of how overjoyed he was when German tanks rolled into Holland. If he hadn't been on a ship in the North Sea at the time, he would have been there to cheer. It was hard to get him back to the escape from Mountjoy, but what he had to say about that in German was no more illuminating than in bad English. Despite his claims to have been instrumental in the plan, which he thought they must accept was a damned fine one, it was clear the Dutchman had done no more than Otto Fürst told him to do. He knew nothing of the woman who collected them after the escape. He didn't know where he had been taken. He had no idea where Fürst was now. The unknown woman picked him up again and took him to the house where he had been arrested. As for the IRA, he barely knew what it was. He continued to imply he had a secret role in German espionage in Ireland, which was the reason for the escape, until Superintendent Gregory told him the Irish government was moving to a policy of hanging spies rather than imprisoning them. It wasn't true, but it didn't need translating into German. After that, it was difficult to stop Jan van Loon explaining how much of nothing he knew – no secrets of any kind – in English and German and, though no one spoke it, in Dutch for good measure.

*

Stefan Gillespie sat opposite Terry Gregory in the superintendent's office. It was now past one o'clock in the morning. Several hours of van Loon had produced nothing. Gregory seemed surprisingly relaxed about this. During the questioning Stefan had sometimes seen him staring at the ceiling with an air almost of boredom, as if he expected nothing from the Dutchman and was wearied by establishing what he already knew. He made no notes of that night's interrogation.

'Write up a report, Stevie. Shove it in here. I can't be arsed.'

'What about Gerry de Paor?'

'What about him?'

'He'll want to talk to van Loon. And to know what he said to us.'

'Will he?'

Gregory got up and paced his office slowly, his mind elsewhere.

'So, what do we do with him, sir?'

'Send the fucker back to Mountjoy. If de Paor wants him, he'll find him.'

'One thing's for sure,' said Stefan, 'none of it helps us find Otto Fürst.'

The superintendent stopped pacing. 'Does that surprise you?'

'I suppose I thought we might get something out of him.'

'We've got something.' Gregory smiled. 'Not from van Loon. All we've got from our Dutch friend is what we were meant to get. That's to say, sweet fuck all.'

Stefan said nothing, but he registered the word 'meant'.

'I don't know who set van Loon up, but he's the sacrificial pawn. Fürst needed him. I don't think one man could have got down that wall on his own. And sawing through those bars was weeks of work . . . and not easy. If he didn't need him, he was sharing a cell. No choice but to bring him in on it. But once they were out, the Dutchman was a liability.

Knocking at the doors of the German embassy, then the Italian embassy, offering secrets about British shipping?' Gregory laughed. 'Get your secrets here, fresh as you like! In Mountjoy, Fürst was stuck with him. But outside . . . surplus to requirements. Herr Fürst and the Boys will be happy he's out of harm's way. Wherever G2 got the tip, it was a very precise one.'

'But the tip-off? Why would the IRA go through Commandant de Paor?'

'I don't know, Stevie. Maybe because G2 wouldn't notice something wasn't right. No sense of smell. Because it's never that neat, is it? Time and place, all on the dot. And there's Leo Hegarty, the IRA man in Hanbury Street. An old warhorse, pretty much out to grass. When was Leo last active? It's years. But that's not the point, is it? While his guest was running a bath, Leo was already hopping over the wall to get away. And I'd say that was before he even had a sniff of us.'

'He could have seen something, heard something,' said Stefan.

'Or he knew we were on our way. If he saw something, you'd think he might have mentioned it to Jan van Loon, instead of leaving the feller there . . . in the nip!'

'So what about Gerry de Paor's IRA informant?'

'What about him?'

'Wouldn't he tell us where the information came from?'

'Ah, but who's using who? The commandant can plough his own furrow. I'll plough mine. He knows more about this than he's saying, never mind informants. If there was someone on the IRA Army Council working for Military Intelligence, I'd know before the IRA. And if one of the Boys wanted to drop something, he wouldn't even know G2's fucking phone number. You don't get it from directory inquiries. I don't know what sort of shite de Paor's shovelling, but he's on my turf. We'll be saying nothing to Military Intelligence. We'll watch what happens. Plain, simple police work, Stevie, that's our task. Didn't Geróid say as much himself?'

There was a tight smile on the superintendent's lips. Stefan knew it well enough by now. Whatever the game was, Terry Gregory was enjoying himself. Quite suddenly he went back to his desk. He searched through several files then opened one up. He read through the first page then turned over several sheets.

'Josephine Kilmartin. You know her?'

'I know she was the woman who dropped van Loon.'

Gregory stepped to the door to the detectives' room and pulled it open.

'Sergeant! Get yourself in here!'

Dessie stood up from the typewriter where he was wearily typing at two-fingered pace. He walked into Gregory's office. The superintendent shut the door.

'Jim and Mack, did they get hold of Emmet Warde this evening?'

'They did.'

'Were they in here afterwards?'

'They were. Out again after the escape. They'd be home now.'

'What happened? With Warde?'

'They gave him the gypsy's warning.' Dessie shrugged. 'As you requested.'

'And how far did they take that?'

'Ask them. It's not my fucking business, sir.'

The word 'sir' was added almost reluctantly.

'You're right, Dessie. I should have talked to him myself. Old fucking habits. Lesson of the day. You never know when something's going to matter. Right, you two go to Capel Street. Pay a visit to the man who is now my favourite private detective.' Terry Gregory glanced round to include Stefan. 'Do you know where Emmet Warde's office is? Last I knew, he lives in a room at the back of it.'

Stefan shook his head.

'I barely know who he is . . .'

'I know,' said Dessie.

'Get him up. Bring him to my house. You'd better offer an apology. If they roughed him up . . . tell him it wasn't what I intended. Say what the fuck you want.'

Stefan knew nothing of this, but he was filling in the gaps.

'A misunderstanding, sir?'

Gregory ignored Dessie's sarcasm.

'It'll do. You might even get a laugh out of him. Get him to my house in an hour's time. Don't tell anyone what you're doing, not even in Special Branch.'

Stefan was puzzled. Dessie, as usual, was always unsurprised.

'I don't know if de Paor really has got ears in the Army Council. I have my doubts. But he does have some in here. Still, they only wag when I want them to.'

'And what if Emmet Warde says, why don't you thank Superintendent Gregory for his apology, Dessie, and tell him that he can go and fuck himself, sir?'

It was evident that Dessie MacMahon enjoyed asking this question.

'You can tell him that I'm offering him an opportunity to do something for his country. If he's uninspired by patriotism, say I'd take his cooperation as a personal favour. Failing that . . . well, I'd put money on it there'll be no failing that.'

5

TERENURE ROAD

The black Ford carrying Stefan Gillespie and Dessie MacMahon pulled up in the emptiness of Capel Street. It was now past two in the morning. They walked to a door next to the entrance to an ironmonger's. It was open. It gave on to a staircase leading up above the shop. Dessie found a switch; a bare bulb lit the staircase and the landing. To one side, inside the door, were several name plates, including one, in dirty brass, that read: EMMET WARDE PRIVATE DETECTIVE. Stefan recognised the tight, narrow stairs and the musty dampness of his own flat across the Liffey.

'You know this feller, Warde, Dessie?'

'I know him. I knew him, anyway.'

'Not many words. But I'd already say you don't like him.'

'I don't.'

'Any reason?'

'A few.'

'I've heard his name,' said Stefan. 'Private detective . . .'

He spoke the last words to himself, wondering what that really meant.

'That's what he calls himself, Stevie. It's only part time.'

'And full time?'

56

'Piss artist and arsehole.'

Stefan Gillespie laughed. 'Well, that's clear enough.'

Dessie added no more.

'Has he done work for Special Branch, for Terry?'

'Not anything I know about. I do what you do, Stevie. Get on with it.'

'But whatever he was doing, he got a clobbering for it.'

Again, Sergeant MacMahon said nothing.

The two detectives were now standing at a door. The paint was peeling, but another blackened brass plate was there, repeating the name and profession. Dessie hammered on the door. He kept hammering, maintaining a rhythmic thud. The purpose was to get a man who was probably fast asleep to the door. Only loud and insistent noise was going to do that. An angry voice called:

'Who the fuck's that?'

'Sergeant MacMahon, Dessie MacMahon, Emmet!'

Silence, then the voice again.

'What the fuck do you want, you gobshite?'

'You know who I am. Open the door!'

'Christ! Aren't you fellers done?'

A bolt was pulled back. Emmet Warde was dishevelled and bleary-eyed. He was still in his clothes, but he had clearly been asleep. His face showed the blood and the bruises he received at the back of Dinnie O'Mara's pub. The smell of whiskey came off him, but he wasn't drunk, and he was becoming wider awake.

Dessie grinned. 'I hope we didn't get you out of bed, Emmet.'

'It's been a while, Dessie. Couldn't you have made it longer?'

Warde looked past him to Stefan Gillespie. Dessie glanced back too.

'This is Inspector Gillespie. You may not know him.'

'I can't say I do, but an inspector's a good sign, even a Special Branch one. In my limited experience, inspectors aren't usually up for giving out a beating themselves. It must be a privilege of rank, getting some other bastard to do it.'

Dessie pushed the door open. Emmet Warde stepped back.

'You'd better come in, lads, as you're coming in anyway.'

The private detective led them into his office, then pushed the door shut. The room had bare boards on the floor. The walls had faded flock wallpaper. Once it had been a drawing room or a dining room. A long time ago. It smelled stale; what wasn't stale was tobacco; what wasn't tobacco was alcohol. There was a wooden desk, too big for the room, stained and cracked; a chair behind it, two chairs in front. There was a metal filing cabinet, the only new thing in the room. The top drawer was open. There was nothing in it but a rack of empty manila files. A shadeless bulb lit the room; more light came from a dirty window to Capel Street.

'As I said, Mr Gillespie, inspectors don't do the hard work.' He turned to Dessie. 'Sergeants are still up for it. Even amiable fellers like Sergeant MacMahon. So, what's the craic, gents? I thought Terry had delivered his message. I received it, as you can see. Where you can't, his telegraph boys dotted the 'i's and crossed the 't's. I'd compliment the lads who make Garda boots. Jesus, they're the business!'

'Terry wants to talk to you,' said Dessie curtly.

'For fuck's sake, what now?'

'He asked us to say he was sorry that things . . . got out of hand.'

It was Stefan who spoke now. Warde looked at him in some surprise. He wasn't sure whether to laugh or spit in his face. Stefan shrugged and smiled.

'That's the new message. Mr Gregory was concerned the first one might have ended up as, well, as a misunderstanding. You know these things happen.'

The private detective looked at Dessie.

'Where'd you get this one? I don't want to laugh. It fucking hurts!'

'Whatever about earlier, this is not the same thing, Emmet,' said Dessie.

'At two in the morning?'

'The car's outside.'

'And if I tell you to fuck yourself, Sergeant?'

Stefan caught Dessie's eye; seeing anger, he replied instead.

'Superintendent Gregory's looking for a favour, Mr Warde. That wouldn't be such a bad idea, would it? Under the circumstances. If I were you, I'd do it.'

Emmet Warde was sharper now. If he had been almost sober when he opened the door, he was fully sober now. And he didn't need any more trouble.

'I need a wash and a change of clothes.'

Dessie looked at his watch, impatient. Again, Stefan spoke for him.

'Ten minutes.'

The private detective walked through the door at the back of the office. Stefan sat down at the desk. Dessie MacMahon stood, looking at his watch again.

'Give the feller a break, Dessie. Those bastards did a job on him.'

'That's not my affair, or yours, Stevie. Terry said an hour, that's all.'

It wasn't all, but Stefan sat back and lit a cigarette. He looked round the room. He didn't know what a private detective did outside an American movie. He'd never met one. The office didn't say a lot for the job. It was a shit hole.

Detective Sergeant MacMahon drove from Capel Street across the river, south to Terenure Road and Superintendent Gregory's home. It was a large, flat-fronted terraced house below the Grand Canal, between Rathmines and Terenure. It was set back from the road, with a square garden of neat grass and gravel. This was the territory of the moderately well-heeled;

businessmen and politicians, doctors and academics. It wasn't a good fit for Terry Gregory. He bought the house after the sale of a farm in Meath, left to him by an uncle who let it fester for the quarter of a century it took him to drink himself to death. The wreckage of the business that had once been a farm was worth nothing, but there was land. The Gregories moved from Northside to Southside. Their children had almost finished school when the move was made; they continued to travel north across the Liffey and to resent the new home they lived in until they left it. The house in Rathmines was what Terry Gregory's wife thought she wanted. That was why he got it. He didn't care where he lived. Much of the time he did little more than sleep there. As husband and father, he was around when needed, but it was Mary Gregory's role in life to ensure he wasn't needed often. A big house in a prestigious suburb was her reward. Naturally, she hated it. She knew no one; neighbours she did get to know, she didn't like. When the children had gone, all Mrs Gregory had was a big empty house. She had the IRA, the advent of war, the Emergency to thank for a way out.

If Ireland wasn't at war with anyone else, it was still at war with itself, in its own Lilliputian field of conflict. The IRA was too weak to embark on a serious campaign of assassination, but the threat was there. From time to time they did something, to show they could. Most of their operations proved, by and large, that they couldn't. The head of Special Branch was a target. The list of targets was long, though the IRA Army Council's will to act on it was short. They were held back by the internment of many of their leaders and their inability to come to a clear conclusion about who they were fighting. Their belief in an imminent German invasion early in the war was equally debilitating. The day of retribution would come when Panzers rolled down O'Connell Street and across the Liffey, to deposit the IRA leadership at the gates of the Dáil and string up Dev. Except that it didn't come and some, quietly, whispered that it never would. Meanwhile, the list was there, and Superintendent Gregory featured prominently. Even with the Boys at their most confused and incompetent, it would still only take the one bullet.

Terry Gregory had no intention of shutting himself up in a fortress. It was the way he did business that he walked round Dublin with only the gun in his shoulder holster as protection. He walked to work as often as he drove, sometimes with an armed officer, sometimes not. If it rained, he used the tram. Gardaí on the beat patrolled past his house, especially at night, and sometimes a squad car would stop outside. Two detectives would sit there long enough to smoke a cigarette or nod off for an hour. But there was no permanent guard. And there was a point to be made by that. However, the point had its dangers, and Gregory was not going to make his wife any part of that point. So, Mary Gregory moved to Cork for the duration, whatever that duration might be, to live with her sister and brother-in-law on their farm outside Skibbereen. She argued against going, but not too hard. It came as a relief from an empty, weary routine. Neither she nor her husband knew they had become strangers over the years, or that moving to a house neither of them wanted to live in was less a new beginning than recognition of a kind of end.

Stefan Gillespie sat in a large upstairs room at the front of Terry Gregory's house. He had been in the house before, but only downstairs, to pick the superintendent up or collect something. Gregory lived upstairs, on the first and second floors. The ground floor was unused. The doors of the rooms there were locked. Behind the locked doors there were dust sheets over the furniture and the shutters on the windows were nailed to the casements. No fortress, but the areas that were vulnerable were closed off. The front door and the door to the back of the house had metal sheeting screwed to the woodwork. It was enough to stop a bullet.

A fire burned low in the grate of the upstairs room. Heavy curtains framed the window. Two lamps gave a soft light. Everywhere there were books. The walls were lined with them. They were piled on the floor and the desk and a round table, and beside the sofas that faced each other in front of the fireplace. Though Stefan had no reason to expect anything from the rooms his boss lived in, this one was unexpected. He sat in an armchair, looking towards the fire, slightly out of the light, wholly out of the conversation. Dessie had proved surplus to requirements and had been sent home. Stefan could see the sergeant was relieved to be out of it, whatever it was. Superintendent Gregory sat on one sofa, opposite Emmet Warde on the other. Between them, on a table, was a bottle of whiskey. The two men drank sparingly and spoke carefully. Evidently there was history between them.

'I should have talked to you myself,' said Gregory. 'It was lazy.'

'Lazy? Jesus, what happens when you're on form, Terry?'

'You've had an apology. Consider the fact you're here another one.'

Warde sipped at the whiskey he was holding. Stefan imagined that wasn't the way the man usually drank. The private detective stared, then shrugged.

'I take it you want something, Terry. Besides telling me to keep my nose out of things you'd rather nobody looked into. When a message is delivered that way, it's hard not to conclude that something smells. I thought those days were behind us.'

'My men are old-fashioned. They were brought up that way.'

'Some of us got past it. That's the point. Shouldn't that be the point?'

'I don't care about the point, Emmet. It's not why you're here.'

'No doubt you'll get to that. But before I do leave it, I'll just tell you you're a cunt. It won't achieve much, but if it's the best I can manage . . . it'll have to do.'

Gregory smiled. But Emmet Warde hadn't finished.

'Josie Kilmartin's a woman who wants to bury her brother. That's it. That's the fucking point. It's been the point for twenty years. She assumes, as anybody would, and as someone, somewhere must know, that when he walked out of Pearse Street with his pal, thoroughly beaten, but not much more, they were stopped and taken somewhere to be finished off. I'd hope just shot. Not because I'm callous, but because it's a better option than being beaten to death. You and I had friends who went that way, courtesy of the Tans. We know what it's about. I've a brother who was on the receiving end of some of that. He was lucky to survive it. And when they went, and we turned to killing each other, it wasn't so different. The IRA killed their share of ours in cold blood. We did the same. That's how those two lads disappeared. Someone must have decided it wasn't the best look for the Free State. That's all I can think. So they were dumped or shovelled into a hole. All I want to find out is where they are. Josie's not looking for revenge. Just a grave and a priest. Her and her mother. Did I go at it the wrong way? If I said help me, Terry, no names . . . point us to the poor fucker's bones, would that work?'

The room was silent. Only the ticking of a clock. Superintendent Gregory leant forward and picked up the whiskey. He filled his glass and Emmet Warde's.

'You always told a good story, Emmet.' The head of Special Branch raised his glass and drank. 'And why the fuck would I know anything about any of that?'

'The same reason you want to stop me. The same reason you keep the gunmen you call detectives in Special Branch. Because they were there. Because they were doing the beating and killing. Because someone in your circus knows someone, who knows someone, who saw something, or fired the shot, or gave the order, or drove the car, or dug the hole. I'm not saying the men who did it are in Dublin Castle now, but they could open the door if you said. I've wasted my time trying to find a way in. I thought if I did, if I came to you with facts, you'd have to look at it. That's all I've been trying to do. To get some evidence I could use.'

Stefan watched the two men from the shadows.

'I never thought of you as a saint, Emmet. I need to think again. But you've had your say. We know the shite we come from. It's still not why you're here.'

'For fuck's sake, Terry!'

'That's what you want, is it?' Gregory's voice was no louder, but Stefan could feel anger behind it now. 'To open up every death, every killing, every brother and father and uncle and cousin who pulled a trigger on a brother and father and uncle and cousin and neighbour and friend and schoolmate? You think there's something to gain from twenty-year-old tales of woe and half-arsed, half-forgotten memories, not to mention the lies and the grudges and the things men did out of fear and blind fucking panic or because they were stupid or vicious or drunk, or because their officers didn't know what the fuck they were doing. That's before we get to the men we executed "officially". And why? To show the other fuckers we could.'

'Two boys, Terry. That's all it is. One of them doesn't have relatives alive. The other has a mother who's next to senile . . . a sister who wants him put to rest.'

Gregory shook his head. It was not denial, but it was refusal.

'It's a small thing, Terry. No one else is interested. Even the IRA couldn't give a toss about it now. Josie's a long-time Republican. They haven't helped her.'

'She not just a Republican, Emmet. She's on the inside.'

Emmet shook his head. 'Does that matter?'

'Come on,' replied Gregory. 'They don't care now because

there's nothing to care about. But if she found her brother, what would happen? There's a piece of propaganda if you like. It won't be in the papers, the censors will see to that. But that's even better. Dev's hiding a murder. Doesn't that prove he's changed sides after all? And that little funeral she wants, with her old mammy, what do you think the Boys would make of it? Fucking thousands of them, tricolours flying, black berets, volleys over the grave. There'd be interned IRA men rioting in the Curragh. And your woman, who doesn't want revenge, would find she suddenly has a lot of friends who do. We haven't had any government ministers shot in a while. I've lost detectives that way. Miss Kilmartin's brother would be a grand recruiting sergeant for the sort of fellers who'd fancy thinning out the ranks of the Garda Síochána.'

'I don't see any of that, Terry. I don't believe that's what she wants.'

'It'll be what the Army Council wants. I'm surprised they haven't the wit to see it's a gift. Are you so stupid you can't see that? Or are you soft on the bitch?'

Emmet said nothing. He heard Gregory's words. He saw something he hadn't seen before. Maybe, in the superintendent's final thrust, there was truth, barely truth at all, perhaps, but enough to question his feelings for Josie Kilmartin.

Terry Gregory saw he had hit something that surprised Warde himself.

'No fool like an old fool, Emmet.'

'She's an honest woman, Terry.'

'She's a believer. If she finds the brother who died for the Republic, she'll believe he can become a hero. He can live again for Ireland. But it doesn't matter. Whatever happened that night, it's gone. I'm not saying you're wrong. Yes, some bastards took those lads out and shot them. They were our bastards. I don't doubt it. But they could be dead. They might as well be for all the chances there are of putting the pieces back together. Remember, no bodies found. If it was meant to be a lesson, there was no one to see it. I'd say it was a fuck-up. Having fucked it up, whoever the men were . . . they buried the memory of the fuck-up with the bodies.'

Stefan still sat in the leather chair in the corner. The older men seemed unaware of him. He watched Emmet, looking beaten, now mentally not physically.

'Leave it, Emmet. I should have talked to you first. A beating saves time. That was a mistake. I also forget that some of the men who work for me are idiots.'

Gregory looked across the room, remembering Stefan.

'You'd have done it differently, Inspector.'

'Horses for courses, sir. But then you wouldn't have asked me.'

The superintendent picked up the whiskey bottle once more. He filled his glass and the private detective's. He stood and walked to the chair where Stefan was sitting and filled his. He turned to Warde. He put down the bottle and smiled.

'Though I say it's time for you to leave it alone . . . it's not.'

Emmet looked up. Stefan frowned, puzzled where his boss was going.

'You're going to tell Miss Kilmartin you're getting some-where. You'll say you have a lead, a clue, whatever. Not much, but something. Maybe not a name, but a place, someone who said something, saw something, that someone remembered. Vague but promising. Pump a bit of urgency into it. You'll need to contact her, to know where she is. If you get a break, she has to know, right?'

Warde was confused now, so was Stefan.

'What sort of bollocks is that, Terry? You just told me—'

'Bollocks is exactly what it is. You'll lie to her . . . at length.'

'What are you talking about?'

'You're going to lie because your client really is the IRA bitch you seem to have parked somewhere along the leafy lane of whatever it is that fills your mind when you're not pissed,

66

Emmet. And I know that's not often. A German spy escaped from Mountjoy tonight. Two in fact. One will be back there tomorrow. The other one, well, I don't know where he is now. But I shall be finding out.'

Emmet laughed. 'Didn't they walk off dressed as women?'

'That's right. You won't find it in the papers like that.'

'No, but I keep my ear to the ground, Superintendent.'

Gregory sat down again, smiling.

'Did your ear tell you the clothes they wore were taken into Mountjoy by Josie Kilmartin? You wouldn't believe that, would you? Or maybe you would.'

Emmet reached forward, amused, and poured another whiskey. It was a surprise, but not one that didn't make sense. He waited. There would be more.

'She had a car,' continued Gregory. 'She picked up one of the men at least. I think she took him somewhere for a couple of hours, either her own place or a safe house, then another safe house that wasn't so safe. We had a tip. We were watching it. When she dropped the man, we collected him without much trouble.'

'What about Josie?' The private detective was no longer smiling.

'She hasn't been arrested. She was gone before we moved in.'

'I see.'

'You mean you don't see at all, Emmet. I imagine she knows where the other man is, a man called Fürst. He's the serious one. The one we caught isn't. I think Fürst not only dumped him as soon as he could, I doubt he'll care that we've reeled him in. It took two to break out. But our second spy was expendable.'

'What's any of this got to do with me, Terry?'

'Your friend Josie Kilmartin knows a great deal. It's likely she knows where Fürst is. I think she's moving him around. She'll know where he's staying and who he's meeting from the IRA. She's playing a part in this. And if I know where she is, if

I know what she's doing, then Herr Fürst won't be far away. You see now?'

'And then you'll pick him up?'

'That's for another day, Emmet. He may be more valuable in the wild.'

'So, I tell Josie a pack of lies. She keeps in touch, keeps meeting me, lets me know where she is, and all the rest. And I pretend I'm about to find her brother.'

'Still sharp, Emmet. That's it. More or less.'

'And why wouldn't I tell you to fuck off?'

'Remember when you served your country, Major-General Warde?'

Stefan registered the title; something else unexpected.

'I see, if a good kicking doesn't do the job, try patriotism. What are you going to do for your next trick, Terry? A tricolour and a chorus of "Amhran na bhFhiann"?' Emmet turned to Stefan, for the first time since he sat down. 'Will you sing along, Inspector Gillespie, or would you have a tin whistle in your pocket?'

Terry Gregory stood up. He moved closer to Emmet, looking down.

'You have a debt to pay, Emmet.'

'Do I?'

'You do. And being a drunk doesn't change that. I'd like to give you the credit of thinking it's one of the reasons you're a drunk. But I might be overstating the case. The romantic in me. But whatever reason you find for doing it, you'll do it. Willingly, or unwillingly. If you think your life's shite, it can get worse, Major-General. As you know already, I have a lot of men brought up with old-fashioned values. I won't say good old-fashioned values. I'm sorry to say some have a personal dislike of you. I don't approve of that in policing, not in a democracy like ours. But we keep coming back to old habits. Like them or not, they die hard, and very hard sometimes. You will do this. So, let's get on with it, Emmet. As the feller says, there's a fucking war on. And we'll do without that sliver of integrity you hold on to. It disappeared into the bottom of a whiskey bottle a long time ago.'

Superintendent Gregory poured himself another drink.

'Drink up. Stevie can drive you home. You've a lot to do.'

He raised his glass.

'Sláinte, from one cunt to another cunt!'

Emmet Warde downed his own whiskey. There were no words, but Stefan recognised what was in the private detective's face. His silence was his consent.

6

BEWLEY'S ORIENTAL CAFÉ

In his office at Dublin Castle, the head of Special Branch scanned the file on Josie Kilmartin. Stefan Gillespie listened as Gregory read sections and filled in the gaps.

'She lives in Crumlin with her mother. Eighteen Cashel Road.'

'Not married?'

'Engaged to Dan Figgis. IRA man interned in the Curragh for the duration. He was big on the Germans-are-after-winning-the-war-for-Ireland front. I don't know if he still is. Probably involved in some planning for the bombing campaign in London. Not sharp politically. More a foot soldier. They've been engaged five years. According to someone who knows him, they're not headed for wedding bells. Word is he sees that happening at some point, but she's the one who's not so keen to get to the altar. A small thing, but interesting. She is loyal, whatever else. Loyal even though she might not like what's going on. She's a bit of the socialist about her. She wouldn't be persuaded by the guns or the bombs, let alone the Nazis. But she's a sticker. She has the faith. And doubt is the first step on the road to heresy. If you don't much like what Republicanism has turned into, it's a test of faith. Believe despite the shite. Don't we all do the same every Sunday at Mass?'

Gregory closed the file and laughed.

'Except for you, Inspector. You get a pass.'

'I make up for it by working for you, sir.'

'Ah, it keeps you human, though, Stevie.'

'Does she have a job?' Stefan kept to the task in hand.

'She was a National School teacher. Principal at a school in Crumlin. But she resigned. The job was one reason she didn't marry Figgis. Maybe it's handy he's been interned since then. The father's long dead, but he owned property in Wicklow Street, a shop and flats. Not a lot, but she has income from it. And she's useful enough to the IRA that they slip her money. She gave up her job to look after her mother, more or less senile. There's an aunt who helps out. If Josie needs time, she has it. She spends that time doing what the Boys want doing. She works as a courier. She's moved arms and explosives. She's busy with meetings and the political side. Works at the Sinn Fein offices part time. Useful woman. And sharp.'

'Did we find out anything about the car?'

'It belongs to the wife of an acquaintance of yours, Francis Stuart. You last saw him in Berlin, working for Goebbels and his pals, broadcasting to save the world from the horrors of democracy, or the British Empire, or American music, and Ireland from the English and itself – or possibly all of the above at the same time. But a man of integrity, like yourself, Inspector. His lady wife, Mrs Iseult Stuart, of Laragh in your own garden county of Wicklow, is a great friend of the German ambassador, Herr Hempel. A frequent guest. She has other guests. German spies drop in to bury parachutes, or recharge the batteries of their radios and share a pre-dinner sherry with lads from the IRA Army Council. Why not?'

'If it's no surprise,' said Stefan, 'shouldn't you do something?'

'Her more unusual guests come my way eventually. But Mrs Stuart has powerful friends. We'd have trouble locking her up. More profitable to let her play her games than stop her.

Anyway, she's lent her car to the Boys to drive our escapees round town. I'm interested in what Miss Kilmartin will do with it next.'

A rap on the door; a detective came in, grinning.

'Visitor, sir.'

'Is that amusing you, Sergeant?'

'It's your man Betjeman, the British press attaché, after you. I put him across the hall, in the front office. I didn't think you'd want him nosing in here.'

'What the fuck does he want?'

The detective shrugged.

'I saw him last night,' said Stefan, 'at the museum. He did say he wanted to talk to you. He had a letter from the IRA. To tell him they're not going to kill him.'

'What?'

Stefan maintained a look of deep seriousness. 'They like his poetry, sir.'

John Betjeman sat in an armchair in a room off the entrance to the Special Branch offices. The entrance was bare and cold. Doors opened off it. There was a broad staircase at one end. A uniformed Guard sat at a desk. There was no great show of security. The Carriage Yard lay within the walls of Dublin Castle, and the gates were policed. Entry was not difficult during the day. As the castle contained offices of government as well as policing and security, it was easy for a representative of the British legation to find his way. In the room where he now sat, the press attaché faced Superintendent Gregory and Inspector Gillespie, holding a sheet of paper.

'It begins cheerfully enough with a cúpla focal in Irish. "A Chara", so polite enough. It goes on. "It has come to the attention of the Army Council of the Irish Republican Army that your activities as British press attaché in Dublin involve the possible surveillance of Irish men and women in a time of war.

72

The Army does not recognise the state of neutrality asserted by the illegitimate Irish government. The Army has made a declaration of war against Britain. From Ireland's point of view the aggressor invaded our shores not yesterday, but centuries ago. It remains in occupation of part of our nation and has made the de Valera regime its tool. We thank God for Germany's fight for a free and progressive Europe. The forces of British imperialism in Ireland are legitimate targets of war, for us here as for our German allies elsewhere. The same is true of any agents of Britain. We believe you are reporting your observations to Britain's spy network. Our Intelligence department has brought you to the notice of the Army Council, as a proper target for assassination. I have argued, on your behalf, that the propaganda you peddle to the gullible only appeals to unimportant groups of people who are already pro-British. I have also argued that a man with your public profile can't be taken very seriously as a secret agent. As someone who has enjoyed your verse, I hope I am right. For the present, no action will be taken over your presence in Dublin, but please take note of the situation. We will know of any expansion of your activities." And there you have it. I'm off the hook, which is something. It ends, "Is mise le meas, P. O'Neil." I'm aware that's just a name, a nom de guerre.'

Terry Gregory stepped forward and took the letter from Betjeman. He scanned it. He turned it upside down. He held it up to the light from the window.

'You won't mind if I keep this, Mr Betjeman?'

'Perhaps you could make me a copy, Mr Gregory. It's not every day I get a letter from an organisation that would cheerfully kill me, in praise of my poetry. I'm not sure about the way he uses the word "verse". Just a hint that he puts me in the second division. Perhaps I'm oversensitive. However, the man has some taste.'

Terry Gregory was still holding the letter up to the light.

'I think it was typed on a machine we're familiar with. That interests me. If it's directly from their Intelligence section, this was probably written by Diarmuid McAlister. Of course, the venture into literary criticism does come with a caveat.'

'I'm simply a press attaché, Superintendent. The harmless in pursuit of the pointless, especially as your press is censored more than we have the stomach for at home. I could put out a piece about a Royal Philharmonic concert at the Albert Hall and find your censor slicing through it, if it singles out German music, let alone, God forbid, British music. If the concert was in Belfast, the piece would disappear in an ocean of black ink. As for my reports back to Blighty, what can I say? Guinness is good, the sherry tolerable, the wine in short supply and barely tolerable at all. I admit that I occasionally suggest Britain will win the war, after the second or third Guinness. The drink talking, or maybe call it poetic licence.'

Superintendent Gregory handed the IRA letter to Stefan. 'I'm in the business of words too, Mr Betjeman, after a fashion. Ones that ring true and ones that don't . . . quite. I have a good ear for it, you might say. Or maybe I'm well versed in spotting a chancer when I see one . . . or even read one.'

'I think you have me there, Superintendent. But don't pass it on to my friend in the IRA. Literary judgements are rarely fatal, but in this case, I'm in your hands.'

Later that day, Stefan Gillespie and Dessie MacMahon sat in Bewley's Oriental Rooms in Grafton Street, with a pot of tea and toasted teacakes. It wasn't a place they often found themselves, but it was here that Emmet Warde was meeting Josephine Kilmartin. It was here that the private detective's job for Josie would turn into the job he was now doing for Superintendent Gregory. Stefan and Dessie sat by the wall on one side of Bewley's big ground-floor salon. The café was full of people. Across the room, only partly visible, Emmet and

Josie sat in a corner. The two Special Branch men were not there to listen, only to watch; to see the private detective was doing as ordered; to learn, later, what he discovered from his client.

'What have you got against this man Warde?'

'We have to work with him. Who cares? There's plenty I don't like.'

'It's not work he wants, Dessie.'

'He can join the club. When did you last do something you wanted?'

'I've no idea what the bloody club is, Dessie. We're tailing him, and he's tailing her, and she's supposed to know where your man Fürst is, because she's been driving him. He's holed up, getting bed-and-breakfast at IRA establishments across the city. And what then? Maybe nothing. Or maybe something our private detective doesn't tell us. I don't know what Terry's threats are worth to this feller, but am I getting the impression you don't think they're worth as much as he does?'

Sergeant MacMahon picked up the pot and poured more tea.

'That's another thing we're used to, Stevie. Nothing happening. Do you care? Most of the time I'd rather nothing happened, you know that. It suits me. So I don't much care whether Mr Emmet Warde's doing what he's been told or not.'

'Tell me more about him. You know who he is.'

'Who he was. Didn't you hear it from Terry? Major-General Warde.'

'A long time ago,' said Stefan.

Dessie nodded and put three sugars into his tea.

'Long enough, Stevie. There was a time anybody who knew which end of a rifle was which could get a snappy uniform and a job in our new army. Emmet was in the British Army till 1918. I don't know why we all thought that was some sort of qualification for something, not when you saw how they fucked up in Ireland.'

'That's what you've got against him?'

'Do you want a list?'

'Yes. If I've got to put myself on the line with him.'

Dessie spoke quietly, with unusual intensity.

'In the Civil War, he decided he'd had enough. He walked out. It got a bit much for the Major-General. It got a bit much for all of us. I lost friends on both sides, like everyone. I never had to kill anyone I knew, but in a way, we all knew each other. Maybe Major-General Warde got some blood on his new uniform. Maybe it didn't come off in the cleaning. But he survived. He even survived when Michael Collins didn't. He was there that day. You might want to think about that.'

Stefan took this in. He looked across to the table where Emmet sat talking to Josephine Kilmartin. There was no reason why what Dessie had just told him need mean anything. Warde had been a soldier. That was all. But it was remarkable information. It placed the private detective at the heart of something in a way that seemed to contradict the shabby office in Capel Street and the stench of whiskey. This was a man who had mattered, to say no more. Once he was someone; now nobody.

'Would you think Mick's death was a reason to walk away?'

Stefan didn't answer. He could imagine it might be a reason.

Dessie lit a cigarette. 'Quite a time to go, eh, Stevie?'

'You're not telling me you think he was in on it? That's some jump.'

'There's plenty thought someone was in on it. We all know what happened at Béal na mBláth. After twenty years we still don't know how it happened. Mick Collins should have been safe in Cork. He should have been well protected. Maybe better protected, though. Nobody should have known the road he'd take to Dublin.'

'And maybe he thought he was too safe,' said Stefan. 'And being a Cork man mattered more than being head of the Free

State Army. Or maybe he believed the IRA would never dare try to kill him in Cork. Maybe he just got it all wrong.'

Dessie shook his head. He was unconvinced.

'While Emmet Warde's raking the muck to find out about Miss Kilmartin's brother, perhaps he should look at the fellers who were with him when Mick died. No one wanted to look too hard at the time. It felt like that. And when the fighting was over, what was the point? You could forget it once Dev took over. But if we don't care who killed Mick Collins, what the fuck is Emmet doing with this kid?'

The past was not something Dessie talked about. He was older than Stefan; old enough to have been an IRA Volunteer at the end of the War of Independence; to have fought the IRA in the Civil War that followed. The fact that he was in Special Branch meant he had been part of IRA Intelligence, then Free State Intelligence. He wasn't in Collins' Squad, but he worked with men who were. Like others in the detectives' room at Dublin Castle, like Superintendent Gregory himself, he carried with him the intimate brutality of a time when Intelligence meant deciding who to kill. None of them spoke of it, but it coloured, quietly, who they were. Stefan stood outside that. It was a wall he couldn't see the other side of.

'I've never heard you say anything about that before.'

'Well, now you have, you'll know why. There's nothing to say.'

'Except that you don't trust Emmet Warde?'

'I don't care about him. He's a piss artist. Never mind the rest.'

'And what is the rest?' asked Stefan.

'What goes with it. Brenda's from Drumcondra, that's why I know a bit. She knew the Wardes. She grew up with Emmet's wife. Your man's a habit of walking out on people. He did it to his missus and his kids a couple of years ago. Not that he was any loss. He liked knocking her about when he was drunk. No shortage of fellers like that, but it's who he is. He's a brother, too, that's in and out of the mental hospitals. Charlie Warde's always relied on Emmet. Emmet got him work. He helped with money. And then Emmet left him to it as well. For the bottom of a bottle. That's the Major-General. The sort to piss off when you need him, whether it's his comrades or his family. So, would you trust him up a dark alley, Stevie?'

Sergeant MacMahon shrugged and stubbed out his cigarette.

Across the café, Emmet Warde and Josephine Kilmartin were getting up. They moved to the front of the shop, where he stopped to pay the cashier. He took Josie's coat and held it as she put it on. It was done casually and easily. It could have been no more than ordinary politeness. But as Stefan watched, it was more intimate than that; in a way neither the man nor the woman seemed aware of. He had sensed it already, glancing across Bewley's at them. He assumed what they were talking about was only the business between them, and the lies the private detective was putting into his client's head; lies that would make it easy to trace her and track her, along with anyone she was with. But the words were only part of the conversation. Stefan Gillespie saw something in the way they sat opposite each other that gave out its own message. It was barely to be seen, but he did see it.

Stefan and Dessie waited ten minutes, then paid the bill and went out into Grafton Street. They walked to Chatham Street and went into Neary's. They found Emmet in a booth, with a pint of Guinness and a whiskey. Dessie went to the bar. Stefan slid in opposite Warde. The private detective drained the whiskey. He offered no greeting. He called across the room to Dessie, who was now ordering drinks.

'A large Powers, Dessie!'

'Is it done?' said Stefan.

'It's done.'

'Did she wonder why you'd been in the wars?'

Warde's face still showed bruises from his beating.

'I told her the truth. I got on the wrong side of a couple of Special Branch detectives. They didn't like the questions I was asking. It carried real conviction.'

He smiled as if demonstrating how thoroughly he was doing his job.

'Did you get my Powers, Dessie?'

Sergeant MacMahon didn't bother to reply. Behind him the barman stepped forward with a tray. He set down the whiskey and two more pints of Guinness.

'So, what did you get from her?' continued Stefan.

The private detective looked from Stefan to Dessie and back.

'You do the talking, is that it? And he gets the drink in?'

'No, he watches you and decides if you're telling the truth. And if he thinks you're not, Terry Gregory will give us an evening off and pass you back to the fellers you met at Dinnie O'Mara's. But Dessie may take convincing, Emmet. He's concluded you're a gobshite and an arsehole. And that's just when you're sober.'

Dessie raised his class. 'Sláinte, Emmet.'

'I wouldn't even argue with you, Dessie. I didn't ask to be here.'

'None of us did,' said Stefan. 'But that's the game we're in.'

Warde drank more of his Guinness, then the whiskey.

'The thing is, she trusts me. I mean in a way that . . . I've done what I could for her. I tried to find a way to help her. I meant what I said, when I told Terry there's no vendetta. For Josie, it's about putting something back that's missing. I'm not asking anyone to look at it that sentimentally. It's a job. I do it a lot. Finding people. Sometimes they're dead, sometimes not. They're missing, though. This one happens to be missing because someone shot him twenty years ago. That's all.'

'Terry's been through that, Emmet,' said Stefan. 'It's not the issue.'

Emmet sat back in the booth and smiled a resigned smile.

'I know. That was my act of penance. So, what did she say? What's she doing? She's busy. Very busy. And she won't be around for a while. She doesn't know how long. She's going down to visit a friend in Wicklow. In the mountains. She didn't say where, and I didn't push. But I'd guess Glendalough and Laragh.'

Stefan looked at Dessie. It was where the owner of the car lived.

'I see you're ahead of me, lads. Do I get points for that already?'

Stefan ignored the remark, but he registered Warde didn't miss much.

'And you told her you'd need to get hold of her quickly?'

'Yes. As asked. I'm on to something. I have a lead. I've found someone who was at Pearse Street that night . . . who remembers something. He's nervous about talking. But I'm working on it. You see, lads, it's turning into quite a story. Maybe I should say it's Dessie. A touch of veracity. A real Special Branch man.'

Sergeant MacMahon leant across the table.

'Fuck off, Emmet. Get on with it. Can you contact her?'

'No, but she'll phone me. I set times I'll be in the office. I asked her if there was a phone where she was. She said no. But she was lying. She's not good at it.'

'How's she getting to Wicklow?' asked Stefan. 'The car?'

'I can't overdo it, Stevie. I can't interrogate the woman. She's close to the Army Council. She knows about secrets. If she gets any hint I'm codding her . . .'

'You don't know how long she'll be in Wicklow?'

'No, but she won't be back in Dublin for some time. She's going over to the west. She says for a holiday. I pushed it to get that out of her. Whatever she's doing, she doesn't want to talk about it. I don't know what the west means. It could be anywhere, but I'd trust what she says. She'll be in Laragh, close anyway, then travelling west. You could plump for Limerick, Kerry or Galway. I threw those at her, talking about holidays I'd had. She didn't pick it up, but she sort of nodded. Whatever she's up to isn't a holiday. She was nervous, as if she'd said too much.'

Emmet stopped. He picked up the glass of Guinness and drained it.

'It's not much when it comes to keeping tabs on her,' said Stefan.

'What did you expect, an itinerary?'

'Maybe more. Like you said, she trusts you. She trusts you a lot.'

Warde didn't reply. Stefan saw what he had seen in Bewley's, that the private detective felt those last words. He was meant to. Stefan knew he cared about Josephine Kilmartin. In their quiet, easy demeanour in the café, he had seen that she cared about Warde. He felt, as certainty – a demeaning, cheapening, degrading certainty – that what this said about the trust between them could be used.

'You'll have to get more out her, that's all. However it's done.'

'It's a big word, "however". She's a long way from stupid.'

'So are you, Emmet. I'm sure you can find all the lies she wants to hear.'

7

WESLEY COLLEGE

What Stefan Gillespie and Dessie MacMahon brought back to Dublin Castle seemed to satisfy Superintendent Gregory. It was hard to know what pleased him more: the information itself or the fact that he felt the game he was playing with Commandant de Paor and Military Intelligence was going his way. Emmet Warde was doing what Gregory wanted, that was clear. The private detective was a throw of the dice, but the number that had come up was good. Warde was unpredictable at best, untrustworthy at worst, not because he owed any allegiance to a German spy or the IRA, but because he was a drunk. He was a drunk who managed to cling on to the idea that somewhere in what was left of his self-esteem there was a bit of integrity not quite pickled by alcohol. Like Stefan, Terry Gregory sensed that Warde cared about Josephine Kilmartin in a way that was about more than the job she was paying him to do. In Gregory's considerable experience of manipulating other people's emotions, such feelings, especially when unspoken, were unlikely not to be reciprocated. That was positive, because it meant that Josie's trust went deeper than common sense and caution might normally admit. But there was a negative side. Emmet Warde's appetite for lying to her would have its limits, especially if the way she was being used could put her in danger. If she ended up providing information to Special Branch, however unwittingly, it could mark her out as an informer and a traitor to the IRA. Warde would know she might cross that line and never see it. If she did cross it, it would be because of him.

Terry Gregory was also pleased because he had his own information, and it fitted neatly with what Emmet Warde had extracted or surmised. Gregory had contacts inside the IRA. No one knew who they were; no one knew how high up the chain of command of the Army Council they went. The information came intermittently. It wasn't always reliable. There were times when the superintendent had to weigh half-truths or deliberate disinformation against his instincts. He didn't always get it right. There were arguments and struggles inside the Army Council that pitted different visions of the war with England against each other; that wrangled over the political fight against de Valera's government in the Twenty-Six Counties; that disagreed about how sabotage in Northern Ireland could serve the ends of a German invasion of Ireland without giving the Irish government a reason to destroy the Republican movement altogether. For some there was only the present opportunity to free Ireland, and the belief, ever more difficult to sustain, that the Germans were coming. For others there was serious doubt about how real that opportunity was, and a corresponding desire to ensure that the IRA survived the chaos. In the midst of all that, there were times it suited one faction to pass Special Branch enough information to ensure another faction was slapped down. There were other times when fear, or money, or personal antagonism, pushed information Gregory's way. Very little of that complex process was visible in the detectives' room. Like any serious magician, Superintendent Gregory kept his tricks to himself. What he knew, as far as most of the men in Special Branch experienced it, made its way to them out of the thin air. That was the case with what he knew now, as Stefan and Dessie sat in his office, reporting on Emmet Warde.

'There's going to be an Army Council meeting next week,' said Gregory, as if there was something self-evident about the statement. 'I don't know where, but Kerry or Limerick. Maybe Tralee, maybe Limerick City. Or anywhere in the middle of fucking nowhere. They may not have decided where. But it's a serious job. The big fellers from the four corners of the country, including the North. And they're the lads to watch. Stephen Hayes still calls himself the IRA Chief-of-Staff but he barely has the Boys under control south of the border, and his relationship with Belfast and Derry is rough. No love lost. Northern Command wants to take on the British. They want serious sabotage in Northern Ireland. They want dead soldiers. Hayes thinks that'll push Dev to take on the IRA in the South and drive a coach and horses through what's left of the organisation outside the Curragh Camp. If the bombing and shooting spills over the border, he's right. They're fucked down here. And there's fellers in the North wouldn't mind that. They want the IRA to take Dev on as well. It's bollocks, but dangerous bollocks. All the sense is on Hayes' side. But they don't see it. They think he's sitting on his arse because he's a coward or because he's a traitor. That idea's spreading. It doesn't help that he's pissed half the time. But the Boys are meeting to thrash the thing out. Next week.'

'And Josie Kilmartin is off west for a holiday,' said Stefan. 'Next week.'

'It seems so,' continued Superintendent Gregory. 'And you'd wonder if she's taking anyone with her. Herr Fürst's timing isn't bad, is it? The Germans are fucked off with Hayes doing nothing. That message is loud and clear. They want what the Boys in the North want. Bombs and bullets, airfields blown up, British soldiers shot. And they've got bugger all. Between Dev and the British, the IRA are still on the branch line they went up in *Oh, Mr Porter.* Seán McCaughey is running Northern Command now. My information is that he pushed Hayes to spring our friend Otto. McCaughey still thinks the German cavalry's over the hill. My bet's Otto will be at this meeting. And Miss Kilmartin will be the chauffeuse.'

'You think she knows she's being watched?' asked Stefan.

'I'd say not, Stevie. She'd be behaving differently if she did. We'll keep an eye on the car, but at a distance. She was out for most of the morning yesterday. We lost her. It doesn't matter. I'm not going to worry about losing her. Emmet's going to help find her again. And if she's driving to Laragh now, she's taking Mrs Stuart's car there. She's good enough at what she does to take back roads and unexpected turns and drive round the houses, not because she's being followed, but because it's how you stay safe. But for now, at least we know where she's going.'

'But not why,' said Dessie. 'It's an odd way to head west.'

'One step at a time,' replied Gregory. 'There'll be a reason. My instinct is that it's about our friend Fürst. She's been moving him around. That's the link. But softly, softly, that's how we tread. I don't want roadblocks in the mountains. I don't want her spooked. And if she's got Otto on board, I don't want some eejit Guard catching him. I want to know what he's at. All the more with this meeting.'

All the more still, thought Stefan Gillespie, since you want to know what Military Intelligence are up to. He smiled at Dessie, who had the same thought. But Dessie was on his own track. Neither Stefan nor Terry Gregory had followed him.

'If she's already got him out of Dublin, she won't have to worry.'

Terry Gregory nodded, catching up; a morning unaccounted for.

'She had time to get to Laragh and back, to Mrs Stuart's.'

'It's possible,' said the superintendent. 'Makes sense of the journey. She might not be going to Laragh with Fürst, but to collect him. They think we're still looking for him in the city and they've already got him out. He's safe. And she can take a long swing through the backroads of Carlow and Kilkenny and Tipperary, to wherever it is she's going. The question is, where is that? So, will Emmet tell us?'

Gregory was looking at Stefan, who had no clear answer.

'What she said is she'll keep in touch. She'll phone him. That's all.'

'Ah, come on. I think we can do better than that, Stevie.'

'He can only ask so much, sir.'

Superintendent Gregory shook his head.

'O ye of little faith! He can hammer harder if he lies harder. Our private detective is going to prove what a hell of a private detective he is. Mirabile dictu, as Ovid has it, he's about to find a feller who really does know what happened to Eamon Kilmartin. No more rumours, the real McCoy. And would you believe it, this feller isn't going to be so very far from where she's taking that little holiday of hers. Not so close that the hand of coincidence falls too heavily, but close enough that you should be able to pick up her trail, Stevie . . . with or without diversions.'

Stefan didn't reply. It was no less unpleasant than he expected, as far as Josie Kilmartin was concerned. But the bigger the lie, the more it would sound like what she wanted to hear. The question was still how far Warde would go with this.

Terry Gregory had read that question in his inspector's face.

'Emmet will do as he's fucking told. He's bought and sold now.'

Stefan nodded. It was true. Somewhere, he almost regretted that it was.

It was late when Stefan Gillespie walked along Wellington Quay to the door next to Paddy Geary's tobacconist's and the

86

stairs up to his flat. The next day, he would be going into the Wicklow Mountains, to Laragh. He was known there, and now there was a new inspector, a man he had worked with when he was in uniform, in Baltinglass, three years earlier. He was someone who would not display the usual suspicious dislike for Special Branch that festered in most Garda breasts, at least while it was Stefan who would be invading his police station, demanding help and information and giving nothing in return. But if Otto Fürst was in the house in Laragh, where Iseult Stuart lived, however well he was hidden, someone would know something; someone would have seen something. There would be no need to name the German or connect an inquiry about Mrs Stuart's well-known Republican shenanigans to the prison break at Mountjoy, which had featured obliquely in the press in any case. There was no shortage of reasons for Special Branch to ask questions about the lady of Laragh Castle. She made a point of her pro-German sympathies. Her home was somewhere a German spy would be made welcome.

The plan was still that Josie Kilmartin would lead them to Otto Fürst and deliver whatever it was that Superintendent Gregory wanted from that, in terms of what the German was doing, what the IRA was doing, or what benefit one-upmanship might bring to his relationship with Military Intelligence. The fact that following the German seemed to offer unlooked-for access to the divisions inside the IRA Army Council only upped the game. The superintendent was not a man to fail to congratulate himself when his instincts proved right. He was congratulating himself already on where those instincts might lead, but the job in hand was a delicate one; a fine web that might collapse at any point. And it was not the stuff of common knowledge in the detectives' room at Dublin Castle. None of this could leak out to Geróid de Paor and G2. Superintendent Gregory was relying on Stefan Gillespie and Emmet Warde to reel something in for him. Stefan knew that his superintendent enjoyed these games against the odds, almost for their own sake. They only made him long for the days when he was patrolling the mart in Baltinglass, checking for irregularities in the paperwork of the cattle on sale.

Stefan pushed open the door to the stairs that led up to his flat. He reached out in the darkness to switch on the light. Nothing happened. The bulb had gone a week before, and still hadn't been replaced; but it was a familiar darkness. As often as not there was no light. At first, he had been irritated enough to change the bulb himself. As time went on, it didn't seem to matter. He was used to climbing up the windowless stairwell in the dark. He turned on to the landing and took out his key. Even though he could barely see it, two years of aiming at the lock, meant he rarely missed. It was as he stepped forward with the key, that his feet touched something. It was soft and substantial. It moved. A drowsy, very hesitant voice.

'Hello, Pa. It's only me, Tom.'

Propped up against the door was Stefan's son, attempting a wary smile.

Tom was left in the flat with a cup of tea, while his father walked to the telephone box on Wellington Quay and contacted the housemaster at Wesley College. The call came just after Tom Gillespie's absence from his dormitory had been discovered. The words were few. There was embarrassment and relief from the housemaster. Stefan was still surprised and confused by his son's arrival. It was enough, on both sides, that Tom was where he was. The real conversation would come next day. Stefan returned to find his son sitting by the window, looking out at the river, anxious, nervous, uncertain what to expect. As yet, almost nothing had been said by way of explanation, and Stefan was more bewildered than anything else. In the weeks Tom had been boarding at the school, he had been home to Baltinglass with him for a weekend and had met him each week to catch up and talk. He had seen no real signs of unhappiness; nothing to lead him to expect this.

'Did you speak to the housemaster, Pa?' asked Tom quietly.

'Yes, the prefect got Mr Henshaw. They'd just found you were missing.'

'He must have been raging.'

'He wasn't raging at all. He was very concerned about you.' Stefan smiled. 'He was also embarrassed. You'd been gone a few hours. I'd say first years leaving the school at night, and no one even noticing, doesn't happen every day.'

The impact of what he had done only really hit Tom now.

'Does that mean Mr Henshaw will be in trouble?'

'I don't know about trouble, Tom, but he won't be looking forward to his conversation with the principal . . . because I'm sure Dr Irwin will know by now.'

Tom looked away from his father, back to the window and the river.

Stefan watched his son for almost a minute. It was no time to push.

'How did you get out?' He asked the question gently, casually.

'There's a window from the box room. And it's easy enough to climb the wall there. Some of the older boys . . . some-times . . . if you leave the catch up . . .'

'Except you weren't planning to go back.'

'I don't know.' Tom looked blank. 'It wasn't really a plan, Pa.'

'No, I don't suppose it was. Did anyone else know?'

Tom shook his head, but he didn't meet Stefan's eyes.

'That's a no that means yes, right?'

'Eric did, Eric Perty. He's the next bed in the dorm.'

'Didn't anyone see you?'

'It was after lights-out. I left my clothes on under the blankets, and then I went out like I was going to the toilet. I left the pillows in the bed. But it's very dark. When they look in, they never come right down the end where my bed is.'

Stefan looked at his son, still puzzled, as much by his own failure to see it coming as by what had happened. He felt he should have done, yet he could find nowhere to see the signs that ought to have alerted him. And he experienced the responsibility that suddenly loaded on him, like a weight he had not known he carried. Tom should have been able to say something to him before it got to this.

'You hungry?'

'A bit,' said Tom. 'I didn't really eat at supper. I was too nervous.'

'It'll be beans and toast. That's all we run to here. A speciality.'

'That's great, Pa. It's better than school, anyway.'

Something was lighter in Tom's voice. Stefan tousled his hair.

Father and son sat at the small table by the window. Tom ate and for some minutes there had been silence. From the street came the occasional sound of a shout, of laughter, as people left pubs and bars. A few cars passed on the Quays. Tom's fear had gone, but his actions hung over him. He didn't know where this left him.

'We better talk about it, hadn't we? Maybe a bit.'

Tom Gillespie looked up and nodded. He didn't want to.

'I wish you'd said something. Before, I mean. Before it got to this.'

Tom looked down again.

'I didn't want to. I thought you'd be angry.'

'I'm sorry you felt that. I wouldn't have been.'

'I thought you'd be disappointed.'

Stefan nodded, recognising, perhaps, that this wasn't far from the truth.

'I thought it would just get better, Pa. And I'd get used to it.'

'And did something start it? Has anything happened?'

'Not really, Pa. It's not anything in particular. That's what made it harder. I didn't want to say anything, but I don't know what I would have said anyway. I thought I'd sound stupid . . . that I didn't like . . . and it wasn't about the German thing really, but I suppose it made it worse . . . It was wishing I was home again.'

Stefan was almost relieved to find something specific to open this up.

'What's the German thing?'

'Doing German, I mean.'

'Is that bad? It was German or French. You chose German.'

'I'm quite good at it.' Tom smiled. 'I know more than I thought.'

'Well, we never really tried to teach you. I know Oma wanted to, but it felt as if . . . I don't know, as if that time had gone. But you must have picked bits up along the way. You've heard it round the house.' Stefan was silent, remembering. He had spoken German a lot at Tom's age, he and his mother. They rarely did now. 'Oma would like it if you spoke some German. It matters to her. And I forget that.'

On his mother's side, Stefan's family was German. It went back three generations now, but that part of his inheritance had been cherished. His mother had grown up speaking German and she made that part of Stefan's life too. He spoke the language fluently. As a child, he had spent summers in Germany with his cousins. But time, as time must, had weakened the bonds. For Tom, the links were tenuous. He called his grandparents by German words, Oma and Opa. There was a Germanness to Christmas that was unlike Christmas in other Irish homes. But there was little more. It was something lost, inevitably, thought Stefan.

'That's how it started, Pa.'

Stefan's moment of reflection hadn't changed Tom's course. 'What did?'

'The teacher asked us if we'd heard any German, or if we could say anything in German. I said a few things and, I suppose, it felt like everyone was quite impressed. He said, how did I get my accent so good and it was better than his!'

Stefan laughed. Whatever had happened couldn't be that bad.

'Then he wanted to know where I learnt it, and I said Oma was German, well, that her family was, and how I called them Oma and Opa because of that.'

'I'd have thought he'd be pleased,' said Stefan. 'I don't imagine teaching German to boys who mostly couldn't care less is a lot of fun. At least he's got someone who wants to do it now . . . and knows enough to get off to a good start.'

'That's what he said, well, sort of.'

Tom ate some of the beans. He seemed surer of himself.

'So, what's the problem?'

'Well, some of the boys at Wesley have brothers and uncles in the British Army. There's two in my class. And a few older boys in the house. Some of them started saying I was a Nazi and calling me Adolf. They kept doing this . . .' Tom put his finger up to his top lip in imitation of a Hitler moustache. He half laughed. It was a mixture of real amusement, hearing himself say it, and nervousness. He was unsure how his father would react. 'And they'd stick their arms in the air and shout "Sieg Heil" and stomp about the dorm goose-stepping. It was things like that.'

'And how long's that been going on?'

'A couple of weeks.' Tom found another smile from some-where. 'You know you're my Nazi dad? That's the gag when I see you. "Been to see your Nazi dad?"'

Stefan laughed. Whatever the pain, Tom could still find some of it funny.

'I wish you'd told me, Tom. Did you tell any teachers? Or Mr Henshaw?'

Tom looked at his father in something like astonishment.

'I don't want to get beaten up as well.'

'Sometimes you have to say something.'

'They'll get fed up, Pa. There's only one who's . . . nasty. The others are stupid. You know how stupid? There's a Jewish boy in third year. He speaks German as well as he does English. He said they did the same to him. When he told them to fuck off—' Tom had never used that word to his father. 'Sorry, Pa.'

'Never mind. Just make sure Oma never hears that.'

'Jesus!' Tom looked appalled at the thought of his grand-mother's response.

The next morning Stefan Gillespie got up early. It wasn't difficult. The sofa he had spent the night on was neither big nor comfortable. He had let Tom have the bedroom. By the time they finished talking, he could see his son was exhausted. It was mostly from anxiety, and the release of some of that anxiety, but he was nodding off even while they spoke. Stefan sensed that Tom had probably slept little in the nights leading up to the events of the previous evening. But he had slept soundly that night in the flat, though Stefan could hear that it was a restless and troubled sleep. Now, as light came in from the window overlooking the Liffey, Stefan went into the bedroom and woke his son up, sitting on the bed.

'You don't need to get up, Tom. I'm going to see Mr Henshaw.'

The name of the housemaster brought Tom fully to consciousness.

'What are you going to say, Pa?'

'I don't know.' Stefan laughed. 'Any suggestions?'

Tom shook his head and smiled sheepishly.

'I assume the answer isn't just to take you straight back to school.'

'Jesus, Pa, everyone's going to know . . .'

'What's done is done. It's only a week till half-term. It's easiest for you to go home early. I'll take you to Baltinglass.

You'll be with Oma and Opa. I'll find some time. It's a break. We can talk. We'll think about what we're going to do.'

A new and unconsidered consequence hit Tom.

'God, what's Opa going to say! He'll be furious.'

'No one's going to say anything till we've all breathed deeper.'

'But I will have to go back, won't I?'

Stefan had not thought this far, but now he had to.

'You won't have to, Tom. That doesn't mean you shouldn't.'

At Wesley College, Stefan was directed to the headmaster's office. He had left a message at Special Branch, to say he would be late. Gregory would have to wait. But there was no waiting at the school. The Reverend Thomas Irwin, principal and Methodist minister, was there to greet him; with him was Mr Henshaw the housemaster. Dr Irwin was struggling to balance several emotions. He was not angry about what had happened, but he was irritated. Anger would have been appropriate in an older boy breaking bounds, but in such cases the boy was likely to be caught, if he was caught, on his return and the matter dealt with by an ascending scale of punishment. The business of running away, though not unknown, was different. The reasons that happened were various, but as they had their roots in a boy's unhappiness, Dr Irwin prided himself that his staff, especially the housemaster and the matron who looked after the welfare of the boarders, picked up problems before they got out of hand, especially with the intake of first years. It was rare that signs of trouble weren't noticed, rarer still that a problem reached the point where a boy ran away. Disappointment also made up part of Dr Irwin's response, as well as a sense of his own failure, as principal and as chaplain. There was a measure of discomfort and embarrassment, too. The boys in his charge were also in his care. Not only had Tom Gillespie been able to leave school unseen, he was absent for hours before anybody noticed. The virtual silence from the housemaster, as the principal apologised and expressed his very real concern, left Stefan feeling mostly sympathy for Mr Henshaw. What there was of anger and irritation in the Reverend Dr Irwin would, undoubtedly, head his way. It wasn't easy for Stefan to say that none of it mattered, since it obviously did, but he knew that the one master Tom really liked at Wesley College was the housemaster. He had no desire to blame anyone. Tom would hate it if it attached to Mr Henshaw.

The outcome was very much what Stefan had worked out during a restless night. He didn't yet know the full extent of Tom's unhappiness, or whether more was provoking it than his son had said. He mentioned the bullying over Tom's German heritage, but he made as little of it as he could. While that might have triggered events, he had to take Tom's word it was not the problem; a broader unhappiness at being away from home in a place he did not yet relate to was the heart of the matter. And it couldn't all be about Tom and Wesley College. The decision to send him there had been difficult because of opposition from a Catholic Church that still laid claim to his son's education and upbringing. Stefan wondered if he had been too keen to take that on, for his own sake more than his son's. He had not looked at what it might mean for Tom, brought up a Catholic, now in a Protestant school. It would be ironic if Tom, having sometimes been bullied at primary school for his Protestant father and grandparents, now faced the same in reverse, in a Protestant school. Neither the principal nor Mr Henshaw felt there was a problem with that, but Stefan was less sure. Maybe his son simply couldn't fit.

There was little more left to say at Wesley College. It was agreed Tom would go home; with half-term he would have a break of two weeks. If he came back, he would come back then. That was something Stefan would have to resolve with his son. The school would give Tom the support it could. Now they all knew, it would be easier. Stefan was unsure. A sleepless night had left other things in his mind. There had been times in the last year when he was conscious he didn't know his son as well as he thought, that there was a distance he hadn't seen before. Absence was a word that had been used a lot that morning. His own absence for much of his son's growing up was not often at the front of his mind. Today it was.

When Stefan got back to Wellington Quay, the unmarked Special Branch Ford was outside. He didn't need Paddy Geary to tell him that Dessie had come in search of him, but Paddy was there, leaning in the doorway of his shop, smoking and reading a newspaper, in the position he spent most of his days, passing time with everyone.

'Sergeant MacMahon's upstairs, Stevie.'

Stefan didn't stop to discuss what he already knew.

'He was out for some bacon and eggs. He'll have breakfast ready.'

That information was more surprising, and as Stefan climbed the stairs up to the flat, the smell of frying bacon pushed some of the usual mustiness aside.

Inside, Tom was tucking into a plate of bacon and fried eggs.

'Do you live on beans?' said Dessie dismissively.

'I don't usually have guests for breakfast.'

'I'm not surprised. You'd even leave your son to starve!'

Tom grinned, then continued eating.

'Terry wants you in Laragh this morning. I brought the car. If there's anything going on with the Stuart woman at all, he wants you sniffing it out.'

'It can wait, can't it? I need some time. I'll talk to him.'

'He's not in the mood. He wants this show on the road. And you and Emmet with it. He's buzzing with it. You'll head west whenever Josie Kilmartin does. She left home in Mrs Stuart's car first thing this morning. She was followed as far as Dundrum. They lost her, but she was picked up again near Roundwood. She couldn't be followed, but you'd put your money on her being in Laragh by now.'

Stefan nodded. Dessie grinned and changed the subject.

'So the boss sent me to get you out of bed and into the mountains. I wasn't expecting to find the son and heir here. And on the run as well. A wanted man!'

Tom looked up, laughing now.

'He told me all about it,' said Dessie. 'But we've sorted it out.'

'Sorted what out?' said Stefan.

'I'll take him to my place. You do what you must. He can stay with Brenda for the day. My lad Noel's on half-term. He's not much older. If your woman goes west, you'll have to go. If Tom needs to go home, I'll take him. All right, Tom?'

Tom looked up again and nodded. He was enjoying himself.

Dessie sniffed. Stefan sniffed too. Smoke rose from a pan on the gas ring.

'Jesus fucking Christ!' Dessie flung himself at the pan. 'The bacon!'

8

LARAGH

Laragh was never an easy place to go for Stefan Gillespie, even if the thoughts it inevitably brought into his head were not so hard to put aside now. It would soon be ten years since his wife, Maeve, died in the Upper Lake at nearby Glendalough. The circumstances of that had faded once, only to return to haunt him in a different way. Time had tricked him, letting his loss subside and then resurrecting it. Most of the years that followed Maeve's death he spent living with the accident that drowned her. It was not long ago that the truth unexpectedly emerged, that Maeve had been murdered. It was a discovery that didn't so much bring finality to her death, as leave it in a darker place. But time, as time does, had softened the edges again. Nevertheless, the town that was surrounded by the mountains he had known since childhood was a place he would not choose to visit. Though close to his home in Baltinglass, it was somewhere, for the most part, not much happened. It was a place that he never needed to seek out. But he sought it out now. And whatever his reasons for doing so, it could only feel strange that, as he drove through the mountains, it was a day on which his thoughts were not so much on Maeve and the past, but on Tom, her son, and the present. He didn't often think how it might have been if, instead of only him and Tom, there had been, down all the years that had gone, Tom's mother with them. The unwanted thought that what his son had lost was more than he had lost was hard to shake off. And the job he was doing here, chasing shadows that chased shadows, in a well of vicious and purposeless circularity, felt emptier than ever.

There had been changes at the Garda barracks in Laragh since Stefan was last there, investigating the murder of his wife, eight years after her death. There was the new inspector, his old friend from Baltinglass; two of the station's most ancient Gardaí had retired; there had been transfers, too. The events of Maeve's death, both the memories of the drowning and the recent events that revealed her murder, were not completely forgotten, but they needed stirring to bring them to the surface, and there were reasons for that. They included Stefan's decision that Tom would never know any truth other than the accident he had always believed cost him his mother. A lot of what had been discovered was left unsaid. By now, whatever baggage Stefan Gillespie brought with him as he stopped the Ford outside the familiar building that was Laragh's Garda Station was his own.

Inspector Downey had worked with Stefan before Terry Gregory claimed him for Special Branch. What the two inspectors had to say to each other at first was about family news and the stuff of war and the Emergency that was everyone's staple diet. Neither man had much to say about work. Stefan's routine did not lend itself to discussion outside Dublin Castle; Patrick Downey's world was one in which little occurred that was worth talking about. So Downey spoke at length about his children, and when he asked about Tom, Stefan talked about him as if the events of the previous night hadn't happened. He didn't know Downey well enough to tell the truth. The conversation was too casual. Not that he knew what the truth was yet. Idle words were soon exchanged for business.

Superintendent Gregory had already spoken to Inspector Downey by phone. It wasn't the first conversation of that kind Downey had known. The comings and goings at Laragh Castle, Iseult Stuart's house, were intermittently of interest to Special Branch and had been for some time. She was a Republican with a public face; she revelled in advertising her allegiances, especially her enthusiastic support for Germany in the war. But an eccentric public profile didn't prevent her providing succour and shelter to Republican elements that posed a more serious threat to the Irish government than she did. As far as Special Branch were concerned, it was unclear when Mrs Stuart was worth watching, or even if it was worth expending precious resources watching her at all. Now it seemed it might be.

'Your super was on first thing,' said Inspector Downey. 'I take it there's no change. You don't want to speak to her. And you don't want the house searched.'

'No, no attention at all. That also means Terry doesn't want your men knowing anything out of the ordinary's going on. He doesn't want anything said, anything asked, that makes this more than routine. It goes with the Emergency and keeping an eye on the usual characters. Ordinary checks. Nothing more than that.'

'That's not a problem, Stevie. Mrs Stuart may not be poor, but like the poor, she is always with us. There's always someone visiting. I couldn't tell you who half of them are, but the German embassy's well represented. Herr Hempel himself, of course, and Petersen, the press attaché. The Republicans are usually the sort they let out in public, assorted poets and half-arsed politicians. Terry sends some of your fellers down every so often to question her and shake things up a bit. There's a few IRA sorts that pitch up from time to time. From the hills when they're training up there. They might stay over. They come and go. We don't take much notice and we don't make a fuss. For the most part we do what your boss tells us. We leave her alone.'

'So, is there anyone there now?'

'Yes. There's a feller who could match the description Terry gave me.'

'You've seen him?'

'He's been seen walking, up above the house. I'm going on what one of my Guards told me. He has sheep there.' Downey laughed. 'Which is handy enough.'

'Your man's not been in the town?'

'No, he's been seen nowhere else. He's not advertising himself. For some reason he must think striding across a mountain makes him invisible. Who is he?'

'It's not important.'

Patrick Downey laughed.

'I don't need to know, you mean. I could make a guess, from the news . . .'

'Well, right or wrong, don't make any guesses in front of your men.'

Downey picked up a pipe and started to fill it with tobacco.

'Ah, Stevie, you fellers do have to justify your wages, don't you?'

Stefan smiled but stuck with the reason he was there.

'What about the woman Terry mentioned – driving Mrs Stuart's car?'

'Yes, she's here. She must have arrived quite early this morning.'

'You've seen her, then?'

'I have, I saw her in the village. But not in Iseult Stuart's car. In another one. It's not one we know. So, if she drove down in Mr Stuart's, she's changed to another motor. A Morris. And there's the registration number.' He pushed a slip of paper across the desk. 'She had it topped up with petrol at the garage, though the tank was three-quarters full. And she had Mick Hogan check the tyres. A journey ahead. Not that I'm any detective, Stevie. She stopped at the phone box to make a call. That would be a strange thing, I'd say, given that Mrs Stuart has a telephone.'

Patrick Downey sat back in his chair and lit his pipe. There was a look of satisfaction on his face. Stefan could see the inspector was not only pleased with what he had just presented, but his smile made it clear there was more to come.

'I'm tempted to ask, Patrick, does a phone number go with the car number?'

Stefan knew the benefits of a small rural telephone exchange.

'Sure, you Special Branch fellers don't miss a trick out here in the sticks.'

Inspector Downey pushed another piece of paper across the desk.

'A Dublin number.'

Stefan Gillespie looked down. He knew the number: Emmet Warde's.

'Can I use your phone, Patrick?'

Downey now pushed the receiver towards Stefan. He grinned.

'You can. And tell Terry Gregory he owes me a favour. We try to keep out of the clutches of Special Branch here. But you can never be sure what's coming.'

When Stefan Gillespie left Laragh, he took the road that would let him drive past the entrance to the house which belonged to Iseult Stuart. It was not far from the Garda barracks. He had no special reason to go that way. There would be nothing to see. Laragh Castle was set a long way back from the road. But he wanted to remind himself where it was. He drove that way for a number of reasons. One was no more than curiosity, but another had to do with the kind of accumulation of information that came instinctively to him. It was instinct that did not have the depth it had in Superintendent Gregory's mind, but it was the same desire to know, to collect information, to make that information complete, however small, however slight the things that made for completeness. There was also a connection that made his curiosity stronger. He did not know Iseult Stuart. He had never seen her. But he had met her husband. It was just over a year earlier, in Berlin, when he was acting as a courier for the Department of External Affairs, carrying documents to the Irish embassy. Francis Stuart ostensibly taught at a German university, but he also worked for German radio, writing for Joseph Goebbels' English-language radio service, and broadcasting himself to Ireland. While there was little communication between Iseult and Francis Stuart, other than what letters dissected by German, Irish and even British censors and Intelligence services allowed, in the way of the most vague and innocuous, it was no accident that a German spy was a guest in the Stuarts' home. There was nothing in any of that, let alone in what Stefan was doing now, that would be illuminated by driving past the entrance to Laragh Castle, but however much he despised the games he had to play for Terry Gregory, however empty they were, he still played them.

He approached the gates to Iseult Stuart's house and the row of trees and untidy shrubs that made up the boundary of the demesne. Hills rose all around, reaching towards mountains that could not quite be seen. He drove slowly. He glimpsed old stone and upper windows; woodwork that even at a distance showed peeling white paint. The pitch of the roof had a Gothic look. He knew the feel of this place. The Republican Stuarts might be a long way from Wicklow's fading Anglo-Irish landlords, but it was the same inheritance. There was nothing remarkable to see, yet he knew the Stuarts better somehow, both of them. And then, as he passed the drive, and the rusting, broken iron gates, there was something to see, in front of an ivy-covered gate lodge he had hardly noticed. It was the grey Morris that Inspector Downey had registered in Laragh. And there was Josephine Kilmartin, washing the car, sponging soapy water from a bucket over the bonnet. Stefan slowed even more, in a way he ought not to have done. But it was barely noticeable; no more than a different tone as he changed gear. It meant nothing to someone who had no reason to be suspicious of a passing car, and here, away from Dublin, Josie Kilmartin had no suspicions. Her own instincts, sharp enough in the streets of Dublin, were softened by where she was and by the things that filled her mind that had nothing to with the IRA or German spies. She looked up, seeing the Ford, for long enough to wave a greeting. Then the car was gone.

Detective Inspector Gillespie and Superintendent Gregory walked from Dublin Castle to Emmet Warde's office in Capel Street. The information Stefan had already passed on only seemed to confirm what Gregory expected. It established above all where Otto Fürst was and placed Josephine Kilmartin alongside him.

'I saw her when I drove past Laragh Castle, sir, cleaning the car.'

'I shouldn't be surprised by what people do,' said Gregory, 'but habits, that's the thing. Always the same. You'd really think she was off on a holiday.'

Stefan laughed. 'I suppose driving a spy about makes a change.'

'We leave it alone now. And trust she's going to keep in touch with Emmet. She's already done that. You told Inspector Downey not to do any more, did you?'

'Yes, sir.'

'I don't care about Laragh and Mrs Stuart now. She doesn't matter. But what we know is that the cars have been changed. It's the Morris Fürst will be going in.'

'Did we get anything from the registration?'

'We did. It's a long way from home.'

'So where's home?'

'It belongs to a priest in Donegal. A Father McLellan, the parish priest in Moville, Inishowen. He's not important but he's on the files. More your pain-in-the-arse Republican than anyone who matters. And he's lent out his car for the cause. The IRA won't be flush with vehicles, so they shuffle these things round Ireland. Who knows how it got down here? But we've some idea where it's going.'

'Do you know what Josie said to Emmet?'

Terry Gregory nodded.

'You'll be going tomorrow. That's when she's leaving Laragh. We don't know her destination, but I think Limerick will do for you. It'll be close enough.'

It was what Stefan expected, but not what he wanted to hear.

'I need some time, sir. Not much, just a bit of time . . . the thing is—'

'I know about your boy. If you're taking him back to Baltinglass, you'll have to fit it in with what's left of today. You've got tonight. You have the car.'

Up the flight of stairs, in the bare, uninviting office, Emmet Warde was waiting. He was looking out of the window as Superintendent Gregory and Inspector Gillespie entered. Gregory opened the door without knocking. Warde was working for him now. No niceties were required. The private detective did not turn round immediately. He knew Gregory was on his way. He didn't offer any niceties either.

'You should get that window cleaned, Emmet. You can hardly see.'

'I thought about it, Terry, but there's nothing worth seeing anyway.'

Only now did he turn round. He sat down at the desk. The two Special Branch men sat on the two chairs facing him. There was an empty glass in front of Warde. There was no bottle visible, but the smell of fresh whiskey was there.

'I'd offer you a cup of tea, but the gas has been turned off.'

The superintendent took out a cigarette. He offered one to Warde.

'I don't suppose you get through a lot of tea, do you?'

The private detective didn't reply.

'I was disappointed I had to call you, Emmet. After Inspector Gillespie let me know that Miss Kilmartin had been on the phone to you. Were you tied up?'

'Since you knew already, Terry, what's the problem?'

'Celerity versus procrastination, Emmet, that's the problem. Procrastination, as you'll know, is the thief of time. "Year after year it steals, till all are fled." You might not know that bit, but you can probably understand that as a policeman, theft is something I abhor. Even Inspector Gillespie, a policeman of a much softer school than the one I attended, abhors it. Isn't that right, Stevie? You can't abide it.'

Stefan knew no answer was required.

Gregory lit his cigarette and leant across the desk to light Warde's.

'Don't fuck me about, Major-General. When you hear from your friend, Miss Kilmartin, you tell me or tell Inspector Gillespie. And you do it with celerity. Fucking celerity. Make that your watchword. And make sure that every single thing she says, every single thing you read between the lines, is reported. Because I could be very tempted to wonder if you were even going to tell me about that call.'

'I'm not hiding anything, Terry.'

'Good, but let's pay the proper attention to time's winged chariot, shall we? You're on my time now. And if you're on my time, you shift your fucking arse.'

Gregory smiled and sat back. The tone was businesslike, even cheerful.

'She leaves Laragh tomorrow morning. You've told me. She'll be wherever she's going in the afternoon. She said nothing to make where clearer than before?'

'No. I said I'd got some information from someone who was at Pearse Street when Eamon Kilmartin was there and remembered him, not a policeman, a soldier. I said he was delivering ammunition. He was leaving when the Intelligence fellers arrived to question the lads. He knew one of them. I told her I've a name and an old address, on the Kerry–Limerick border. The man doesn't live there now. He sold a farm and moved somewhere else. I'm following that up. I might get more.'

'Jesus, Major-General, you sound like you almost believe it yourself.'

Warde continued in a monotone, as if he was being interrogated.

'I said I thought this man had moved to a bigger farm. It could have been in the same area, or further away. I thought Kerry or Limerick still, but it could have been Clare to cover wherever Josie might end up. I said I hoped I might get an address for him, either from the owner of the place he sold or from the auctioneer.'

When Warde finished he shrugged and stubbed out his cigarette.

'I'm impressed, Emmet,' said Superintendent Gregory. 'Aren't you, Stevie?'

Terry Gregory barely seemed to notice how uneasily the elaborate lie sat on the private detective's tongue, though Warde didn't hide it. He only showed amusement at how neatly it went together. But what Gregory took in and what he didn't was based on well-established principles of efficiency. He didn't need the emotion that went with this unless it added useful information. And it didn't.

'She said she wouldn't be far from where I was going,' continued Warde. 'She wants to know as soon as I find out anything. For her, this is the first solid evidence in twenty years. The first time there's a name that might link directly . . .'

Emmet Warde let the thought drift away.

'How will she contact you?'

'I've booked a hotel in Limerick. She can get me there. I've booked a room for Stefan. I don't know how close that's going to be to Josie. But it'll be a start.'

'It'll do, Emmet,' said Gregory, nodding. 'Stick with Limerick, I'd say.'

'Is that a guess, Terry?' asked the private detective. 'Or do you know more?'

'I'm not in the habit of guessing. But that's all I have.'

The superintendent got up.

'That'll do for now. Miss Kilmartin leaves tomorrow and so do you two.'

Stefan Gillespie stood up too.

'So what's the aim of this, Terry? If you already know something about where this Army Council meeting is, what's Josie going to add to that? If there's some feller giving you information, he'll know a fuck sight more than she does.'

'It's the man she's driving, Emmet. That's her contribution.'

Warde stood up, taking the empty glass from the desk. He walked to the filing cabinet and opened a drawer. He produced a half-empty bottle of Powers.

'I'd offer you a drink, lads, but apart from the fact that there's not a lot left in the bottle, I've been advised I should be more selective about who I drink with.'

'Just be sober in the morning, Emmet,' said Gregory quietly.

As the superintendent turned to leave, Stefan had a question.

'Didn't she ask where you got this new information about her brother?'

'I said I got it from a feller in Special Branch. A man I have some dirt on. And that's not hard to believe, is it? If I was so inclined, there's a lot of dirt that would be easy to put together. I know no one minds very much who you boys shoot, but there are other things that are nasty enough. Wouldn't you say, Terry?'

'There are, Emmet.' Gregory smiled. 'And you do have to protect your sources. After all, a private detective of your calibre has a reputation to maintain.'

Emmet Warde raised his glass and drank the whiskey down in one.

'Cheers!'

He filled the glass once more as the two Special Branch men left.

The house on the North Strand where Dessie MacMahon lived with his wife Brenda and his four children was small and cluttered, comfortable and busy. Just now it was noisy not only with the offspring of the MacMahons but a selection of children from surrounding streets who moved through the kitchen in shifts, eating as quickly as they could in order to return outside to play. The fact that more children were eating than Brenda MacMahon had counted that day did not faze her. The portions were a lot smaller, the mess a lot bigger. As Stefan Gillespie pulled up outside in the Ford, with Dessie in the passenger seat, the front door was open and a trail of children of all ages was emerging. Tom Gillespie was there, laughing loudly, deep in conversation with Dessie's oldest boy, slightly shorter and slightly older. The two were about to break into a run and disappear. Tom had not noticed his father. Dessie grabbed Noel by the collar. He was spattered liberally with mud.

'I take it you didn't manage to wash for your dinner?'

'Didn't have time, Daddy!'

'You're filthy. Top to toe.'

Noel looked at his father blankly. This was self-evident, surely.

'And so's Tom. Jesus, and in his fecking school uniform.'

Tom's Wesley College flannels and blazer were if anything dirtier and more mud-spattered than the clothes Noel MacMahon was wearing. Tom only grinned.

'We were down on the shore. By the docks. Tom's never seen it.'

'Well, he's seen it now,' laughed Dessie. 'Sorry, Stevie!'

Stefan laughed too, simply relieved how different Tom was from the boy he left in the flat that morning. The day had rescued him. He had forgotten to worry.

Brenda MacMahon came out on to the street.

'He's had a good day. You can tell from the state of him.'

'I can.' Stefan's voice was quieter. 'Thank you, Brenda.'

'He's welcome, any time. And he may put some manners on my crowd.'

Tom frowned, as if this was a truly humiliating idea.

'We need to go home. I've told Oma and Opa we're on our way.'

Tom Gillespie nodded, now more subdued; he was back in the real world.

'I don't know if they've told Jumble. He'll know soon enough.'

Tom smiled broadly again. Whatever else, there would be Jumble, his dog.

9

THE RICHMOND ASYLUM

On the journey home to Baltinglass, little was said between Stefan and Tom, but there was nothing uncomfortable about the silence. Tom was not in a car so much that it wasn't still a simple pleasure to look out at the world. He was relieved that the acceptance of what he had done seemed to involve no repercussions. There was none of the anger he had anticipated. The future was there, but not now. And that was enough. Stefan was only concerned that his son would be back in the place that mattered to him. What happened next would depend on Tom; he must find a way to help his son make the best decision. It would not be difficult to send him back to Wesley College. The event was already less significant, even in Tom's mind, than it had been; a boy breaking bounds to see his father. That was how the school wanted to see it. It would be forgotten. But if Tom couldn't find a way to believe he would be happy at the school, the problem would still be there. In a way Stefan recognised, because he had it in himself, Tom thought too much about things that needed moving round rather than pushing through. If anything, Tom carried that thinking with a greater intensity. Where Stefan could let a problem go, he was beginning to see that his son couldn't.

Tom would have to believe that returning to Wesley was what he wanted; he would have to make it his own.

Even as father and son came home to the farm below Kilranelagh Hill, the lines were being drawn between Tom's grandparents, David and Helena, in ways Stefan might have anticipated. They were less than useful. Helena felt Wesley College had been a mistake. She saw Tom's deeper sensitivities more clearly than Stefan. The fact that she missed her grandson more fiercely than she could have expected didn't help her bring much objectivity to that conclusion. David had not been keen on the school initially. He didn't want the fight with the Catholic Church that in the end never came. Now he had come to believe the college was the best of the few options they had. He wanted more for Tom than the secondary school in Baltinglass could offer; the end to education at fourteen or fifteen. He had persuaded himself there must be change; Wesley College was that change. Despite David's love for his grandson, the idea that the decision would have to come from Tom himself was not something he saw. Homesickness was natural, but time would cure it; Tom had to buckle down and get on with it. Surely that was the reality.

Stefan had felt the two approaches in the bud, even from a phone call home. By the time he got back with Tom, they were fully grown. These two opposing views were not, in their extremities, what Stefan wanted to leave Tom with. Helena would offer a deceptively easy way out, while David would put his grandson's back up. There was time to work things out, but not as much time as Stefan needed alone. Yet he couldn't be there. He would be back, but a lot would happen while he was away. What Stefan wanted, as he prepared to leave Tom at the farm, was for nobody to say much at all until he got back. He gave what instructions he could. The subject of school was to be left to settle, like milk, so that the cream of the right solution might come to the top. But it was not something he could rely on; from his mother, his father or his argumentative, stubborn son.

Meanwhile, for the one night Stefan was home, the house was full of the vitality that only this son and grandson could bring to it. Tom had spent what was left of the daylight in the fields and woods with Jumble. He came in full of everything he had missed, wanting to know all that was happening on the farm. He would be up early the next morning to help with milking. There was a list of jobs he wanted drawn up. He was throwing himself into the farm with an enthusiasm that was an expression of his love for his grandparents. But it was also about putting aside the problems he was still unused to shouldering. Neither Helena nor David believed their grandson's proposed workload would be maintained for more than a few days, but they enjoyed his good intentions. He brought a lightness to their lives that wasn't always there now. Stefan felt, almost physically, how close his grandparents and his son were; although he was at the centre of things for this one night, he was still slightly outside that. He wondered if when he got back from Terry Gregory's wild goose chase – that's what it felt like more than ever – even his father's views on Tom returning to Wesley College might shift closer to his mother's opposition. The last thing he wanted was a consensus that excluded him.

For now, Stefan had done what he could. The days that were to follow belonged to Superintendent Gregory and the man he had to travel to the west of Ireland with, a man he didn't much like and didn't think could deliver the kind of information Terry Gregory was looking for, whatever that was. The head of Special Branch had little trouble sending his men on operations that had no clear purpose. Often enough, there was only a place to sniff or an itch to scratch. This journey west, to see if something or nothing happened, offered endless opportunities to fail and no idea what success would look like.

Stefan Gillespie stood out in the farmyard at Kilranelagh that night, smoking a cigarette. He had watched Tom's light go off upstairs. He thought his son would sleep well again, after what must have been a lot of nights of barely sleeping at all. He could hear the clatter of plates from the kitchen, as his mother and father washed up. He heard their laughter too, and he thought how quiet the evenings at Kilranelagh must be for them, without their grandson. He walked across the cobbles, breathing in the air of the farmyard and the countryside beyond it, listening to cattle shifting in the barn. He felt the urge that came more often than it had, to find a way to leave Terry Gregory and Garda Special Branch behind. But there was no way to do that right now. The Emergency that was the war in Ireland meant there was no resigning. He smiled, wondering, as he always did at such times, whether it suited him that way. The urge was easy when he couldn't act.

There was a rumble, deep and heavy, somewhere in the darkness, far off. It felt as if it was to the south. It wasn't unlike the sounds that came from the mountains when the red flags flew on the approaches to the Glen of Imaal, and the Irish Army was firing on the ranges, in preparation for whatever it was they prepared for. Not long ago the idea that the Germans would come, or the British, or both, had hovered over Ireland distinctly. But these seemingly very real possibilities had already faded, an irrelevance set against the vastness of the Russian steppes and the deserts of North Africa. The artillery still sounded in the Wicklow Mountains for the battles that would never come and could never have remotely been won. But the sounds Stefan Gillespie heard now were different. They were longer, lower, and if the ground did not actually shake, the way they travelled in the night air created the impression that it did. He knew the sound. He had heard it closer than this, but far off too. He had been in London and in Malta when bombs were falling. He stood in the farmyard and listened. There had been one blast, then another; a gap and now a third. And then there was nothing but the silence of the night. He saw David in the light of the kitchen door.

'I'd shut the door, Pa. No point showing a light.'

It was an instinct his own experience gave him that seemed out of place, but his father pulled the door behind him and walked out into the dark farmyard.

'There's enough lights out there, Stefan. One won't matter.'

'I know. It's a habit. Once you've got it . . .'

'You think it's bombs, then?'

'It is. I don't know where. Somewhere south. I don't know how far.'

The night was quiet. Then there was the screech of a vixen from the opposite hill, a sound that cut through the darkness, familiar yet always strange, and now reassuring. Father and son smiled at a noise that belonged to the dark.

'It's not the army, would you say – on an exercise?'

David was still looking for an explanation for the noise that didn't belong.

'It's the wrong direction. And it's a different sound. I know it.'

Stefan turned back towards the house.

'Seems like the end of it, Pa.' Stefan smiled. 'So, perhaps not an invasion.'

The two men went inside, dismissing the incident, even though it had no place in the stillness of an Irish night. The thought that there might be people at the end of those explosions did not enter David Gillespie's head. The moment, unexpected and disturbing as it was, had gone. The morning would bring an explanation. But the thought was in Stefan's head for a time, as he went upstairs to bed. He had seen what the wrong end of all that looked like. But soon enough the blasts had gone from his head, too. They were distant and transitory, however troubling. They were replaced, as Stefan fell asleep, by his own preoccupations.

Three bombs had fallen south of Carlow during the night. Three people were dead. There was no further detail. In the absence of information, speculation made the bombs variously German or British, dropped by mistake or dropped on purpose, depending on the prejudices of the speaker. While it was possible to argue that a German plane could have lost its bearings and made an error, it was, naturally, harder to conceive that a British bomber could mistake Ireland for somewhere in occupied Europe. Stefan Gillespie reached the Carriage Yard to discover that two more bombs had fallen that night, in South Dublin. Two houses had been destroyed but no one had been killed. There were only minor injuries. It was the business of the government to maintain a proper level of neutral indignation, directed with scrupulous fairness, publicly at least, at both combatants, while at the same time minimising the significance of the incident. However, the proper place for indignation was in the diplomatic notes that would result from further investigation. Public indignation, directed at only one belligerent, was unhelpful.

'They're all German bombs,' said Superintendent Gregory, shortly. 'The Germans will say they don't know anything about it. Down the road, when most people have forgotten, they'll say the pilot mistook us for Bristol or Blackpool.'

The subject was of little interest to Terry Gregory. It wasn't his remit. But he still cast the bombs, as he cast almost everything, in a mould that measured chance against coincidence and incompetence against conspiracy. Behind every incident there was almost always something you couldn't quite see. Sometimes these things mattered and sometimes they didn't. But you needed to hold on to the strands of information and misinformation long enough to be able to judge which was which.

'But even a mistake does no harm in the right place, Stevie.'

Terry Gregory was looking down at a file as he spoke, turning the page. The issue of bombs, wherever they fell, was only occupying a tiny corner of his mind.

'There's three people dead,' said Stefan Gillespie. 'Isn't that harm enough?'

'Harm enough, but not too much.'

The superintendent looked up, smiling.

'I don't get the point, sir.'

Stefan wasn't smiling. His boss's idle, empty words irritated him.

'It does no harm to remind us there's plenty more where they came from.'

'Is that likely?'

'Possible, likely? You never know what's likely. Take last night. I had to send Jimmy Fallon and Mick Harris out to Kilmainham. There was a feller holed up in his house with a fucking revolver, screaming he'd shoot anyone who tried to take him. The Guards wouldn't go near him. He'd already sent a shot past a detective from Rathmines. I think it was Jim Guthrie, so you couldn't altogether blame the feller. I wouldn't mind a shot myself. Anyway, that was after the bombs. Your man wasn't anywhere near, but he had it in his head there was artillery along the Liffey and the IRA were coming for him. He thought he was surrounded.'

Stefan looked at his boss, unsure how to respond. The story wasn't finished. Gregory's tone suggested the end would call for laughter, but you could never tell.

'So what happened?'

'Mick knew your man, and between him and his wife, they got him to put down the gun and open the door. He didn't fire again. And they carted him off to the Richmond Asylum. Not his first visit. I'd say he's been in and out a fair bit.'

And the tone had changed. Superintendent Gregory was more reflective. The smile on his face had disappeared. He stood and walked to the window. He looked out into the Carriage Yard. He turned and shrugged.

'That's how it goes. And that's why you'll be collecting Emmet from the madhouse this morning. The feller they carted off is his brother, Charlie Warde. Emmet's there with him now. He'll be waiting for you. Keep me in touch. And don't scare the culchies. All I want to know is more about our friend, Herr Fürst.'

Stefan Gillespie was still taking in the story he had just heard, even as Terry Gregory was pushing it out of the way; its job done. He wasn't sure where to place Emmet Warde. He had the story Dessie MacMahon had told him in Bewley's, that suggested a difficult, maybe unreliable man. This was just strange.

'And watch Emmet, Stevie.'

'Does that mean you don't trust him, sir?'

'In the face of all the facts, he thinks he's an honest man. So no, I don't.'

Stefan drove to Grangegorman and the Richmond Asylum. He knew the building, though it was a long time since he had been inside it. As a young Guard he had taken people there. He remembered the jokes, or at least the joke; there only really was one. If you went to prison, you'd serve your time and be released. If you went into the asylum, with no court and no judge, you'd be lucky if you ever came out. That wasn't strictly true, but it said all you needed to know about the place. Approached along an avenue of trees and lawns, the eighteenth-century pile didn't look very different from Leinster House, the seat of the Irish Parliament. It had the same simple, Georgian elegance. It was a similarity that didn't go unnoticed. It offered at least one more joke about a building still popularly called the madhouse.

Emmet Warde was sitting on a wall at the front of the asylum as Stefan stopped the car. Emmet opened a rear door and put in an overcoat and a small suitcase. He waited, the door still open, making no attempt to close it and move to the passenger door. When he did close the rear door, he still didn't open the front one. Stefan leant across the car and pushed the door open for the private detective.

'I'm sorry about your brother, Emmet.'

'He has his ups and downs. But before we go, I've a job for you, Stefan.'

And still Warde didn't attempt to get into the car.

'What do you mean?'

'A favour.' Emmet Warde slammed the passenger door shut. He walked round to Stefan's side and pulled his door open. 'I need someone with a Garda warrant card, especially with a bit of Special Branch clout. Will you come on?'

'Come on where?'

'Into the madhouse. I have to get my brother out before we go.'

Emmet Warde pushed open the heavy door into the Richmond Asylum. He walked in with a kind of breezy assurance, smiling at the male nurse who sat at the reception desk, smoking a cigarette. Stefan followed, less breezily and less assured, but having to quicken his pace to keep up with the private detective.

'Can we just walk in here?'

'You're here in your official capacity, Inspector Gillespie.' Emmet laughed. He seemed almost to be enjoying this. 'I've been in and out. They're used to me.'

He stood by a locked door at one side of the hall, smiling at the nurse.

'I'm back in to see my brother, Padraig. I've Inspector Gillespie with me.'

The nurse got up and walked towards them with a heavy bunch of keys. He seemed less concerned about their presence than irritated at having to get up.

'I thought you'd gone, Mr Warde. Didn't Dr Moylan say—'

'I have to go back and see him. You know there were shots fired last night?'

The male nurse grinned. 'I heard that one.'

'Inspector Gillespie has to talk to Charlie and get a statement.'

'Good luck with that, Inspector!'

Some sort of response seemed required. Stefan shrugged.

The nurse unlocked the door. It opened into a long corridor, Emmet and Stefan walked through. The door was locked behind them. The corridor had windows on one side. It was brighter than Stefan expected. But the stonework was dark and heavy. It was part prison and part hospital. The smell sent the same mixed message. Cold stone, tobacco, boiled cabbage, urine, but something cleaner that cut through all that, the sharper scents of antiseptic and disinfectant. The noise from the wards that opened off the corridor was low and constant. A buzz of conversation. But as Stefan Gillespie and Emmet Warde walked on there were stranger sounds; a cry, a shout; from somewhere much further away a high scream.

'I still don't know what you want me to do, Emmet.'

'You lie, it's easy enough. You lie. You lie and we take Charlie out.'

'You think I'm just going to do this?'

'You are, aren't you? You're here.'

'I'm here to pick you up for a fucking job. We're driving west.'

'So, now you've got another job. First things first, Stefan.'

'I don't even know what you want me to say!'

'I told Charlie's doctor you're on your way. Superintendent Gregory needs to question my brother at Dublin Castle. On matters that are, well, of importance. Urgent, even. You can't say what. Security, and so on. Come on, Stefan, don't look so glum. This is your bread and butter, isn't it? You can spout that sort of shite all day long. A Special Branch inspector like you! With a qualification in bollocks!'

'And why would I say any of that, Emmet?'

'Quid pro quo. Because I'm doing Terry Gregory a favour.'

'You're doing him a favour because you haven't got a fecking choice.'

Emmet Warde stopped. Stefan stopped too. Warde's mood, which had been jokey, co-conspiratorial, changed. He looked at Stefan with solid determination.

'I have a choice. And I know what it could cost me. Maybe I can't be arsed to make it for myself, but I've got a reason to make it for my brother. If you want to go back to the Carriage Yard and tell Terry I said he could fuck off, just do it.'

'Why are you pushing this now? I don't know what the problem is with your brother, Emmet, but Terry said it's nothing new. He's had . . . he's been . . .'

'He's been in and out of the bin. Is that what you mean?'

'It's not how Terry said it.'

'Who cares how you say it?' Warde walked on briskly. 'It's true.'

Stefan hurried again to catch up with him.

'And he's in again,' continued the private detective. 'And this time he's been committed after firing a gun and nearly starting a fucking shoot-out. He thought the IRA were after him, or the Black and Tans, or whoever else he keeps in his head. But tomorrow he'll be grand. He'll be himself. He already is. Over the years he's been in and out for treatment. But we've kept him away from places like this. We've paid for it privately. That's what's stopped them banging him up in this shite-hole, with odds against him ever getting out again. Money and what's left of my name. Major-General fucking Warde. Now they want to keep him here. And treat him. And when they do, I'll tell you what it'll be. Wires on his head and electricity through his brain. If that doesn't work and they get to hold him, it could be there's another way to put his fucking brain right. By cutting a lump of it out.'

Emmet Warde had stopped. His words were quieter again.

'So just say what you have to, Inspector, and we take him out of here.'

'All right, Emmet. And you think they'll let us do that?'

Warde smiled. It was relief. Stefan was now on his side.

'Whatever kind of bastard he is, Terry Gregory's a good judge of men. You carry conviction, Stefan. Jesus, I'm sure you almost had me convinced of something. I can't remember what. But that's the art. What it is doesn't matter!'

The private detective pushed open the doors into a big, long room. A drone of voices, in different timbres; low buzz, high-pitched, staccato words; a loud shout, almost a roar. The eyes of an old woman were fixed on Stefan's face. They were blank, as if they were looking through him, but they held him. Somewhere behind the eyes was a question, or maybe a silent appeal, a cry for help. Suddenly, the woman pulled up the skirts of her dress, a black, stained, shapeless thing, that she now held over her head. Grey underwear sagged on scabby, bone-thin legs.

'You can't be in the men's ward, Kathy. How did you get in?'

A woman in a nurse's uniform appeared and put her arm round the woman. She rolled the dress down from the woman's head with a gentle, familiar, almost tender touch. The woman's expression had not changed. Her eyes were still fixed on Stefan. As the nurse led her out of the ward, she looked back. She was crying, very quietly.

As Stefan continued into the room, Emmet Warde was talking to a male nurse. The man was frowning, and shaking his head, as Warde spoke cheerfully and confidently, before heading down between the rows of beds. The nurse went past Stefan, giving him a curious, concerned nod, before hurrying into the corridor.

In the ward there was a line of beds against each wall, maybe forty in all. The room was surprisingly light, with high windows and a high ceiling. The smell of antiseptic was stronger, cutting through the staler scents. A group of men stood in the centre of the room talking, gesticulating, some of them laughing. Two or three were doing the talking. Others were listening. Some were muttering to themselves and not listening, even though they laughed, uncomprehendingly, when the others laughed. One man stood outside the group, shouting over the laughter, words that were indistinct, however loud, and maybe were not words at all. Stefan took them in as he passed the group. Some of the men looked at him quizzically, confused. Some smiled. Someone poked at him, smiling.

'What do you want?' The man was young, in his early twenties.

'I'm visiting someone,' said Stefan, pointing down the room. Emmet Warde was walking slowly towards a bed that was last in the row on the right-hand side.

'He's just in,' continued the young man, walking beside him.

'Right,' nodded Stefan.

'He's a cunt. He is. Don't look at him. A cunt!'

Stefan passed three men at a table, playing cards. An old man looked up.

'He thinks everyone's a cunt. I'm not saying he's wrong.'

On one of the beds a man had his knees up, clasping them, rocking himself.

Emmet Warde stood by the last bed. A man sat on the side of the bed, facing the wall, dressed in a crumpled suit. Next to him on the bed was a hat that he was stroking slowly. His back to the room. He was staring at the floor.

'Charlie, I'm back,' said Emmet, looking down at his brother.

The man on the bed turned his head. He was younger than Emmet, with pale, thinning hair. The difference in age was not in his face or his stature. If anything, the lines on Charlie Warde's face, and the stocky build, suggested he was the older brother, but in his eyes there was something more boyish, despite his forty years.

He had a look of bewildered innocence in this strange place. By comparison, Stefan thought, looking from brother to brother, Emmet's face was harder.

'They don't want to let me out, Emmet.'

'No, you told me, Charlie. I was only just here.'

'I know you were here. You can cut the shite. I want to go home now.'

'The gun's the problem, old son,' said Emmet Warde gently. 'We could normally get you straight home, or at least to a private hospital. But you took a shot at a Guard, Charlie. That takes a bit of sorting out. I've talked to the doctor, and the hospital superintendent, and they want you here. It's not going to be easy.'

The look of bewilderment was replaced by something more anxious.

'Fuck that, Emmet. No fucking shock. I'm not having the electrics!'

'I know. We'll get you out.'

'It was like there were guns. That's the thing, Emmet. Last week, I seen fellers watching me, following, outside the house. They still have the gunmen.'

'Lay off that, Charlie. It's best to keep your mouth shut in here.'

Emmet put his hand on his brother's shoulder.

'Who's he?' asked Charlie abruptly, only now noticing Stefan.

'Stefan Gillespie,' said Emmet. 'He's a friend. A Guard.' The private detective looked round, then leant in closer. 'Special Branch. You can trust him.'

The younger brother looked hard at Stefan.

'Will he get me out of here?'

'I think he will, Charlie.' Emmet laughed. 'Isn't that right, Stefan?'

Stefan nodded and smiled, still with little idea what he was supposed to do. He turned as Emmet Warde turned. Walking towards them were two men in suits. An elderly man, bald, spectacled; a younger, slight and nervous, as if he had dragged his superior into something uncomfortable. The older man spoke.

'It's Mr Warde, isn't it? Mr Emmet Warde?'

'Mr Dunne,' said Emmet politely. 'I'm sorry you've been disturbed in this matter. Dr Moylan felt he didn't have the authority . . .' He glanced at Stefan. 'I should have introduced you. Detective Inspector Gillespie, from Dublin Castle.'

'Inspector Gillespie.' The hospital superintendent was unsettled by Stefan's presence. This was a situation in which the clear lines of authority were confused.

Emmet read that whisper of confusion and expanded on it.

'His superior is Superintendent Gregory, of Special Branch. When Mr Gregory contacted me about my brother, he did ask me to extend his apologies, for intruding into hospital matters, but there are political issues involved in the questions he needs to . . . Well, obviously some discretion is necessary.' Warde smiled, as if this was, indeed, obvious. 'Perhaps you'd better explain, Inspector.'

'Thank you, Mr Warde,' said Stefan sourly.

'I don't understand,' said the hospital superintendent. 'If you want to question Charlie, it should be done here. The Gardaí brought him in, after all.'

Stefan caught a wink from Emmet. He had to deliver something.

'The thing is, Mr Dunne . . . the questions that Superintendent Gregory is interested in asking Charles Warde may not specifically relate to what happened in Kilmainham last night. And the gun itself . . . may be pertinent to further inquiries.'

Emmet smiled. Stefan registered a thumbs-up.

'It's all very irregular. I can't take responsibility for releasing—'

'I'm sure Superintendent Gregory will take full responsibility.' It was Emmet Warde who interrupted. 'Wouldn't you say so, Inspector Gillespie?'

'I'm sure he would . . . if necessary . . .'

'Why don't you phone Special Branch, Doctor?' said Emmet.

The hospital superintendent was becoming nervous. References to political issues and weapons of dubious origin were hitting home. These were areas of life that no one wanted to go near. As for Dublin Castle and Special Branch, it was a world that carried the smell of a past that, in its darker manifestations, no one wanted to remember. Suddenly, it seemed as if whatever it was that had brought Inspector Gillespie into his asylum really would be better dealt with outside it.

'I'm sure that's grand,' said Dunne. 'Exceptional circumstances, and so on. I think if you can provide your bona fides, Inspector Gillespie, you can proceed.'

Stefan looked at the hospital superintendent blankly.

'Warrant card, Inspector Gillespie,' said Emmet Warde, grinning now.

Stefan produced the card.

Dunne nodded, as if this provided proper cover for any loss of dignity.

'That appears to be in order. Thank you, gentlemen.' He turned away, with a momentary look of disapproval at Dr Moylan, who had remained silent, as if the thing was entirely his junior's fault. 'Charles Emmet is in the custody of Inspector Gillespie. I shall leave the paperwork to you, Dr Moylan.'

Dr Moylan sniffed and watched his superior leave. He had no idea what paperwork might be involved in dispatching the patient, but he'd find something.

★

Charlie Warde left the Richmond Asylum, supposedly in the custody of Detective Inspector Gillespie, en route for questioning by Superintendent Gregory at Dublin Castle. He didn't make that journey. Stefan drove him home. No one would come looking for him. That wasn't how the asylum worked. Either you were in it or you were out of it. Now Charlie was out, and in the short span it took to travel the distance from Grangegorman to Kilmainham, he seemed to have become a different person. By the time his wife opened the front door, whatever derangement hung over him as he sat in the madhouse had gone, at least as far as outward appearances went. And while Charlie returned to the normal world, his brother and Stefan Gillespie were leaving Dublin, heading to Limerick, and the world Superintendent Gregory had dispatched them to, which was barely normal at all.

'We could maybe stop for a piss in a bit, Stefan?'

'If you mean we could maybe stop for a drink, we won't.'

The private detective laughed.

'Who said anything about a drink?'

'It'll save you asking,' said Stefan. 'I wouldn't want to disappoint you.'

'You already have.'

Emmet stared wearily out of the window.

'What's the point of this, Stefan? It's not as if I don't know who your man is, the German. Josie's driving him somewhere, but you knew where he was yesterday. You could have arrested him. If Terry wants the Army Council, he can lay his hands on most of them. He doesn't need Herr Fürst. What's the game?'

'It's the usual one, Emmet. It's not how many of the Boys Otto meets. It's the others, the ones who might surprise you. What are they up to? Are arms coming in? Will Stephen Hayes sit on his arse for the rest of the war or do they break out the gelignite? How many other German agents are roaming the country? Not many or dozens no one knows about? And if anyone's going to tell us the truth about all that, it'll be Otto. I'm just guessing. But Terry wants him on a long line.'

'That's not a bad try, Inspector. You almost have me convinced.'

'If there's more, I don't have it, Emmet. That's Terry's way. Information and more information. The more you get, the bigger the chance you might find something. If it's mostly bollocks, there's the bit that isn't. You'd know yourself.'

'Why the fuck would I know, Stefan?'

'I'd say an ex-general would know the rules of the game.'

'Maybe I've forgotten. Maybe I know it's not mostly bollocks, it all is.'

Emmet looked out of the window again, silent for some minutes.

'Terry plays the game because he enjoys it. Why do you, Inspector?'

'It's my job. You don't have a choice this week. I don't any week.'

'Ah, a reluctant recruit.' Warde pushed up his coat collar and slumped back into the seat. 'A drunk and a bashful Special Branch man. Who's the bigger fool?'

The private detective pulled his hat down over his face.

'Don't wake me up unless you change your mind about that drink.'

PART TWO

WITHIN THE GATES

The Irish Republican Army refuses to recognise the present neutrality of Ireland, because of the fact that the aggressor has already invaded Ireland. Consequently, the Army declared war on the aggressor, which is being waged since January 12th, 1939. In spite of the assertions of neutrality made by the present Irish government, the Army will continue its warfare against Britain until the ultimate victory is won . . . The Army welcomes every nation which at this time is fighting the British enemy. Without favouring the ideology of National Socialism, the Army regards with satisfaction the success of the German forces in their struggle against the common enemy.

IRA War News, 1939

10

LARAGH CASTLE

The house that was called Laragh Castle was not a castle.
It lay behind the small Church of Ireland church of
St John, with good views of the mountains, and only visible
from the road when the leaves were off the trees. It called itself
a castle because it was converted from a militia barracks that
had been built in 1798, along the Military Road the British
drove up into the Wicklow Mountains to disabuse Irish rebels
looking for safety there of the idea that they couldn't be killed
as easily on the top of a hill as at the bottom. When that work
was done, the building remained. Some of the stone was used
to rebuild the chapel of ease that had until then been Laragh's
Protestant church. That became St John's. At its dedication,
the Archbishop of Dublin made a point of separating the
church from any common or profane uses, though he was
unclear what those might be, but what remained of the barracks maintained its profanity as a house. The façade, newly
filled with windows, was given crenellated parapets and two
towers with arrow slits, to ensure that a Gothic reincarnation
would remove any suggestion of the common.

The house was smaller than it looked. Behind the curtain
wall and the arched entrance, there were only a few rooms, still

heavy and dark, despite the windows that pierced the barrack walls. Outside, the paint peeled; several varieties of red and black lichen stained the parapets. Inside, the plaster on the walls crumbled beneath layers of wallpaper and paint, but the stone was solid. Whereas other decaying barracks still stand along the Military Road like fortresses, Laragh Castle had shrunk in size and changed in appearance. As a barracks, and a symbol of the subjugation of the mountains, it had been forgotten, though a hundred and fifty years on, Mrs Iseult Stuart and her husband Francis still called the enclosure at the back of their house the Prisoners' Yard, as every owner before them had done.

Josephine Kilmartin was not enjoying her short stay at Laragh Castle. Her job was to drive the German, that was all. Having got him to Laragh Castle, she now had to take him across Ireland to a meeting of the IRA Army Council. She had replaced the car that belonged to Iseult Stuart with another car. If necessary, another car would replace that, but it was assumed enough had been done in terms of false leads and dead ends to leave Garda Special Branch searching for Otto Fürst in Dublin. Josie was only given instructions, never details, whether she was acting as a courier, or a driver, or passing messages and money, or smuggling weapons, or sheltering a man on the run. The relationship she had with the men who ran the IRA made her endlessly useful, but never quite a participant. At political meetings, her views and her arguments were listened to, even respected and applauded, but where action was concerned, she took instructions. When it came to discussing any jobs she had to do, the men talked across her, or dispatched her to make the tea. She was often party to conversations that were confidential, simply because of a kind of invisibility. They were not called the Boys for nothing. It wasn't so different at Castle Laragh, but here it was Mrs Stuart who ignored her.

Iseult Stuart was polite and even, intermittently, charming, but she spoke to Otto Fürst across Josie as soon as the talk turned to the struggle, or to the war, or to anything that had to do with serious politics and the business of Republicanism. However, she offered Josie her most practised smile when she asked her to be a perfect darling and help the housekeeper bring in breakfast, or lunch, or tea. On more than one occasion Josie heard her reflect emotionally on the importance of women in the Irish struggle for freedom, as the mistress of Laragh Castle gave Herr Fürst history lessons he had no interest in. She could only smile that Iseult thought her not worth a conversation with about anything that mattered.

The room they mostly sat in was part sitting room and part study. It was packed with old, dark furniture that needed negotiating to move even a short distance. It was a warm, comfortable room, though the fire of smouldering, never-quite-burning peat smoked continually. The walls were lined with bookshelves, and books, old and new, were piled on most of the surfaces. When Mrs Stuart came in to find Josie looking along the shelves, she smiled apologetically and said there would probably not be much there that would interest her.

As little was said to Josie when she sat with Iseult Stuart and Otto Fürst, she took the opportunity to walk in the woods and take the dogs that filled the house with her. They, at least, were good company. When she did sit in the study, mostly unregarded, for much of the time she was an observer. Among the many things she observed was the fact that while Otto Fürst engaged politely, even enthusiastically, in the stream of conversation that Mrs Stuart seemed able to produce, almost without taking breath, she irritated him in a way his smile could not hide. At least not from Josie. Iseult Stuart was unaware of that truth.

The German had little to say to Josie either. In the journeys around Dublin, and during the drive down to Laragh, he sat in the back of the car. It was as if she was chauffeuring him. She had no difficulty with that. He was a man with a lot on his mind, that much she could tell. And what was on his mind wasn't her business. That was how it should be. It felt as if they had a relationship, a professional one. She did her job, which was to help him. She would not be required to do it for long, but while she did it, it would be done carefully and efficiently. What she offered the struggle wasn't much. She knew that sometimes. Others risked their lives. One reason she was there, doing whatever small or insignificant task she could, was because it had cost her brother his life, when he barely knew it could. Her commitment recognised the modesty of what she could offer, and that modesty meant never questioning how much or how little was asked of her. She had played her part in the escape from Mountjoy. She had picked Otto Fürst and van Loon up and kept them moving around Dublin. When it seemed that every trail was dead, she drove Fürst to Laragh. She had driven the other man too, the Dutchman, who had been caught shortly after she delivered him to the safe house in Hanbury Street. She had been surprised that no one in the IRA was put out by this. It was a failure, but it seemed van Loon was expendable. Josie couldn't help feeling that his role had been to help Fürst escape. Only the German mattered.

By now Josephine Kilmartin had walked Iseult Stuart's dogs to exhaustion. She had cleaned the car she would be driving to Limerick. Everything was in order for the journey. As much as she could, she kept away from the study, the chattering Mrs Stuart and the mostly laconic Herr Fürst. If he had much on his mind, she had her own thoughts to deal with too. She drove into the village for petrol when the car didn't need it. She had found a telephone box and contacted Emmet Warde in Dublin. It was not something she felt she could do from Laragh Castle, even though Mrs Stuart had a telephone. She had called her aunt from there, to make sure her mother was all right. But that was different. It was always difficult leaving her mother, though her aunt was there to help. Kathleen Kilmartin was aware of what was going on around her most of the time, and she was not frail physically, but suddenly she could lose all sense of where she was and who the people round her were. Josie saw the fear in her mother's eyes, as if incomprehensible emptiness drained her consciousness. It was happening more.

Keeping in contact with Emmet Warde was something Josie had not expected to have to do. It should have been enough to leave him with his work and see him again when she returned to Dublin. In the months he had been working for her, little had happened. She was already coming to the conclusion that he was getting nowhere, as she had got nowhere herself for years. At first, the private detective had brought new hope into the long and fruitless search for the truth about her brother's death. Her determination not to abandon that search had become a kind of faith over the years, however futile it often seemed. It was her mother's obsession too, but it had driven Josie's life. And for a short time she thought she did see hope when Emmet Warde agreed to investigate. He had looked where she was unable to look. He had spoken to people who would never speak to her. But maybe she had deceived herself. He found only more dead ends. She was aware that her conversations with Emmet were becoming circular. He revisited her own dead ends and added more cul-de-sacs. Yet those conversations gave her something. Talking to him had come to matter. She didn't know why. Sometimes what they talked about had nothing to do with Eamon's death, or with anything. She looked forward to seeing him when there was little else she looked forward to. She had wondered if she was almost paying for somebody to talk to. But now, out of nowhere, when she felt certain nothing would come of it, he had found something. After all the pointless years, it astonished her.

It was happening fast. Emmet had found someone to talk to. He had warned her that it was a fragile link, but it was real. He knew it was real. And now he was going to talk to someone who might cut away the long darkness and shine a light. She told herself that she shouldn't assume too much. But Emmet had never given her hope where there was none. She knew she wanted to believe in what was happening too much. But she had to believe. She trusted Emmet. And she had to keep in contact with him. She had to know it all as soon as there was something to know. She could not tell him where she was or what she was doing, but she would tell him what she could. And now that he was heading west with her new hope, their new hope she felt, she would not be far away; it was as if this was how it was meant to be. She would be close, surely, when he found something. She would say nothing to put at risk what she was doing for the IRA. All Emmet knew was that she was taking a holiday. And she would be calling him. If she needed to meet him, he would have no idea where she came from. What she was doing would remain a secret, as always. But she had her own secrets now and her own hopes.

All this was going through Josie's head as she sat in the study at Laragh Castle after dinner; it had been going through her head all day. She took no notice of the conversation between Iseult Stuart and Otto Fürst. There was no need. She was barely aware that Iseult was twisting the dial on the radio and a crackling voice was speaking. The conversation had stopped. Iseult and Otto were listening intently. Josie's attention refocused as Mrs Stuart called across to her.

'Do listen to this, Josephine. It's Francis. He's speaking on Radio Berlin.'

Josie nodded as if she knew what her hostess was talking about. She didn't. She had some idea that Francis Stuart was a Republican who was now in Germany. She smiled in response to Iseult Stuart's excited, conspiratorial smile, and listened.

'. . . and as I talk this evening . . . an ordinary Irishman in Berlin, with no desire to make propaganda, I speak of what I see and have seen. When I first came here, I learnt of Hitler and the new Germany. I was fired with enthusiasm. Here was someone with the vision and courage to free life from the money god that controls our world. The* word dictator did not frighten me. Better to be ruled by one man whose word could not be doubted, than by the gang of international financiers. I had heard the jibes against this man that filled the English press and spread to our own, and I saw that Ireland could never develop a truly free cultural life while subject to the cheapness that comes from the gutters of London. We want none of the cant they call idealism. We shall remain neutral, of course, but if we have to fight it will be for no so-called ideal. We know their sickening ideals . . . the liberal materialism that is only the tyranny of money. We see the spiritually dead civilisation of England and the USA. We only want to separate ourselves from that and recover our stolen counties in Ulster, as Hitler recovered German land. We want to live simply on clean Irish soil, free of the money god. When Chamberlain stepped into an aeroplane at Munich, and said, "This means peace in our time", it seemed a horrible joke. An elderly, complacent businessman without a drop of passionate blood, what did he know of German people's longing to be united again? Or of the determination of our own people for unity? Chamberlain is dead and forgotten, but Germany has its lost provinces. Passionate desires will always triumph. Now, even in Ireland life is in the grip of politicians and international financiers. It need not be that way. In the streets of Berlin, all that is gone. I say to our fellow citizens in Belfast, under foreign rule, endure a little longer. The end of this war will give us back our national unity. The struggle that began its latest phase on an Easter Monday in Dublin will triumph. Most of us may not have a vision of what an Irish nation can be. All that matters is that there are a few with the vision and energy to plan for the whole nation. They are planning, now!'

The voice stopped. The crackling from the speaker increased. The sound of an orchestra faded in. Mrs Stuart got up, delighted, and almost bounced to the radio to turn it off. She turned to look at Otto Fürst, expectantly. She ignored Josie again.

'It's very good, Iseult, very good indeed.'

Josie could hear the German saying what he was expected to say.

'But you can tell he's a novelist,' laughed Iseult. 'Too many niceties and circumlocutions. He does dance around things so! I have to say, if I was in Berlin, I'd be tempted to knock him on the head and tell him to call a spade a spade.'

Otto Fürst gave another one of the many smiles he had produced in the course of his stay at Laragh Castle, which more or less said that he didn't understand what his hostess was talking about and didn't much care.

Josephine Kilmartin recognised the look and smiled too.

Mrs Stuart reached over with some wine and filled Otto's glass. She then filled her own. It didn't immediately occur to her to fill Josie's. Fürst noticed, however, and as Iseult put the bottle down, he picked it up and looked at her.

'It's all right, Mr Fürst, I've had enough.'

'I'm sorry, my dear,' said Mrs Stuart, 'it's stretch or starve here!'

Iseult turned to Fürst again.

'Sometimes Francis needs a kick. You're not writing a novel, darling, there's a bloody war on, as the British never tire of telling us. You're not addressing a seminar of literary critics, for God's sake. This is for the hoi polloi. They need to know what's what. Not just in Germany and Britain. Everywhere!'

Otto Fürst nodded, happy for silence to signify agreement.

'It's all very well dancing round these phrases about international finance and the tyranny of money and bloody liberal materialism. We get the code, but I'm damned if I understand the need for it. You don't have any of that shilly-shallying with dear Ezra!' Iseult fixed Fürst with a questioning look. 'You've heard Ezra?'

The German frowned, uncomprehending, but unable to hide it now.

'Ezra? I'm not sure that I know—'

'Ezra Pound. You know Ezra Pound! Of course you know . . .'

Mrs Stuart looked almost indignant at the possibility Fürst didn't know.

'Ah, yes, dear lady. The poet, yes, of course.'

The German spy was stretching himself to pull this from his memory.

'He's in Rome. Playing his part, on Rome Radio. You haven't heard him?'

Otto shrugged. He hadn't. He only barely knew the name.

'Ezra and I were lovers. You may know that. I was very young then.'

Iseult looked from Otto to Josephine, with an expression of something like half-forgotten defiance. Her days of shocking people were behind her, but this was a moment when that old passion briefly flared up in her again.

Fürst was indifferent to this unwanted information. Josie found herself thinking that the second bottle of wine had been a mistake on Mrs Stuart's part.

'Ezra was never a man for euphemisms. He is of the let's-call-a-spade-a-spade school. In this case the let's-call-a-Jew-a-Jew school. We all know it's what international financier means, so why Francis needs to quibble when millions are killing each other at the Jews' behest, I've no idea. He's not in a place where they keep the truth about these people under a bushel. We struggle to pick up Radio Rome here. Berlin's much easier. But I have heard Ezra's talks. He's as outrageous and funny and perceptive as he always was. He tells the Americans where they're headed, the English too. He says if Churchill and Roosevelt aren't kikes, they should be. They're sucked dry by the Jews who run their countries. You have to decode when Francis mocks liberal materialism, but Ezra has a poet's indifference to the niceties. "The big Jew's rotted every nation he's wormed into!" Wonderful!'

Iseult roared with laughter at this, looking again from Otto to Josie. Neither of them responded. Josie was startled by the vehemence. Otto looked weary.

'But I don't need to tell you any of that, do I, Otto?'

'No, you don't need to tell me any of that, Mrs Stuart.'

There was a silence, interrupted only by a further giggle from Iseult.

'I think Francis should get to the point . . . he should get to the point . . .'

Her words trailed away. She had expected the German to say more. She couldn't understand why he didn't find what she said funny. It was true, and Fürst, as a German, would know that as well as anyone. But it was also funny. She didn't think much of Herr Fürst. He had little to say about anything. She had probably been wrong to imagine a spy would be interesting, let alone entertaining. There were few people now who were entertaining. The bloody, bloody war had made the world she inhabited a dull place. She did her best. She had done her best with Fürst, but she would be relieved when he was gone. She wanted to believe she was playing her part in a war that was a war for Ireland. But it felt like nothing. The trouble with the Irish was that beneath the bluster and the fury and their righteous anger against the English, too many of them were like the English: lifeless, thoughtless, dreary, ordinary. And this German spy didn't seem so far away from that. Not to mention the mouse-woman he had brought with him.

Iseult picked up the wine bottle again. It was empty.

'Francis is doing his bit. Ezra, too. I do what I can as well, Herr Fürst.'

Somewhere in the dregs of the bottle, first names had been forgotten.

'I'm very grateful, Mrs Stuart. Germany is very grateful.'

Mrs Stuart got up, with a graceful smile. It was a curtain on the evening. She had no more to say to Fürst, and she certainly had nothing to say to Miss Mouse.

'I'm tired, very tired. I'm sure you can find your own way to bed.'

The German stood up. He gave a slight bow. Iseult left the room.

Otto turned to the desk where there was a decanter with whiskey in it. He brought it back to the low table where his empty wine glass was and poured some.

'A nightcap, Miss Kilmartin?'

Despite having only spoken a few words to Fürst, Josie felt more relaxed now. Even not talking to Iseult Stuart had been a demanding experience.

'I wouldn't mind. I only have the wine glass.'

'We won't worry about that.'

He poured a whiskey into her glass and sat down.

'You have a lot on your mind, Miss Kilmartin.'

'Enough.' She was aware how observant he was; it was unexpected.

The German made no attempt to ask more.

'Good. I shall enjoy the silence of the journey tomorrow.'

Josie smiled. 'I'm sure she means well, Mr Fürst.'

'I wouldn't count on it, dear lady. I wouldn't count on it at all.'

Josie laughed.

Otto Fürst sat back into the cushions of the sofa and sipped his whiskey.

'You didn't look entirely convinced that the Jews run the British Empire and the United States, and may even, God forbid, be pulling Mr de Valera's strings.'

'I hope it didn't show,' said Josie.

'I'm sure not. I don't imagine she sees much of what anyone else thinks.'

'Good. I didn't want to be rude.'

'Nobody does, dear lady, not when it comes to the Jews. Best to agree.'

Josie couldn't decide whether he was sneering at her or Mrs Stuart.

'I'm sorry, Herr Fürst, I don't understand. I'm sure it doesn't matter.'

'I simply mean that when it comes to the Jews, no one with any sense of history would want to be so impolite as to suggest that they're really not a bacillus that is infecting the world with disease. After all, we are in decent society here.'

He sat back, sipping his drink, smiling, as if he amused himself.

Josie didn't much like what Iseult Stuart had said, but the ideas behind the words were not unfamiliar. She heard them at meetings. She read them in Republican newspapers. She accepted them as she accepted many things she didn't like about the Nazis, as a kind of necessary solidarity with Germany. But she heard versions of the same things elsewhere, in the Church too. The Jews, after all, were behind the evils of Capitalism and the terrors of Communism. Josie's own inclinations had once pulled her towards Republicans who saw socialism as a way forward, but those voices had disappeared. She had swallowed less palatable ideas in the belief that Ireland's freedom stood outside mere politics. If she couldn't contribute much in other ways, she could at least contribute her faith. That faith now meant supporting Germany in the war. She almost felt Fürst was testing her.

'I know nothing about it, Mr Fürst. Politics don't interest me.'

'Ah, Miss Kilmartin, you're a woman after every German man's heart!'

She felt now he was just laughing at her.

'We have a long drive tomorrow, Mr Fürst. I'll say goodnight.'

'Take no notice of me, Miss Kilmartin. Or of what I say. Sometimes, I simply try things. It's easy to forget who you are in this job. Sometimes, for the hell of it, I look at the nonsense I'm obliged to spout, and I dig down to find some different nonsense. I have all sorts of nonsense in here.' He tapped his head. 'And some of that must be me! But which bit is it?'

Josie really was ready to go to bed, but for the moment she stayed.

'I'm not laughing at you, Miss Kilmartin. I have a job to do, like everyone else . . . and some of the time . . . I don't even know what it is. That's not easy. It takes me where it takes me . . . to collect, to stir, to make trouble, to find things out.'

The German reached for the whiskey. He was drunk. Josie realised that but she let him talk. She felt in some way he needed her to, even if she couldn't understand. Meaning seemed unimportant. If he was laughing, it was at himself.

'Make no mistake, dear lady, I'm here to serve my country. If that means it is necessary to believe the unbelievable and stomach the unpalatable, I'm a German. If you can die for your country, it can be no great hardship to lie for it. If war is deceit, we can have no qualms about deceiving ourselves. To do, you only have to believe in part, but that part, even that little part, must dispose of doubts. We do what we can, Miss Kilmartin, for Ireland and Germany. Damn the rest!'

He stood shakily and moved to the door.

'I shall say goodnight, Miss Kilmartin.'

As he stepped forward, he staggered. Josie stood up.

'Shall I help you?'

'Not at all, dear lady, no! Do you know the song that goes, "We're here, because we're here, because we're here, because we're ..."' He spoke the words slowly, as if considering them carefully. 'Do you know that song, dear lady?'

'Yes. I've heard it.'

'The Tommies sang it, going over the top. It's a wonderful language English, don't you think? Such great sentiments out of nothing. I admire that. And we are, you know, we are here . . . because we're here. Never forget it, liebe Dame.'

The German chuckled. He went out, humming the tune to the words he had quoted. Josie listened to him climbing the stairs. She finished her drink, not really wanting it. As she turned to leave, she felt tears in her eyes. She had no idea why.

11

LOUGH DERG

Set among the tall trees that marked it out as, in the previous century, an adjunct of a large Anglo-Irish estate, the fishing lodge looked out on Lough Derg, the long narrow lake that the Shannon River formed among the low hills of Galway, Clare and Tipperary. It was a small, neat building of cut stone, arched windows and elaborately carved Victorian barge boards, several miles from the village of Whitegate on the lough's western shore. The lodge was surrounded by trees on three sides; on the fourth were the waters of the lake. It had flourished for a hundred years while parties of affluent Anglo-Irish aristocrats and considerably more affluent businessmen gathered to fish on the lake. It had fallen into disrepair and been abandoned around the turn of the century when the Anglo-Irish not only ran out of money but power. The lodge had been reincarnated as a hotel for fishermen by Fintan Corcoran just before the Great War but had never made any money. It passed into the hands of Mr Corcoran's son James, who was more interested in Republican politics than fishing, and survived, or at least stayed open, slowly decaying, until he was taken into custody by the Free State, in 1939, for using the lodge's cellars to store rifles, ammunition and explosives for the IRA. Now, along with hundreds of his IRA comrades, James Corcoran was interned in the Curragh Camp in Kildare. The fishing lodge continued to decay, but it was occasionally visited by some of his old friends. The party of a dozen men who had recently arrived there by car from various parts of Ireland, including the North, and by train to the station at Killaloe nearby, had brought no fishing rods with them. The ones who wore heavy trench coats and took turns patrolling the woods around the fishing lodge, and the track that led to it through the woods, carried revolvers in their pockets, and also took turns wielding the single Tommy gun they had, more as a signature of who they were than in anticipation of a skirmish. Fighting was no more in the minds of the men at this IRA Army Council than fishing. The correct procedure, in the event of a police raid, was to get out and to get out fast.

Among the men who had gathered at the fishing lodge, the most important was the Chief-of-Staff, Stephen Hayes, who ostensibly led the IRA in his position as head of the ruling Army Council. He was a man who had come to the top more through the various failings and mistakes of his predecessors than because of his own talents, in particular those of Seán Russell, who was dead or not dead according to a number of stories that had him variously on the run in America, training German spies in Berlin, or at the bottom of the Atlantic off Galway after dying on a German U-boat as he was about to land in Ireland. Variations on these themes were believed and disbelieved to different degrees and at the same time none of them were believed on the assumption that they had all been spread by British Intelligence anyway. The short version was that Hayes was there because Russell wasn't, but that at some time, if he wasn't dead after all, Russell might return as Chief-of-Staff.

Stephen Hayes' own failings were generally known and generally tolerated. He drank too much. He had no real plan for what the IRA was actually meant to do in the war it had declared on Britain in 1939. With a large part of the member-ship interned by the Irish government and the organisational structure in Britain broken up by overreach and incompetence as by British action, Hayes seemed more concerned with keep-ing the IRA in existence than fighting a war. Mostly that meant doing nothing. And for a time, doing not very much, while waiting for Britain to be invaded by Germany, was a winning strategy. The invasion would see an all-Ireland Irish Republic presented to the IRA by a grateful Adolf Hitler. It was never clear what he would be grateful for, but it was assumed that in the absence of anything tangible, hating the English would suffice. When Stephen Hayes did do something, it never quite worked. The spectacular Christmas Raid on the Irish Army's Magazine Fort in 1939 had gained the IRA huge quantities of guns and ammunition but led to little celebration. Most of the weapons were recovered within weeks and the internment of hundreds of IRA men that followed drove a coach and horses through the leadership. Hayes was noted for his incompetence; it was sometimes considered a level of incompetence that was remarkable even for an unimaginative drunk. And there was no question that Garda Special Branch often had good intelligence on the IRA. Outside the Dublin leadership, some people felt that intelligence leaked from the very top.

There were others at the fishing lodge by Lough Derg from Southern Command, but the most significant of the leaders, and the man who was most hostile to Stephen Hayes, was Seán McCaughey, head of Northern Command. Northern Ireland, as the part of Ireland still under British control, had its own command structure. Nominally under the authority of the Army Council, it frequently took its own course. Its leaders saw themselves in direct conflict with the British enemy. The men of the North had a real war to fight. They looked across the border and saw indolence and laziness that stood in the way of that war.

*

It was to Corcoran's Fishing Lodge that Josephine Kilmartin had brought the German spy, Otto Fürst. She had driven from Wicklow with him by quiet roads, priding herself on the way she went. She worked hard at such things, whether she was carrying people or documents or weapons across the country. Nobody much noticed the care she took but her reliability, if unremarked, was unquestioned.

Now that she had delivered the German she had another role to fulfil. The IRA men who were camping out in the bare bedrooms of the fishing lodge came with little more than a few guns and some ammunition. There was no food. And even though the meeting would only last two days, some provisions had to be provided. It was Josie's job, and not an unfamiliar one, to drive into Killaloe to gather up the bacon and eggs and tea and milk, along with replenishment of alcohol and cigarettes. Back at the lodge, she would spend much of the time shuttling between the kitchen and the dining room where the Army Council would hold its sessions, to consider developments in the war Stephen Hayes was conspicuously not fighting. She would be, as always, more or less invisible.

The morning after her arrival with Otto Fürst, Josie was bringing in new cups and new pots of tea as the Army Council sat around a large heavy table that filled the dining room. Stephen Hayes was introducing the German spy. The escape from Mountjoy was something that had worked well. Hayes was not only comfortable diverting attention from his own inaction to the action that the presence of a German agent might at least suggest was happening, but he was also keen to take credit for the escape itself. He had not organised it. He had approved it reluctantly, though that reluctance was not forgotten. He was unsure who had organised it. But all went smoothly. The success was now his success. And a success was the right place to start the meeting. It was also something that gave him the opportunity to shift discussion from what he wasn't doing in Ireland to what the Germans should be doing in Ireland. When in doubt, it was always a good idea to move on briskly to blaming any failure on the inability of the Germans to deliver the weapons and explosives they had been promising the IRA for over three years.

Sadly, Otto wasn't keen to play the game as Hayes required. His response, when the Chief-of-Staff asked him what would happen next, was to return serve.

'What next? I think you need to tell me what next, Mr Hayes.'

The Chief-of-Staff smiled unconvincingly and ignored the question.

'Shall we leave the misters and the herrs, Otto? Is that best?'

'Of course, we're all friends, so why not, Stephen?'

Fürst smiled, looking round the room at all the faces. He didn't need great resources of perception to feel that the atmosphere was less than friendly. The mood had been there as the Chief-of-Staff introduced his colleagues on the Army Council. It wasn't that many of them didn't trust him. They didn't trust each other. He would work out who stood with who in time. For now he just felt the tension.

'I don't want to repeat old conversations,' said Hayes. 'You and I talked before you were arrested. I've asked for the same things from other Abwehr agents. Weapons! Apart from money, and never enough of that, there's fuck all.'

'Ah, now, Stephen, there are things Germany wants too . . .'

Hayes could see that Fürst was not going to give him the advantage he had expected. The German hadn't even thanked him for the escape from prison. If Hayes was slow to act much of the time, he was fairly quick to find irritation. He was unaware that Otto was simply gauging who was with Hayes and who wasn't.

'There's no point blaming things on us when your lads have a habit of asking Guards for directions to the nearest IRA man, five minutes after they get off the submarine or drop from the sky. Those fellers we don't even get to meet so.'

'It's not easy to coordinate these things,' said Fürst blandly.

'Don't give me that shite. I know what goes to Berlin. We're a bunch of incompetent arseholes who couldn't run a piss-up in a distillery. But we're a fuck sight better at hiding your fellers than they are at hiding themselves. And what do you do when you get here? What do you bring? You can find a U-boat to drop an eejit in Dingle, but what about dropping guns and explosives? We're still waiting. You want to know why we're not attacking the British in the North? We were told to wait for a fucking invasion. Where were you, Otto? We're still here waiting.'

Stephen Hayes stopped, looking hard at the German. He was pleased with the speech. It made it clear who was in charge. Clear to the Abwehr man and clear to other IRA men in the room. When they spoke, they would speak to his agenda.

'The invasion of England had to be postponed,' said the German. 'A strategic matter. Action in Ireland must wait. The Führer decided to destroy the Soviet Union. That is happening as we sit here, gentlemen. Stalin is finished.' Otto Fürst looked at the men around the table with satisfaction. It was a statement of German power that was unassailable. 'We hear little in Ireland out of the fog of war, but I think we hear enough. I'm with you because Ireland matters to Germany, but this war is about something too great for us to let impatience drive our ambitions. This is a war for civilisation. When the Communists are wiped from the face of Europe and all of Europe is free, as most of it now is, it won't be hard to tidy away the English. If the English fight on, they will be swept away like the Soviets. In Berlin I think the feeling is that the destruction of Russia will put an end to Churchill and his warmongers. The English will make peace. They came close before, I'm told. But whether they fight or surrender, Irish unity will come.'

He sat back in his chair. He was pleased with his speech, too. It was rousing and it was convincing enough, surely, for these ragtail clowns and their non-existent army, on this tiny island at the edge of everything, involved in nothing but its own incestuous concerns. There were those in Berlin who believed Ireland could be made to matter. He wasn't one of them. Ireland might irritate the British. It might embarrass them. It might misdirect precious resources. It might stir the pot of chaos in some small way. The Abwehr made larger claims, but he was not convinced that the men who sent him to Ireland believed them. They had their own games. He didn't know which ones were real and which were not. He had no desire to know. He wasn't a believer. The chances and the choices that had brought him here were the nearest thing he had to purpose or direction. To be in motion was better than to be still. And he wasn't sorry that the game the Abwehr chose for him was this one. Whether he was here on the run, or interned, or imprisoned, the game could be played with a safety he could have nowhere else. He would not hang. Capture, even for the second time, meant no firing squad. And whatever else he did to while away the hours with his friends in the IRA, he would not be crossing the border into Northern Ireland. From Germany's point of view there might be something worth doing on British soil, but there was also the hangman's noose to consider. It was better to talk. And as Fürst knew, talking was what the IRA Army Council did best. However, the conversation so far was not what Hayes wanted.

'Fuck the Russians. If you want us to act, we need the means. Not the shite.'

The German continued to speak calmly. He would keep control.

'Information, Stephen. At the moment that's what I need. That's what I can send to Berlin. Information about the North. Troop movements, army camps, naval bases, coastal defences.

There's never enough. And it's never precise. What am I supposed to do, get a train to Londonderry and count their ships myself? When Germany comes, all that is essential. We'll need you then, but we need you even more now. To prepare the way. You may be Ireland's soldiers, but you have to be Germany's spies, dear friends. And that's before we get to the issue of sabotage.'

Otto Fürst smiled. The ball was in their court. It had never left.

'There's a lot of talk about sabotage, Herr Fürst. But nothing happens.'

The man who spoke was Seán McCaughey. He made a point of addressing the German formally. Fürst had barely registered the men Stephen Hayes had introduced him to on his arrival. He would judge each in turn as the meeting proceeded. He would know who mattered and who didn't. McCaughey's slow, northern voice didn't need to say much before the German knew he mattered. He also knew that this man was there to oppose Stephen Hayes.

'You've had information. Years of it. I don't know what you fellers do with it, but I know there's a lot of waiting and even more doing sod all. I'd wonder sometimes if anyone wants us to do a fucking thing. I don't just mean your pals off the submarines, Herr Fürst. Whatever we come up with in Northern Command, the word comes back from the Boys down here, "Sit on your arse, lads. Sure, aren't there great days coming?" Wouldn't you say so, Stephen? Isn't that about right?'

McCaughey turned his eyes to the Chief-of-Staff with a wry look.

'A quick chorus of "We're All off to Dublin in the Green, in the Green" and then it's back to the pub for another round and another plan for making plans.'

'We've half our men interned down here, Seán. It's the same for you in the North. There's a limit to what we can do.' Hayes turned back to Fürst. 'That's why we need the materiel. That would change things. That sabotage would be realistic.'

'It's a modern war,' said the German with a shrug. 'Information first.'

Seán McCaughey looked round the room at the council members.

'Don't these two make quite the double-act? Otto says, "Jam tomorrow, lads", when Stephen gets the house in order. And Stephen says, "Jam tomorrow, boys", when Otto has one of his U-boats deliver the jam. And is that the way of it, so?'

Several of the IRA men laughed. Several didn't. The rest looked awkwardly from Stephen Hayes to Seán McCaughey, aware that laughter, even a smile, was not about the joke, but about which side you were on. Otto Fürst, who had already smelled the division, now saw it went deeper than he had realised. He grinned. He had no problem with the Army Council falling out. As an ingredient in the Irish game, little was required of the IRA. They were less important to Germany than the Irish government's neutrality. If there was an invasion, whether it came to Northern Ireland or the whole island, the IRA might count for something, but even then it would be under German control. Their value was as an irritant to the British, and a warning to Éamon de Valera not to move any closer to Britain. That was all.

Stephen Hayes also registered the laughter and the subtle change of mood it represented. The edge in the relationship between the IRA in the North and the South could be felt. In the North, after all, British troops were everywhere, as was the Royal Ulster Constabulary and its Special Branch, run by people whose antagonism against the IRA included a religious hatred that was worn as a badge of honour. In the South there was a bridge between the IRA and the men who hunted them. It was fragile and crumbling but it could still be crossed. At least one side could see the other across its span. There were no such subtleties in the North. For Seán McCaughey the lack of action in the war against Britain was an unanswered question. Why, with the old enemy's back against the wall, weren't they fighting?

'When the weapons come . . . when the time's right . . . when . . . if . . .'

Those were the words Stephen Hayes heard himself saying again. They were the only ones he had. He could see those words, and the platitudes that went with them, were not well received, even by his own. The discontent was already there, he knew that, and McCaughey was stirring it, he knew that too. He sensed how few words it was taking to alter the mood in the room. It was only now that the Chief-of-Staff realised the men from the North were not alone. The silence from the other men in the room, his own men, expressed growing dissent. And it wasn't coming out of nowhere. It had appeared too quickly for that. It had to be organised.

'Do you have a plan, Stephen?' said McCaughey in a tone of contempt. 'A new one, maybe. You're a great man for the plans. Plans to send to Germany to help with the invasion. The one that's waiting on the demise of Josef Stalin and the Red Army. Wasn't there a time our grandfathers were waiting for Napoleon to get back from Moscow and put an end to the English for us? And what about the plans for robbing banks and robbing the Irish Army's weapons. Never a peep. We nearly got there a couple of years ago. All our Christmases at once. Until the Guards grabbed every fucking gun we took, as if they knew where we were hiding them. And all the camps and the police stations and the ships north of the border, that you had plans for us to attack, what about that? We don't hear of those now. And when we come up with our own? If you don't put them on the long finger, you piss on them. A thousand reasons to say no, and never a reason to say yes. Am I wrong there?'

The nods and murmurs of assent went round the table. There were only two men, beside Hayes himself, who remained stony-faced and unmoving. The rest showed different degrees of agreement, but they showed them, nevertheless. It wasn't the first time Stephen Hayes had faced criticisms. This was more concerted, certainly, but the same remedy applied. He would agree. And when he agreed, some dissenters would move back in his direction. He would make a decision that sabotage had to come higher up the agenda. He would look to Otto Fürst for support. Again and again, explosives, better explosives, had to come from Germany. Fürst, like other German agents, would promise to put pressure on Berlin. There would be new plans, new enthusiasm, new determination. It would be exactly what Seán McCaughey had described. Jam tomorrow was the truth.

It was also true that the Chief-of-Staff had produced many plans. In his head, they merged into one another. They had revolved for so long around the belief that a German army would land in Ireland and as that vision receded, Hayes could see nowhere to go. He had his faith, but he was no longer sure what it meant. It felt less and less real. He drank more and he did less because he had lost any sense of what he was supposed to do. The one thing he had left was an unshakeable conviction that he had to hold the IRA together; that one day, even if it wasn't to be this day, even this war, their day would come. His army was falling about him, whatever McCaughey believed. And anything that pitched the IRA into full-blown conflict with the British in the North, or de Valera's government in the South, would destroy the organisation. He couldn't say that. He couldn't say his overarching plan was to do as little as possible, and thereby save their arses.

In the silence that followed Seán McCaughey's challenge, Fürst watched as an interested outsider. The knives were out. Such things always intrigued him. He looked at Stephen

Hayes and read his face. Containment was the necessary course.

'All right, Seán, I know how you feel. I am listening to you.'

McCaughey laughed again.

'For fuck's sake, Stephen. A lot of us at this table have been listening. A long time. There's a God-awful chattering of birds. You don't so much hear it as feel it, slipping by you on the breeze. No one knows where it comes from but there's a lot of the Boys have a good idea where it goes. It whistles into Dublin, from every one of Ireland's four green fields, and it finds its way along Dame Street, through the Dublin Castle gates, to the Castle Yard, where Superintendent Gregory has a way with the twittering of birds. He knows what they're saying.'

'If that's meant to be funny, you'll need to explain it, Seán.'

'A lot gets out. I'd go back to the Christmas raid on the Magazine Fort. They didn't collect up those lorry loads of guns because Terry Gregory was on Santy's nice list. He knew. He knew because he was told. And that's only the beginning. There's no shortage of operations that went wrong because the Guards were waiting. In the North, too. Operations that were planned down here. I know the RUC gets tip-offs from Dublin Castle. That's one for the dogs in the street. But where does Dublin Castle get its tip-off, though? That's the one that presses on my mind.'

'Mine too.' Hayes shrugged. 'You shut one door and another opens.'

'That's one way of looking at it,' replied the man from the North.

'And what's the other way? If you've got the answer, tell us.'

'What I'd say, General Hayes,' the word general came in quotes, 'is that if the singing bird is high enough up the tree, there's not a lot of point shooting the poor bastards who are on the branches down below. And if he's right at the top . . .'

The room was quiet. This was no argument, it was accusation.

'I don't think you want to push your luck much further, Seán.'

Stephen Hayes' voice was hard. Containment and agreement wasn't what this was about. In the faces of many of the Army Council there was suddenly less sympathy for McCaughey. He had moved too quickly from concerns they all felt to an attack that he could not expect be supported, except by his own men. Even they looked at him doubtfully. They knew this was too much, too soon.

'Enough of the birds, lads.' Seán McCaughey grinned. 'I'm only making a point, Stephen. We're leaking, North and South, and it's coming from somewhere. The quality of the information that's getting out means it's coming from high up. I'm not saying someone in this room, but someone who can't be far away. We need to stop it. It's not coming from the North. There's too much of it. The bird's in your tree, Stephen, and you're the Chief-of-Staff. You need to find the bastard.'

Hayes nodded. It wasn't exactly an apology, but it was all he was going to get. If McCaughey had stepped sideways the accusation was still hanging. Only the men from the North felt comfortable. For the rest, it wasn't the first time they had asked questions about the way Special Branch accessed information, but it was always easier to believe the leak came from lower down the chain of command than the Army Council. But McCaughey had a point. The unwelcome knowledge that a traitor could be sitting with them made further conversation stilted. It was clear that the meeting was going to break up with little achieved. Effectively, Seán McCaughey had put an end to what he started. For Hayes, trying to see a way through the mess, the atmosphere of mistrust had its benefits. If McCaughey had arrived with some of the men from the Southern Command turning his way, they were now less keen.

It didn't matter why McCaughey's attempt to force a hotter war in the North had been stifled. The diversion into accusations had achieved that. Hayes was surprised that his northern counterpart had squandered his advantage.

The meeting was over. There were a few administrative issues to discuss, but no one was going to try to push anything else substantial. There would be more discussions with Otto Fürst, but the German would not want to say much about his plans in front of the whole Army Council. Stephen Hayes was content that his position had not been challenged seriously. He remained in the dining room, tidying up his papers. The others had drifted outside in groups or were looking for food in the kitchen. Josephine Kilmartin was clearing the big table. Only Otto Fürst and Seán McCaughey remained, as the German told the story of his escape from Mountjoy yet again. McCaughey had already heard it, but he seemed to want to stay. He caught Hayes' eye as the Chief-of-Staff stood. He had something to say.

'You know there are American soldiers in the North.'

The words were addressed to both the Chief-of-Staff and Fürst.

The German looked genuinely surprised.

'Stephen knows.'

Hayes nodded.

'What are they doing?' asked the German.

'I don't know. Advisory roles,' said McCaughey. 'Laying the ground.'

'For what?'

'The arsenal of democracy, I suppose. You've heard that shite?'

Otto nodded. The Chief-of-Staff frowned, unclear what this was about Seán McCaughey was still talking to Fürst.

'They can help the British as much as they like. It's hard to

157

think anyone's going to stop that now. God knows, our people have tried hard enough in the States. But I don't know if the battle's lost altogether. American soldiers have no more right to be on Irish soil than the English. And what's Dev doing about it?'

McCaughey turned to Stephen Hayes, who shrugged.

'I think there has been a protest made, but it's all secret. It's not in the papers. It hasn't been raised in the Dáil. As far as possible, Dev's going to pretend it's not happening. And who cares? Dev being pissed off won't bother Roosevelt.'

'But what if something did bother him, Stephen?'

'Like what, Seán?'

'Like some consequences. Like some dead bodies to carry home.'

'What the fuck are you talking about? You want to shoot Yanks now?'

'No, not at all. But it's time we reminded the British that they can't use Ireland to do what they want. There's a cost. And they haven't been paying it. If a couple of American soldiers got caught up in that, there'd be all hell, I'd say. I don't think Roosevelt's persuaded Americans they want to get into someone else's war. You read they do in the English papers, but it's not the message I'm getting from New York or Boston. You must hear the same, Stephen. And we need to use that.'

'I don't know what you're talking about, Seán. This is bollocks.'

'Do you think it's bollocks, Herr Fürst?'

The German responded slowly and cautiously. He didn't like this.

'I don't know. Like Mr Hayes, I don't know what you mean.'

'Foynes. On the Shannon. You'll know it's where the flying boats land.'

Fürst merely nodded, none the wiser.

'What about it?' said Hayes.

'Every couple of days a flying boat from America comes into Foynes and heads off back across the Atlantic. And who's on those planes? Well, we all know. Everyone knows. And everyone in Dublin pretends it's not happening. British ministers, British generals, British admirals, British businessmen. Not to mention all the American businessmen who are supplying the British with weapons. And a few American army sorts to make up the numbers, along with the agents and diplomats and all the other buggers the British need to keep America on their side.'

'It's not news, Seán. And it's not news Dev's turning a blind eye.'

'It would be news if one of those flying boats exploded, I'd say.'

The Chief-of-Staff said nothing for a moment, then laughed.

'Is that what you've been waiting for? Is that your big idea?'

'It's bigger than some, Stephen, a lot bigger. And worth a thought. It would take out some very big British names, soldiers, politicians, all sorts. You wouldn't get a haul like that anywhere else. Jesus! Why wouldn't that be worth doing?'

'We couldn't even get into Foynes.'

'I've got someone in Foynes right now,' replied McCaughey.

The German spy watched, looking from one man to another. It was not his business, but it intrigued him. McCaughey had the confidence. Hayes was uneasy.

'It's not your turf, Seán. You keep out of the South.'

'It's just a bit of luck, Stephen.' The head of Northern Command smiled. He was playing this for what it was worth. 'A friend of a friend. A solid Republican.'

'If you have information from Foynes, you need to pass it on.'

'That's what I'm doing. It needs keeping quiet . . . the last minute.'

'What does?'

'With so much leaking out, I'm telling you now. No one else knows.'

'Then fucking tell me!'

'There's a bomb. The feller will get a bomb on the Yankee Clipper.'

The IRA Chief-of-Staff looked at McCaughey in astonishment.

Otto Fürst was tempted to applaud. It was a bold move.

'Oh no,' said Stephen Hayes. 'That's out of the fucking question!'

'And why?' said the head of Northern Command, looking puzzled.

'Not without my say-so!'

'It won't be without your say-so. Now you know, you can give it.'

'I said no, Seán! However you've done this . . . you'll stop it! Now!'

Seán McCaughey looked at Otto Fürst.

'What would Berlin think, Herr Fürst? Bigwig British soldiers and politicians dead. What would the Abwehr say? Would Herr Hitler object to that?'

The German smiled. It was well done. He could hardly tell Berlin he had said or done anything to stand in the way of delivering a blow like this to Britain. And once he had agreed, was Stephen Hayes going to say it couldn't happen? Would the Chief-of-Staff want that to go back to the Abwehr? It was bolder than anything he had ever suggested. He couldn't simply stop it. It was checkmate.

12

THE ROYAL GEORGE

Emmet Warde came back from the phone booth. As he sat down at the table he nodded across to the barman. He slumped back in the armchair, staring at the fire, saying nothing. Stefan sat opposite him, reading a book. He said nothing, waiting for the other man to start the conversation. It wasn't his place to ask. It was the first night in Limerick for Stefan Gillespie and the private detective. They were there, at the Royal George Hotel, to wait for the phone call that would come, if it came, from Josephine Kilmartin. Wherever she was, whatever she was doing, Terry Gregory's information was that she was somewhere in the same area. There was a meeting of the IRA Army Council; that was where she had taken the German, Otto Fürst. It was still Fürst the head of Special Branch was interested in. And Josie was his driver. She was the connection. It would not be the only route Superintendent Gregory was exploring. It was simply one handful of seed that had been scattered.

Only when the barman put down a whiskey, did Emmet look up.

'You can bring a bottle. It'll save your legs.'

The barman nodded and walked away.

'Terry can pay for that,' said Warde, smiling at Stefan.

'I'm sure he can.'

The private detective sipped at the whiskey.

'Your brother's all right?' asked Stefan.

'He's at home. And he'll be grand for a time. Then he won't be.'

A bottle of Powers was placed on the table.

'What . . . happened to him—' Stefan stopped. He didn't know whether it was a question he could ask or if it was even the right question. 'Is that the right word?'

'You mean has he always been crazy?' Emmet laughed.

'That's not what I meant. Forget it. I'm sorry.'

'Well, we've got to talk about something. Why not my mad brother?'

'I said forget it, Emmet.'

Warde took the bottle. He looked at Stefan, who shook his head.

'Ah, you've a job to do. You need to stay sober. I've a job to do as well if Josie phones. I have my list of lies at the ready. I need not to stay sober. Cheers!'

'I'd say you're hoping she doesn't phone. Is that it?'

'It would suit me. I don't mind wasting my time or your time or Terry Gregory's money. If she does phone, you only have my word for what she says.'

'I think you're too far in for that, Emmet.'

Warde nodded slowly, then stared for some time into the fire.

'You know I was in the British Army?'

'Yes, I heard that.'

'Middle East and then the Western Front. It's an odd thing, but you hear fellers say they had a good war. I've said it myself. Maybe it's like a lot of things, relative. If you came out alive, well, you had a better war than the bastards who didn't. So, I missed 1916. I missed the years afterwards. And when I came back, I was in demand, you might say. The cause wanted experienced men, officers like me. I even had a medal to prove I knew what I was doing. As if anyone in that shite-show knew what they were doing. But being in the British Army always hung over you. There was always a question. No one asked it, but I could still hear it.'

'Is that why you left . . . in the Civil War?'

'It was there. I had a lot of reasons. Maybe the one that held the rest together was just how many years I'd spent watching men die, sending men out to die, and doing my own share of killing along the way. By the time we were killing each other for the glory of Ireland, I'd been at it, one way or another, for six years. And then came Béal na mBláth. You know I was there when Mick Collins was killed?'

'Yes.'

Stefan remembered the way Dessie MacMahon told him that, as if simply being there and surviving asked severe questions about Emmet's loyalty. There was silence again in the bar. The private detective poured himself another drink.

'There was a pat on the back and a shake of the hand and all the tears and commiserations to share. For a few minutes, for the rest of us who were there, we were almost heroes. You shot it out with the buggers. You were by Mick's side at the end. You did your best. But, well . . . was your best good enough? And why . . . were you alive when Mick wasn't? And that was a question I heard. Not to my face. Behind my back, but not so far behind . . . not far at all. How did they know exactly where he'd be? It was true. Someone did betray him. I know it. But I watched him die. That day, I'd have taken his bullet. I might even have handled the crap that came afterwards . . . if I'd still believed in what I was doing. I didn't.'

At intervals, Emmet slowed his words and topped up his glass.

'I left because I'd had enough. We all should have had

enough . . . still, whatever it did to me, it did worse to Charlie, even if he never saw a trench.'

Stefan didn't ask what that meant, but Warde could see the question.

'Shellshock, that's what we called it in the war. Cowardice was another word, though it got harder to say. Men who'd been in the trenches for years, who survived bombs and bullets and saw their friends shovelled up in pieces or strung on the barbed wire or drowning in the mud . . . it got in their heads. I don't know what makes some of us take it and others break, but that's how it was. When it came, when you saw it in front of you, you weren't looking at cowards or fucking malingerers. You were looking at men with heads in a madhouse. They tried putting them in prison, or forcing them over the top first, or shooting them. But they couldn't stop it. I saw it. And I knew plenty who brought it home with them and had to live their chirpy, cheerful lives as if it wasn't still there . . . when it was.'

Stefan reached across and took the bottle. He poured himself a drink.

'And what's that got to do with Charlie, you're asking me?'

Emmet Warde sat back in the armchair, looking at the fire. Stefan thought he wasn't going to say any more. He thought the whiskey had lost the rest. But then Emmet seemed to take control of his thoughts again, and he continued.

'You don't have to be in a trench. You don't have to walk into machine-gun fire across no man's land. You don't have to have artillery battering your eardrums. You don't have to throw yourself in a hole when a shell goes off and find your pal's brains all over your face. I know what shellshock is. It's what Charlie's got left with. He found his in Dublin's fair city and the four green fields of Ireland. He's been shooting and being shot at, killing and bombing, since he was seventeen. It doesn't make him any different from the rest of us. We all stand in the same place. Some slip through as if nothing

164

happened. Others have their minds fucked up. Charlie lives his life as if nothing's wrong. He cracks jokes about the old days with the best. Then . . . often for no reason you'd see . . . it's in his head.'

Emmet stopped. The impulse that made him speak had gone. He poured a glass of whiskey for himself and one for Stefan. Whatever had made him say it, Stefan could see he would say no more. There would be little further conversation, about all that or about anything. The private detective raised his whiskey glass.

'To the dead who are never forgotten, and the living who are.'

Stefan drained his glass. He thought Emmet would sit up with the bottle.

'I'm going up to bed, Emmet.'

Warde nodded, now thoughtful.

'She won't phone tonight, will she? It'll be tomorrow now.'

Stefan shrugged. 'You'd know better than I do.'

The private detective didn't respond. He looked into the fire again. There was something bleak and empty in his face. The shutters were down, but Stefan had a sense that they hid nothing, because there was little there to hide. He walked out of the bar and went upstairs. He couldn't help feeling that if Charlie Warde had paid a price for what he gave his country, in a different way, so had his brother.

When Stefan came down next morning, Emmet was there, drinking coffee and eating fried eggs. Like a lot of drinkers, he seemed awake and bright. He was well scrubbed and smartly dressed. His words were businesslike. It was business.

'Josie phoned.'

Stefan nodded. The waiter caught his eye.

'Just some tea and some toast.'

'Wherever she is, she drove into the town. She said Killaloe.

She was buying provisions, she said. Make what you like of that. Her friends in the Army Council, I guess. So, I delivered my news. The man I met yesterday in Limerick, who knows a man who was in Pearse Street . . . Let's not do it to death, eh? You like a bit of poetry, I know. "I saw a man who wasn't there . . . He wasn't there again today . . . I wish that he would go away." But the job's done. I said I needed to talk to her. And she's keen. Dear Josie, what a girl! She has to drop a friend at Limerick Station.'

'So what did you say?'

'I said Limerick Station would suit me down to the fucking ground. So we have a date, tea and buns in the station buffet. That's where I tell her it all went wrong . . . and I couldn't find the feller who was at Pearse Street. So nearly there, and just at the last minute . . . Still, I'm doing my best, I'll say. My fucking best!'

'Don't overdo it, Emmet. You need to keep her onside.'

'I will, Inspector, don't you worry. I've plenty more lies.'

They said nothing as the tea and toast arrived. Stefan poured the tea.

'What time will she be at the station?'

'Around one o'clock, just before. There's a train then.'

Stefan took a timetable from his pocket and flicked through it.

'There's a train to Dublin at quarter to one. Nothing else fits that time. It's tight. But it'll be done before she meets you. She said she was dropping someone?'

The private detective poured more coffee.

'For a train. Yes, that's what she said.' He grinned. 'It could be her cousin Katie from Killaloe. She could be on a little holiday after all. And this whole thing could be a bloody farce, couldn't it? What about that? No spies, no gunmen, just a lonely woman who should have forgotten about her brother being murdered and led some sort of life . . . But what would be the fun in that for any of us, Inspector?'

Stefan Gillespie sat in the black Ford in a corner of the fore-court of Limerick Station. There were other cars parked close by; there were taxies waiting at the entrance; there was a stop for buses that came and went. He was as inconspicuous as he needed to be. He didn't know what he was waiting for yet, only that Josie Kilmartin was coming to the station. She would meet Emmet Warde, as arranged, but that had no significance. What mattered was who she was bringing to the station. Since she was no more on holiday than her private detective was uncovering buried information about her brother's disappear-ance, the reason Josie was at the station had to do with the real business she was on. There would be a passenger in the car she was driving. It would be someone from the IRA Army Council or the man she had brought from Dublin to the Army Council meeting, Otto Fürst. Stefan's instructions meant he had no interest in any of the IRA men, however high they ranked in the pecking order. His target was the German spy.

It was Fürst who had brought Josie to her journey west; Fürst was the man Superintendent Gregory wanted to know about. If she was dropping him at the station, he would be get-ting the Dublin train. And Stefan would take the same train. The IRA meeting must have concluded. At least the German's contribution, whatever that was, was over. There were other places to go, but for a German spy the capital made more sense than most. There was a fast train to Dublin due. He wasn't leaving much time to catch it, but it would always be the busi-ness of a man keeping a low profile to catch a train with little time to spare. Hanging about on platforms, or waiting any-where too long, was one way of asking to be noticed.

Emmet Warde had not left the hotel with Stefan. He would make his own way. They would have no contact in the street or at the station. He was again a private detective, meeting a client to discuss progress in an investigation or, as he would now explain to Josie Kilmartin, the unexpected and disappointing lack of progress. Having produced something out of nothing, he would now reverse the trick. He would meet her in the station buffet. When their business was done he would return to the hotel. She would drive to wherever she had come from. She would probably say something about friends she was staying with. He might have to suggest a lead he wanted to follow up in the vicinity, to make sense of what he was doing. He would know she was lying. She would assume he told the truth.

If Josie's passenger was Otto Fürst, Stefan would be on the German's train, following him. The only purpose was to see where he went and if he met anyone. If the spy seemed suspicious the job was to be abandoned. Assuming Stefan had a German to follow, Emmet would collect the car that night and drive it to Dublin.

It was half past twelve when Josephine Kilmartin pulled into the station forecourt. Stefan knew the car already. He had no trouble identifying Otto Fürst as he got out. There was a heavy overcoat and a turned-up collar, along with a grey trilby shading his eyes, but the photographs of the face were sharp enough in Stefan's head. He was amused that when Josie took a small suitcase from the back of the car, clearly Fürst's, he walked on into the station, leaving her to carry it.

Stefan leant across to the glove compartment and took the Webley revolver, pushing it into a brief case. It was less about a need to be armed than leaving the gun in the car. He put the keys in the glove compartment for Warde and headed into the station. He bought a ticket to Dublin. He would not use his warrant card and advertise himself. If the German was going somewhere else, he would work round it. He bought a newspaper to give himself something to do and reached the platform. Five minutes until the Dublin train. Otto Fürst was there. He had his suitcase and Josie Kilmartin was walking away from him. She passed within feet of Stefan Gillespie, heading for the buffet and her meeting with Emmet Warde.

The train approached. Steam hissed; tracks rattled. Carriages shuddered to a halt. People got out; people got in. Stefan moved along the platform. He saw Otto Fürst walking through a carriage. He hunched over a cigarette, glancing up. The German sat at a window seat. Stefan would get on board, finding a seat not too far away, but not too close. A distance that would not create proximity or eye contact.

It was as he turned toward an open carriage door that he saw the man sitting opposite Otto Fürst. It was Commandant Geróid de Paor, out of uniform, in a suit of Donegal tweed of the kind that suggested a fishing holiday. The two men, German spy and Irish Intelligence officer took no notice of one another. De Paor was reading. Fürst looked out at the platform and lit a cigarette. Stefan took this in in seconds. He turned his back and walked rapidly out of sight. De Paor would recognise him as instantly as he had recognised the G2 officer. There was no point getting on the train. Not only because he would be spotted, but because he had done what he was there to do. He knew that immediately. He had found out what Terry Gregory wanted to know and had almost certainly suspected. There could be no coincidence in what he had just seen. The two men were not sitting opposite one another on the Dublin train by any chance. They were there by arrangement.

By the time the train pulled out, Stefan was heading out of the station. He stopped at the buffet. Through the window he saw Emmet and Josie, walking from the counter, carrying tea. He waited until they sat down. Then he went in. At the counter he bought twenty cigarettes. The private detective and the IRA courier were in a conversation that had immediately become quiet and intense. Emmet was delivering a neatly packaged lie about a man he had tried to find in Adare who proved a false lead in respect of events of twenty years ago.

Josie would be experiencing the disappointment of false hope. Stefan made a point of brushing past their table to catch Emmet's eye and let him know he had not taken the train.

In the booking office he went to a telephone booth and called Superintendent Gregory. He gave his news in a few oblique words. He felt the sense of satisfaction at the other end. It was what his boss had wondered about from the moment he stood in an empty cell at Mountjoy. Then, perhaps, it was something he might have said he half-suspected. Now, it would be something that he had known all along.

13

FOYNES

The telegram from Superintendent Gregory arrived at four in the morning. Stefan was woken by the hotel porter, who looked at him with unconcealed irritation. If Stefan had been asleep, so had he. It was unlikely, thought Stefan, that some conversation between the porter and the postman who brought the telegram wouldn't have asked questions about who he was. Stefan and Emmet had registered as something in a vague civil service department, but hotel porters always knew more than the available information told them. It was improbable this one hadn't got a good idea Stefan was a police-man. But by this stage it didn't matter.

FOYNES RAIL STATION TOMORROW SEVEN AM STOP IF ASSOCIATES IN BLUE THERE RADIO SILENCE STOP LEAVE EW BEHIND NO EXPLANATION REQD STOP DUBLINTG

It was easily translatable. Gregory wanted him at the railway station at Foynes, some twenty-five miles away, that morning. Associates in blue meant there would be local guards; he was not to engage in any conversation about why he was in the area. He was amused. He imagined that as he was in Limerick undercover, there might be an indignant inspector or superintendent asking what the fuck he was up to on his patch. For the rest, he was to leave Emmet Warde at the hotel, with no explanation. That wouldn't be difficult. The private detective would be asleep when he left. As long as the tab at the bar was open, he wouldn't care anyway. A brief note telling him to stay put would be explanation enough.

Stefan lay back on the bed not so much tired as weary at the prospect of more events that involved the unknown, the inexplicable and probably the unimportant. Going back to sleep wasn't worthwhile. He'd be lucky to get more than an hour and he'd be dead on his feet driving to Foynes. He got up and took out the roadmap. He knew Foynes from one visit, when he had flown to New York on the Yankee Clipper with an extradition warrant for a man who had disappeared by the time he arrived. In the course of finding him, he had met a woman who, for a time, had meant something in his life. And then she'd gone, and she didn't mean something any more. It would have been the same for her. That's how it happened. He wondered where she was. It was the last time a woman had mattered that much. It was a thought that simply came from the name of a place. He wondered if she ever thought of him. It was a reflection from nowhere, fonder than he expected.

Inspector Gillespie arrived at Foynes railway station to find two black patrol cars and a large Rover that belonged to a burly, uniformed superintendent who stood beside it, proprietorially, watching Stefan's Ford approach. The superintendent was neither cheerful nor welcoming. Stefan walked towards him. That was clearly the expectation. The superintendent was a mountain to be approached with deference.

'I take it you're Gillespie.'

'Yes, I am.'

'I'm Superintendent Mackay.'

'Good to meet you, sir.'

The superintendent eyed him, as if searching for sarcasm.

'I had a call from the Commissioner. He said you were in Limerick.'

Stefan nodded. He was.

'I suppose it would be pointless me asking why you're in Limerick at all. You know you've no fucking business here, not without informing me. Unless of course you're on holiday. Would that be it? Bit of a jolly away from the big city?'

Finding no obvious sarcasm in this inspector, he was trying his own.

'I'm sorry, Superintendent, you'd have to take that up with Mr Gregory.'

Mackay took out a cigarette.

'Don't worry, I shall. Jesus, Mary and Joseph, you're a shower of cunts.'

He lit the cigarette.

'Do you know what this is about?'

'I have no idea, sir. Superintendent Gregory didn't say.'

'A bomb on a fucking Yankee Clipper. An IRA bomb.'

'Jesus!' Stefan was now able to look genuinely surprised.

'Jesus, indeed. Still, at least we've you handy. It's odd, isn't it? Put a Special Branch man in a Limerick hotel, for no reason anybody's ever likely to tell me, and out of nowhere, a bomb. Were you expecting one? Or have you a nose for fucking bombs? That'd be Terry Gregory's explanation for most things. His fucking nose!'

The superintendent turned to the station. A train was approaching.

'Anyway, Inspector,' Mackay grinned suddenly, 'welcome to Foynes.'

The meeting that followed, between Superintendent Mackay and Detective Superintendent Gregory, though far from warm, was more cautious on the Limerick man's part than his response to Stefan Gillespie. While he would have liked to show the head of Special Branch the contempt and irritation he felt, it was not advisable; Gregory was too important. He held the same rank, but even on Mackay's turf he had to be handled with care. A cold eye would have to suffice.

A convoy of police vehicles drove the short distance from the railway station to the flying boat station, where the seaplanes that crossed the Atlantic anchored. Superintendent Gregory was in the Ford Stefan was driving. Sergeant MacMahon was in the back. No words were needed for Stefan to understand that though these events seemed to have nothing to do with why he was in Limerick with Emmet Warde, that operation was still a secret. Dessie was there because he was the only Special Branch man who knew of it, or who even knew Stefan was in Limerick.

'You know we're looking for a bomb, sir?'

'On a flying boat. It's a first for the IRA. It has me scratching my head.'

Stefan nodded. It was nothing if not unexpected.

'If this went off with passengers on board,' continued Gregory, 'the damage to Ireland . . . These planes are full of American generals and senators now, never mind the Imperial bigwigs. You might say, why wouldn't the Boys want to fuck Dev that way? And killing British politicians . . .? The more the merrier. But if the IRA wanted to bugger themselves in the States, they couldn't do any better.'

Terry Gregory was genuinely puzzled. It wasn't right.

'How did you find out?' asked Stefan.

'Ah, now that's a strange one. The information came from an unlooked-for source. For once, our friends in G2 are on top of things. I don't normally expect Commandant de Paor to know much about the IRA, but this one came from him.'

'Yesterday?'

174

'Last night.'

'I see.'

'Last night. Not so long after you saw him on a train with his prize spy, Herr Otto Fürst, who'd arrived, hotfoot, from a meeting of the Army Council, where McCaughey and the Boys from the North were kicking Stephen Hayes up the arse and demanding action, that's to say something, somewhere . . . blown up. You'd think they meant a British camp across the border, but it seems, according to Geróid, that blasting a Yankee Clipper out of the air is from Northern Command.'

'So they've got someone in Foynes?'

'Not just in Foynes . . . someone who can get on board.'

'So you think Fürst heard this at the meeting, and told Gerry?'

'It's not what Commandant de Paor said. Didn't want to reveal his source. But as I knew anyway, well, that didn't last. He only held his ace for a few hours.'

'Well, at least we know, sir. Looks like Otto's going to be useful.'

Terry Gregory nodded thoughtfully.

'Gerry doesn't know how I found out about the German. He doesn't know you saw them together on the train. He has no idea you were there at all. Right?'

'I assumed that.'

'Ah, he's the fast one, always the fast one, Dessie!'

'He has his moments,' replied Dessie from the back seat.

'Thanks, Dessie! You'll keep me straight so.' Stefan looked back at Gregory as the car pulled into Foynes' main street. 'And what's happening here now?'

'The Clipper's held back. Gerry has a bomb disposal team searching it. He drove down last night. We need to look at every bastard who's been near the plane since it docked. If the IRA are serious about this kind of sabotage, it's big. The British can't afford to lose the Atlantic connection. And if we can't police that . . .'

Stefan was surprised by the tone.

'Whatever it's worth, it's hardly worth a war in Ireland.'

'Who knows what it's worth? Our job's to make sure we don't have to find out. It's also to shut down any information . . . about any bomb . . . on any plane.'

'You might want to mention that to Superintendent Mackay, sir. I wouldn't think there's a Guard in County Limerick doesn't know what's going on now.'

'Am I right, Stevie, in thinking Jack Mackay called my brave boys a bunch of cunts?' Gregory leant back in the seat, shaking his head. 'Surely he wouldn't!'

Stefan and Dessie laughed.

'Ah, well,' said the head of Special Branch, 'I'll take pleasure in telling Jack the necessary home truths. Keeping his fucking mouth shut will only be the start.'

The convoy of police cars drove along the main street of Foynes that looked as much like a row of ordinary houses as an airport, since that's all many of the buildings were. They stopped at the Garda Station. A sergeant emerged, simultaneously officious and flustered. He got to Superintendent Mackay's car in time to open the door for his superior. Mackay got out, smiling and then, deciding too much cheerfulness wasn't a good look, nodded gravely. In the black Ford, Gregory stubbed out a cigarette and sniffed, watching Mackay, who was now waiting for him. He made him wait longer than was necessary. He turned to Stefan.

'You go to the dock. The bomb fellers have been on the Clipper since the early hours. No news, so they haven't found it. Go on and see what's happening.'

'Thanks, sir,' said Stefan, smiling. 'I'll poke about, shall I?'

'Ah, I'm sure if anything's going to go off, they'll shout.'

'Maybe lay off the fags when you're on board, Stevie,' said Dessie.

'If de Paor's there,' continued Gregory, 'just listen. He'll have a lot on his mind now, but he'll still be wondering how I knew about his dalliance with Otto.'

Terry Gregory got out of the car. He walked to the station with the Limerick Superintendent. The two men were immediately in deep conversation, but as they reached the door, Gregory patted Jack Mackay's shoulder and laughed. Driving away in the Ford, Stefan Gillespie and Dessie MacMahon grinned. They knew the smile of the crocodile. That amiable pat on the shoulder was the prelude to a bollocking. The head of Special Branch was about to establish who was in charge.

Stefan drove on through the airport to the dock, where the flying boat was at anchor. Dessie saw the Yankee Clipper for the first time. Stefan had been here before, but the size and grace of the plane was something that didn't lightly diminish by seeing one again. There were few things so big and so new that were so beautiful. Dessie felt it now.

'That,' said Sergeant MacMahon, 'is fucking something!'

Where the River Shannon below Limerick leads out to the Atlantic, after its long and circuitous journey through Ireland, a small town became, in 1936, the unlikely focus of the world's newest technology of international travel. It was a question of fuel. The flying boats that had opened up long-distance air travel from Europe to America, Africa, the Far East and Australia had a limited range. When they flew from America, across the Atlantic, the Yankee Clippers and the Empire Flying Boats reached that limit with the coast of Ireland. Out of the need to refuel and let passengers connect to planes and trains bound for Britain and Europe, or further afield, the Shannon-side town of Foynes provided the mix of airport and harbour the flying boats needed. It was travel for the wealthy and powerful, the property of politicians, tycoons and magnates, and Hollywood's most famous stars; the great and good and not infrequently the not-so-good. The luxurious Yankee Clippers of Pan-American operated only a few years before war stopped flights, but even as war in Europe approached, the clientele through Foynes was changing.

Flying west there were more people from Germany, and not just Germany, who were escaping what was coming and had the money to leave in style. In both directions the seats of the wealthy were also taken by politicians and diplomats, industrialists and businessmen, senior military personnel, and no small number of those whose vaguely defined professions covered intelligence work. Then, for a short time, the flying boats didn't fly. But the airbridge between Britain and America was vital to Britain's war and to American support for it. Quickly, the Yankee Clippers were flying again. Foynes was back at the hub of routes that connected America to Britain and Britain to Africa, the Middle East and beyond. The passengers were more and more politicians and the military, though at first uniforms were not seen in the terminal at Foynes. The passports many of these passengers travelled on were false. Almost everyone who passed through Foynes had something to do with the war. Whatever about neutrality, Ireland facilitated it.

There was no wall, no barbed wire round Foynes, but Shannon Airport was no ordinary part of Ireland. Most in the town worked for the airport in one way or another. British and American aircrew were based there; so were British Intelligence officers. Foynes Garda Station had its own Special Branch men; G2 its own Intelligence officer who listed every passenger. No journalists were allowed. No one could use a camera. Even local visitors were stopped and questioned. Foynes had a separate existence to the rest of Ireland. It was meant to be invisible.

However, a bomb blowing up a Yankee Clipper full of British and American VIPs would put an end to invisibility. It would embarrass Ireland's relationship with Germany, which chose to turn a blind eye to Foynes. It would disrupt relations not only with Britain but America. An unspoken arrangement guaranteed Shannon Airport was secure. Failing in that would be more than embarrassing. Franklin Roosevelt, the American president, was already unhappy with de Valera's even-handed neutrality, set against his one-sided version. Dead Americans, especially important dead Americans, would sour relations in unpredictable ways.

Stefan Gillespie was on board the Yankee Clipper, walking through the passenger accommodation. The inside of the plane had been taken to pieces. Everywhere panels had been removed to expose the struts that held the flying boat together. Men were out on the wings, where engine cowlings had been removed. The men searching the plane were soldiers and engineers. Stefan met Commandant de Paor in the cockpit, sitting in one of the pilot's seats, poring over blueprints of the plane.

'Two options, Stefan. Wild goose chase or they're too fucking clever.'

'What do you think, Gerry?'

'On the basis that it's me has to give the all-clear?'

'I didn't know.'

'That's what it's going to come down to. Is Terry here?'

'At the Garda Station.'

The G2 officer looked at Stefan quizzically for a moment.

'You were already in Limerick?'

'By chance. Bit of a break. It didn't last long.'

Stefan smiled. Geróid de Paor returned the smile, unconvinced.

'Well, let's go and exchange notes.' De Paor stood up. 'Terry can tell me what I'm doing wrong and take no responsibility for anything at all, and I can decide whether this fecking tub's safe to take off. Are you a betting man, Stefan?'

'No.'

'Me neither,' said Commandant de Paor.

At the Garda Station, an upstairs office had been taken over by Superintendent Gregory. He stood there with Stefan Gillespie and Dessie MacMahon and the Foynes' Special Branch men, alongside Geróid de Paor and his bomb disposal officer and G2's Foynes' Intelligence man. It was de Paor who was speaking.

'We're at the end. The plane's been searched over and over. The engineers have been through it. Bomb disposal's been through it. Every bit of engine, every cubby hole, every crack and cranny. It's not going to be so small you wouldn't see it. We had a diver down as well. I don't know that the IRA are up to something underwater, but we couldn't even do that ourselves. Everything's been covered. Besides, the Clipper's been delayed. There's no fuse that wouldn't have gone off.'

Gregory nodded, no less puzzled by all this.

'If they have the access, Gerry, if they have someone who could be on board for any final checks, for anything that gets done just before the thing takes off . . .'

'It's a very small number who'd have that kind of access,' continued the commandant. 'Even smaller since flights resumed. Once the thing's docked, a few engineers, cleaners. That's it. When they're getting ready to take off, there's the flight crew, engineers again, people taking on food and drink . . . but most of that's done by the crew now. Nobody just wanders on board. The jetties are patrolled day and night. Gardaí and Military Police. You'll have a list of everyone with access.'

The superintendent gestured at two detectives at desks behind him.

'I have those names. I've looked further, too. All vetted. I can't say how thoroughly. But more thoroughly now. No one that stands out. My men are going through files at Dublin

Castle. We may find a few old IRA men, from fucking donkey's years ago. What does that mean? Isn't that most of us in this room!'

'And your man here's heard nothing?' asked de Paor.

'No more than your feller, Gerry. Has he got anything to offer us?'

'No.'

'What about the others?' said Gregory. 'Whoever our friends across the water have here, MI5, MI6. You'd know better than me. And the boyo who calls himself the American consul's secretary. The view in the station is you wouldn't get far if you asked him to take shorthand. It's a lot of ears to the ground, Gerry.'

'They'd hardly know what the IRA's up to,' replied de Paor shortly.

'But your source would know, Commandant. He was very sure, wasn't he?'

The G2 man was uncomfortable.

'If you want to discuss that, Terry, this wouldn't be the place.'

'We're all friends here, Geróid, but I take the point. My point is that however sure he was, he was wrong. If the job's done, and there's no bomb, then what's it about? Did the Boys change their minds? Your source . . . how reliable?'

'I've no doubt he believed what he told me. He had it from the IRA.'

'I think you're right, Gerry. So again . . . what the fuck does it mean?'

'I don't know.'

'Me neither. We've made a grand show of ourselves, scurrying for a bomb that isn't there. We can keep the details secret. But not what we've been doing. It doesn't say much for our security. There'll be shaky conversations between the British and Yanks and our elders and betters in Dublin. Don't we look like fools?'

Commandant de Paor did not reply. He was aware his information put this show on the road. But if he had panicked, he felt it had been for good reasons.

'The passengers were all taken to the hotel in Adare last night. They don't know what's been happening yet. You won't have seen the passenger list, Terry?'

'No, I haven't.'

De Paor turned to the man beside him and took a file.

'You might recognise a couple of the names,' the commandant said, handing Gregory a sheet of paper. 'You'll have seen them in the papers, maybe. Not all the names are real. Two of the false names are American admirals. I could go on. But we should look a lot worse than fools if that list was at the bottom of the Atlantic.'

Superintendent Gregory handed back the piece of paper and laughed.

'Fair play to you, Geróid. You have me convinced entirely . . .'

That evening, shortly after dark, the Yankee Clipper moved out into the waters of the Shannon and taxied along the river. A channel was marked by two lines of flares that stretched from Foynes into the darkness. The Shannon, as it spread out into the Atlantic, was a long way from the war, a long way from German aircraft, but there were risks. The flying boats never took off in daylight. The engines were revving now, louder and shriller, until the sound was a roar. The hull cut through the water like a boat. Then it lifted, its elegant lines, still visible above the rows of flares, lighter than its size could possibly make it. It could be seen, moving west, rising into the night. And then it was gone, swallowed by the darkness. The hum of the engines could still be heard. Finally that was gone too.

Stefan and Dessie watched the flying boat take off. Many of those who worked at the airport, who would not normally wait to watch what they had seen so many times, had stopped to look that night. Sure as everyone was that there was no danger, some still gazed up after the Yankee Clipper had disappeared. For Dessie it was a vision of unexpected grace and beauty that silenced him. For Stefan there was something in the way the Clipper sailed into the darkness, rising from the reflecting flames on the water, that made the marriage of the machine and the vastness of the night beyond a vision too. There was space and freedom. It was a fleeting glimpse of nothing. But it made the place he stood in shabby, confined.

Superintendent Gregory was not at the dockside to watch the take-off. He had closeted himself at the Garda Station for hours with a telephone, alternating calls to Special Branch with calls to numbers only he knew. Most of the unexpected visitors to Shannon Airport had left. Commandant de Paor was driving to Dublin. Superintendent Mackay was in Limerick, having played no real part in the day. He was writing the Garda Commissioner a letter of complaint about Terry Gregory.

Something had been eating at Terry Gregory. It started before he got to Foynes. Perhaps even as Commandant de Paor had delivered the news about the bomb at Shannon Airport. The information should have been solid. Whatever about de Paor's dipping a toe into the muddy waters of spies and double agents, and the G2 man's relative unfamiliarity with the IRA Army Council, this was information that came, surely, straight from the horse's mouth. Yet Gregory's first reaction, the one that came from his not inconsiderable gut, was 'Bollocks!'

He would have been hard pressed to come up with a more unlikely IRA operation. His response was to question the source. But he couldn't. And there was no time. If the information was accurate, action had to be taken. That was all he could say to the Garda Commissioner, and all Commandant de Paor could say to his superiors. And it wouldn't have stopped there. Even Dev would know before the night was out. The embarrassing cock-up might have all sorts of justifications, but cock-up it was. Gregory's stomach rumbled. Something wasn't right. And now that the outcome of all this had been precisely . . . nothing, he wanted to know more.

It took a long time to piece something together from the back and forth of oblique and inconclusive phone calls Gregory devoted his evening to. There was no single thing that explained why reliable information had proved unreliable. But the more he looked at where it came from and how it arrived and put that together with consequences, not for him, not for the Irish government, not for Britain or America, not for agents or spies, but for the IRA itself, the more the head of Special Branch saw a picture. He built it from contradictions and whispered resentments; from his deep knowledge of struggles within the IRA. It wasn't a full picture. Maybe it wasn't true. But it was a sketch of something that made sense.

Stefan Gillespie sat with his boss on the terrace off the bar at the Royal George Hotel. It was not a cold night for October, but they were alone. Stefan was staying one more night at the hotel with Emmet Warde. Dessie MacMahon was on his way back to Dublin. Superintendent Gregory had decided to stay in Limerick too. For reasons Stefan could not yet understand, he was talking through what had and hadn't happened at Foynes at length. He started with where the information came from, and he kept returning to that. What Fürst had told de Paor was very specific.

'The point isn't Seán McCaughey announcing this spectacular bomb on the Yankee Clipper, it's how he does it. Who's there. And Otto was very clear about that. He was there, McCaughey was there, and Stephen Hayes. No one else. McCaughey has said nothing during the Army Council meeting. He's argued about sabotage and bombs and all the things Northern Command want to happen. Hayes cuts him off.

At least he shuts him up. That's the routine. McCaughey demands war and the Chief-of-Staff says not today, maybe tomorrow or the day after. It's been going on for years like that. So, if Seán has this up his sleeve, why doesn't he use it? Why doesn't he say, fuck you, Stephen, you idle, drunken bastard, don't tell me we can't mount a serious operation. I've just mounted one. I'm going to blow a whole plane load of British bigwigs and assorted Very Important Arseholes out of the sky over the Shannon. I'm going to show Dev he can't even police the country. And I'm going to show our German allies what grand fucking fellers we all are!'

Gregory chuckled. He liked the sound of that.

'The reason would be that there was no bomb,' said Stefan.

'So, why say it? And why only to Hayes?'

'And to Otto Fürst, sir.'

'Fürst doesn't matter. Well, he does matter, because he's the man who reported the conversation. But McCaughey has no idea about that. The only reason Fürst is part of this tête-à-tête is because he's going to support McCaughey when the Chief-of-Staff says fuck you, call it off, we're not blowing up any flying boats. He's going to be asked whether Germany would approve. And what can he say?'

'Well, presumably, he says, yes.'

'So how does Hayes stop it? He doesn't want it to happen. But McCaughey has come very close to turning a lot of Army Council men down here against him. People don't like him. People don't trust him. He's only there because no one else wants to take on the shite. So, what happens if he calls the Army Council back together and says a decision has to be made to stop this mad operation at Foynes? What happens if McCaughey wins the argument and it goes ahead? Hayes is finished. And what Hayes knows, but McCaughey is too manipulative to understand, is that the IRA's finished too. And that's what's in Hayes' mind.'

'But McCaughey's talking bollocks. There's no bomb!'

'That's the point,' said Superintendent Gregory.

'How, sir?'

'If Hayes can't risk losing an argument that might see McCaughey take over anyway, there's only one way to stop the bomb. To inform. To tell me. And since Seán already believes his Chief-of-Staff is a traitor, that's what he thinks will happen. When it does, he has his proof. There was no bomb. No one, anywhere in the IRA, knows a thing about it. It never existed. But Stephen Hayes thinks it does.'

'Hayes and Otto Fürst,' added Stefan.

'As I said, Seán doesn't know about Otto's promiscuity.'

'And would Hayes have passed on that information . . .'

Terry Gregory shrugged.

'I don't know . . . he didn't. But as far as McCaughey's concerned . . .'

'He did.'

'Yes, he did. The whisper is out. McCaughey's coming for him. It's unlikely he won't take him now. A court martial and a bullet. Not necessarily in that order.'

'Won't someone tell him?'

'They might be slow to. If he's on the way out . . . why go with him? Still, if no one else is going to give him the gypsy's warning, I suppose we might as well.'

Terry Gregory was heading back to the bar. Stefan followed.

'You don't want him shot then, sir?'

'I don't much care, but why not stir it up even more?'

The two policemen walked back into the bar. Emmet Warde sat at the table by the fire, reading a book, or at least flicking through the pages as he drank.

'The more mere anarchy they loose at each other, the better, Stevie. Hayes is in Ennis. The sieve still leaks. McCaughey just doesn't know where the holes are. His car's at Hogan's in Francis Street. Warn him . . . and give him my regards.'

'So, I walk in and say . . . what, sir?'

'To get back to Dublin fucking fast. That'd be a start.'

'You think a chat with a Special Branch inspector will help his case?'

Terry Gregory laughed, then stood for a moment, looking across the bar at Emmet Warde. 'Never waste anything. I knew there'd be another job for Emmet.'

'He thinks he's finished. And why wouldn't he?'

'He knows me better than that. Bring us over some drinks.'

Gregory walked to the table and sat down opposite Warde. The private detective looked at the Special Branch man's smiling face and leant back, drawing in his breath slowly. If he thought it was all finished, he already knew it wasn't.

14

THE VATICAN

Stefan Gillespie and Emmet Warde left Limerick early. Stefan drove north into the County Clare town of Ennis. By ten o'clock the black Ford was parked in Francis Street. The bar that was called the Vatican was at the other end of the street. No one knew why it was called the Vatican, but it was assumed it had been an idle joke that simply stuck. Fifty years earlier the proprietor had changed the name from his own, the usual naming convention for a pub, to the loftier, more distinctive and still humorous name that had found its way into common usage in the town. It remained the Vatican, a dingy and uninspiring frontage of grey cracked rendering, grey windows – the glass as well as the paint – and a yellow front door that bore a faded painting of the papal mitre and the keys of the kingdom. It was here, according to Superintendent Gregory's sources, that Stephen Hayes, Chief-of-Staff of the IRA, had been staying since the Army Council meeting by Lough Derg.

The town was still quiet, but there were enough people and cars and carts about to make the parked car inconspicuous. It would be Emmet's job to go into the pub and warn Hayes that if he didn't move fast he would be lucky to get back to

Dublin. It seemed likely that the IRA man would know something of what had happened at Foynes by now. He would be relieved that there was no bomb and bewildered by the behaviour of his counterpart in Northern Ireland. However, it was unlikely he had any idea that Seán McCaughey now felt he had the evidence that marked him out as a police informant and that he was about to act on it.

For the moment, Stefan and Emmet watched the Vatican from a distance. A man in his twenties leant against the doorway, half in and half out, smoking a cigarette. He occasionally looked up and down the street, idly, but still with purpose. He shifted from foot to foot; there was a certain nervousness, Stefan Gillespie thought. The man repeatedly checked his watch. The bell of an unseen church began to strike the hour. The man stepped out of the doorway. He looked up and down the street again. Then he turned sharply and walked rapidly away. He took the first turning he came to and was gone. Stefan was puzzled. Emmet was watching too, but he had no interest in what he was looking at. It meant nothing.

'That was one of Hayes' fellers,' said Stefan.

Warde nodded.

'I'm assuming your man's still in there.'

Warde shrugged.

'If he isn't, he isn't,' continued Stefan. 'A few minutes and then go in.'

'Then you take me back to Limerick?'

'I can still take you to Dublin, Emmet.'

'I'll take the train. I arranged to meet Josie at the station. She phoned the hotel last night. She doesn't have the car, whatever that's about. I'll go with her.'

'What'll you say to her?'

'I can't say anything. I just have to keep lying about all those false leads . . .'

'All right, give Hayes the message. Tell him he owes Terry Gregory one.'

Emmet took out a cigarette. He put it between his lips, unlit.

'Are you sure Terry wouldn't rather he was shot? He's a gobshite.'

'I don't imagine Terry gives a fuck whether they shoot him or they all shoot each other in turn. He must think there'll be some benefit in keeping him alive.'

'Fair enough. If being a gobshite was all it took to get yourself shot . . .'

The private detective laughed. He lit the cigarette and got out of the car.

Stephen Hayes sat on a stool in the dark, empty bar. In front of him a half-drunk pint of stout and a whiskey. He took a sip from the stout, then sank the whiskey. The barman, who stood some way down the bar, polishing glasses and whistling tunelessly through his teeth, put down the cloth and glass and walked to where Hayes was sitting. He picked up a bottle of Powers and poured more into the chief's glass. The IRA man drummed his fingers on the bar. He couldn't understand the whole Foynes fiasco. He had been forced to accept something he would never have approved, to save face. He had been put on the spot in front of the German, too, with McCaughey producing an operation that looked impressive, never mind the consequences, and on his turf. The man deserved a bullet, but he had people whispering instead; people who wanted more action; people who thought the Boys in the North had it right. He had tried to get his own man in Foynes to find out what was happening and stop it. Yet there wasn't a sniff of a bomb on a flying boat. There was not even a rumour about someone Seán McCaughey had in Foynes, someone Southern Command just didn't know about.

The thing had a smell. Hayes felt it was dangerous. He had been close to putting a word where he knew it would find its way to Terry Gregory, if that was all he had left to stop it. He didn't inform, but it was a fine line. There were people at the top of the IRA who did and he found it useful to leave them in place. However, the information was out anyway. Special Branch and Military Intelligence descended on Foynes with a bomb squad. And there was nothing. It gave the Free Staters the runaround, no one could argue with that. But why? It was aimed at him, he was sure of that; more at him than giving Dev a fright. Whatever McCaughey was playing at, if it was meant to make him look like a cunt, it had.

Hayes glanced round as a man entered the bar. He didn't know him. The man smiled, heading towards him. He nodded across at the barman, still polishing.

'I'll have a Powers.'

'We're closed,' said the barman.

'It'll be grand,' said Emmet Warde. 'Put it on Mr Hayes' bill.'

'Who the fuck let you in?' The Chief-of-Staff stood and took a step towards the door. 'George! George! Get in here and do your fucking job, you bastard!'

'George isn't there, Mr Hayes. I think he had an appointment.'

'Who the hell are you?'

The barman moved back down the bar, picked up a small glass, and poured another whiskey as asked. The newcomer's business wasn't any business of his.

'I've a message for you, Stephen.'

'What the fuck is this? Do you know who I am?'

The barman returned to his glass-polishing post. Warde lowered his voice.

'Terry says Seán McCaughey's coming for you. You need to get out and safe home to Dublin. You're running out of friends in the West. I wouldn't wait.'

The private detective picked up the whiskey and drank it.

'Is this another joke?' said Hayes.

'I wouldn't say so. But what was the first one?'

Stephen Hayes felt the danger now. He couldn't fit it all together. The bomb that didn't exist still didn't make any sense, but surely it was part of this. However McCaughey was using it, it was a deeper game than making him look like an arse. He walked to the back of the bar and pulled open a door on to a dark staircase. He had made his decision. Whoever this man was, he was listening. And he had heard.

'Davey! Shift yourself. We're going!'

No reply came from upstairs.

'Get the car started at the back. Come on, you fucker. We're going now!'

There was still only silence.

'He's gone, Mr Hayes. He went a while ago.'

The barman shrugged.

'What do you mean, he's gone? He's driving the car!'

The door from the street opened. Three men came in. Two of them wore the trench coats that ought to have announced their profession to any Guard who passed them in the street. One held a Webley revolver. Hayes recognised them only as Seán McCaughey's men from the meeting. McCaughey himself, in a dark suit and trilby, spruce and clearly self-satisfied, came in last. He held an automatic.

'Stephen Hayes, I'm arresting you on charges of treason.'

The Chief-of-Staff gazed back at the Ulsterman.

'You'll come with us. I'm here on behalf of the Army Council.'

The shock only had seconds to register, but Hayes was not without courage, or at least the kind of bloody-mindedness that would serve almost as well.

'I am the fucking Army Council, you tosser.'

The man with the Webley stepped forward and hit the Chief-of-Staff across the face with the barrel. The blow was hard. It broke the skin down one cheek. Stephen Hayes fell to the floor. McCaughey walked forward and peered down.

'No you're not, Stephen, not any more.'

As Hayes got to his feet, Seán McCaughey finally looked at Warde.

'And who are you?'

The private detective's mind was racing. What he said now mattered. It mattered a lot. Nothing he said could let these men think, even for a moment, that he was something to do with Terry Gregory and Special Branch. There was a whole scenario shaping itself in his head that would end very badly. He had no interest in how badly it might end for Stephen Hayes but for himself, he had to think quickly. There had to be a reason he was here that wasn't about that at all.

'I asked you a question. Who the fuck are you?'

'My name is Warde . . .'

Emmet was still thinking. He had to tell some sort of truth, something simple that explained enough to be convincing but to make him harmless. He had to find a reason why he was with Hayes, and it had to be about who he was, or who he was meant to be. Emmet Warde, second-rate private detective, unsuccessfully working on a case and asking questions about the past; a past that could have nothing to do with any of this. He had to trust that Hayes had the sense to know that any mention of Special Branch and Terry Gregory would be a disaster. All he could find to say would be about Josie Kilmartin, even though everything inside him said he should keep his distance from her. Wherever this was going, he didn't want her dragged into it. There was no choice. That piece of truth was all he had.

'Emmet Warde. I'm a private detective.'

The three IRA men looked at him, puzzled. McCaughey laughed.

'A private detective! Jesus, Mary and Joseph, I've heard it all.'

'I know him, Seán,' said one of the Ulstermen. 'So do you. Emmet Warde!'

The head of Northern Command recognised the name now.

'Major-General Emmet Warde. What would be the odds on that, eh?'

'I'm not a general in anyone's army. I haven't been for twenty years.'

'But here you are. Ex-general talking to ex-Chief-of-Staff. What were you doing, comparing notes on campaigns? Free State soldier and Free State informer. That's a potent combination, Mr Warde. Wouldn't you say that beats all, lads?'

McCaughey glanced at his two men, grinning. Then he stopped grinning.

'What were they talking about?' He barked the words at the barman.

'I couldn't hear, Mr McCaughey. But Mr Hayes was looking to leave.'

'Is that right, Stephen? What did the major-general have to say?'

'I don't know the man. I only know the name now you say it . . .'

'General Warde, then,' said McCaughey, 'you tell me what you had to say.'

Emmet Warde felt the growing fear in his stomach. There was no avoiding it. He had to say that truthful something that would be enough but not too much.

'I'm helping a woman . . . who's trying to find out what happened to her brother, twenty years ago. He was shot by Free Staters.' Warde used the term Republicans always spat out with distaste. 'They took him for putting up posters, and he disappeared with another lad. They were only teenagers. The bodies were never found. Everyone knew they were dead, but no one ever said who did it, soldiers, detectives, Collins' men. She wants to bury him, that's all. She wants a body. She tried every way to find what happened. She tried to find out what the IRA knew. It never got her anywhere, any of it.' Emmet paused. Enough, but not too much. 'She's paying me to see if I can do anything. I was over here to see someone I'd heard might remember something. He didn't or didn't want to. I've been up a dozen blind alleys with Guards and old soldiers. I wanted to go back and see if there was anyone you boys could point me to. Anything she missed. Anyone who'd remember. I'd hardly ask questions about the IRA without the go-ahead.'

That would do. Anything else he said, he would say in answer to questions. He had not even looked at Stephen Hayes, but he was giving him the story too.

'And how did you find our Chief-of-Staff?'

'You think it's that hard?'

It wasn't an answer, but it would do too. It wasn't that hard. If he was pushed, there would be enough confusion in a chain of acquaintances and bar conversations to cover it. The danger wasn't there. He still hadn't used Josie Kilmartin's name.

'It's a good story, General, not bad at all. And who's this woman?'

There was no choice.

'Josephine Kilmartin. You should know her.'

'We know her well enough,' said Stephen Hayes, 'and you do too, Seán.'

One of McCaughey's men spoke.

'She drove the car down to Lough Derg with . . .' The next words were to be 'the German' but these were words to be careful with. 'She's Cumman na mBan.'

'Josie?' said McCaughey. He only knew her by that name.

'She was even at Lough Foyle a few years ago, at your brother's place, bringing in gelignite . . . with Dan Figgis. He's in the Curragh. Isn't that right?'

The Ulsterman looked at Hayes, who nodded, puzzled by

the direction the questions were taking, but only glad they weren't coming anywhere near him.

'And this story?' continued McCaughey. 'What about that?'

'I've heard her talk about her brother. I don't remember what she said.'

McCaughey stared at Emmet Warde for some seconds.

'I don't think you came up with that out of thin air, Emmet. But I don't like it. Maybe I just don't like who you are. It's not every day I could go out to reel in a traitor and find a Free State major-general on the end of the line. And the two of them drinking whiskey at an ungodly time of the day.' He turned towards Hayes. 'But then it's always time for you, Stephen. We'd all know that well enough.' He turned again to the private detective. 'I need to know more. It worries me. The Chief-of-Staff's on his way to a court martial. You may come with us, General.'

Emmet knew there wasn't going to be any argument.

'I know nothing about any of this, Mr McCaughey. I'm no use to you.'

'We'll see. We'll see what you have to say later.'

The head of Northern Command looked round at his men.

'There's a car in the yard behind the pub. That's the one Hayes brought from Dublin. You take these two in that. Route as planned. I'll drive up to Inishowen in the other car with Tadhg. We'll go first and take the main road. If anyone's watching, us they'll see me go and we'll lose them along the way. I'm not worried about the Guards at all, but our Chief-of-Staff may have a few friends left. Just not many.'

The two men were now prisoners in the back seat of a Rover. The car was at the back of the bar. Their hands and feet were bound. The rear passenger doors were still open. Outside, Seán McCaughey was giving instructions, pointing out circles on a road map. A fourth man had joined him, carrying a

Tommy gun that protruded from a sack. He gave it to one of the men who would be driving the prisoners. He then went to the gates to the street and pulled them open. In the car Emmet spoke to Hayes without moving his head. He spoke in Irish. It was poor Irish, but it was all he could find. He was taking a risk that the Ulstermen's would be even poorer.

'A bhfuil Gaeilge agat?'

'Tá.' The Chief-of-Staff breathed the word.

Emmet continued in halting Irish.

'Do you think these lads will have Irish?'

'From the North? A good chance they won't.'

Seán McCaughey was walking away now, across the yard.

'All you know is I came in and asked if I could talk about something that happened twenty years ago . . . some simple questions. And that's as far as we got.'

As Emmet finished, the man with the Tommy gun was getting into the car.

'What are you fucking saying?'

'Nothing,' said Emmet.

'It was fucking Irish.'

The other man leant into the car. His fist smashed into Emmet's face.

'Don't come the clever bastard, General. Shut up and enjoy your ride.'

Along Francis Street, Stefan waited. He had waited with Emmet Warde when the IRA man at the door had walked nervously away. He waited as Emmet went into the Vatican. He waited when a car pulled up outside and three men had gone inside, leaving one at the door, a new sentinel. He knew the car was the one Josie Kilmartin had driven from Laragh. He was still waiting when one of the new arrivals came out again, got into the car with the sentinel, and drove away. He did nothing because he didn't know what to do. He didn't know if something was wrong, or if these comings and goings were just whatever IRA business Stephen Hayes was transacting. And he couldn't find out. There were four or five IRA men in the pub at one point. He couldn't take them on if Emmet was in trouble. There were too many and Superintendent Gregory's orders were not to interfere. So, he still waited. And now no one came and no one went. There was no sign of Emmet.

Then someone appeared. A man in an apron. He yawned, looked and went back in. Stefan could wait no longer. He had sent Emmet Warde in. Either the private detective was still there or something had happened. He sensed that the pub was now empty; something was over. The barman was about his business.

Stefan leant across to the glove compartment of the car. He took out the Webley and pushed it into his overcoat. He started the engine and pulled out into the street, stopping at the Vatican. If there was a need to get out fast, the car would be there. He put his hand in his pocket, to hold the pistol, and walked into the pub.

The barman looked up with a grunt; a greeting of sorts.

Stefan scanned the room. No one to see. Only the barman, awaiting an order.

'Where are they?'

The barman frowned, puzzled for a second or two. Then a look of weariness replaced the frown. He thought they'd all gone. Here was another one.

'Where's who?' The words were said by rote.

'Don't fuck me about,' said Stefan. 'I'm to meet Stephen Hayes here.'

The man in the apron eyed Stefan cautiously. Which side was this one on?

'He's gone.'

'Gone where?'

'How the fuck do I know? It's not my bloody business.'

'It's my business, you cunt. And that makes it your business.'

Stefan took out the Webley and put it on the counter, his hand resting on the grip. He had the measure of the barman. The man had nothing to do with any of it, whatever it was. But he had information. And he would give it easily enough.

'He was staying here, that's all. He always stays here.'

'So where's he gone?'

'Why would they tell me?'

'Don't ask me another question. Do you get that, you gobshite?'

Stefan let his hand stretch to grasp the gun, though he didn't pick it up.

'He didn't go out the front door, did he?'

The barman shook his head.

'So who did?'

The barman said nothing.

Stefan picked up the gun now.

'Who did? Who were the two fellers who went out the front door?'

'Mr McCaughey. He was just here.'

Stefan nodded. It had already happened. He had been too slow. But he couldn't have stopped it. If it was even his business to stop it. He didn't care what had happened to Stephen Hayes. But he knew they had taken Emmet Warde too.

'McCaughey didn't leave with Hayes. So where is he?'

'They went in the other car.'

'What other car?'

'It was in the yard.'

Two cars; one he hadn't seen; he couldn't identify it.

'And the other man?'

The barman frowned again. There were a lot of other men.

'The one who came in on his own. To see Mr Hayes.'

'They took him too.'

'Where?'

'I run a fucking bar. That's it. They didn't discuss it with me!'

'North, south, east, west? What did they say?'

Stefan put the gun back in his pocket, but his hand was there with it. It was still pointing at the barman.

'North. Someone said Donegal, Inishowen. That's the only thing I heard.'

The call Stefan made to Superintendent Gregory was short. It was unsurprising that, since the warning had been too late, Gregory quickly abandoned his interest in what happened to Stephen Hayes. He had given the man a lifeline. He should have been quicker at using it. That was the end of any obligation he had. Whether the Boys in the North shot Hayes or the Boys in the South caught up with them and shot McCaughey was now solely in the hands of the Boys themselves. The stew would be gratifying, however it played out. As for Emmet Warde, if he had the sense to be the eejit who'd stumbled into it all by accident, he'd probably get out of it with bruises and some broken teeth. He was of no concern to the IRA. And now he was of no concern to Garda Special Branch either. Terry Gregory wasn't about to send his own men out to rescue Stephen Hayes from his disgruntled comrades. He would not be risking one Garda life for him. Emmet would have to trust to luck.

Stefan, who had sent the private detective into the Vatican to warn the IRA Chief-of-Staff of his danger, was not convinced crossed fingers and a Hail Mary were all Special Branch owed Emmet Warde. But Superintendent Gregory was not for turning. He regretted his decision. He should have left Hayes to reap his rewards. Warning him hadn't even been important. Stefan did hear regret in his boss's voice, or was it irritation? The warning had been a whim; a game Gregory couldn't resist adding a twist to. He was sorry they'd involved Warde, but what was done was done. Stefan almost saw the shrug. Emmet was of no significance. Who cared? Gregory still saw no reason for McCaughey not to let Emmet go.

That was the end of the conversation. Gregory was already forgetting his mistake. It was less easy for Stefan. The orders had been Gregory's, but he had delivered them. Emmet could end up with a bullet in his head as easily as walk away. That was the other role of the dice. But the Ennis barman was the beginning and end of the trail. There was nothing without action from Gregory.

Then he remembered the car that left from the front of the pub, carrying Seán McCaughey. Another car had left, with Emmet Warde and Stephen Hayes. They must be going to the same place. He knew about the first car. He knew its number. He knew where the man who owned it lived: a priest in Moville. And that was close to what the barman in the Vatican had heard: Donegal and Inishowen. It was a trail. It might be the wrong one, but it was there. It was precise information, more precise than he might have anticipated. It could mean nothing or it could say everything. There was someone to question about that. There was Josie Kilmartin.

15

LUIMNEACH

She came into the station buffet at exactly three o'clock. She looked round at the tables for Emmet Warde, then went to the counter and ordered a cup of tea. Stefan Gillespie stubbed out the cigarette he was smoking and waited. She walked away from the counter and sat at a table by a window that looked out to the Dublin platform. Stefan drained his own cup and got up. He was still unsure what he should say, what he could say. He could not anticipate her response, but his instincts told him, from the little he had seen, and from what he thought he had read behind Emmet's words, that there was something between the Republican courier and the private detective that meant what he had to say would matter to her. It was by no means impossible she would spit in his face and in Emmet's too. However carefully he skirted the details, he would have to tell her who he was. He would have to explain that the man she believed was helping her in her sacred quest for the truth about her brother's death had not only lied to her, but did so to allow the police to follow her. Emmet had betrayed her so that she would inadvertently betray her brothers-in-arms in the IRA; wasn't that the only way she could see it?

The more he turned these ideas over, the less sure he was that the care and empathy that connected Emmet Warde and Josephine Kilmartin would matter. The more he tried the tepid half-truths he was arranging and rearranging, the more he believed anger and contempt would be her reasonable reactions. But Josie was all he had if he wasn't going back to Dublin and leaving Emmet to the whim of the Boys from the North. Those were his orders. He had reasons to disobey them, but the balance hung uncertainly. If Terry Gregory had decided he owed Warde nothing, was it his business to take up the cross on behalf of Garda Special Branch? Was he even serious? He wondered if he wasn't just going through the motions of trying to help Emmet, knowing it was out of his hands. What could disobeying Gregory achieve? What would he do? At least if Josie spat in his face and told him to fuck off, it would bring it all to an end.

She looked up at him. She knew the stranger had something to say to her as he stood by the table. Her look was quizzical. She was already unsettled by him.

'I have a message from Emmet Warde.'

Stefan sat down.

'He won't be here to catch the train. He can't be here.'

'I see.'

He heard disappointment; more than he might have expected.

'I need to tell you what's happened to him.'

'What do you mean? Is he all right?'

'I don't know ... I'd say ... I think he's all right at the moment ...'

Stefan let the implication that Emmet 'being all right' was a state of affairs that wasn't necessarily going to last hang over the space that followed his words. Josie heard the seriousness that was in that space. She knew this was no idle conversation. She also knew, instinctively, that asking if there had been an accident wasn't the right response to what this stranger had told her. It was something else.

203

'Who are you?'

'I don't think this is something we should talk about in here, Miss Kilmartin. I've a car outside. If we sit there, I can explain. It would be better. And safer, too.'

Josie was used to a world in which what was said had to be said in the shadows or at least where there were no other ears to hear. She was used to what had to be hidden, whether it was a gun or the command to use one; a man on the run or the evidence that might expose an informer. The stranger's tone didn't surprise her as it would have done most people. These were the kind of words, oblique and full of unspoken suggestion, that often hovered at the margins of her life. But making a connection between those particular shadows and the man who should have been meeting her in the buffet, to travel on the train back to Dublin, didn't fit at all.

'Are you from the Army Council?'

She spoke the words quietly, as if they already troubled her.

'No, I'm not, Josie.'

'I don't understand. How do you know me?'

'I'm a policeman.'

She sat up straighter. Her first reaction was defence; not far behind was anger, undirected, instinctive. Her body was tense. She breathed deeply. If she had been followed, it was hard to see where from, what for. There was nothing she carried now that related to the IRA. The Army Council had dispersed. The German would be in Dublin. She would say nothing. Those were the instructions. Silence.

'I'm not here as a policeman. I'm here because of Emmet Warde. Because he's not safe. There's a good chance he'll be killed. If that matters to you, Miss Kilmartin, you'll want to talk to me. If it doesn't, the Dublin train will be in soon.'

She didn't reply. In her head, without any explanation as yet, her different worlds were colliding. The collision was a quiet one, but she felt its strength. She also felt that she had no choice but to listen to the stranger sitting in front of her. She looked at him hard, wanting to see something that would tell her she was right to do so, despite everything she knew about how to respond to any Guard, anywhere. And she knew without telling that this wasn't any Guard, anywhere.

'It's up to you,' said Stefan. 'I can't make you listen. I don't even know what you'll say if you do listen. But if you want me to piss off, it's what I'll do.'

He got up and stood looking at her. It was up to her.

'It's the black Ford, just to the left as you come out. I'll wait.'

Stefan sat in the car, in front of Limerick Station, for several minutes. He wasn't sure she would come. But she did. She came and walked straight to the car. There was no hesitation. He could see that she acted decisively once she had made her mind up. That was useful. If she knew anything that could help him find Emmet, she would have to make her mind up again. And she would have to do something.

She opened the car door and got in. She shut it gently.

'I'm Stefan, Stefan Gillespie.'

'And a Guard?'

'Detective Inspector.'

She looked at him, trying to read more than she could see.

'Special Branch.'

She took out a cigarette, then a lighter from her bag.

'That's grand, Mr Gillespie. That's just what I need.'

She lit the cigarette.

'And what have you got to do with Emmet? Are you one of the fellers that beat him up behind Dinnie O'Mara's? You didn't seem worried about him then.'

'Those would have been some other fellers, Miss Kilmartin.' Stefan smiled.

'Shall we leave the craic, Inspector? I'm only here because of Emmet . . .'

The last words were quieter, less decisive. She was feeling her way towards something she didn't understand and already knew she didn't want to understand.

'I'll start at the end,' said Stefan. 'You decide how much of the beginning you want. Take it as read I know you were ferrying people about at an Army Council meeting. I'm not here to ask about that. It doesn't matter how I know. No one was watching. But today, Seán McCaughey kidnapped your Chief-of-Staff, Stephen Hayes, to try him as an informant. They'll call it a court martial and I guess they think they have evidence. It's not my business. You may consider it's not yours. You'll have seen enough of the Boys and their squabbles to get on with your job and keep your head down. Well, we all do a bit of that. I'm not here because I give a shit about Hayes and McCaughey. Nor to arrest anyone. I'm here against my boss's orders. Superintendent Gregory . . . you'll know who he is.'

She nodded. He stopped. She was good at not showing her feelings, but he could see the tension. If nothing else he knew she was unaware of what had happened. But the lines in her face, the moment almost of absence as she looked out through the windscreen at the station forecourt, told him that something was connecting in her head. If she knew anything, she was only now beginning to realise that she had seen things, heard things, meaningless at the time, that started to make a kind of sense. None of it interested Stefan unless it helped find Emmet.

'All I know is that McCaughey has Hayes and they're taking him north. I don't know where. I have some idea maybe, but whether it's right . . . that's where I need help. The thing is, Josie . . . The reason I want to know where . . . the reason I do, is not because I care if your friends shoot each other . . . or because anyone in Special Branch does . . . let alone where they do it . . . it's because your Northern Command lads have taken Emmet, too. He's a prisoner, along with Stephen Hayes.'

Josie turned towards him now. There was real shock.

'What do you mean taken Emmet?'

'He was in a bar in Ennis when they came for Hayes. He was with him.'

'That's mad!'

'It seems mad enough looking back . . . but he was.'

'Emmet's got nothing to do with the IRA.'

'No, he hasn't.'

'Then why . . . why would he be with . . . ?'

'Does why matter?'

She was calmer. She shook her head.

'Don't try to be clever with me, Mr Gillespie. Why?'

'Someone thought it was a good idea to let Mr Hayes know his friends from the North were after him. You know enough about these things, Josie. So I won't try to be clever, and maybe you won't pretend you don't know the shite that goes on. At my end and yours. Well, now and again, the shite's in your face. Emmet has nothing to do with it, you're right. He was carrying a message he didn't want to carry, because he'd been forced to do things he didn't want to do. It's mostly about keeping an eye on a German spy. I don't know whether Stephen Hayes is an informer, but at the top, whatever side you're on, giving information or getting it is just another way of staying in control. If you win, you're a hero; if you don't . . . it gives some other fecker a reason to knock you off your perch. My boss and your Chief-of-Staff and McCaughey could have a cheerful evening in a pub comparing notes. You and I haven't got time. Emmet's in a car, heading north, with a man who will be shot. But do McCaughey and his lads shoot Emmet . . . what are the odds?'

Josie looked out through the windscreen.

'I don't understand. It doesn't make sense. Why would Emmet go . . . ?'

'Because he was told to. Because he thought if he did it, that would be the end and he could maybe even get Superintendent

Gregory to leave him alone when he was asking questions about what happened to your brother . . . a favour for a last favour. He went . . . for no reason, in the end . . . because I was there to make him.'

'I can't take this in!' There were tears in Josie's eyes. 'Fuck it!'

'How much of an explanation do you want?' said Stefan.

She looked back at him, her face harder.

'Emmet was working for Special Branch?'

She said the words slowly, still not quite wanting to accept them.

Stefan was weighing how much of the truth she would take and still care what happened to Emmet; arranging what could be exaggerated, what omitted.

'He got a beating for asking questions in the wrong place. People are sensitive, even twenty years on. He tried another way, getting Superintendent Gregory to give him access to old records. He got a bite. There was something my boss wanted. A feller who escaped from Mountjoy. You were driving him about.'

Josie looked at him coldly. She knew enough to know the truth was only going to be part of what this man was telling her. She had to decide whether there was enough truth to make her do any more than get out of the car and walk away.

'I had no reason not to trust Emmet. I couldn't have imagined he would . . .'

There was more disappointment than anger; she had lost something.

'Doesn't everyone watch everyone, Josie? Aren't your friends at it? Ask Stephen Hayes what he thinks. Emmet had no choice. And what did it amount to? We don't know where Otto is. We don't know how much of what Emmet told us was even true. He's played the game before. There'll be a lot he kept to himself.'

The mix of half-lies and half-truths was as good as Stefan could manage.

'Am I supposed to believe that, Mr Gillespie?'

'That's up to you,' said Stefan, well aware that he wouldn't have found it convincing in her place. And yet it was a kind of truth. 'I think Emmet cares a lot about you. He cares that he's been banging his head against a wall for you and getting nowhere. I don't know what else to say. He didn't ask to get dragged into this shite. He wouldn't have been, would he, if he hadn't been working for you?'

For the first time there was a laugh from Josie Kilmartin.

'It's my fault he was informing on me?'

'Well, at least it's not your fault he's been kidnapped by your Northern Command, along with the man they want to shoot. I suppose that'd be my fault.'

'Your superintendent owes Emmet a favour. I'm sure he can save him.'

'You do think he needs saving, then?'

She said nothing.

'Superintendent Gregory couldn't give a fuck. As long as the Boys are at each other's throats, the more, the merrier. A consummation devoutly to be wished. And why let someone as unimportant as Emmet get in the way of that?'

Stefan knew that she wasn't going to get out of the car. If she was going to help him help Emmet, it would be because of what she felt, not because of how she might score what had already been done. He had to push what was happening now.

'They left Ennis two hours ago. Two cars. Including the one you drove from Laragh. Whatever Emmet is now, they won't like what he was once . . . a Free State general in the Civil War. If his life hangs on that . . . I can only do something if I know where they're going. That's all I have. Donegal and Inishowen. Your car that belongs to the priest in Moville. If you know anything else, you have to tell me.'

She nodded. Her mood had changed.

'Inishowen could be right, I'd say.'

Stefan realised she had made her decision.

'So, you think they might be going there . . .'

'Seán might want to get Stephen out of the South. There'd be plenty down here who wouldn't want Seán McCaughey taking over, even if they don't like Stephen. And Seán's very strong in Inishowen. His brother has a farm across Lough Foyle, in Derry. I've spent time there . . .' She stopped. She had made a decision to help this man find Emmet, but he was still a policeman. 'It's where the McCaugheys have their support, both sides of the lough. It's a safe haven. Even the Guards in Inishowen wouldn't be too particular looking into what he gets up to.'

Stefan turned to the back seat. He picked up a book of maps. He put it on his lap and flicked through pages, taking in roads leading from the west to the north.

'So, Donegal and then Inishowen . . . and Moville . . . somewhere there . . .'

He waited. He was already aware that she was a mine of information. She would only give him what was necessary. She would not trust him. But he realised what her work for the IRA meant; all that carrying, ferrying, delivering, and all the time barely visible, even to the men of the Army Council. She travelled the island, the North and the South. She knew IRA men everywhere. She knew homes, farms, supporters, secret ways and safe houses. Even Gregory didn't grasp what she was.

'I don't know about a route.' He shook his head. 'How would they go?'

'They'd probably avoid big towns,' said Josie. 'Too many Guards.'

'Is that what you'd do?'

'I would if I had two men tied up in the back of my car.'

Stefan laughed. Josie didn't. He looked at her hard.

'Not that we could catch up. This is all there is, Josie. It's still a guess.'

She stubbed out her cigarette. She took the map from him.

'It's the only one we have, Inspector. Hadn't you better start driving?'

16

MOVILLE

The journey from Limerick to Inishowen would take them something like eight hours, depending on the roads they used. There was no point doing anything other than take the straightest route. The IRA cars might take lesser roads but trying to second-guess their journey would achieve nothing, even if Josie's knowledge might have gone some way to doing that. The men from Northern Command were at least three hours ahead; there was no chance of catching them, even if Stefan and Josie stumbled on the right route. Nevertheless, Stefan knew that whatever the different routes, they would all be travelling the same roads at times, especially as they came into Donegal and headed for the narrow strip of land that provided the only road into Inishowen from the Republic. The Inishowen peninsula, bounded by Lough Swilly to the west and Lough Foyle to the east, was almost sliced off from the rest of the Republic by Northern Ireland and in normal times the best roads in and out went through the North and the city that was called, depending on your inclinations, Londonderry or Derry. Stefan thought something might come of those same roads. Cars were not so common that a garage wouldn't remember a customer. Filling a tank required ration coupons, so more time and conversation. Somewhere on the road might be signs of the cars they pursued.

Josie was not hopeful.

'They won't want to be fiddling with coupons. Why would they?'

'I know what you're going to say . . . with two men tied up . . .'

'They don't need to. There are friendly garages along the way if you know where to go. There'd be a tank of petrol, no trouble, and no coupons asked for.'

'Would you know those places?'

'Not so much over this way. And we'd be better avoiding them anyway . . .'

Stefan nodded in agreement. But he wasn't convinced there was no point asking questions. Cars could be remembered for all sorts of reasons in a main street that saw few enough, let alone the cars of strangers. As they journeyed north he made a point of stopping at intervals for a gallon of petrol, rather than filling the tank. He had no shortage of ration coupons. One book identified him as an officer in the Gardaí, another as a travelling salesman; that was the one he used. He had an amiable story about catching up with salesman colleagues in Sligo, or Donegal Town, or Letterkenny, depending on where they were. It was easy enough to ask if a car had stopped earlier to fill up. No one had, at least no one in a car that fitted.

Two questions preoccupied Stefan and Josie. The first was whether they were right about where they were going. She was more confident about that than he was, even though the idea had come to him first. It made sense to her in a way that was full of connections he could not make. But that couldn't make her certain. And even if they were right, there was still the leap that had to be made from the general to the specific. Moville was easy to find; a house, a farm, somewhere, any-where, was something else. Stefan had developed a trust in what Josie knew, about where IRA men lived and where safe houses were situated, that let him believe she would find what they were looking for. She was less sure. She would need information. The second question was what they did if they found where Emmet Warde and Stephen Hayes had been taken. Stefan said almost nothing about this. In his head was the idea that if he knew where Emmet was, he could force Terry Gregory's hand and make him do something. Or maybe he could play his Special Branch card and push a local inspector into taking action. But the local angle seemed unpromising. If Inishowen was the sort of place where the Gardaí and the IRA left each other alone, what were the chances? There was another way, of course. To try to get Emmet out. But that involved risks he was not ready to think about. Without support, without back-up, again, what were the chances? Whatever he owed Emmet Warde, it didn't reach that far.

Josie didn't ask Stefan what he would do if the time came. He was a means to finding Emmet. That was her purpose. It was a purpose that had grown as the miles passed on the road north. The image of a dark place, a frightened boy, a gun and a hole with earth shovelled over it, had been part of her life for so long that she almost remembered no time it wasn't there. The circumstances that brought Emmet into the hands of men who were her colleagues and her comrades had been pushed out by that image now. Even her recognition that her feelings for the man she had employed as a private detective were now personal, in unexpected, unfamiliar ways, had been pushed aside by that image. She saw not her brother in that dark place, awaiting the shot, but Emmet. And it felt as if she had put him there.

'If we find where they have them . . .'

Josie spoke after a silence of more than half an hour.

'Hmm?' Stefan glanced round.

'You'll have to stay out of it. I don't know what they'd do to you. And it wouldn't help me, would it? It would only confirm what they think about Emmet.'

'I'm not with you, Josie.'

'I have to go in and get Seán McCaughey to let Emmet go.'

She spoke as if this was not only obvious but simple.

'I don't know if it can be that easy,' said Stefan.

'I can tell them who he is. I can say he's nothing to do with the police, or the IRA, or anything, except what he was doing for me. Stephen Hayes is something else. It's not for me to . . . But if they know I've found them . . . and if they know it's no secret what they're doing . . . people already know in Dublin. What use is Emmet to them? They'll have more to think about than Emmet . . . or me . . . won't they?'

'You'll just walk in. And Mr McCaughey will say, "Grand." And that's that.'

'Why wouldn't he listen?'

'Why would he listen?'

'Because I'd be right. And he'd be wrong.'

Stefan would have laughed at any other time, but she meant it.

'It's not much of a plan, Josie.'

'When you come up with something better, Stefan, let me know.'

They drove on again in silence. It wasn't much of a plan. Even as it stood it could backfire. If Seán McCaughey thought his attempt to take over the Army Council was collapsing and he could be on the end of bullets from his friends in the South, it might push him to act sooner rather than later. If he shot Hayes in panic, he would not scruple over Emmet Warde. But it was all speculation. Except for one thing. He knew that Josephine Kilmartin would do exactly what she said.

The journey north felt slower than it was. As time passed, Stefan's doubts about where they were going increased. Josie hung on to the instincts that were born of some knowledge. More and more Stefan faced the idea that if they were wrong they would be a very long way from anywhere, for nothing. But then something happened, against the odds, and against Josie's belief that he was wasting good time stopping too often for a gallon of petrol and idle conversation.

They were a long way towards Inishowen. They had driven from Limerick to Ennis; on to Athenry and Claremorris; to Swinford and Sligo and Bundoran, where the strip of the Republic between the sea and the border with Northern Ireland was only a few miles wide. Now they were in Donegal. And it was at Bundoran that Stefan stopped for the fourth time for a gallon of petrol and to tell his rambling story about catching up with some fellow travelling salesmen. And the car had been there that afternoon, the priest's car, the Morris Josie had driven from Laragh. The garage owner chattered as he pumped in petrol. Two men, heading north, maybe for Donegal Town. They didn't say. They called in for oil. And a good job. The sump was almost empty. A leak. Slow, but it would get faster. Still, Morrises were hardy. It would get them where they wanted.

'Did you know you had a leak? I thought you'd have spotted it.'

'I should have done, Stefan,' said Josie. 'It's handy that I didn't.'

One question, at least, seemed settled. There could be little doubt now that the cars that carried Seán McCaughey and his men, as well as Emmet Warde and the soon-to-be-ex-Chief-of-Staff of the IRA, really were aiming for Inishowen and Moville. They would be there now. And Stefan and Josie would be there soon enough. But any satisfaction was short lived. It was time to move on to what to do next.

It had been dark a while when they drove into Moville. Stefan didn't know it, but Josie had been there on IRA business. She had a place to start: the priest.

The town wasn't large, though it was the biggest on the peninsula's Lough Foyle coast. But it was big enough, Stefan thought; strangers would not stand out too much. It was a place people came on holiday, though fewer came since the border to Northern Ireland had virtually closed. He drove into Main Street, then down to the harbour. From the harbour the road took him back to Main Street. He slowed as he reached it, not knowing where to go. He was in Josie's hands now.

'So, we're here.'

She put out the cigarette she was smoking.

'What now?'

She pointed ahead.

'Too late for Mass, but let's hope Father McLellan's at home.'

A little way out of Moville, as the road to Greencastle climbed a gentle incline, was the Catholic Church and the priest's house, solid and dignified. Stefan, following Josie's directions, had stopped at the gate that led up to the house. They stood looking up the drive. At the front of the priest's house was the car Josie had driven to Lough Derg from Laragh Castle, delivered back to its owner, Father James McLellan, and not long ago. It was the car that had left Ennis with Seán McCaughey. It left at the same time as the one carrying Stephen Hayes and Emmet Warde. They must both be close; the IRA Chief-of-Staff and the man who stumbled unwittingly into his kidnapping. How close? Where were the two men now? They could be anywhere on Inishowen. In the darkness, Stefan and Josie had to face the fact that however right they were about the destination, they were starting again.

This was strong IRA country. It was not only the territory of the Northern Command, it was Seán McCaughey's particular domain. Safe houses were not difficult to find and in the empty interior of the Inishowen peninsula, there were plenty of isolated farms where IRA men could do whatever they liked, unseen and unremarked. It was a place where the loyalties of not every member of the Gardaí could be guaranteed, and even the most loyal policemen pursued the sensible policy of never asking too many questions or poking too hard to see what was going on at the end of every boreen. And blind-eye-turning was even more firmly established along the coast of Lough Foyle, from Muff to Redcastle, from Moville to Greencastle and Inishowen Head, by the long-established enterprise of smuggling goods across the water into the British jurisdiction of Northern Ireland, given a new lease of life by a war that imposed rationing on the North and meant that some of the most basic foods were in high demand at happily inflated prices.

But it wasn't only goods that could be smuggled. When necessary, as Josie knew, a small boat and cover of darkness provided a route, also unseen and unremarked, in and out of the North. That was the other possibility: the two prisoners were no longer in the Republic. Across the lough, little more than a mile from the Derry shore, Seán McCaughey's brother had a farm. Of all the safe houses close to Lough Foyle, none was safer for the head of Northern Command. And if the water had to be crossed, the coast near Moville was the place to do it. They had to know whether the two men were on Inishowen or on the other side.

Stefan and Josie were still watching the priest's house. He had his car again. It had only just been delivered back. And since the priest was an important man in Republican Inishowen, it was unlikely no one stopped to thank him for his aid in loaning the cause his vehicle. It was unlikely he would know the IRA Chief-of-Staff was there, let alone en route to execution, but he would know something.

'I've met Father McLellan. Here and in Dublin. He knows who I am.'

Stefan nodded.

'He'll remember . . . he'd have no reason to doubt me.'

'Would he know what's going on?'

'Not at all! But he wouldn't be a man with much love for Stephen, I'd say. He wouldn't be weeping at the funeral. But it doesn't matter. I'm not going to ask him about that. I'm just going to say I have something urgent to bring to Seán McCaughey. And they sent me to Moville to try and catch him. The fact that I know Seán was here won't make him wonder what I'm doing. Just the opposite.'

'So, you'll ask him where McCaughey is?'

'It's worth a try.' Josie smiled. 'He's a priest. He has a high opinion of his importance. He wouldn't want a woman to believe they never told him anything.'

'All right. If it's all there is . . .'

'I'd hardly know anyone else here, Stefan.'

'You keep the car for now, Josie. If you've been sent up here, it'll look better if there's some evidence of how you came. I'll walk back into the town.'

'Where will you be?'

'I've only seen the main street and the harbour. Let's say the harbour.'

Stefan gave Josie the car keys and she walked up the drive to the priest's house. He watched her. Probably there was no risk in what she was doing, at least not now, but she had a kind of easy fearlessness. He wondered how deep it went.

He walked past the parked car and down the low hill to the town. There were few people about. There was the buzz of noise in pubs as he passed. He noted the largest, McKinney's, on the corner of the road to the harbour. A notice advertised rooms. Whenever Josie came, they would need somewhere to stay the night now.

In the harbour, only one fishing boat was getting ready to go out. A man untied a rope at the quayside. He wound it into a coil and threw it on board. The engine chugged noisily. It was one of the bigger boats, but not big. There was a wheelhouse and a cabin, but most of it was taken up by a stern full of nets and lobster pots and fishing tackle. Stefan took little notice. He walked along the quay, lighting a cigarette, looking out into the darkness where the Derry shore, invisible in the cloudy night, lay across the water. He looked round to see the black Ford pull up. Josie got out. As he stepped towards her he raised his hand and stopped. A lorry's horn sounded. He was caught in the lights; then the harbour was dark again.

In that moment, as Stefan Gillespie stepped back to let a lorry pass, Emmet Warde saw him. The private detective sat on a wooden bench in the cabin of the fishing boat Stefan had glanced at. He was gagged; his hands were bound. Next to him was Stephen Hayes. Emmet had turned his head to the small cabin window, half below deck, pressing his face against the glass as the quayside and its dim lights receded. He knew the boat was crossing Lough Foyle to the North. He had a good idea what that meant for Hayes, but he had no real sense of what it would mean for him. Ignorance, of everything and anything, was all he had to cling to; that and the hope that he couldn't matter to anyone. And it was as those thoughts went through his head, for the hundredth time, that he picked out the man caught in headlights on the quay at Moville. He saw Detective Inspector Stefan Gillespie. How the policeman came to be there he could not begin to imagine. Then he saw another figure. A woman walking towards Stefan. He knew her, too, immediately. He didn't see her as clearly as he saw Stefan. The headlights were on her for seconds before sweeping away, but he knew her with the certainty only someone deeply cared about can be known. How she moved was enough. Josie was with Stefan. That extraordinary fact meant there was another hope, a stronger one, to hold on to.

PART THREE

THE PLOUGH AND THE STARS

Oh; here's to Adolf Hitler
Who made the Britons squeal,
Sure, before the fight is ended
They will dance an Irish reel.

Now they're casting longing glances
At the manhood of our land,
But for Ireland – Ireland only –
Will that gallant manhood stand.

IRA War News, 1940

17

LOUGH FOYLE

The fishing boat that carried Stephen Hayes and Emmet Warde across Lough Foyle unloaded them, along with the four IRA men, in shallow water off the Derry coast, below the cliff-like mountain that rose up suddenly and steeply from the flat coastal plain. This was Binevenagh. Its grey, fortress-like walls were clearly visible from Inishowen, even in the darkness. The high pillars of horizontal stone, lighter than the surrounding night, reflected back what moonlight there was. Now, as the six men walked through fields on the Derry side of the water, their goal was Binevenagh's craggy slopes. They had seen no other vessels on the short crossing from Moville. The Northern Irish coast was patrolled, on land and offshore, but it was done with a touch that was, if not light, less intrusive than war might have warranted, and with threats of invasion fading away, that touch was becoming more unobtrusive. There was a small army camp to the north, near Magilligan Point, where the soldiers concentrated on the approaches to Lough Foyle. Their routes and their habits were well known. Further down the Derry side of the lough, patrols of the Home Guard and the occasional RUC constable on a bicycle, more infrequently a squad car from Limavady, were considered enough. The entrenched business of smuggling across Lough Foyle remained outside the exigencies of war and defence as far as almost everyone was concerned. It was in nobody's interests to interfere.

Where the boat from Moville had landed its prisoners, a thin strip of sand led from the shore to fields and scrubby woodland. On the beach stakes and barbed wire were visible in either direction, but there were gaps at intervals, and the six men walked through them easily enough. The night was not dark. There were small farmhouses across the fields. There was the smell of peat smoke in the air. They walked in silence. Only one gun was in evidence. The Tommy gun that followed Stephen Hayes and Emmet Warde. After almost an hour negotiating fields and stone walls, they came to a road. They crossed it where the ruins of a church stood out against the rising woodland beyond. A man was waiting there, sitting on a wall and smoking a pipe. As they approached, a van pulled out from behind the ruin. There were short, businesslike greetings. Hayes and Warde were pushed into the back of the van. Two of the IRA men, including the man with the machine gun, got in with them. The van pulled away, taking a narrow turning that led up into the woods and towards the hills above. The remaining IRA men followed the same route on foot.

The road the van took was narrow and steep and soon became a dirt track. The journey wasn't a long one. The two prisoners were pulled out and pushed across a farmyard. A sheep dog circled them, barking furiously. There were dim lights from a single-storey house. There was a long stone out-building and a Dutch barn full of hay. At one end of the outbuilding was a stone outhouse. The prisoners were flung through the door on to a dungy floor. The square room was empty, except for some broken bales of straw. There was no window, only a small opening, a foot square, high up on the back wall. A little moonlight came through.

'We'll bring you some food and some water.'

Those were the only words spoken. The door closed. A bolt was shut.

'Where the fuck are we?' said Emmet.

'I know where we are,' answered Hayes, barely visible in the darkness. 'It's a farm that belongs to Seán McCaughey's brother. I've been here before. Years ago now. It used to be a weapons dump. It's halfway up a fucking mountain.'

'So, what happens next?'

'God knows about you, but I'm going to be put on trial. Don't laugh.'

'I'm not,' replied the private detective.

'No. I'd be tempted to . . . if the joke wasn't on me . . .'

Hayes fumbled in his coat and pulled out a packet of cigarettes. He took one and lit it. The blaze of light only accentuated the dark when the match went out.

'I'm nearly out of fags,' was all the IRA Chief-of-Staff had to say for some seconds. He sat back and inhaled. 'Least they can do is get me some fucking fags.'

The following afternoon the court martial took place in the long stone barn. Along one wall a line of a dozen cattle stalls ran, divided by rusting iron bars. It was a milking parlour, long disused, and rusting too were the chains that had once slipped over the heads of the cows as they were being milked. One of them had been wound round Stephen Hayes' legs and fixed with a bright new padlock, as he faced the end wall of the barn, where a trestle table stretched. Four men sat in a row on one side. Seán McCaughey, Pearse Kelly, Nick McCarthy; the fourth was Liam Rice, who would keep the record. In front of Rice were several pamphlets that contained IRA regulations, as well as a copy of the Bible. None of these would be opened. In front of McCaughey, who would prosecute, was a collection of notebooks, handwritten documents and a sheaf of newspaper cuttings. Somewhere among these items was the evidence that proved Hayes' guilt. None of it would be required. Stephen Hayes had requested no defence; none was offered. The only other items on the long table were a bottle of Bushmills whiskey and five glasses. Behind the trestle table, above a hay rack on the wall, two flags were stretched out. The Irish tricolour and the deep blue banner that was the Plough and the Stars.

The Chief-of-Staff stared in silence at the men behind the table. Emmet sat close by. The prisoners had been brought across the farmyard from their cell. Emmet, too, had a rusty cow chain round his legs. He had no idea what role he was supposed to play in this game. He had nothing to say as far as anyone in the barn was concerned. He had his story. They knew it, whether they believed it or not, whether they cared one way or another. He wouldn't change it. To Hayes' right, on a hay bale, an IRA volunteer sat with a Tommy gun. At the barn door stood another, leaning on a rifle, a belt of ammunition across his chest, smoking a pipe.

The men at the table shuffled papers and lit cigarettes, and there was a murmured conversation about the procedure, which hadn't quite been worked out. In the end it amounted to little more than who went first. Eventually, Pearse Kelly took a hammer from his pocket and struck the board with this makeshift gavel.

'We're here to try Stephen Hayes, former Chief-of-Staff of Óglaigh na hÉireann, on charges of treason against the properly constituted government of Ireland, as established by the Second Dáil. This is a military court. All procedures, and judgements, as well as any punishments, will be carried out accordingly.'

'This is shite, Pearse, and you know it full well. Procedures my arse.'

Hayes spoke quietly. It was not defiance, more helplessness.

'The prisoner will speak when required to speak,' said Kelly.

'You're here to shoot me, lads. And what the fuck for? Do youse know?'

Pearse Kelly banged the hammer down again. The volunteer

with the rifle walked from the door, turning his rifle so that the butt was pointing towards Hayes.

'Jesus, is it more of those procedures? You gave me a beating before first light, a beating for breakfast, another beating after that. Is those your regulations?'

Emmet Warde said nothing, but he had his own bruises.

'You'll get your chance, Stephen . . .'

Hayes looked from the rifle butt to the table and shrugged, silently.

'Will you read the charges?' Kelly turned round to McCaughey.

The head of Northern Command stood up. He held a piece of paper in front him. For a moment he looked down, reading it through, his lips moving. He cleared his throat and read the charges in the tone of legalistic seriousness he had heard in many courts before. He coloured it with an expression that all the faces at the table now mirrored; they were here, tragically, more in sorrow than in anger.

'The charges are, firstly, that you, Stephen Hayes, conspired with the Irish Free State Government to obstruct the policy and impede the progress of the Irish Republican Army. Secondly, that you, Stephen Hayes, are guilty of treachery for having deliberately forwarded information of a secret and confidential nature, the activities of the Irish Republican Army, to a hostile body, to wit the Irish Free State Government, at a time when the Irish Republican Army is at war with Britain.'

'Stand up!' The words were barked at the Chief-of-Staff by Pearse Kelly.

McCaughey looked round, startled.

'He should be standing up for the charges, Seán.'

There was a murmur of agreement along the table.

'Now, lads, don't forget your procedures,' said Hayes, rising to his feet.

Seán McCaughey resumed his seat.

Pearse Kelly stubbed out his cigarette.

'The prisoner can sit down again.'

'Isn't the next procedure that I plead? Not guilty, Liam.' Hayes sat down, looking at the man who was making notes. 'You might want to record that, so.'

The tribunal looked out at their former Chief-of-Staff, like a trimmed-down version of the Last Supper, each man's face frowning, as if scarcely believing the finger of suspicion really had come to rest on one of their number in this way. The man cast as Judas sat on a wooden bench, propped against a stack of hay bales. He was weary from lack of sleep; the bruises on his face were replicated by many more under his clothes. Somewhere in his head he was trying to believe he could talk his way out of this, but it was a belief that struggled with what he knew about the organisation he so recently controlled. There were those in the South who would still support him; that was why they had brought him into the North. Even if his own men knew what was happening, it would be over before anyone could act. The North was McCaughey's. He was invulnerable here. And if he fell to the bullet they had waiting for him, Hayes knew that nothing else would matter. The law of the gun, whatever the politics, whatever the personalities, had always shaped the IRA and it still did. No one would dare oppose McCaughey once Hayes was dead.

Emmet Warde sat on a kitchen chair at Hayes' right, still with a sense that he had slipped into something unreal. He was at the trial, he was told, in case he was required to give evidence. He felt he was seen as a kind of physical proof of the accusations about to be thrown at the IRA Chief-of-Staff, even though he could have no connection to them. Whatever they were, they could mean nothing to him. But he knew he was expected to say something, to prove something. It was conceivable Stephen Hayes had been giving information to Terry Gregory; it was equally likely he hadn't. Emmet had been close enough to all this, years before, fighting the British and fighting the same kind of men who were here to judge Stephen Hayes. He knew it was only about what those who held the guns wanted it to be. There was no one in the barn who didn't know that. He had been told his own case would be dealt with in due course. His cooperation would determine the outcome. He knew cooperation meant giving evidence Hayes was a Special Branch informer, and he was a Special Branch go-between. Whether he would be shot or let go he had no idea. The decision would be made at McCaughey's whim.

The story he had come up with, to explain why he was with the Chief-of-Staff when McCaughey's men came for him, just about stood up. He had to stick to it. The truth was far more dangerous. If he had nothing to do with Stephen Hayes, he was still working for Special Branch. He regretted telling enough of the truth to involve Josie. If McCaughey chose to believe he was some kind of spy, what would it mean for her? On the other hand, she would confirm his story. All he was doing was looking for information about a boy the Free State shot in the Civil War.

So far, several beatings and pistol-whippings had not induced the private detective to confess either to the story Northern Command wanted him to tell or to the real reason he ended up in a bar with Hayes. He knew it irritated the IRA men that he offered no evidence against the man on trial. It seemed doubtful he would be called as a witness. Perhaps, as there would be no witnesses, he was a kind of token that witnesses existed somewhere. His physical existence, even without any confession, was an outward, visible sign of Hayes' inward, invisible guilt. Emmet Warde had been, after all, a general in the Free State Army; that was enough. He thought that for some at the trestle table it was still a reason to shoot him. He might be guilty of nothing else, but that would do. The hope he had was that he didn't matter. But there was another hope. The two faces he saw from the boat at Moville.

He could not understand what it meant, except that Stefan and Josie knew. When his head was spinning after a pistol smashed the side his face, he wondered if he had imagined those faces. When he woke from the snatches of sleep he drifted in and out of, he wondered if the faces belonged in his confused dreams. But they were real. And something had to come of it. It would have to come soon, surely. They wanted Hayes to confess, but no confession had emerged from the fists and rifle butts. The trial would have to do the job. Emmet had no doubt where the trial would lead, any more than Hayes did. Whatever time there was was running out. If Stefan and Josie were going to do something, whatever it was, whoever else it involved, he needed to slow things down. He couldn't even guess how they had come together, but they must know what was happening. He was in Northern Ireland, yet barely a few miles across Lough Foyle. They had found where he was. They couldn't have lost him. It was what he had to keep saying.

Emmet Warde came out of his reverie, back into the barn and the trial.

Seán McCaughey had been speaking for some time. He held a wad of notes in his hand, but he used them as a prop rather than for reference. He had stepped out from behind the trestle table. He stood closer to Stephen Hayes, waving the papers for emphasis, whenever his words picked up the rhythm of indignation.

'And so it goes on. The man who was given the sacred task of leading the army of the Republic, party to the most heinous conspiracy of crime in Irish history! When the bomb went off in Coventry, were we really supposed to think this was the carefully planned implementation of the Sabotage Plan in England? Was that attacking their institutions, their transport systems, their politicians, their military, in the lead-up to the war? No, all that would have brought some fear to Britain's leaders. A fifth column in their midst, ready to act. And what would it have done to our relationship with Germany? It would have made solid allies. Instead of which, under this man who called himself our Chief-of-Staff, the Germans see us as a collection of incompetent clowns led by a piss artist. Coventry wasn't a great plan that went wrong, was it? It wasn't a bomb that went off in the wrong place. It went off where this man intended it to go off, to discredit the IRA and slander our reputation as soldiers fighting for a just cause. And it put paid to the whole bombing campaign. Then we come to Christmas 1939, and the raid on the Magazine Fort. Well, that seemed to go well. All those guns, all that ammunition. But within a week, it was back in Free State hands. Because Special Branch sniffed out every place arms were hidden. Like magic. Also like magic, the Magazine Fort raid persuaded the last politicians in the Dáil who stood in the way of Dev putting hundreds of Republicans in his Curragh concentration camp to change their minds. That was what our Chief-of-Staff was doing to us!'

McCaughey pointed his finger theatrically at Stephen Hayes.

'I'm not going to list every contrived betrayal. They're here. Every bank robbery that saw volunteers caught red-handed. Every useless explosion that never blew anything worthwhile up but sent volunteers to their deaths at the end of a Free State bullet or the English hangman's rope. And how many men in England have been arrested? How many hanged? You'd think someone provided lists of names. And you'd be right. Then there are the agents our German allies send. Does anyone think it's an accident that agent after agent is arrested when he's barely set foot on Irish soil? No wonder the Germans think twice about sending money. All this – all this – is the result of one man's treachery. A man we trusted most betrayed us all! I set a trap for him. I told him about an operation I knew he would want to stop. It was never real. But I knew what he'd do. He was the only IRA man who had the information. I told no one else. And within hours the Free State knew everything.'

Seán McCaughey shook his head, looking hard at Hayes. Again, the more-in-sorrow-than-in-anger momentarily wiped the fury from his florid cheeks. There was a murmur of approval as he returned to his seat. All eyes were on the Chief-of-Staff, who looked pale, shaken by the vehemence of the words. If he had any doubts about where he stood, they had been swept away by the verbal torrent.

'Do you have anything to say?' said Pearse Kelly.

'It's still bollocks, Pearse. The lot of you. Who says any of this happened? As for the fucking circus at Foynes, what's that about? I didn't tell anyone about it. I didn't need to. I already had a good idea the thing was a game. Do you think I don't have people at Foynes? Do you think I wouldn't know if there was a bomb?'

'Foynes is neither here nor there,' said Kelly. 'It's all the rest. Look at it!'

'Look at what? None of it happened. Not one of his fucking lies!'

'Can you prove that?'

'What kind of a fucking question is that? I thought you'd brought me here to prove it did happen. Where is the evidence, the witnesses? Did I do it on my own?'

For some seconds there was silence. The accusations alone were the case.

'We know full well you didn't do it on your own, Stephen,' replied McCaughey. 'That's why we need you to confess. If you have any regard for the sacred trust that Ireland gave you, you'll give us the names of the people who worked with you. We have to rebuild after what you've done. The whole Southern Command is infected with rot. The least you can do is say who was in it. We've asked you to do that. We asked you to limit the damage. We asked you to confess.'

'You beat the shite out of me, you mean. Isn't that how it's done? Beat me till I'll say anything and then shoot me anyway.

I've done nothing but put the interests of the IRA first, while you bastards play at soldiers and spies. I'm the one who's trying to keep the Republican movement together. If it was up to you, there'd be no one left standing. You'd give Dev every reason to execute anyone he fancies and see every man jack that's left in the Curragh. None of it's true. I've got nothing to confess to. As for the fucking Germans, they don't need help getting themselves arrested. They land them with a swastika stuck on their bloody heads.'

Hayes took a breath. He had found some words, but he was shaking.

'Give me a fag, Pearse. I'm fucking gasping.'

Pearse Kelly nodded towards the volunteer with the rifle. The man left the gun leaning against the barn door and walked across to the bench. He took out a packet of Player's and gave one to Hayes. He lit it with a match. As he turned back to the door, he looked at Emmet Warde. The private detective shook his head.

'Is that it, Stephen?' said Kelly.

'You're joking, you gobshite! You think I can't drive a coach and horses through everything Seán's just said? There's not a word of truth, not one word!'

'Let's save some time, Stephen. Seán's given us a list of accusations as long as your arm. You're going to tell us they're all shite. Well, we'll take that as read. So, all shite, Liam.' Kelly turned to Liam Burke. 'You can record that as the prisoner's response to the charges in detail. And you put next to it "bollocks", with an exclamation mark, as a complete response to his response by the court martial.'

There was laughter along the tribunal table.

'You're not the only one who specialises in information, Stephen. You specialise in giving it to Special Branch, we specialise in collecting it and keeping it where it belongs, inside the Army Council. I think we've all heard enough.'

Kelly looked each way along the table. He met only nods of agreement. Hayes sank down on to the bench. The resources of anger and determination he had dragged out of himself were used up. His knowledge of how his organisation worked, with the beatings that had weakened his body, had brought him close to breaking. And as a man who drank too much, who always drank too much, he was shaking not only because of his helplessness, but because of the need for alcohol.

'For fuck's sake! You can't stop me defending myself!'

'Emmet Warde, stand up,' said Kelly, suddenly changing tack.

The private detective got to his feet. Kelly looked at McCaughey.

'We've had some word from Dublin,' said the Ulster commander, 'from two Cumman na mBan women I'd trust. They haven't got hold of Josie Kilmartin. But the story about Eamon Kilmartin is true. As far as it goes, no one has a bad word to say about Josie. She's been a Republican all her life. She works hard and she's not afraid to take risks. I don't know if we helped her as much as we should have done, about her brother, but I don't think anyone had any information. And as the years have gone by . . . It was a long time ago. We all honour the past. We can't live in it.'

Seán McCaughey was silent for a moment. He didn't like the story. He felt, somewhere, that they could have done better by this woman and her dead brother.

'So, we have established that she was paying Warde to work for her. We have some material from his office, including bills she's paid. I don't know what the going rate for a private detective is, but the general seems to come quite cheap.'

For a moment, all the men at the table laughed.

'He was doing what he says he was doing. One thing that's certainly true is that our ex-general wasn't getting far. But he was making himself unpopular. There were people in Special Branch who didn't like the questions he was asking. And Terry Gregory had two of his lads beat the general up, to make that point.'

Emmet felt a rare surge of gratitude towards the superintendent.

'Won't that do?' asked Pearse. 'If what he says stands up . . .'

'Does it stand up?' said McCaughey, gazing at Emmet. 'Something isn't right. He knows more than he's saying. If he doesn't, he knows too much now. If we end up in a Free State court, there he is, witness-in-chief. He knows enough to hang us. If he was in the wrong place at the wrong time, it happens. He can't go free.'

The head of Northern Command spoke firmly, decisively. He wasn't asking for any other views. Not everyone was comfortable. Pearse Kelly certainly wasn't.

'I don't know, Seán. If the man's done nothing . . .'

'There are a lot of dead people who did nothing, Pearse. But I'd say he's done enough. He might have walked out of the Free State Army, but he'd left enough dead Volunteers behind him. I don't think we're going to shed any tears.'

Kelly still didn't like it. But no one else spoke.

'Why would I want to give evidence against anybody?' said Emmet. The words were quiet, only just audible. He did not expect them to be listened to. As he continued, his words were not for the IRA men. They expressed his own bewilderment. 'I left that behind a long time ago. I'd be a witness to nothing.'

No one answered.

For Seán McCaughey, his work was done, the trial finished. And although Pearse Kelly sat at the centre of the trestle table, as chairman of the tribunal, beneath the tricolour and the Plough and the Stars, it was McCaughey's court.

'Take the prisoners out,' said Kelly. 'Both of them. We're done.' He met the eyes of the former Chief-of-Staff. 'We will be considering our verdict. You might want to give some serious consideration to what lies ahead, Stephen. If I was a priest, I'd know what you must do. You may confess. There's a cancer to

235

root out. You created it. I won't say it'll save you. It might save what's left of your soul.'

Under different circumstances Emmet might have laughed.

Stephen Hayes and Emmet Warde stood as a Volunteer undid the padlocks that fixed the chains to their legs. The tribunal looked on. McCaughey reached for the bottle of whiskey on the table. He undid the cap and filled four glasses. Hayes seemed very detached now. What little attention he had was focused on the bottle.

'Jesus, is there a drink, lads, for fuck's sake?'

McCaughey walked over to Hayes and gave him the bottle.

The two gunmen led the prisoners out into the farmyard. It was dark. As they crossed the yard a cluster of hens spread out in front of them, clucking irritably. The Chief-of-Staff held the bottle close. Emmet was trying to push McCaughey's words out of his head. He was thinking about Stefan and Josie.

The barking of the dog and the little light that came into the outhouse from the high window told Emmet Warde it was morning. But he had not slept. Stephen Hayes was still snoring in the straw that served as a bed. The private detective had left the whiskey to the Chief-of-Staff. For once, he had no appetite for it. Hayes finished the bottle. It was enough to let him sleep after a fashion. Now, as he woke and sat up, yawning, sour-mouthed, it was with the sudden realisation of where he was and what was happening. He leant back against the wall and closed his eyes.

'Fuck it.'

Emmet moved across the outhouse and sat beside him.

'You need to change the rules, Stephen. You have to make us some time.'

Hayes looked at him and shook his head.

'You may be all right, I don't know. But I'm fucked.'

'You need to do what Seán McCaughey wants you to do, Stephen.'

'All that bastard wants is to fucking shoot me.'

'He wants you to confess. The others want that more than he does . . .'

'I've got nothing to confess to. He knows that.'

'Maybe, maybe not. But what if you do have something to confess?'

Hayes' eyes were blank and uncomprehending.

'Give him a confession. Start with whatever bollocks he came up with . . . if that's what it is. And give him more. Say, yes, that's what I did. These are the people who did it with me. These are the peelers and the Special Branch fellers. And you go on. You give so many names that most of the Army Council and half the volunteers in the twenty-six counties are in on it. You make up plans and plots that never happened. But the main thing is names. Put it in writing and give them plenty of it. If McCaughey knows most of what he's accused you of is bollocks, the rest don't. He's told them all you're a traitor. Now you're confessing. So, what you say must be true. But if it is, then there's hardly a fucker south of the border who can be trusted. And you're not a solitary informant, you're the star witness.'

Hayes let Emmet Warde speak. At first he was puzzled, but as the words took shape, he understood. He still felt a bullet wasn't far away. But time was something. Time could change things. Seán McCaughey couldn't stick him up against a wall if he was giving information the man claimed he wanted. And the more complicated it got, the messier, the more confused, the more time it made.

The Chief-of-Staff came to his decision quickly. It was something where there was nothing. He stood up and went to the door. He hammered on it hard.

The bolt outside was pulled back. A grinning face appeared.

'It's a wee bit early for breakfast, Mr Hayes. The chef's not up yet.'

'Tell Seán I'll talk to him. Pen and paper. I'll give him what he wants.'

18

BINEVENAGH

It was some years since Mrs McKinney had seen *The 39 Steps* in a cinema in Derry. Trips to the pictures had always been rare, but with the border effectively closed, access to films had been shut off. Mrs McKinney did not believe that the unpleasant journey to the picture house in Buncrana, on the other side of Inishowen, was worth the effort. She was impressed neither by the place nor by the films. She had seen other films in Derry, of course, but Robert Donat and Madeleine Carroll had stuck with her. She had a romantic disposition that found little outlet in the pub on the corner of Main Street and Quay Street. When Stefan Gillespie arrived late one night with a woman she took an instant liking to, she responded to his request for two rooms with a smile and, if not a wink, a pleasantly knowing look. She said that two rooms was difficult. Some rooms were closed up for the season, not that the season amounted to much these days, and they weren't aired. There was a good double room, though, the best really they had to offer. There would be no problem if they wanted that room. It certainly didn't matter to her what names they put in the register. She didn't put it that bluntly, but her unwavering smile of welcome said it anyway. And it occurred to Stefan that Mrs McKinney's romantic imagination was by no means unhelpful. Even if no one was asking for explanations about who they were and what they were doing, an explanation that demanded secrecy was not to be spurned. If they were illicit lovers, as Mrs McKinney had decided, it was a role that insisted on a low profile.

Josie had been startled to find herself in a large room with a large bed and Stefan Gillespie. She had not paid much attention to his negotiations with Mrs McKinney. She had assumed they would have a room each. But the decision made sense. She was satisfied that the room's uncomfortable sofa was his for the night.

At the priest's house, Father McLellan had been helpful and forthcoming. He was rather pleased that the Republican movement was paying him so much attention. It wasn't always like that. But it was gratifying that Seán McCaughey himself had brought back the car he had generously lent out and that when a messenger from the Army Council in Dublin came looking for the head of Northern Command, it was to his house that she came, as to a fount of discreet knowledge. It seemed that even in Dublin there was recognition of who he was and what he did for the cause. It was a pity that Miss Kilmartin had not arrived a few hours earlier. He didn't know where she would find Mr McCaughey, but he was afraid she was too late to find him in Moville. He was fairly sure that your man had crossed the water. Father McLellan lowered his voice as he spoke of crossing the water, even though he was in his house. The near-whisper was meant to imply that Josie would know what he meant. And he was right. She did know.

Neither Stefan nor Josie slept well. She was comfortable enough, but too much was on her mind to allow her more than a few hours' sleep. He had plenty on his mind, too, but since he wasn't comfortable at all, he got no sleep. He got up as soon as it was light. He dressed and walked down to the harbour. He sat for some time, watching two fishing boats unload their catch, mostly lobster pots. The decision had been made the night before. They would have to cross Lough Foyle. If finding Seán McCaughey on Inishowen had been a daunting task, what lay on the other side of the lough, in Northern Ireland, was simpler. The farm that McCaughey's brother had was the obvious place, the only place. It was close; it was isolated; it was inaccessible and yet easy to escape from. It had all the familiarity and security required for Stephen Hayes' court martial. If there were people in Dublin who might want to put a stop to what was happening, they were too far away. There might even be those in Belfast who were uneasy about Seán McCaughey going the whole way with this. By the time they even knew, it would be done. If it was to be done, then doing it quickly would still any dissident voices.

The question of what precisely would happen once Stefan Gillespie and Josephine Kilmartin found their quarry remained where it had been for some time. But Stefan accepted that. Only when he had seen the place could he move forward.

And there was still the water to be crossed. Josie's knowledge about smuggling, men and goods, made it clear it could be done easily enough, but it didn't provide the name of someone to do it. It was certain that Moville's fishermen would be involved. Anybody with a boat might be involved. The question was how to find somebody who could be persuaded to take them across. Questions would inevitably be greeted with suspicion and denial. But the availability of money would probably open things up eventually. There was not a great deal of money, but Stefan had the car. For someone who was already in the business of smuggling, a car to sell would not be a problem. And even if it had to go cheap, it was a lot of money for a few miles across Lough Foyle.

Stefan already had in his head that James McKinney, the proprietor of the pub, might be the place to start. He was a man who would know everyone as well as everything.

It seemed unlikely he wouldn't know the men who were smuggling into the North. It seemed unlikely Stefan hadn't already seen some of them in the bar.

As he walked back from the harbour, Stefan found his instincts more than confirmed. He entered McKinney's through the open gates at the back of the pub. A van was parked by an outhouse. Two men were unloading into the outhouse. What they were unloading was food. There was nothing unusual about that; what was unusual was the quantity. As he glanced into the van and through the open door of the outhouse, he counted half a dozen sides of bacon. There were trays that must have held hundreds of eggs. There were boxes that contained packs of butter that must have also numbered close to a hundred. There were dozens of packets of sugar. That was more remarkable. Sugar, unlike everything else, was rationed even in the Republic.

Although he barely paused to take in what he saw, the two men unloading the van looked at Stefan uncomfortably. He smiled and walked on into the pub. But he noticed that one man walked down to the open gates and pulled them shut. It hadn't bothered them before, but now that they had been observed, it seemed as if the men had decided that what they were doing was better done behind closed gates.

Stefan and Josie sat in the bar a little later that morning, finishing breakfast. Mr McKinney was behind the bar bottling up and cleaning, preoccupied with the start of his day's work. He was barely aware of them. They were the business of his wife. She was very much aware of them, chatting happily about nothing in particular as she brought in the tea and the food. She had gone now and Stefan looked across at Josie. They had already discussed McKinney's abundance of provender. The conclusion that this was exactly what was likely to be smuggled into Northern Ireland was irresistible. There, everything was rationed; everything was hard to get. A short boat trip would make the contents of James McKinney's outhouse worth a lot of money. Josie shrugged as Stefan looked at her, then nodded. He walked to the bar. He leant on it and spoke in his best conspiratorial tone.

'I'm looking to get across Lough Foyle.'

Mr McKinney looked up from stacking bottles.

'What's that, Mr Gillespie?'

'I'm looking to get across the lough, to the other side.'

The publican wiped his hands on a bar towel, eyeing Stefan.

'It's easy enough.'

'Is it?'

'You've a car. You can drive down to the border at Muff. It'll take you half an hour, not much more. If your papers are all in order, you're in Derry in no time.'

'I was thinking more about the coast . . . and Limavady.'

'You drive out of Derry, along the lough. Maybe you'd have a map.'

'It wasn't the way I wanted to go.'

McKinney looked at Stefan more cautiously.

'It's the only way there is.'

'I was wondering about a boat.'

'I'd have thought you'd know that's not possible now, Mr Gillespie.'

'I know it's not allowed. I wouldn't be sure it's not possible.'

'Well, you'd know more than me, in that case.'

'I have reasons to get across without anybody knowing.'

James McKinney shrugged.

'That'll be your business.'

'And what about your business, Mr McKinney?'

'This is my business.'

'You must use a fierce amount of butter and eggs from what I've seen. Not to mention the bacon and all that sugar. Jesus, it'll be some breakfast you do here.'

The publican smiled.

'The thing about business, any business, is to mind your own, Mr Gillespie.'

'I need help,' said Stefan. 'We need help. There's some money in it.'

'You pay your bill when you leave,' replied McKinney, 'and that'll be good enough money for me. It will be tomorrow you're leaving, didn't you say that?'

'I didn't.'

'I think tomorrow would suit us both. Today might be even better.'

James McKinney walked away. The conversation was over.

Stefan went back to Josie and sat down.

'That didn't get us very far. He wasn't biting.'

'Can we try the border?' she asked.

'It won't work. We have identification, but we need permits.'

'We know there are boats going out, Stefan. If we keep asking . . .'

'I don't know.' He shook his head. 'There's no time . . .'

'What about the story?'

'The story?'

'Hadn't you something in mind, Stefan? Aren't we running away?'

She smiled. They had a story. They had something like a reason.

'I can tell a story to anyone who'll listen. It's finding someone . . .'

Josie's smile had gone. She knew time was not on their side.

'I'm going to go out myself. Someone will do it. Someone has to.'

She walked out. She was not angry with him, but she was angry.

Stefan drank the last of the tea. It was cold. She was right. Yet inevitably they would draw attention to themselves. He felt the more attention they attracted, the less likely anyone would take the bait. But a boat was still the only way.

The door behind the bar opened and James McKinney reappeared. Behind him was his wife, Kathleen. The publican lifted the flap and came over to Stefan. He sat down. Mrs McKinney sat by him. She smiled. McKinney was more open.

'What's so special about getting into the North, Mr Gillespie?'

Stefan sat back; the story could be told.

'We need to get out.'

'There's a lot of ways to get out. Get a visitor's permit. Get a visa for a job. It's not that hard to do. You'd maybe find it easier going to England from Dublin. Why would you come up here? That's all I'm asking. It's a funny way to get out.'

'I didn't choose the way, Mr McKinney. But Josie and me . . .'

Stefan paused, working through versions of the story he had created. 'We're . . . well, you'd have to say we're running . . . that we're . . .'

Reluctance seemed right. It had to feel like he didn't want to say it.

'You're running away?' said Mrs McKinney.

While her husband waited for more, unmoved and not much interested, Stefan could see that his wife was leaning forward, intrigued, almost expectant.

'Josie's been separated from her husband for some years . . . I don't want to say it, but if you want to know why we're here, then I have to say something . . .'

'Did I say I wanted to know why you're here?' grunted the publican.

'Just listen to him,' snapped Mrs McKinney.

'He treated her badly,' continued Stefan. 'I won't say more than that, but I mean badly, Mrs McKinney.' He focused on her eyes, his own eyes full of a meaning he left to her imagination. 'I met Josie in Sligo. She'd moved there to get away, after he'd put her in hospital one time . . . and I was working there . . . Well, we were two people on our own, not as young as we were . . . I suppose both lonely enough. You might say she was a married woman. I'd say what was that worth?'

He showed a little defiance. He sensed Mrs McKinney would want that.

'But the only way we could be together was to leave Ireland.'

'Is that so hard?' said Mr McKinney, still unimpressed.

'Her husband found out what was happening. He put private detectives on to us. It's not that he wanted her, but he has property that's really hers, from her family. He needed her to get access to it. So she had to come back to him. And these private detectives – well, that's what they called themselves – their job was to frighten me off . . . and maybe break what bones it took to send me on my way.'

'Jesus Christ,' exclaimed Mrs McKinney, crossing herself.

The publican smiled. He was finally impressed, if not wholly convinced.

'I've said more than I should. But running was all we had.'

'And what are you going to do in the North?' asked Mr McKinney.

'I've a brother in Belfast. He can get us papers for England.'

It was Mrs McKinney who spoke next. She was more than convinced. This was more romantic than she had anticipated; this was better than butter and bacon.

'There could be a way to get you across . . .'

Stefan adopted a look that he thought expressed hope and gratitude.

'What would you pay?' she continued. Business was still business.

'I haven't much cash. But I've the car. Isn't that more than enough?'

'It's not so easy to sell a car these days,' said the publican.

'I'm sure you'd find a way, even if it wasn't, let's say, the normal way. If you got half what it's worth, you'd do well . . . better than sugar and trays of eggs.'

'I'll maybe see what I can do, Mr Gillespie.'

'I'll need transport the other side. Can you do that?' Stefan smiled, but he spoke strongly. 'You'll have people who bring home the bacon. A lift to the train?'

Again, there was a glance between Mr McKinney and his wife. The nod that came from her was so slight as to be barely discernible, but it was definitely a nod.

Stefan walked to the harbour. He thought he would find her there. She sat on a wall, looking across Lough Foyle at the cliff-like mountains on the other side, smoking a cigarette. The quay was quiet. The fishing boats tied up there would not go out till late. There was little work anyway, with the restricted access the fishermen had to the lough and the sea, in the shadow of the conflict that made the other side of Lough Foyle the territory of the British Navy. On one boat a man washed down the deck. At the water's edge two men were stringing lobster pots.

'We're on, Josie. Whatever it is we're on for . . .'

'You found someone?'

'The smell of money was more than Mr McKinney could resist.'

'That's grand.'

Stefan didn't know if grand was the right word.

'The smell of money and dancing cheek to cheek.'

'What?'

'Just remember we're in love, Josie. Mrs McKinney has a romantic heart, as long as the money comes in too. The occasional loving glance wouldn't go amiss, or your head on my shoulder. You won't have to keep it up for very long.'

'That's something.' She laughed. 'No consolation, but something.'

246

They gazed out from the harbour, their eyes caught by something across the water. It had appeared suddenly, though they would have seen it if they had been looking up the lough towards the sea. It was a grey British warship heading into Londonderry. It was a frigate, small enough in the hierarchy of warships, but bigger than anything that sailed out of the Inishowen coast. It cut through the water at a steady speed. The barrels of gun turrets pointed ahead. They watched the boat as it passed, a reminder that across the lough there was a different place, that they were entering in secret, with all the risks and uncertainties that entailed.

As Josie saw the warship pass, Stefan knew she was not thinking what he was thinking. In her head was the foreign presence of that ship; the power of the old enemy made manifest. For him, it was yet another question about what they were doing. Still in his head was the question of the police. There was no forcing Superintendent Gregory's hand now. There was no Inishowen inspector to batter into action. If there was a police force to turn to, it would be the Royal Ulster Constabulary. And if the Gardaí were an anathema to Josie Kilmartin, the RUC was the British state at its most vicious. He could have no idea whether the RUC would care much more than Terry Gregory about IRA volunteers shooting each other. They'd more likely want tickets. They certainly wouldn't care about an ex-major-general in the Irish Army. The best Stefan could hope from them was to be arrested himself. Whatever he had left to turn over in his mind, the options were no clearer than they had been driving north with Josie. They might know where Emmet was, but Stefan certainly had no dice to throw here. At least Josie had a plan. And maybe it was the only one there was. Maybe she just had to walk into the farm where Emmet Warde was a prisoner and tell the head of the IRA's Northern Command to let him go. She would do it. But why would McCaughey agree?

That night a small boat pulled away from a jetty below the harbour at Moville, into Lough Foyle. It was no more than an open dinghy powered by a smoky outboard motor. It was steered by one of the men Stefan had seen unloading contraband destined for the black market across the water. James McKinney looked out from the prow at a light and useful mist. Stefan and Josie were in the middle of the boat with their suitcases. Josie sat close to Stefan, leaning against him. It might have been to maintain the fiction of their relationship, but it was also because of apprehension that made the night seem colder than it was. They saw no other vessels once a fishing boat sailing north from Redcastle had passed them. There were moving lights, barely visible, further north on the Derry coast at Magilligan Point, but a long way off. The boat was aiming for a creek where the narrow River Roe flowed into the lough. The river would let them push a short way inland. As McKinney brought the boat close to the shore, the cliffs of Binevenagh were there in front of them; what had been a long black hulk between dark water and dark sky came into focus as the steep cliff face of the mountain.

Stefan had removed from the black Ford everything that had identified him as a policeman or asked questions about who he was. In his case, along with such useful things as the maps and the binoculars, was the Webley revolver and a pair of regulation-issue handcuffs, along with a variety of at best confusing identity documents and ration cards, some in different names. Mr McKinney was pleased with the deal. However he disposed of the car, it was a good return for little work.

Shortly after the boat entered the river the outboard was switched off. The man at the stern still steered, but the oars were shipped and Stefan and McKinney rowed on in the darkness for perhaps another half a mile. Then the boat turned into the bank and came to a halt on a small beach of black mud. McKinney took out a torch. He shone it at the high grass in front of him and switched the light on and off several times. Some way off a pair of lights also flashed on and off. The publican regarded his passengers with a satisfied grunt. They were standing, ready to go.

'Straight towards the lights. You'll find Eddie Walshe's taxi there.'

'It's appreciated, Mr McKinney,' said Stefan.

'Yes, thank you,' said Josie.

James McKinney smiled benignly. He didn't have his wife's romantic imagination, but he did share with her the satisfaction of money for nothing. It was unfortunate, though he couldn't know it, that it was unlikely to be long before the Garda Síochána came in search of the black Ford resting in a shed at his pub.

There was a kind of path through the high grass and the reeds beside the river. It led to a piece of bare, flat ground at the end of a dirt track. A man in his sixties leant against a grey Hillman. He stubbed out the cigarette he was smoking and opened one of the back doors. Stefan and Josie walked on, their feet caked in mud.

'That's good timing. I only got here fifteen minutes ago.'

'Mr Walshe, is it?' said Stefan.

'It is, but no names, no pack drill, I say. You may get in. We're safe enough here, but you don't want to be hanging around along the coast for no good reason.'

Stefan and Josie got into the back with their cases.

They drove along the track, between low stone walls, and reached a road.

'You know you're too late for any train from Limavady . . .'

'I imagine so,' said Stefan.

'And from what Jimmy said on the phone, you'll not want to book into a hotel for the night. Maybe I'm wrong. I don't know what identification you have.'

249

'No, we won't want to do that.'

They were on the road now, driving towards Limavady. The cliffs of Binevenagh rose up to their left. Stefan and Josie were looking that way.

'You can wait at my garage. It won't be very comfortable, but you're out of the way. I'll drop you at the station first thing. There's a Belfast train at seven.'

Stefan looked at Josie. There was no plan to take a train anywhere.

'We've something to do before we think about trains, Mr Walshe. We need a couple of days here. I'm not sure how long. We'll be spending some time . . . here.'

The taxi driver was surprised. It wasn't what he expected.

'Up to you. I got the impression you needed to get to Belfast.'

'You hire out cars, Mr Walshe?'

Eddie Walshe glanced at his passengers in the mirror.

'I do hire cars . . .' It was a wary, cautious answer.

'We'll need one. I don't know how long. Three or four days maybe.'

The response was a snort of laughter.

'You're joking, aren't you?'

'Why would I be joking?'

'You're smuggled across the lough. I don't know you from Adam. According to Jimmy McKinney there's some feller somewhere after you. If you're not on the run from something, it's as near as dammit. I'd say you've got no permit to be in Northern Ireland. And you think you'll drive off in one of my cars. I'd put good money on the fact that I'd never see the pair of youse again.'

'I'm sure we could come to an agreement. I'll pay over the odds.'

'You can leave a deposit that's the price of a new car, can you?'

'I can leave you twenty-five pounds, plus the hire.'

'You may stick to the train. I wouldn't take the risk. I'm sorry . . .'

The response was not unexpected. This time there was no collateral to offer. But they had to have a car. Somewhere close, on the slopes of Binevenagh, was the McCaughey farm. They could make their way up on to the mountain by foot, to the road Josie knew that looked down on the farm, but they would be helpless. They needed a vehicle. It didn't seem likely that Mr Walshe would provide it. The other option was to steal one. It wouldn't be so hard in Limavady. They could exit the town in the middle of the night. On a little-used mountain road that was barely more than a track, the car could be hidden. If they could use it to get Emmet away, however that was done, it didn't matter that they were picked up by the RUC. In a way, that was a guarantee of safety. If luck failed, and the police stopped them before they did anything, Stefan would take a chance on the only thing left, telling the RUC what was happening, and hoping they would choose to do something.

It was Josie who spoke next. She had noted certain things about the interior of the Hillman. A rosary hung from the rear-view mirror. In the well between the front seats, under a packet of Woodbines, there were several cards, printed with black edging, that looked like Mass cards. She could also identify the small badge she had noticed on Eddie Walshe's lapel, that said he was a Knight of St Columba. What it meant was that he was a Catholic in a place where antagonism between Protestants and Catholics bubbled beneath the surface, whatever about the business of everyday life that meant pretending it wasn't there. He was also a Catholic who, whether this small world turned a blind eye to it or not, was involved in smuggling.

'Do you know the McCaugheys, Mr Walshe?'

'I'd know some McCaugheys. There's a few of them.'

'I'm thinking of Tony McCaughey. He's a farm back there, isn't that right?'

The taxi driver didn't reply. The questions were oddly specific from someone who shouldn't know anything about this area. It was also a name that made him uneasy. It wouldn't always do that, but here, with these two, it did.

'And would you know Tony's brother at all, Seán McCaughey?'

Walshe said nothing. If he didn't know him, he knew enough of him. This was taking a strange direction. One thing he felt sure of: his passengers were something other than the pair of ill-starred lovers he had been told they were.

'It's to do with Seán McCaughey and some friends of his . . . the little bit of business Mr Gillespie and I have to see to here . . . It won't need to concern you.'

'Look, I don't know who the fuck you are, or what that man McKinney thought he was doing . . . I don't want to know about this. I have no truck with politics, anybody's fucking politics. I keep myself to myself. I get on with my neighbours, Catholic or Protestant. It doesn't bother me. I'll drop you in Limavady. You can do what you want and you can go where you want. It's all there is to say.'

Stefan looked at Josie and smiled. She was good at this.

'No one will stop you keeping yourself to yourself,' said Stefan. 'We need the car. We'll pay. If they were here, Mr McCaughey and his friends would guarantee you won't be out of pocket. They'll remember you helped us tonight . . .'

The last words carried the implication that Mr McCaughey and his friends – and Eddie Walshe knew exactly the kind of people those friends were – would also remember if the taxi driver didn't help. That would not be appreciated at all.

The Bishops Road, which ran over the top of the mountain of Binevenagh, was once a track for shepherds and turf-cutters. During the Famine it was bedded with stone for part of its route, not because it went from anywhere to anywhere that couldn't be reached more easily by other ways, but because it provided the pointless, backbreaking work starving people had to do to receive the food that kept them alive. The glorious views of the Derry coast, Lough Foyle and the mountains of Inishowen were little appreciated by those who made the road in baking heat and freezing cold. Now, in so far as the Bishops Road was used at all, it was a place where farmers looked for lost sheep and a few hardy walkers came to admire the scenery. But it was on to the Bishops Road, following Josephine Kilmartin's only half-remembered directions, that Stefan drove Mr Walshe's Hillman from Limavady. They came at a snail's pace in the dark. And as dawn broke they found their way to an outcrop of rock at the low, southward end of Binevenagh that looked down on a small, isolated farmhouse. They could drive close to the edge and hide the car among heavy, sprawling gorse. They were able to see the place where they now believed Emmet Warde and Stephen Hayes were prisoners.

19

THE BISHOPS ROAD

A long day looking down from Binevenagh. Below the crag the sheer rock gave way to patches of hazel and ash woodland. Beyond that fields bounded by tumbled stone walls and barbed wire. Along from their vantage point, the rock wall stopped and there was a slope running downhill that turned into a track through a belt of trees to one of Tony McCaughey's fields. The track had been walled; the walled way was still visible lower down. If the track was steep it was easy on foot. A tractor might get up it; in dry weather even a car. It was a track Josie climbed when she stayed at the farm three years earlier, with the man she was supposed to marry, now imprisoned by the Irish government in the Curragh. She stood with him where she now sat with a Special Branch policeman. She thought then that she loved Dan Figgis. As she looked down from the same cliff she reflected that the last time she visited him, behind the banter and mutual concern, she came away feeling that he was a stranger to her. She didn't know him now; she never had.

The view of the farmyard was clear, along with the back of the house and a Dutch barn full of hay. It was a long way, but the binoculars let them identify some IRA men and, importantly, to count. There were seven men. Seán McCaughey and his brother; five others. Josie thought one was a man called Pearse Kelly. There was another she had seen at Lough Derg; she didn't know his name. And they saw the prisoners. Several times Emmet Warde and Stephen Hayes came out into the yard to walk around and smoke, watched by one or two gunmen. There were two cars in a lean-to; also a tractor. There was a track that must lead to the coast road.

For the rest, work on the farm continued. Tony McCaughey moved several dozen black cattle from one field to another and put out hay with the help of two IRA men. At one point three of the Volunteers, including Seán McCaughey, spent over an hour at the back of the house. It looked like they were nailing boards across the back door. Afterwards they cut a square of pig netting and nailed it, with a great many nails, to a window. It had to be the room where the prisoners were held.

There was little said between Josie Kilmartin and Stefan Gillespie about the next move. They were preoccupied with working out what was happening; all the more intensely because of their inability to see a clear way forward. Stefan got Josie to sketch a plan of the house, as far as she could remember it. The room where Emmet Warde and Stephen Hayes were being kept was a bedroom. It led to a large kitchen and living room. On the other side of that were two smaller rooms, maybe bedrooms too. A door at the back of the kitchen led to an extension containing a bathroom and some storerooms. After dark there was no light to see in the yard. The farm had no electricity. The lack of telegraph poles also meant there was no telephone. But there was light. A low light shone from the window that had been secured with pig netting. And it stayed shining when it was close to midnight.

Stefan had already reconnoitred part of the path down from Binevenagh and the Bishops Road to the farm. He decided to go closer. There was plenty of darkness. There had been no movement at the farm for hours. He took a torch, but he would not use it unless he had to. He made his way slowly, painstakingly, down the track and along the walled way. He came to the first of the fields. In the second he walked through the herd of cattle. They showed little interest. A group of them followed him to a wall close to the back of the house, but when he climbed over they turned away. The back window and the room lit by an oil lamp was close. He moved forward, crouching. He could see into the room. It wasn't easy to see. There were no curtains or shutters, but the glass was dirty and cobwebbed. He could make out a man, probably sitting at a table, maybe writing. He thought it was Hayes. For a moment the window was blocked. A man stood with his back to it. He felt sure it was Emmet. But he was reluctant to go closer. He could risk no sign. There was every chance that there was an IRA man with a rifle in there.

A low growl made him turn his head. A sheep dog was on its belly, sliding towards him. Its teeth were bared. It would be moments before the barking started. Stefan moved slowly away from the house. He hissed some commands at the dog.

'Come-bye, come-bye, boy! Come-bye!'

The dog stood up, uncertain, confused. The calls used for herding with a dog don't vary a lot, nor does the tone, which matters as much as the words. The calls Stefan would use in Wicklow would be close to the ones this dog heard every day.

'Away!' hissed Stefan. 'Away-to-me, boy!'

The dog's head tilted sideways. Here was a stranger, but here too were the commands he knew. And two different commands at once. Did he go left or right?

'Lie down!'

The dog seemed to accept the last command. He dropped to the ground.

Stefan turned and walked quickly away. He had only bought himself a few more seconds, but they let him over the wall into the field before the dog got up and started barking. The barking would follow him up the track. He would still be able to hear the sound when he reached the top of Binevenagh. But nothing else happened. It was a sheepdog barking in the middle of the night. It meant nothing.

The next morning, while Josie resumed the vigil from the rock, Stefan drove the car back along the Bishops Road to the metalled road that wound down to the coast road between Limavady and Coleraine. There he found the track that led to the farm. The buildings were out of sight. There were more fields, more ill-maintained walls, and some ditches and hedges badly in need of cutting. There was nothing to see here; there was nothing to help. But what did strike him was the confidence of the IRA men, even in an area where Protestant farmers were Tony McCaughey's closest neighbours. They felt safe. All day watching the back of the farm they had seen no sign of Volunteers patrolling; the front was the same. Maybe they were right. If there was no one unusual to see, there was nothing for anybody to notice. But Stefan was not at the front gate of the farm to look for sentries. On the way from Limavady, the night before, Josie had pointed out the entrance. He had registered the broken gate and a metal box on a pole for post. That was what he wanted. He had with him an envelope that had contained his various ration coupons and identity cards, and in it was a book he had spent some time reading at the Royal George Hotel. Emmet Warde had picked it up and looked through it one evening in the bar. It hadn't impressed him, but it had been the source of some jokes. He would know the book. He would know whose it was. On the envelope Stefan had written, 'McCaughey, Nr Limavady'. He had stuck on an Irish stamp from his wallet. Josie had scrawled across it,

'Not Known. Try Binevenagh?' The arrival of the book would mean nothing except a misdirection. Whether the book found its way to Emmet was a longshot; if it did he would know Stefan was there. He would at the least be ready for something, whatever that was.

Later that morning, John Betjeman's volume of poems, *Continual Dew*, arrived in the kitchen of Tony McCaughey's farm. The apparently misdirected package caused more amusement than it justified, but the IRA Volunteers were bored. There was nothing to do. The urgency of the kidnapping and the drama of the trial had dissipated. For those awaiting a quick bullet for Stephen Hayes, the situation had become less transparent than it was twenty-four hours earlier. Seán McCaughey had looked for a confession from the Chief-of-Staff, but all he required was Hayes' admission of the charges against him. What was emerging from the bedroom at the end of the farmhouse was sheet after sheet of information; names, dates, times, places. It all laid claim to widespread informing and pervasive cooperation with the police. It piled confused and unverifiable assertions on top of the few facts that the head of Northern Command thought proved Hayes' guilt. It created a chaotic stew that was entirely the product of the Chief-of-Staff's imagination, stirred and seasoned by whatever Emmet Warde could add. There were mutterings of discontent. Seán McCaughey wanted the thing done. There was more than enough to justify Hayes' execution. Why wait? But for others the sheets of paper from the bedroom had become mesmerising. There wasn't only betrayal, there was conspiracy. How could they move till every name was known? This mix of boredom, irritation and confusion wasn't the clean break Northern Command was looking for. Stephen Hayes' life, and now Emmet Warde's, hung on the toss of a coin. Was the Chief-of-Staff for the bullet or the witness stand? And it was in the middle of this that the post brought the book. Something to laugh about, however briefly. The laughter caught Emmet's attention as he walked to the toilet and back. The guard was quite lax now. The prisoners were secure in the bedroom. There were guns in the kitchen if they caused trouble. The trial was done; the beatings served no more purpose. So, when Emmet recognised the book, it was easy to pick it up. If he wanted to read it, no one else did. He took it into the bedroom. He saw that various phrases in various poems had been underlined. None of them seemed to have anything to tell him, except, he thought, that they were disguising something, somewhere that might. He found it in the poem, 'The Arrest of Oscar Wilde at the Cadogan Hotel', where the underlining of 'A thump and a murmur of voices' and 'Two plainclothes policemen walked in' let him know that Stefan Gillespie was somewhere close. And that something was going to happen.

Above the farm, on the crag beside the Bishops Road, there was no more avoiding a decision. Stefan still had very little. He knew the layout of the farm. He knew the room Emmet Warde was in. From what he'd seen, he felt the chances were that there were no IRA men in the bedroom. The back door was barred; the window out was nailed tight with hard pig netting. The kitchen must be full of armed men. There was no way out. But he couldn't be sure the guard wasn't closer than he thought. The window was the one weakness. He had pliers and tyre levers in the Hillman that would get through it, but the window might need breaking after that, maybe from the inside. Even if the two prisoners were on their own, the noise would bring IRA men out of the house; if there was a guard in the room, it would not only happen quicker, it would probably mean Emmet Warde would be shot before he got to the window, along with the IRA Chief-of-Staff. Certainly, they would not get anywhere near the track to Binevenagh without bullets flying.

There must be a way to do it, but the risks were high. He didn't want to take them.

Josie was still convinced that her arrival would be enough to release Emmet. Her plan had developed. She would claim she had been sent by men in the Army Council who were sympathetic to Seán McCaughey. Their message was that Hayes' execution was not only acceptable, it was overdue. But they wanted no loose ends and no other deaths to cause trouble with the police, on either side of the border. Josie thought the fact that she was there would prove that some Army Council men in the South knew where Hayes was. That might provoke some panic, even in the heartland of Northern Command. She wouldn't have to explain anything. She'd been told to go there by IRA men at the border. They had driven her to Limavady and on to Binevenagh. They were in Limavady now. She would be picked up at a certain time on the main road, with Warde. It would then be up to Northern Command to negotiate with the Army Council. She didn't know where their information came from. They had sent her because she was neutral in any conflict and because she knew the farm.

Stefan had to admit she had a way round explanations. Whether Seán McCaughey would buy any of this, he couldn't know. But there were other IRA men there. Some resolution with Dublin would be required. In the middle of all that, why wouldn't they just let Emmet Warde go? Stefan had almost decided to agree. But if it didn't work, it wasn't where he would leave it. He would give her time. He would watch the farm. And if nothing happened, he would go to the RUC as much in hope as expectation. That was something he didn't say to Josie, but he doubted that she wouldn't know it.

The vantage point on the mountain and the apparent indifference of the men at the farm to the possibility of observation had left Stefan Gillespie more confident than he should have been. As the afternoon of the second day passed, he lay on the rocks, looking down at the farm, still running through what could be done, still fixed on that one weakness that was the bedroom window. Josie was in the car, hidden by a circle of gorse, trying to get some sleep. The next day, they had decided, they would have to act. They had spent enough time watching. Meanwhile, although Stefan had been down that track that led to the farm, it did not occur to him that anyone would come up it. The IRA Volunteer who did so came more out of boredom than anything. The atmosphere in the kitchen was argumentative. He left them to it and walked the perimeter of the farm. He had no intention of climbing the slope to the mountain, but as he walked through the fields he saw something glinting there. It stopped. Then there it was again. It was evening sunlight on Stefan's binoculars. That wasn't what came into the Volunteer's head, but something was odd. He walked up the track to the Bishops Road. It didn't take him long to see Stefan, lying on the crag, looking down through the binoculars.

'Are you getting a good view from there?'

When Stefan turned round, there was a rifle pointing at him.

'You better stand up, mister.'

Stefan stood up.

'Do you have a weapon?'

Stefan shook his head.

'Why would I have a weapon?'

'Why would you be here?'

It occurred to Stefan that he might say something about the view. It wasn't going to be convincing. But he had to say something. As he looked behind the IRA man it became all the more important to keep talking. Anything would do.

'I'm only walking up here. It's a beautiful place to walk.'

'You've been looking below for some time, I'd say.'

'I have. And why not? You can see Inishowen from here.'

'And is Inishowen what you're looking at?'

The IRA man was not entirely convinced he'd found a spy.

'Who are you? Where are you from?'

It was then that Josie, approaching the IRA man without a sound from behind, smashed the Webley on his head. She did it with remarkable force.

The IRA man was handcuffed and gagged. His legs were bound with a pair of Stefan's torn-up trousers. A tow rope from the Hillman tied him to a thick trunk of gorse beside the car. On the top of the crag, with dusk now falling fast, Stefan shook his head. He had been careless. Events were forcing their hand. For Josie to walk into the farmyard now, with one of the IRA men missing, was a very different proposition. They would certainly be looking for him once it was dark.

'How long before they decide he's missing, not out for a walk?'

Josie could only shrug.

'I think it's the window,' said Stefan.

'What do you mean?'

'You can't go in there now. We'll give Emmet a chance to get out, and Hayes too if he can take it.' He picked up the Volunteer's rifle. 'Can you use one?'

She nodded.

'If they're behind us, you'll have to let them know you're there.'

She nodded again. Having seen the mess Josie had made of the IRA Volunteer's head, he felt confident she would do exactly that if she needed to.

He started with the cars. A hammer and a clasp knife. They were not parked close to the house, but at the farmyard's far end. Each one had four flat tyres within moments. He moved to the rear of the barn and skirted it to reach the back of the house and fields he had already walked through from the track to Binevenagh. He had opened two gates and now he was driving Tony McCaughey's cattle through the first. They had been reluctant to move, but he had them going soon enough. And when the dog arrived, growling as before, it was too absorbed in the excitement of doing its job to care who this particular man was. Stefan hissed instructions as he slapped the rumps of the most recalcitrant bullocks. The cattle were picking up speed, and with the dog enjoying a more reckless approach to his job than usual, they were careering through the second gate and into the farmyard. Only now did the noise reach the men in the farm kitchen. The whole yard was full of cattle, heading out of it at the other end, on the track to the road. The dog had lost any interest in the stranger in the field. He was as out of control as the milling bullocks. The farmyard was suddenly not only full of cattle but full of men. How many men, Stefan could not anticipate, but he thought most of them, surely. And he was right. There was a mix of laughter and cursing. The cursing came from Tony McCaughey, the laughter from almost everyone else. It had livened up the evening if nothing else, and as they tried to gather the stumbling, pushing bullocks, it was a mad game. Tony McCaughey and his brother tried to get ahead of the cattle to turn them back from the road to the farmyard. Others were trying to herd some of them into the fields they had escaped from, fighting the instinct of the beasts to stay together. And while this was happening in front of the farmhouse, at the back Stefan was cutting through the pig netting that covered the window and levering it back with a wrench. There was no one else in the bedroom, and so far whatever noise he was making was covered.

Emmet saw him immediately. He was by the window, trying to push up the sash. It was jammed. It hadn't been nailed shut, but it hadn't been opened in years. Inside the bedroom, he told a bewildered Stephen Hayes to push a chest of drawers against the door. Emmet picked up a chair and smashed it against the window. It broke not only the glass but the rotten frame. Suddenly he was climbing out, pulled through the gap by Stefan. Behind him came the Chief-of-Staff. They might not want him; he was coming anyway.

As the three men ran, over the wall and into the black fields, a shot came from inside the house. It had been fired through the bedroom door. The noise of the breaking window had not been drowned by the cattle. Stefan knew there would be more shots within minutes. And they would not come from inside. They could only run for the track up the mountain, hoping that darkness and the winding path and the broken walls would hide them. There were shouts behind them in the field. There were torches. There was the crack of rifle and revolver fire. They scrambled over the wall of the second field and there was enough light to see the opening that led up to the high track. It was enough light, and too much. They could be seen.

And the shots came closer.

'Keep going,' screamed Stefan. 'Up, just up. Keep by the walls!'

He crouched down and took out the Webley. He fired three times.

There was a short silence. Gunfire was coming the other way now. However well armed the IRA men were, they had to go slower; they had to look for cover. They couldn't race across the field. But they were still coming, still firing, as Stefan followed the other two men on to the track. They fired again; a rifle, a pistol. Stefan ran on. He was sure they weren't all there yet. Some of them would still be running back, maybe pushing their way through the cattle in the yard.

It was then that rifle fire came from the crag above. It was regular and it was effective. Josie wasn't firing at anyone. But every time one of the IRA men fired, she shot in that direction. For Stefan and Emmet and Stephen Hayes, the race up the steep road was becoming faster and faster. They fell and scrambled, sometimes running, sometimes on hands and knees. But the top was getting closer, and their pursuers were not, moving from cover to cover in the face of the shots from above.

When the three fugitives reached the top of the track, Josie had moved round from the crag. She knelt and fired twice more into the darkness. A shot sounded in return. The Hillman was a little way off, the engine running, the Bishops Road only a few yards away. Emmet and the Chief-of-Staff ran to the car and got in to the back. Stefan turned to Josie. The job was done. They were clear.

She staggered towards him. Then she collapsed. She had been shot.

In a corridor at Limavady Hospital, Stefan Gillespie stood outside the doors of an operating room. On a bench sat Emmet Warde and Stephen Hayes. They were bloodied and bruised from the scramble up the mountain. Their clothes were torn. They all, in their different ways, looked bewildered and distant. They did not speak. Stefan looked up as the doors at the end of the corridor opened. Three men in Royal Ulster Constabulary uniforms entered, hesitantly. One held a rifle. The man in an inspector's uniform held a pistol. Stefan knocked the Webley that was lying on the bench next to Emmet on to the floor. He kicked it along the corridor.

'What took you so long, Inspector?'

'What the hell is going on here?' said the RUC man.

'At the moment our friend is having a bullet taken out of her back. Not as bad as it looked. She'll be OK. That's more or less it. Do you want our hands up?'

'Keeping still will do. Who the fuck are you?'

Stefan realised that in terms of taking the situation out of the hands of Limavady's finest, and propelling it higher up the chain of command, to someone in the RUC who would pick up the phone to Dublin, it would be better to go straight for the hung-for-a-sheep rather than the hung-for-a-lamb approach.

'Well, I'm Detective Inspector Stefan Gillespie, of the Garda Special Branch. My colleagues are Major-General Emmet Warde, Óglaigh na hÉireann, retired . . . and to show what a broad church we are in the South, Mr Stephen Hayes, the Chief-of-Staff of the IRA . . . if not retired, I'd definitely say very close to it.'

20

McKEE BARRACKS

It took little more than twenty-four hours for the circumstances surrounding events in and around Limavady to circulate upwards into realms in which police commissioners, Special Branch heads and governmental ministers on both sides of the border decided that there was easy resolution to something that embarrassed everyone but had no real significance to anyone, or at least anyone outside the IRA Army Council, which, unsurprisingly, was not party to the discussions. The solution was to do nothing. Detective Inspector Stefan Gillespie, Emmet Warde and Stephen Hayes left Limavady by train and changed for the mainline to Dublin. Josephine Kilmartin was well enough to be taken to Dublin's St Vincent's Hospital on Stephen's Green by ambulance. The RUC had no interest in visiting Tony McCaughey's farm below Binevenagh. There would be nothing to find and no one to see, except Tony and his black cattle. Since much of what had happened had, for various reasons, not happened, there was every reason to think it would be some time before the head of the IRA's Northern Command looked in on his brother.

The very least Stefan Gillespie was expecting was some kind of disciplinary action. It had not occurred to him until he was travelling back to Dublin that he might have done enough to get kicked out of Special Branch. He probably knew that Superintendent Gregory was too bloody-minded to do something that he would have no objection to. And he was right. The Commissioner, Ned Broy, was only concerned to get the politics out of the way. Once that was done, he left the rest to Terry Gregory. The head of Special Branch had a lot less to say about what had happened than Stefan expected. As far as punishment was concerned, he had little more to offer than a predictably wry smile. The best punishment, he said, would be to leave Stefan Gillespie exactly where he was; still in the Carriage Yard.

It was unsurprising. Nothing had changed. And it seemed nothing would change. He still had a life to lead that Dublin Castle played no part in. And that was playing out better. In the time he had been away, Tom Gillespie had found that his time at home was not what he thought it might be. He recognised, maybe only intuitively, that he didn't want everything to stay the same; or perhaps he recognised that it couldn't. When Stefan came back to Baltinglass, the decision was already made, and Tom had made it. He would go back to Wesley College. It wasn't that he wanted to please his father, it was that he wanted to make it work.

Emmet Warde had returned to his office in Capel Street. Josephine Kilmartin was able to leave hospital within days and was back with her mother. No one in the Republican movement knew anything about her part in what had happened to Stephen Hayes. There were reports about the kidnap, the trial and the escape, but Emmet, Josie and Stefan were invisible. In Ireland, censorship on both sides of the border meant newspaper articles were even shorter on detail than they were in length. The conclusion of the reports amounted to little more than Hayes walking out of his incarceration when no one was looking. In America, where the IRA was always a topic of interest and censorship had no hold, the accounts were even closer to fiction. One report had him leaping from a speeding car to escape.

For the rest, Superintendent Gregory let things lie. There would come a time when both Hayes and McCaughey would no longer be useful enough to be left at large. For now, chaos in the IRA was allowed to run its course. But that didn't mean he was happy with what had occurred. He said it only to himself, but there was something lazy, feckless in the way he had dealt with the IRA, and people at its periphery like Josie Kilmartin. Warde wasn't even that. It irritated Gregory that Stefan had been right. If Hayes didn't matter, he had let other people get pulled into danger, when what was at stake was little more than his own amusement. He felt a need to make amends. But Terry Gregory was Catholic enough, in whatever passed for his soul, to know that confession and absolution were private matters. He would offer something up in penance; no one would ever know that's what it was.

For several evenings Superintendent Gregory searched the boxes of unordered and unrecorded papers in the cellars of McKee Barracks, the headquarters of Irish Military Intelligence, G2. He was looking for anything that might give a clue to what had happened one night in 1922 to Eamon Kilmartin and Brendan Davey.

Commandant Geróid de Paor didn't like Superintendent Gregory poking around in the Intelligence archives, whatever he was up to. He had no good reason to refuse the request, but he did mention it to his commanding officer, and on the second night, Colonel Dan Bryan wandered down to the cellars, as if he often took an evening stroll in that direction. He exchanged a few empty pleasantries first.

'I hope there's no trouble in this, Terry?'

He wasn't seeking information, only reassurance.

'There's nothing that'll trouble the government. I'll make sure of that. It's a private thing. And I may find nothing. If I do, it's to close a door, not open any up.'

Colonel Bryan nodded. His own view was that the privacy of almost everything in these cellars was best maintained by keeping all the doors locked.

Terry Gregory was not expecting to find any record of specific events. He thought it was unlikely he would find the boys' names. In those days little had been written down and that had served the Irish state well. With nothing to find, there was no reason to look. But some things did exist. There were duty rosters and accounts and pay slips. There were details of weapons and ammunition signed out. All these things recorded dates and times and places. And somewhere in all that, Gregory found names to put together with some dates and places. Nothing recorded any actions that had been taken, but he had a good idea now of at least one officer in Intelligence who had been there and had done something. The times were right. The place was right. The visit to Pearse Street was right. What wasn't right was that if he had found what provided a way to close a door for Josephine Kilmartin, it would open a door to something dark for someone else.

It was to open that door that Superintendent Gregory walked from McKee Barrack to Capel Street and climbed the shabby stairs that led to Emmet Warde's shabbier office. Nothing had changed. The room still smelled of whiskey and it looked as if work in the private detective business was much as it had been, non-existent.

'There was a favour you wanted from me,' said Gregory.

Emmet wasn't clear what the superintendent meant.

'Josie Kilmartin. Her brother . . . you asked me to look.'

The private detective was surprised. When he asked, Gregory's words had been, 'I'll see.' He didn't believe that he would see. He was certain nothing would happen. That's what he told Josie Kilmartin. And at the same time he told her there really was nowhere to go. He wanted to help her more than ever. Whatever anybody else owed anybody else, he owed her something. He owed her because of the lies he had told her. He owed her because in spite of that she had very probably been there to save his life. In doing so she ended up risking her own. She gave him no reason for that. He was almost puzzled by what had been done for him by a woman he informed on and a policeman he hardly knew, who probably saw him as not much more than a chancer and a drunk. Neither of them showed any interest in being thanked. He wasn't sure they knew why they'd done it. But whatever had happened, whatever had been done, it was over. The last thing he expected was that the head of Special Branch would have something more to add.

'I asked you, Terry, but you'll know I wasn't holding my breath.'

'I have something.'

'On Eamon Kilmartin?'

'And the other boy, Brendan Davey.'

'You know what happened?'

'I know the name of one of the men who picked them up, after they were released from Pearse Street. There's a daybook in the G2 archives that records who was in and out of the barracks. It includes details of patrols, vehicles that went out. It doesn't tell you about arrests or interrogations. But cars and lorries were precious. It records what they were doing, where they were going, who was driving. That night a lorry went to Pearse Street to look into the arrest of two Fianna boys. The entry's scratched out, but you can read it. There's no record of the lorry returning, or anything else for the rest of that evening. It starts up again a couple of days later. Apart from that the log's complete for the period. It wouldn't be unreasonable to think there was material they didn't want to keep, and that whatever that was . . . it covered almost exactly the time the two lads disappeared.'

'So you know who took the lorry to Pearse Street?'

'There were three of them. Two dead and one . . . who isn't.'

'So, do I get to speak to the one who isn't dead? Or will you?'

'I've done enough, Emmet. It's up to you.'

Emmet Warde was puzzled by Gregory's tone. He seemed almost saddened.

'Was he Free State Intelligence?'

'He was one of Mick Collins' boys, from the Squad. A gunman since he wasn't much older than Eamon Kilmartin and Brendan Davey. You could be tempted to fill in what went on so. A ride into the mountains was the favourite.'

'So, where do I find this feller?'

'I'll give you his name. You can decide what to do next.'

'Will he talk, though?'

Terry Gregory took a piece of paper from his pocket. He passed it across. As the private detective looked down, he saw the name of his brother: Charles Warde.

21

THE RED COW

They were the last men I killed. Though you could say they weren't men at all, fifteen and sixteen. It seems younger than it did then. And that only comes into my head now. It wasn't part of the reckoning when it happened. I'd killed my share when I wasn't much older than the two lads from Clondalkin. The first time, I was seventeen. I don't say I looked at it like that back then. None of us looked at what we did. We looked at what we had to do. What we were told to do. It was duty. It should have been harder when war against Britain became civil war, harder not to ask questions about what it was for. It felt different for a while, but not so hard.

We saw the lists of the dead. Everyone knew someone. We all had a friend, a cousin, a brother, a father, someone, some-where. If we didn't see a name we knew one day, we drank with those who had. We counted their dead too, the IRA's. We knew them. You might think that shoved the pointlessness of it all in our faces. On a good day, maybe. Most days it only made us more bitter towards the feckers who now killed us and made us kill them. We were angry. We needed anger because we didn't have what our new enemy had, the belief and passion they paraded about and hurled at us with the bullets and explosives. We believed what we were fighting for was right. The people had voted for it. We were fighting to save Ireland from fanatics, who the blink of an eye ago had been the same as us.

All that was easy to say. But it wouldn't bring tears to your eyes as the Plough and the Stars fluttered in the wind. We were killing and dying for an honourable compromise, not the sunlit horizon of the Republic. You heard it in the streets, not from the Republicans who shouted abuse at the Free State soldiers, but from the people who put us where we were and asked us to defend them. Ah, but you'd have to give those IRA fellers some respect. Fair play to the Shinners! You might not agree, but aren't they fighting for what they believe in? And we were fighting for an Ireland that was only there because everyone was tired of fighting for the one that wasn't. The IRA, with the sacred martyrs in their heads, were killing us for defending a compromise nearly everyone wanted and nobody was satisfied with.

I kept doing what I had done since I was seventeen. And so did most of Michael Collins' Squad. If a few men we knew disappeared to the other side, there weren't many. At Wellington Barracks we were no longer the Squad but Military Intelligence. We were no longer the liberators, but the protectors of the state. With the power and authority statehood brought, there were still people to be arrested and imprisoned. There were, sometimes, men to be killed. But every raid or shoot-out now had the stamp of official action. We didn't have to pull the trigger in quite the same way as we used to. We acted as ones who shot with authority. An arrest, a military tribunal and a firing squad gave the business of execution a legitimacy never enjoyed before. These were perks of nationhood.

Sometimes there was a point to be made in familiar ways. Legitimacy didn't sap the gunman from our souls. When the Civil War dragged on, when the aimless back and forth of murder persisted, and when the cries to end it all at any price meant louder, harsher orders, we fixed on those orders and made them our own.

The turning point came when Michael Collins died in the fire from IRA bullets. Anger became fury. Resentment and frustration became hate. The Civil War that had always been coloured by revenge now became sanctified by it.

By then the IRA had little strength in Dublin. I fought in the streets of the city to cleanse it, and somewhere I shot and killed a man I had fought beside only months before. I don't remember his name. There were probably others I didn't even see. But the heart of the war was elsewhere by then. It was our business in Intelligence to ensure it stayed like that. It was up to us to sit on the IRA and the people who propped them up. The gun that might kill a soldier or a Special Branch man or a politician on his way from Mass was never far away. Increasingly we were pushed to clamp down on all rebel action, however small.

Some days, across the city, posters would appear calling for the destruction of the Free State and the enemies of the Republic. Someone, somewhere in the government, or in the army, would decide that couldn't be tolerated. The people who put them up, the women and girls and the teenagers of the Fianna, were still part of the IRA's war. In the aftermath of Collins' death, there was a mood for a harder war. We knew there would be more executions. And a poster that defended the IRA was a call to murder. That's what we heard. We weren't in the front line, but the anger and the grief we knew in the face of the death of the man who had been our leader since the beginning of the war against the British hit us. We wanted to hit back. A report came in that two boys from the Fianna were caught putting up anti-Treaty posters. I was sent to Pearse Street to question them.

I don't recall who sent me, but I went with two other Intelligence officers. I don't even know now if anyone did send us. Perhaps the decision was ours. Teach the fuckers a lesson. I know those words were said. We said them ourselves, the three of us. Maybe someone higher up said them too. Maybe someone higher up made it clear that teaching them a lesson should make a point in a way that the rest of the bastards couldn't miss. Sometimes, now, I see myself repeating those words. Sometimes I see a knowing smile from my commanding officer. Sometimes I can only picture myself driving from Wellington Barracks in a van with two other men.

The aim was to interrogate the boys and see what names we could get out of them. I say it was the aim, but I'm not sure it ever was. And they gave us no names. I doubt they knew any. A sheaf of posters and a pot of glue was probably all they ever knew. We knocked them about in the cell at Pearse Street. The Dublin Metropolitan Police had done some of that themselves, but we gave them more bruises and drew more blood. They were afraid, but they could take a beating. They saw it wasn't going to get any worse. And when they heard they'd be released, they found their courage again. They were a little bit cocky. They even re-found their contempt for us. It didn't matter. We hadn't finished with them yet.

We left Pearse Street and sat round the corner in the van. We drank, I remember that. There was some whiskey. I don't say we were drunk. Drink was a part of our lives. We were used to it. It was a habit no one thought of as a habit. Over the years, I think a lot of us learnt to drink more than we knew. Our days were often idle, or at least they would have seemed that way to anyone looking in. We talked. We asked questions. We followed. We collected information. We watched. We spent hours discussing what we'd seen, what we'd heard, what we'd collected. We put it all together and discussed it again. Sometimes it was something. Often it was nothing. We didn't always know the difference. But all that talk could as easily happen in a bar as in a barracks, and very often it did.

The two lads from Clondalkin came out from the police station. They were cockier than ever, laughing and full of themselves. They must have felt they'd won something. They were blooded and they'd survived to tell the tale. I had known that feeling once, in different circumstances. I made no connection then. We saw them first in Townsend Street. We followed them towards the river and picked them up in Poolbeg Street. We tied their hands and put them into the van. It stopped them laughing, but I don't think they were really frightened. Not yet. They had taken two beatings. If there was another one, they would take that too. I don't know. Maybe they were already frightened. Maybe they already suspected more. I say they weren't because, years on, I still don't want to look inside their heads.

Most of the men I shot, I shot quickly, often at a distance. The ones that took time, the ones whose eyes I held in mine, are the ones that aren't so easy to forget.

We drove out beyond the edge of Dublin, to the Red Cow Inn. There was waste ground not far from there. It was close to where the two of them lived, to where they had been arrested. And it was even closer to where the first Republican soldier was shot at the start of the Civil War. If it was a sacred place for the IRA, it was our place too. It was a place to make a point, to give a reminder. But I still can't say, all these years on, what was in our heads. I know the point, of course, as I knew it then, though I can't remember if we knew how we intended to make it. Yet maybe we did, even if the words had never been spoken. I could say now that it was a pistol-whipping that went wrong. I often have told myself that. But didn't the three us have more in mind? Didn't we already know where we were going? Didn't we want all the Republican fuckers to understand what they had coming?

In the darkness, away from the road, away from the lights, away from everything, suddenly the boys were afraid.

There had been few words. They had asked what was happening, where we were going. We didn't reply. But when we took them out of the van they didn't speak. Maybe by then they couldn't speak.

I don't know who took a gun out first. I won't say it wasn't me. I still can't say, as we all took out pistols, whether we would have pulled the triggers or simply beaten the bloody shite out of the boys and left them. I still want to say we didn't intend to kill them. I can't. Then it was too late. One of the lads started to run. I fired. The other two fired. And the boys were dead. The boy who ran and the boy who stood still. It was done. And there was our point. Bleeding on the ground. But now we had a reason. One of them had run. We fired to stop them. Any shite will do sometimes, especially if you're not that bothered to excuse what you've done.

And that was it. We drove back to Wellington Barracks. We didn't say what we'd done when we walked in. That might have told us we weren't as pleased with ourselves as we thought. It was late by then. We'd stopped on the way to finish the whiskey. But something did have to be said. And when I told the commandant, the response wasn't what I expected. If there had been a nod, if there had been an unspoken look that sent us out to do the thing properly, to take it all the way, it had come from him. But whatever went before, it was different now. I don't think he cared much about the consequences of what had happened. He certainly hadn't got a conscience about the lads. Anyway, there would be no consequences, not for him, not for the three of us who fired the shots. No one was going to know about it.

There would be no records. The conversation I was having with the commandant would go no further. If no one had seen anything, it was enough. The dead bodies of two teenage boys weren't what anybody wanted. The implication, unsaid, was that 'anybody' meant people higher up the chain of command.

Even if no one could be held responsible, the killings weren't so much a message now, as an embarrassment. It was an embarrassment that couldn't be passed up the line, except to say it was resolved. So the three of us were sent back to the Red Cow, with some shovels and a pickaxe. The job now was to disappear the evidence.

We put the boys' bodies into the van. It was tougher going back to their corpses than it had been to walk away from them. We drove south to Blessington and the edge of the Wicklow Mountains. A place came out of the silence as we drove. One of the others knew it. It would do. A small bridge over an isolated river. It had been repaired recently, after the parapet collapsed on one side. There was the ruin of a barn on a slope above. Some of the stone had been used for the repairs. There was loose rubble and freshly dug earth, easy to work. The bridge was on the way from nowhere in particular to nowhere else in particular. Not long ago it had led to a valley outside Blessington that had been flooded to create a reservoir. Now it led to a dead end at the new lake and a track into the hills. So, we carried the bodies from the bridge to the barn. We buried them as deeply as we could. We heaped loose stone to hide where we had dug. And we drove back to Dublin. The next day we carried on as we always did. There was a war on.

The names of the other Intelligence men don't matter, the two who were with me, the commandant, maybe a couple of others. I don't know how many knew. My name is enough. Sometimes, when I think about that night, I wonder if my shots hit either of the boys. I know they did. That's the truth. I had been shooting men a good stretch. I was long past missing. It's a kind of fantasy, that my bullets went wide, and it makes no difference to what happened. But when I look back at my first killings and my last killings, I remember that the shots I fired, that first day, at British soldiers manning a checkpoint, brought me an exhilaration I had never known.

Then, even though it was possible that my bullets hit no one, I was desperate to believe they had done. I needed to know that I had killed. My last shots, my final shots, were fired at two teenage boys on a black piece of ground not far from the Red Cow Inn, and twenty years on I want to believe that I didn't hit them. I can't count the men who died between those two events, either because I killed them or because I sent others out to do it. I don't know how many. I've forgotten who most of them were. But somewhere in my head, they are with me.

22

THE NORTH STRAND

Emmet Warde could not think very clearly about what he would say to his brother. He took in what Superintendent Gregory had told him. That was hard enough. Either the rest would come or it wouldn't. He could only speak the words that would start it. He couldn't know what his brother remembered. He couldn't know what was buried in ways that meant memory had no access to it. He couldn't know what the confusion and chaos in the dark corners of his brother's mind would do with the journey he had to make him take. It wasn't long since the last attack had left Charlie Warde waving a gun at people in the street and put him back in an asylum. He wasn't sure that if Josie Kilmartin was someone else, he wouldn't walk away. Terry Gregory had done the work, perhaps against his better judgement, but he had left the decision about what to do with the information with Emmet. That decision included the option of doing nothing. That might be the right judgement. When time had taken away the rest, maybe only the dead were fit to bury the dead.

However, Josie Kilmartin wasn't someone else. She had not been simply anyone from the beginning. After what had happened, she could never be that now.

So Emmet walked through the south of the city to Charlie's house in Kilmainham. His brother was there. Jobs came and went with the mess in his head. The mess, now, was lying low, but there was still no job. Emmet found Charlie on his own, which was better, but the house was no place for the conversation. Open air and somewhere without people seemed right. The brothers walked to the Grand Canal and along its banks. Emmet had said nothing about events in the North. He wanted to make less of it than he might have done anyway. His version for general consumption was light on detail; one more thing to leave behind. And its closeness to the fantasies that erupted in his brother's head, of Black and Tans and IRA gunmen, often undifferentiated, searching for him, gunning for him, was more than enough reason for silence. But in terms of the past, the twenty-year past, there was no escape. He was there for the death and disappearance of Eamon Kilmartin and Brendan Davey. The effect of that on Charlie was something that had to be faced.

At first, they talked about not very much. A job Charlie was hoping to get; the family; the war in Europe in a loose idle way. But Charlie knew his brother. He didn't see him very often. He understood there must be some reason for this walk.

'So, what is it you want, Emmet?' Charlie Warde smiled. 'It's something.'

Emmet said, in few words, what he had to say. He explained he had been working for Josephine Kilmartin for some months. He did not say where the information he now had came from. His brother didn't ask. When Emmet finished, they walked on along the canal in silence for many minutes. There was nothing on Charlie's face that showed anything. There was no surprise, no bewilderment; no pain, no fear that spoke of turmoil. It seemed as if he was simply, quietly, looking inside and organising what he found there. Then he told Emmet what had happened, in words that were a simple statement of facts.

He was calm. He said he would meet Josie if that's what she wanted. He knew where the bodies had been taken. He remembered well. He thought he could find where the boys were buried.

The following day, the walk along the Grand Canal was repeated. This time the two people walking were Charlie Warde and Josephine Kilmartin. She walked slowly, using a stick. The wound in her back was healing quickly, but movement was harder than she showed. Emmet watched the two of them move away. He wondered if, when it was over, this would be the last time he spoke to her. It wasn't just wondering; he was afraid it would be the last time. How would she feel about a man whose brother had murdered her brother? He didn't know the answer. She had responded with deep silence to his words. He only sketched the outline. He left the detail to her meeting with Charlie. He saw that in her silence was the reality of facing the last moments of Eamon's life. After all the years of searching, she was unprepared for it. Seeking the truth, imagining the truth, was a different thing to meeting it head-on. What she now faced was the final, terrible piece of a jigsaw that wasn't so much being put together, as being broken apart. In some ways the search for her brother had forged her identity. It was so much of who she was, who she had been for twenty years, that she was no longer sure of who she was outside that. She didn't know that meeting her brother's killer would make her life easier or harder. She was adrift. The things she held on to were disappearing.

What Charlie told Josie, Emmet didn't know. Perhaps it was the same words he had already heard. It couldn't be very different, but what her questions were, and how his brother answered them, he never knew. When it was over, and they came back, Josie calmly, with almost studied politeness, thanked Charlie. When he walked away, heading home on his own, she thanked Emmet in the same way. And then she went. He had already told her what Superintendent Gregory had told him. The place where Eamon Kilmartin and Brendan Davey had died would remain unidentified. So, too, would the burial site. The recovery of the bodies would be carried out by Special Branch and other Garda officers. Josie would not be present. There were reasons why Gregory insisted on that, but it wasn't for Emmet to explain them. He expected her to protest, but she only nodded. Perhaps she didn't want to face those places herself. Perhaps the funeral was all that mattered. Whatever was in her head, it was something that no longer involved him.

The bodies would be found with very little difficulty. Charlie Warde's memory was good. His directions were precise and clear. He had forgotten nothing.

Stefan Gillespie drove Emmet and his brother to the bridge over the King's River. Charlie paced the ground on the hillside above the bridge, where the ruins of the barn still stood. The stones that had been piled over the graves were now a mound of grass. A party of Gardaí from Dublin Castle, along with several Special Branch men, dug through a morning and completed their task. There were only bones, and remnants of clothing almost indistinguishable from the black earth. A van was there to carry the bones to the morgue, where they would be washed and arranged in something like the forms of skeletal bodies. The bones of Eamon Kilmartin and Brendan Davey would each have a coffin to carry their remains to the funeral parlour. There they would await their removal to the church for the funeral Mass, and then to the cemetery. It would all happen quickly, and quietly. Those were Superintendent Gregory's instructions. The burial of Josie Kilmartin's brother, and her mother's son, had come with instructions. Gregory visited the funeral parlour to reiterate them and ensure they were complied with.

The coffins sat side by side in the funeral directors' chapel of rest. The lids were screwed down. Josie had looked only once at the white bones in Eamon's coffin. She didn't need to look again. They were not him. She didn't want her mother to look. Now on Brendan Davey's coffin a tricolour was draped. Over Eamon Kilmartin's lay the blue flag of the Plough and the Stars. It was one of the few things that was left of him. Once it took up most of the wall above his bed.

Josie stayed by the coffin for most of the day before the funeral. Her mother came and went, sometimes clear about what was happening, sometimes confused. There were no close relatives of Brendan Davey, only some cousins who had never met him. People came in and out, mostly neighbours, and mostly old. In the afternoon, Terry Gregory came too. He came, he said, to pay his respects. Josie knew he had something to do with finding her brother. She thanked him in the same quiet and courteous way she had thanked Charlie and Emmet Warde. She felt very little as she sat in the funeral parlour, and even as she shook the hand of the man she ought to despise as the head of Special Branch. Once, she had imagined this time. She imagined the passion and pride and anger and the dozen other fierce emotions that would fill her. She had imagined resolution. There was none of that. It was aching and empty sorrow. The images she saw were her brother as a child.

'Perhaps you'd step outside for a moment, Miss Kilmartin.'

Superintendent Gregory was more awkward than he usually was.

Josie nodded. She got up and followed him out to the street. She saw Stefan Gillespie a little way off, in the driver's seat of the car that had brought Gregory. She smiled. He nodded back. There was nothing else to pass between them then.

'I'm sorry about the restrictions I had to ask for, Miss Kilmartin . . .'

She looked at him, puzzled. She hardly remembered what had been said.

'I mean about visiting any of the locations . . .'

The superintendent trailed off. He had to repeat these things and to insist that the funeral the next day would happen as discreetly and as uneventfully as it must.

'It's not important, Mr Gregory.'

'I hope not. It's a requirement that the government . . .'

He didn't offer explanations. She knew what it was about. There were to be no plaques, no memorials, no Republican wreaths to mark the places of execution or burial as the sacred sites of martyred heroes. The sites would remain unknown and unrecorded. That was why she wasn't told where they were. For the state, this was no time to stir up the memories of old atrocities and play to the IRA gallery. The government wanted nothing that would nourish any kind of sympathy. It wasn't that these atrocities were owned by the government; far from it. Most of the men who served the state had fought on the anti-Treaty side themselves. But nothing was simple any more. There were still IRA men in prison, interned in the Curragh Camp in the South; interned by the British in the North. And there were still IRA men to try to execute. The chain of command that went from Gregory to the Garda Commissioner to the Justice Minister and Dev himself demanded that the pond remain undisturbed. Even for Eamon Kilmartin's coffin to go to his home for a wake was inappropriate. As few people as possible were to be part of this.

'And the funeral itself,' said Gregory, 'no parades, no banners, no marching. It's how it has to be. The times we're in . . . no oration, no rifles over the grave.'

'I know all that. It's already been said.' She looked at him more coldly, with a flash of what had been there till recently, not contempt, but a considered disdain. 'I suppose you'll have your men there to make sure that doesn't happen. But you

286

needn't worry, Superintendent. I don't think the IRA are interested. I ought to be surprised by that, but I'm not, not now. Everyone has more important things to be thinking of. It's not much, is it? I thought . . . it would be much more . . .'

She shook her head. The disdain had disappeared as quickly as it came. She had nothing else to say. She turned to the funeral parlour. Gregory went to the car.

'Is she all right?' asked Stefan.

'I don't know. You'd know her better than me.'

Stefan started the car and pulled into the road.

'What did you say?'

'The same shite. Rules of engagement.'

Gregory took out a cigarette and lit it, gazing through the windscreen.

'I don't suppose it matters in the end,' said Stefan. 'At least it's done.'

'It is. For what it's worth. Miserere mihi peccatori.' The superintendent drew in a lungful of smoke. 'But that was in another country, and besides . . .'

Weeks had passed, and the normal business of Special Branch had resumed for Stefan Gillespie. People to be watched, embassy officials to monitor, meetings to attend where the loudmouthed and indignant were recorded. Ministers and senior civil servants to be chaperoned and guarded. The ever-decreasing circles of observation that no longer kept up with the correspondence or movements of those who had left Ireland, visibly or invisibly, to fight for Britain. There were the checks on who came and went across the Irish Sea that had been more and more left to the mailboat crews. There were still spies of various stripes. Most of the Germans were imprisoned. The few who were still at large were there because, like Otto Fürst, they were of some use, wittingly or unwittingly, to Special Branch or Military Intelligence. Britain's agents were kept in sight, but largely left alone. When it suited both sides, they worked quietly and efficiently with G2 anyway.

The IRA were invisible after the fiasco in the North. Internecine conflict was nothing new but the chaos and recrimination that surrounded the attempt to execute Stephen Hayes had left the Army Council weak and fragmented, with trust in short supply and even less sense than before of what they were supposed to be doing. The men who might have brought order to the organisation were in the Curragh detention camp, squabbling with their captors as their comrades outside squabbled with each other. It was evident to all but the most gullible that the Germans were not coming. Even with the press and radio more heavily censored than in Britain, and an insistence that the conflict had to be reported either with perfect balance or not at all, the idea of Hitler's invincibility, which flourished in the early days of the war, was unsustainable. The baize curtain had been pulled back in the skies above Britain. As Christmas 1941 approached it was torn down. The German invasion of Russia had frozen solid in mud and ice outside Moscow. No point in scouring Irish newspapers for that. Yet this truth was in the air itself.

It was in the early hours of a Friday morning that Stefan Gillespie was woken by the sound of shells exploding. He knew anti-aircraft guns were firing as he got out of bed and went to the window that overlooked the Liffey and the north city beyond. In the distance he saw the beams of searchlights, reaching into the night sky. He could not tell where the anti-aircraft batteries were firing, but the noise repeated itself in short rhythms. Then, east along the river, he saw flares shoot up and burst, lighting the darkness, one after another. The first flare green, the second white, the third orange; a St Patrick's Day firework display. He opened the window, and between the sound of the ack-ack guns, never before fired in anger, and the bursting flares, he heard the heavy hum of engines overhead. The flares were sent up to tell the pilots they were flying over neutral Eire. Whatever city they were looking for, they were lost. The warning flares were repeated, over and over again. For an instant, as he watched, he remembered the Yankee Clipper at Foynes, gazing into the night with Dessie McMahon. Grace and beauty. An illusion; he knew that. All things could be turned to destruction, even the very air.

He looked down on to Wellington Quay and saw people lining the pavement, gazing up at the sky and across the river. The instinct he had learnt painfully in London – that you didn't look, you ran for shelter – was not a part of Irish life. There was no need. They were safe. The few mistakes that had been made were very few, and small, and accompanied, eventually, by such concerned apologies from the German government, that no one felt anything serious could happen. But this was different. Stefan heard the buzz of voices from below, a mixture of surprise, even awe; yet still little sense of fear. It wasn't real somehow and the bursting of the tricolour flares seemed to demonstrate that.

It was then that a different noise shook the city. This was no anti-aircraft battery or exploding flare; it was a bomb, deep and resonant. There was a glow on the horizon for a moment. And then another blast, another bomb. The force could be felt. It was not far off. People turned to move away, but with none of the assurance Stefan had seen in London. Did they go back into their houses? Did they stay in the street? Did they look for open spaces? But wherever they went, only a few people remained on the Quays, still looking north and east where the bombs had fallen. The staccato of the ack-ack guns continued. But between the shells, the city was quiet. Stefan listened for the engines above. He thought he couldn't hear them. There was a third blast. A third glimmer of light. The anti-aircraft fire stopped, abruptly. He heard the sound of bells, far off and close. Ambulances and fire engines, all heading north and east across the river.

Stefan pulled on his clothes in the darkness and hurried down the stairs. He came out on to the street to see the same uncertainty he had felt from his window. People were hurrying past, some with purpose, others clearly confused, while others stood across the road, by the Liffey, talking in small groups; some stood transfixed, staring at the sky. In the doorway of his shop, Stefan's landlord, Paddy Geary, was smoking a roll-up, looking on with the curious, phlegmatic expression he maintained for all occasions, great and small.

'Do you know where they dropped, Paddy?'

'North Strand. Somewhere there. That's the word.'

Stefan's first thought was that it was where Dessie lived.

'It'll be grand,' said Paddy. 'After the Jerries tell us it must have been the RAF, they'll say their fellers took a wrong turn after all and give Dev an apology.'

'Those were big bombs,' said Stefan, shaking his head.

'Then it'll be a big apology. Sure, Dev'll give them a real talking-to.'

Stefan turned to walk away. Paddy Geary's misanthropic observations on the view from Wellington Quay were to be avoided at the best of times. It was now around two in the morning. Stefan was heading for Dublin Castle and Special Branch. The duty officers would know what had happened. They would also know what help was needed. The bells of ambulances and fire engines still sounded. A dark car pulled across the road suddenly and stopped. Stefan barely saw it coming. No headlights were on. The driver's door opened. It was Superintendent Gregory.

'I was coming to make sure you hadn't slept through it, Stevie.'

Stefan walked round and to the passenger seat.

'The North Strand? You've heard that?'

As the car pulled away again, Gregory nodded. His idle words had been a kind of knee-jerk. He pushed them away. He already knew the situation was bad.

'What do you know, sir?'

'A bomb in Ballybough. A couple of houses demolished, but no one was killed, they think. A bomb on the North Circular. Just a crater. The North Strand's different. A lot of houses have gone. There's some dead, too. Some and counting.'

'Do you know where?'

'Between Seville Place and Newcomen Bridge.'

Stefan gazed through the windscreen. They were crossing O'Connell Bridge.

'It's close to Dessie.'

'Yes, it's close enough, Stevie.'

The smell came first, before the noise and smoke and heat and finally the sight of the collapsed street. It was a smell Stefan knew. He had smelled it in London, coming out of the Underground in the mornings after bombs fell. It hung about the streets all the time, until you hardly noticed it. And he had seen what went with it. He had dug the dead out of the rubble in the confusion of smoke and steam and water and fire and bells; in the clamour of falling brick and cracking timber and shouting and screaming. And it was the same. Only the people who stood at the edge of the chaos were different. In London there was little shock and no surprise. Everyone knew what to do. Here, in an ordinary street in a place that had never seen it, there were crowds of onlookers who had no words, who could not take in that this had happened. Beyond them, in the rubble and the smouldering flames, firemen and ambulance men and Guards and dozens of men and women, filthy from the black fumes and the dust, dug into piles of brick with shovels and pickaxes, pulling them away with bare hands. There was no order, only desperation.

As Stefan stood watching, it was Terry Gregory who was unable to take in what he was looking at. He might have told himself what to expect; it was worse.

'Jesus Christ!'

Two men pushed past, carrying a stretcher; a woman, broken, bleeding.

'You two got nothing to do except fucking gawk!'

Stefan knew the voice before he recognised Dessie MacMahon. The face was black. He wore only a torn shirt and trousers. He rushed on to the open doors of an ambulance. The woman was lifted inside. Dessie and the other man turned back to the wreckage of the street. Stefan pulled at his arm as he passed, shouting.

'Dessie! For fuck's sake, you're all right!'

Sergeant MacMahon stopped. Only now did he see Stefan and Gregory.

'Jesus, Stevie . . . Jesus!'

For an instant the sight of his friend brought Dessie out of the adrenalin-stoked fury that had been driving him into the rubble to find the people trapped there; living, dying and dead. He was still. There were tears, quickly gone.

'I'm all right. I'm . . . all right.' He nodded at the super-intendent. 'Sir.'

'You're all right, I mean. Brenda and the kids . . . ?'

'We're grand. We're . . . no more than broken windows. We were all at home. Noel's in Malahide with his uncle. But, God save us all, we could have been . . . You told me, Stevie, about London. You hear it, but you don't . . . I mean, you can't . . .'

'Who's in charge, Dessie?' said Gregory.

'I don't know. There was an inspector just now, who was . . .'

Dessie looked round for a uniform. He saw no one and shrugged.

'I'll find him,' said the superintendent. 'And see what he needs. More men, I guess. And he wants to get this perimeter sealed off and shove some of these buggers out of the way. If they're not doing anything, they'd be better not here.'

Gregory walked away towards the ambulances and fire engines.

'I best get back to it, Stevie,' said Dessie.

'I'll give you a hand.'

Stefan smiled. He walked with Dessie MacMahon towards the wreckage. He didn't do it as easily as the smile suggested. He knew what lay under the rubble.

The next morning, Stefan ate breakfast in the police canteen at Dublin Castle. He had not slept and had only been back to his flat briefly. The dead on the North Strand now numbered more than twenty; men, women and children. The search was still in progress in the wreckage of the houses, but there was little hope that anyone would be found alive. There were still people missing. There were still prayers to be said. But it was quietly assumed that there were only bodies left to recover. The canteen had been a silent place that morning. Stefan spoke to no one. He returned to the Carriage Yard with a heavy sense of the pointlessness of his job. A familiar feeling; normally he had familiar ways to ignore it. Today he didn't.

As he turned into the archway and Special Branch offices, he glanced left, along the roadway to the Palace Street Gate. He saw Terry Gregory walking to the gate with Dessie MacMahon. There was no reason why they shouldn't be walking where they were or leaving Dublin Castle by the gate Special Branch always used. But something in the way they moved, slowly, purposelessly, made Stefan stop. The superintendent and the sergeant paused. Gregory put his arm round Dessie's shoulder. It was not a gesture anyone who knew him was used to. Stefan watched his friend go through the gate. Dessie was a big man, physically and in character, but now his back was hunched. He was smaller, more fragile, in a way that didn't make sense.

Terry Gregory watched Dessie walk through the gate into Dame Street. Stefan waited. His eyes met the superintendent's; he knew he was right to.

'What's wrong, sir?'

Stefan could see Gregory was shaken.

'It's his boy . . . Noel.'

'What do you mean?'

'Dessie thought he was with his uncle last night, in Malahide . . .'

'I know.'

'He wasn't. He cycled back to the North Strand with a friend of his. It was late when they got there, so he stayed at the other's lad's house. He didn't bother to let Dessie or Brenda know. He was safe enough. The parents were good friends . . .'

Stefan already knew what Terry Gregory was going to say.

'It was a house in Seville Place. They found the body this morning.'

23

ST PATRICK'S CATHEDRAL

Why they were meeting was unclear to both of them, except that they needed to. She phoned him and said something about unfinished business. He was waiting for the call. There was no unfinished business. There was only finished business. And that included Emmet's own. The detective agency was done. The shabby office in Capel Street had closed its door. He said he had an offer of a job. It would take him to England, for a time at least. She didn't ask what it was. He did most of the talking and she let the words wash over her, watching his face but not really listening to what he said. He didn't say that one of the reasons he was taking the job in England was because money was needed to keep his brother at the private asylum he was now in. There had been a relapse. It was odd that the events of twenty years ago and their repercussions, which had been all the two of them talked about for many months, were barely mentioned now. But he did say he had spent time back at home, with his wife and his children. He had made the decision to face his responsibilities. It wouldn't be easy, but he had to change the way he lived. He was putting his life back together. She said that was a good thing. He didn't tell her he had stopped drinking, but she knew it. And she knew that would not be easy. She said almost nothing about herself, except that everything was going along. Her mother was no better, but she was calmer. Something was easier in her soul. Josie's own soul was calm too. She didn't say that or that it was a calm that seemed to come from an empty place. She didn't say she had been to visit her fiancé in the Curragh Camp and had broken off the engagement. It had been a long and odd engagement. There was commitment without passion; maybe not even much commitment. She would have liked her fiancé to show that ending it mattered. If he had, she might have felt there was something to hold on to. He was surprised, but untroubled. Truthfully, she wanted him to fight it. He didn't. He said he was sure they'd always stay great pals. She didn't tell Emmet that the end of the search for her dead brother had become the beginning of the end of the life she had built around the Republican cause, which had been her faith and her family. It wasn't that she no longer believed in her country as she always had, but it wasn't enough. Now, where there had been a framework to her life; where there had been an unquenchable determination to find justice, or at least peace, for her brother Eamon; where there had been usefulness and purpose in the cause he died for there was an empty space. Something had gone. She said nothing of any of that to Emmet. Everything, she told him again, was going along. And then, after his many words and her few, there was no more to say. They sat in silence for long minutes. Then they got up and walked out to Grafton Street. They stood still, facing each other, close to each other, as people hurried round them and traffic clattered. They both knew that in a different world it could have been different; it should have been. But they had never said anything to express those barely realised feelings. The only world was the one they had. Here it was. She looked up. For an instant she thought he would kiss her. He moved his head almost imperceptibly. He stopped. He reached and took her hand. He smiled. She smiled.

They walked in opposite directions along Grafton Street. They would not see each other again.

*

In the days that had passed since the bombs, shock had already given way to grim acceptance among those who were directly affected. The list of the dead stood at twenty-eight. Beyond the North Strand there was a sense that, bad as it was, it could have been worse. Anger would be dissipated by a governmental statement of deep and dignified outrage, and the recognition of what everyone really knew, that this meant nothing beyond the shores of Ireland. And even outrage had to reflect the restraint demanded by Irish neutrality. Edouard Hempel, the German ambassador, expressed sympathy for the relatives of the dead and horror at what had happened. He showed every sign of meaning it. His message to Berlin requested that no cheap propaganda be made blaming the British. He didn't need evidence to know where the bombs came from. Joseph Walshe, Secretary at the Department of External Affairs, was grateful for Hempel's concerns and keen for a rapid apology from Berlin. The Germans, he felt, should say the incident was under investigation. If it became clear the responsibility was theirs, they would express their profound regret. As he balanced his words with the pace at which a response should be forthcoming, Walshe had a photograph of a bomb fragment from the North Strand in front of him; it bore the words, 'Hier Nicht Anheben'. The Irish ambassador in Berlin had already received an aide-memoire from the German Foreign Office to say the competent authorities had no reason to believe German aircraft had dropped bombs on Irish territory. Hempel and Walshe knew otherwise, as did everyone else; they also knew that time would soften the truth.

Other events were crowding out the North Strand bombs in the tortuous pursuit of the neutral tone necessitated by an ever-increasing disconnect between the Irish government and the outside world. With no declaration of war, the Japanese had attacked the American Pacific Fleet. Pearl Harbor meant the United States entering the war. The shock in Ireland was real, as was the confusion that went with it. Tiny, neutral Ireland sat on one side of the Atlantic; on the other was America, the great, neutral democracy that was Ireland's friend. There was a bond in that neutrality, that Ireland saw and believed because the voices it heard were Irish-American. But the neutrality of the American president, Theodore Roosevelt, never had anything to do with Éamon de Valera's vision of balance. Roosevelt had done everything to support Britain against Germany. Brazenly, publicly, he called the United Stated the arsenal of democracy. Not only did he have no time for Ireland's secretive cooperation with Britain, he had no sympathy for Ireland's kind of neutrality. Where the English at least understood de Valera's position, even if they didn't much like it, Roosevelt showed irritation, impatience and anger. Like everything else in Ireland, the newspapers expressed none of that, but the air carried the whisper of it, as of other realities. Now, with America as Britain's ally, there was not so much a sense of world war coming closer, as of de Valera's rigid neutrality pushing Ireland further into an isolation ever-curiouser and curiouser.

In the midst of this, the world at war was not much on Stefan Gillespie's mind. The night on the North Strand, and the news that had followed it, left personal feelings too close to the surface. His instincts were to go to see Dessie, but he had experienced in his time too many well-intentioned friends who didn't know when to simply stay away. Dessie was still at home. He sent a note, but he would go when it was right. However, for several days he had also avoided going to Wesley College to tell Tom about the death of Noel MacMahon. The two boys had only recently become friends, but it would have to be done. Stefan had decided a trip home to Baltinglass would be the time, rather than when Tom was at school. He recognised that he was putting something he didn't relish doing on the long finger.

With those thoughts in his head, Stefan found himself walking towards St Patrick's Cathedral, en route to Dublin Castle. A straggle of people moved from Patrick Street to the cathedral. He realised it was a service for the dead and injured of the North Strand. He turned in too, almost without making a decision to do so.

Looking up at the Gothic walls, the cathedral pulled him in. It was his place in a way, or had been. He didn't often think about that. He never went there, close as it was to where he worked. He had no belief to take him through the doors. But he had an affection that touched him from time to time. This was the Church of Ireland cathedral he sang in as a boy, before his father and mother left Dublin for the farm outside Baltinglass. He knew the smell of stone and ancient oak in the high, cold interior. And he heard the music of the choir sometimes in his head. It was a corner of his life that had left few marks, but it had laid some foundations.

Stefan sat in a pew at the back of the cathedral, looking down the knave towards the choir where he had once sung. He watched as the buzz of conversation subsided and the organ sounded, as if it was somehow chiming and humming with the stone walls and columns. The choristers appeared, boys and men, making their way to the stalls in front of the altar. He gazed up. High above, hanging limply, ragged and faded, some almost crumbling to nothingness, were the colours of Irish regiments that had fought in Britain's wars; the Dublin Fusiliers, the Connaught Rangers, the Royal Irish Regiment. Flags that had been carried at Salamanca and Waterloo, in the Crimea and across the globe; flags that commemorated men who died in their tens of thousands little more than twenty years earlier. Stefan had known these things simply as part of the fabric of the cathedral. They had a strange incongruity, yet an equally strong sense of belonging, as the choir began to sing and the neutral dead were remembered now under the old battle honours overhead.

He knew the music, Stanford in C; always there when the choirmaster had to make a decision at short notice. He knew the notes. They washed over him, finding a place of peace in his head. It was no bad place to be for the short time it lasted.

It was as Stefan stood waiting to leave the cathedral that he saw the British press attaché ahead. Nothing surprising about that. From his brief meetings with John Betjeman he knew the Church of England and the Anglican liturgy were part not only of his Englishness, but of his poetry. St Patrick's was a place you might expect to find him. Whether he was there because he wanted to be, or because a point was being made on behalf of the British government, his presence had no significance. But as Stefan moved outside, where some people drifted towards Patrick Street and others stood talking, he registered the press attaché again, walking with a man. He recognised the man, though he couldn't name him instantly. His instinct was to query, not knowing why. As the man turned, he knew.

There was a thin moustache where there had not been before. Something different in the hair; perhaps it was dyed. But there was no mistaking Otto Fürst, the German agent and G2 double-agent he had tracked weeks before. He saw an envelope pass from Betjeman to Fürst, then the German was gone. Stefan had no interest in following him. Fürst was free because he was allowed to be free. The German knew that and his presence, even if unexpected, showed the confidence he had in his invulnerability. That didn't matter. But seeing Herr Fürst in the company of the British press attaché was another thing altogether. And that did matter.

Betjeman turned to light a cigarette. As he did, he saw Stefan Gillespie.

Stefan was already in motion. He had moved quickly, knowing that if the poet saw him standing still, watching, he would suspect something was wrong. Betjeman didn't know, but the expression on his face told its story. It was there only for seconds; surprise and discomfort. Then it was gone. The amiable press attaché walked towards Stefan, smiling broadly. Stefan returned the smile. He knew what was happening. Betjeman had to gauge whether his meeting with Fürst had been observed. He wanted a sense of why the Special Branch man was there. Was he being followed? Had he made a lazy mistake? Had he been too careless?

'Not a place I'd expect to see you, Mr Gillespie.'

'And why would that be, Mr Betjeman?'

Stefan was glad to play along. The more idle the conversation the better. Betjeman had no reason to believe he would have recognised the German agent, even if he'd seen him. And Stefan wanted to give every reassurance that he hadn't seen anything. His reasons for being at St Patrick's were simple enough. They happened to be real. He was happy to let the press attaché know what they were.

'You do know it's a hotbed of Anglicanism, Inspector?'

'I have heard that. It always was, even when I was at the choir school.'

The press attaché was disarmed and interested. It was not what he would have expected. He was not a man who believed he saw the world around him in stereotypes, but he was as guilty of that in Ireland as most English people were.

'That does surprise me. It shouldn't, should it?'

Stefan shrugged, all in good humour.

The two men walked on to Patrick Street. The poet's interest in things that had nothing to do with his role as British press attaché and spy put paid to his suspicions. He expounded briefly on the music of Charles Villiers Stanford and the little-known glory that was Anglican liturgy. Stefan responded accordingly. John Betjeman might be a better spy than the IRA Army Council gave him credit for, but he didn't take the job as seriously as he was meant to. Beyond the cathedral, poet and policeman exchanged more serious words about the bombing of the North Strand, and then went their separate ways. Betjeman had already forgotten about the German. Stefan walked directly to Special Branch offices and Terry Gregory.

In the superintendent's office, Gregory was laughing. The news Stefan had brought from St Patrick's had not come from any work he had done; it was chance. But the head of Special Branch was a believer in the serendipity that came, if you kept your eyes always and everywhere open, on any favourable breeze. The eyes had been Inspector Gillespie's, but the serendipity was what made fruit drop from the trees into the superintendent's lap. One way or another, it was fruit well earned.

'Stevie, boy! So, who's going to tell me now there's no place for a black Protestant in the ranks of the holy, Catholic institu-tion of Garda Special Branch!'

Stefan was aware that his superintendent's satisfaction, even delight, came not only from the useful information that the German double-agent regarded by Commandant de Paor and Military Intelligence as their prize catch was also working for the British. In the game played between G2 and Special Branch, de Paor had previously got one over on Gregory. Now Gregory had clawed back the advantage.

'I've no idea what John Betjeman was handing over, sir.'

'It doesn't matter,' said Gregory. 'Unlikely our popular poet would be involved in the information trade. He wouldn't get his hands dirty. Besides, information comes the other way. That's what the British are paying Herr Fürst for. As are our lads at G2. I'd say Mr Betjeman was delivering a message, that's all, or maybe money. And since Otto, contrary to the beliefs of his friends in the IRA, can wander around without being watched, let alone arrested, as a pet of Geróid de Paor's, a busy public place would feel safe enough, especially a busy and very Protestant place. I imagine the idea of St Patrick's amused Betjeman. Hubris, wouldn't you say?'

'He was surprised to see me. He covered it well, though.'

'Did he think you'd spotted Fürst?'

'I don't know. I'd say not. I guess, by the end, he just thought he'd bumped into me. I'm not sure he'd have any reason to think I'd even know who Otto was.'

'Yes. He'd be at the edge of this. He's no MI5 man. Whatever the reason for using him as a messenger, he's not a serious agent. Just an invisible one. You should go to church a bit more, Stevie. A weather eye on the Church of Ireland!'

Terry Gregory laughed again, enjoying the joke.

'You know why I was there,' said Stefan, not enjoying the joke.

'I know,' replied the superintendent. 'And you know I do.'

It was a quiet reprimand, but Stefan heard it.

'I don't think I'll sit on this,' said Gregory, lighter again. 'It's an option. But we'll do G2 the courtesy of letting them know that their feller is two-timing them.'

He picked up the phone.

'Put me through to G2.'

He waited, humming. Stefan started to get up. Gregory shook his head.

'Commandant de Paor, please. This is Superintendent Gregory.'

The call was answered.

'Ah, Geróid, it's Terry. Are you up for a drink? Something you might want to know. You may already, in which case it would have been helpful to say. But I'm guessing that I'm ahead of you. It concerns your German friend's friends.'

Stefan could almost hear the mix of irritation and exasperation coming from Geróid de Paor at the other end. He would know Terry Gregory had something that was going to embarrass or deflate G2. And the superintendent would not give up the information without savouring a bit of mystification and self-satisfaction.

'It's hardly a telephone job, Geróid.' Normally the head of Special Branch called his G2 counterpart Gerry, but at times like this he liked to stress the Irishness of de Paor's name, as if it was somehow in quotes. 'You'll know it's said that a man cannot serve two masters, for he will hold to one and despise the other. But what about three masters? It's also said, don't let thy left hand know what thy right hand doeth. Which hand are you . . . left, right, or one you didn't know about?'

It was evident that Commandant de Paor's final reply was curt.

'That's grand. The Brazen Head in an hour.'

Superintendent Gregory put down the receiver.

'He'll be put out. He won't want it to show, but he will be. If you can betray your friends, it's not hard to betray anyone. And we should know, shouldn't we?'

Gregory reached for his cigarettes. The last words, as Stefan knew, were not directed at him. They were thrown to an indifferent wind, maybe meaning something, maybe nothing. It was another game Gregory played, mostly with himself. Stefan had heard it all before. He was in no mood to join in. The poet-spy and the triple-spy and the superintendent-spy, whatever damage they could do each other, or anyone else, seemed a long way away. In his head he still heard the music of the choir of St Patrick's, and words he had sung in the choirstalls as a boy, when they meant little. 'I held my tongue, and spake nothing: I kept silence, yea, even from good words.' He heard his own silence. In his head, too, were the words he would have to say to his son. He had waited when he should not have waited.

'Have you seen Dessie at all?' Stefan ended Gregory's reflection.

304

'He didn't want to see anybody. I've left it.'

As Terry Gregory lit his cigarette, he pushed aside the game. Stefan nodded. For now, he had made the same decision.

'The funeral's Tuesday, Stevie, you know that?'

Stefan was still thinking about Dessie, and the last time he had seen him; the distant, defeated back of him, walking slowly through the gate on to Dame Street.

'I'm taking Tom home tonight . . .'

He left the thought that accompanied that unfinished. But Terry Gregory knew what it was. He knew more than anyone assumed he knew about his men.

'Were they close, Tom and Dessie's boy?'

'I wouldn't say that. Who knows with kids? Tom's not a great one for friends, not since he got older. They got on. There was a plan about Dessie's boy coming down to the farm after Christmas.' He shrugged. 'That's enough, isn't it?'

Stefan collected Tom from Wesley College. Father and son walked down Grafton Street, past Trinity College to O'Connell Bridge, then along the Quays to Kingsbridge Station. The bombs that had fallen only days ago had already receded in Tom's mind. They were talked about so intensely at school that they had been almost talked out. The boarders had heard them when they fell across the river. They came out to listen and to see some of the light that was briefly in the night sky. There was more excitement than fear, at least for the boys. There was fear enough for the staff, who had no idea whether to keep everyone outside, or go back in, or move away from the buildings and take the boarders into Stephen's Green. But it was over quickly, for those who were far from it, and it was only the next day, when the day pupils came in, that the truth about what had happened was revealed, to be confirmed by the principal at morning prayers.

The sense of shock was real, but without seeing the demolished houses and ambulances carrying away the dead, it felt further away than it had been. The news about the Japanese attack on Pearl Harbor had followed within days. Watching from Wesley College was like watching from anywhere in Ireland, struggling to see round a corner from a long way away. But even for the boys in Tom's dormitory everything felt closer than it had done. Something had changed.

So as Stefan and Tom walked through Dublin and along the Liffey, it was the war and America that the questions were about. But Tom knew quickly that his father didn't want to talk. His questions were answered with more don't-knows than he was used to. One question about the bombs on the North Strand produced no answer. It didn't matter. Tom was pleased to be going home for the weekend. He was happy to take in the sights and the noises of the city, too. There would be more to say at Kilranelagh. At least his father wasn't asking him how it was going at school. It was all right. That was as much as he could say. And all right would do. He didn't want to be cross-examined on it, though. The war was an easier conversation to have, even if today he seemed to be the only one having it.

The train pulled out of Kingsbridge into the darkness. The carriage wasn't full. Stefan and Tom sat opposite each other, both looking out for several minutes and seeing only pinpoints of light and their faces reflected back at them.

'It'll be Christmas next time I come home.'

It was a new subject. Tom announced it brightly.

'So, is it still on, Pa?'

'What?'

'Noel coming down after Christmas. You said and Mr MacMahon said . . .'

Tom's words faded out. He registered a strange look on his father's face.

'No, Tom, it's not. I'm sorry. I should have told you this straightaway . . .'

24

THE ALIENS OFFICE

Dublin, May 1947

The war had been over for almost two years. The Emergency ended in Ireland as it began, with a bewildered and slightly petulant whimper. Having sat outside the chaos, or at best watched it through a long telescope, little had changed. That wouldn't be true for long. But for now, Ireland seemed to sit at the edge of a world it was barely on nodding terms with. It was a quiet place, and for those who weren't taking the boats, and soon planes, to ferry them to a life somewhere else, everything was familiar. There were those who fought in the war nobody had much to say about and returned. They kept a discretionary silence about what they had seen and done. The easiest way to get on back home was to pretend it hadn't happened. If you had the decency to say nothing, family and friends, workmates and colleagues would have the decency not to ask. The dead, naturally, did not return; their silence was assured. And there were many who simply didn't come back. Whether they left to fight or work, they stayed in England and further afield. At Dublin Castle, Superintendent Gregory and his men spent some time establishing whether returning ex-soldiers qualified for prosecution, but ultimately it was felt that since there was little to say about the war, there wasn't much point.

With no German invasions to dream of, and no Nazi powerhouse to bring the British Empire to its knees – a job the Empire had embarked on itself now – the Boys of the IRA were being rehabilitated. They could be viewed with fondness; a mad uncle who could be let out of the attic. They might be seen as the steely bastion of Republicanism, lurking in the shadows to keep mainstream politicians on their toes. And even in the shadows Republicans had friends again. If Sinn Fein and the IRA still struggled to find a place on the narrow spectrum of Irish politics, they had left their limpid version of National Socialism behind for new directions. With a Cold War drawing its iron curtain across Europe, the only way to be on the opposite side to Britain was to embrace socialism again; the red variety rather than the black. The glories of communism inspired souls that had cheered Hitler's march into the Soviet Union as the salvation of the civilised world. This new product would not sell well in Catholic Ireland, yet it was somewhere for Republicanism to go. And songs still sounded in the bars of Dublin and Belfast, London and Liverpool, New York and Boston. If the ideology was shaky, the tunes held. It would be a while before the road was straight again. It would come, though. As ever, it would be the bloody-minded stupidity of Britain that primed the pump.

For now, Republicanism was half asleep. In Special Branch, Terry Gregory's finest found themselves putting on weight and drinking with the Boys they were arresting and occasionally shooting only a few years ago. Meanwhile, Ireland's children grew up and left its shores in ever greater numbers. Those who remained did so uncertainly, waiting for Éamon de Valera to die, or fade, with respectful indifference. Dancing at the crossroads was in its decaying half-life. Dev's own Geiger counter buzzed with less and less frequency. The Church stood firm. The gates of the atheistic Hell of the world beyond would not prevail. Yet.

It was on a day in May 1947 that the Garda Commissioner, Ned Broy, asked Superintendent Gregory to meet him at Garda HQ in the Phoenix Park. It was a bright day, cold for May. But a good day to be out. Gregory walked, as he almost always did. He had not stopped walking in Dublin, even when that carried serious risks, but he enjoyed the sense that now there were none. He carried no gun. Life was easier, but less interesting. Being bored amused him for a while, but he drank more, smoked more. He spent a lot of time doing nothing. There was nothing to do.

As he reached the gates of Garda HQ, he met Broy coming out.

'Jesus, it's cold enough for May, Terry!'

'I'd rather that sometimes. It wakes me up.'

'Do you need waking up?' said Broy, laughing.

'I'd say I do, Ned. Too often now.'

'Let's walk. We can wake each other up.'

The two men strolled into the Phoenix Park. They said little, except for a few more words about the weather and the trees and the new flowers. Terry Gregory was waiting. Broy had something to discuss. He was biding his time.

'I will be retiring in a couple of months. It's time.'

'You've had enough?'

'I had enough a long time ago. I stuck with it because I expected everyone else to. War, Emergency, the days when it felt like anything could happen. I don't know if we built them up ourselves, German invasions, British invasions. It gave us a kind of holy justification in the face of all that chaos. We had the incense of integrity. A little nation pitted against the giants who were tearing the world apart.'

'Isn't that what we were?' Gregory laughed.

'A bit of it. Maybe too much of what we wanted to be.'

'Do you ever think it was a mistake, Ned?'

'I think it was what we had to do. Maybe we sat on the fence too long when we knew it was the barbed wire round the death camps. Dev's a stubborn man. It's been his strength, but sometimes he can't walk away when a bus is coming at him. He built himself around what Britain was to Ireland. But if it got more complicated . . . the idea there was a moral streak in their war . . . he wouldn't see, even at the end. You didn't have to abandon neutrality to tell the decent truth.'

'The words said one thing, Ned,' said Gregory. 'But we know the work that went on with British Intelligence. We know there wasn't very much neutrality in all that?'

'But no one can say it. That's one of my last jobs. Destroying the evidence. Same in Military Intelligence. Everything goes. You might think it wouldn't be bad to know that even in the middle of doing the best thing, maybe the only thing to keep the country in one piece, we saw the Nazis for what they were. Dev knew about all that. He chose not to see too much. Now it's our dirty secret.'

'Aren't all our secrets dirty?' said Gregory.

'We've plenty that are. It makes us no different to anybody else. But Dev's a believer. You must never forget it. In Holy Ireland, what's dirty never really was.'

Gregory didn't reply. They walked silently for several minutes.

'I think of the past more than I did,' said Broy. 'I think of dead men. And I find myself less pleased with who I am than I thought I was. I find myself looking at the need for it all in the way my accountants look at the figures I give the government. It's a cold calculation, however it's added up. It's not about regret. But I remember more. I take less satisfaction than I did in knowing we were right.'

The superintendent shrugged. Broy wasn't looking for an answer.

'What about you, Terry?'

'Me?' Gregory smiled. 'I trail more dead men behind me than you, Ned. And dirty secrets are mostly all my balance sheets contain. Someone has to know what they are. We might still be here without them, but I'm not sure what we'd be. That's it for me. I'm not in the business of reflection. It's why you put me there.'

'Yes, it is. But I think those days are gone.'

'Have they? I'm not so sure.'

'No one's going to say there's blood on our hands, but there's always a little bit under the fingernails, Terry. And the scrubbing brush doesn't quite get it out.'

'I thought we did that for Ireland?'

'That's why we need to go. The heroes are dead. What's left, the rabble that never quite made Olympus, well, I'm not sure we're altogether decent. We should take our pensions, shut our mouths, and be wheeled out with our medals at Easter.'

'Is that an invitation for me to join you in your retirement bash?'

'No.'

'That's a relief. I've got enough clocks on the mantelpiece.'

The Commissioner stopped. His words had a purpose now.

'Not an invitation, an instruction. From the minister. We have too much baggage. The same for a lot of your men. It's only war that kept you there. Special Branch won't be run the way we let you run it. You've the scent of the gunman.'

'That's one way to go, Ned. A bad smell. It wasn't what I was expecting. Don't I get even to say, "I have done the state some service, and they know't."'

'They do know it. That's the trouble. Now they want to forget it.'

Commissioner and superintendent turned back towards Garda Headquarters, walking across the close green sward of the Phoenix Park, between budding trees. In front of them a herd of a dozen fallow deer parted, unfazed by their approach.

'I have wondered why I do the job, Ned. Faced with the bollocks piled round me, I have asked myself. And I've found reasons, all sorts of reasons. Even good ones. But in the end, I forgot how to be anything else. The truth is, it's all I am.'

'I'm sorry, Terry. That's the price . . . isn't it?'

Gregory took out a cigarette and lit it. He drew deeply, then grinned.

'"You are old, Father William, the young man said, And your hair has become very white; And yet you incessantly stand on your head – Do you think at your age it is right?" Just one thing, Ned . . . make sure there's no fucking clock.'

Detective Superintendent Terry Gregory sat at his desk, looking out through the glass wall that separated him from the detectives' room. The room was quiet. It was often quiet now. Three detectives sat at their desks. They were doing something, but what they were doing probably didn't matter very much. His men were increasingly working on ordinary crime. He was lending them out to other stations to do investigative work some of them weren't very good at, the older ones anyway. There was no doubt the place had to change. If there was a murder in Kildare or a bank robbery in Dundalk, knowing which IRA men drank in which pub in Dublin, and who you could batter into giving you information, didn't count for much. He had detectives who could handle the painstaking gathering of evidence, but they were carrying the rest, more at home in a bar than at a crime scene. And he wasn't that different. Ned Broy was right. He'd never thought of himself as a gunman, but he wasn't sure, looking back, that he'd ever been much more. Two new detectives had joined Special Branch only a week earlier. They were young and enthusiastic, and he was uncomfortable with them. There were IRA men who would have cheerfully shot him years earlier that he found it easier to drink with. Half a dozen men had retired since the Emergency. He hadn't taken that in. Now he would go the same way. This was his place. Not any more.

A knock at the door. He looked up. Detective Inspector MacMahon.

'There's a problem at the Aliens Office. They want you.'

'Me? What the hell for?'

'There's a feller causing a row.'

'Get a bloody Guard to throw him out! Jesus Christ!'

'They've got him in a room. He wants to talk to you, sir.'

'Does he? You can call them back and tell them to fuck off!'

'The man's Otto Fürst. He's the German—'

'I know who he fucking is! I'm not senile yet, Inspector.'

The response was angrier than Dessie had any reason to expect.

'I'm sorry, Dessie. Not a good day. Otto . . . let's see what he wants.'

Gregory walked from the Carriage Yard to the building that housed the Aliens Office, where civil servants and some of his own men generated the paperwork that regulated the outside world's access to Ireland at a time when that world had little interest in it. It was a place normally subject only to the industrious shuffling of files that circulated and re-circulated at a tempo that still owed much to the inheritance of an empire built on paper and rubber stamps. On those stamps the Lion and the Unicorn of His or Her Britannic Majesty had been replaced by the Harp, but little else had changed. Today, however, the order of the Aliens Office had been disrupted by an argument at the reception desk. A German resident in Ireland, about to be deported, had forced his way in, Gardaí had to restrain him. The man was now in an interview room. Two Guards stood watch as he paced the room, muttering and swearing in English and German. Now that he had been arrested he demanded to see Superintendent Gregory, the head of Special Branch. The superintendent, he insisted, would prove that he had served the Irish state. He would prove this was all a very grave mistake. And he would stop the deportation.

Terry Gregory came into the room with Dessie MacMahon. Otto Fürst had met Gregory shortly before the end of the war, when he was finally arrested. There had been some hours of interviews, but the espionage activities of the agent of a country that already lay in ruins had little interest for anyone. A few months later Fürst was released. He stayed in Ireland and assumed he could make his life there. No one seemed inclined to stop him. That had changed. Now the Irish government had decided he must leave. Fürst nodded at Gregory, recognising him.

'Mr Gregory, yes? I remember you now.'

'Mr Fürst.'

'This is all a mistake. You can tell them it is. You know it is.'

'You're causing a bit of a row.'

'You can resolve this, Superintendent. You know who I am!'

'I know who you are.'

Gregory smiled. The German saw nothing reassuring in that smile.

'I will not go back to Germany. You can stop it.'

'You don't have a choice, Mr Fürst. There's an order for your deportation.'

'No. I don't accept that.'

'It's done. There's no argument to have, Otto.'

Fürst shook his head. His lips tightened.

'I gave you help. During the war, I put my life at risk. I saved other lives. The information I gave saved lives. I was on your side. You know that. When I escaped from prison, it was your Military Intelligence that made it happen. Mr Bryan, Commandant de Paor, they know how I worked for Ireland. I worked against the IRA, against my own country. For years I passed on information. Where are they? Where's Geróid de Paor. He can vouch for me. I have tried to speak to him. Why

314

isn't he here, now, to stop this? I cannot be sent to Germany!'

Gregory sat on the edge of the desk.

'There's not a lot of point looking for G2, Otto. Gerry's doing something else now. They've mostly been disbanded. There's a few fellers in an office in a barracks somewhere in case the Russians invade.' The superintendent laughed. 'And they'd only know that if the CIA phoned to say the Reds were on the way.'

Terry Gregory took out a packet of cigarettes. He offered one to the German. Fürst shook his head angrily. The superintendent shrugged and lit one himself.

'Happy days are here again. We're all out of it. You, too.'

'I only ask to stay in Ireland, to live here. I deserve that.'

'Do you?' Gregory shook his head. 'You'd be better to ask the British.'

'What the hell does that mean?'

'In fact, I think you did ask. We did feel a need to keep an eye on letters abroad for a bit, once the war was over. You sent several letters to an address in London, which isn't a long way from the offices of MI6. You'll remember it.'

The German frowned, shaking his head hard, as if he didn't remember.

'I don't know what you mean. I don't understand you, Mr Gregory.'

'They weren't interested either. I don't think you got a reply. Right?'

Otto Fürst stared at the policeman.

'We are in the same kind of business, Herr Fürst, after a fashion. At least we were. I know there are spies and agents who ply their trade for the noblest of motives, even if those motives seem a lot less than noble to the casual observer. But let's not pretend you were in that category. When you arrived in Ireland, you recognised the IRA were a bunch of incompetent gobshites. After you were captured, you were turned by Mr de

315

Paor and his friends in G2. They engineered your escape from Mountjoy, or at least let the IRA do it. You returned to your role as German spy but paid by Irish Military Intelligence. I think paid was very much to the point. And you were also being paid by British Intelligence. I'm sorry to say my old friend Gerry was slow to spot that. But one day, one of my officers saw you with the British press attaché. Remember him, Betjeman? You were so sure you were protected that you didn't worry. You knew G2 wouldn't pick you up. You knew I wasn't allowed to arrest you. You knew the IRA believed in you as the messenger of Adolf Hitler. You were invulnerable. I don't know what Mr Betjeman gave you that day at St Patrick's, money maybe? Certainly not a slim volume of verse. We both know how the game's played, Otto. You played every side. The side that mattered would always be the one that was on top – the British.'

Fürst shook his head, but he didn't argue. He took a cigarette from the packet that still lay on the table. Terry Gregory struck a light and lit it for him.

'I needed to know what the British were doing too, Mr Gregory.'

'That won't wash, Otto.'

'It doesn't alter what I did for Ireland. I gave good information.'

'I'd say you gave us only what MI6 decided you should give us.'

'That's not true. I put my life at risk!'

'Well, you wouldn't be alone in that,' said Gregory. 'It's one of the more miserable truths about a war in which millions of people died, that there aren't very many people who even care. Especially in a country that was only playing at it.'

'You know what could happen to me in Germany?'

'I have a fairly good idea. Not much. You weren't shovelling bodies into ovens or shooting prisoners of war. You'll be of little interest. You'll be questioned by somebody from British Intelligence. They already know your story and they couldn't give a fuck. They'll know you were on MI6's books. You might have to sit in a classroom for a lecture on denazification, but I'd say you were more a chancer than a Nazi. But they won't send you to the Russian Zone, where I imagine it's a lot less accommodating. And that's about it. I don't see you have a problem. Guinness will be in short supply, but they say the Deutsch beer's decent enough.'

'You don't understand. There are still people who remember. They'll know. They'll know I was . . . a traitor. You don't think these things just get forgotten!'

Terry Gregory laughed.

'Bollocks! You were in the spy business too long, Otto.'

'It's not a joke? I mean it. They are still there. The fact that they lost doesn't mean they don't want revenge. People who helped the enemy. Those people die!'

Superintendent Gregory was unconvinced. He didn't know much but it wasn't the Germany he read about. It seemed unlikely that in a Germany trying to escape from its past and begin again, there were squads of killers looking for people as insignificant as Otto Fürst, traitors or not. Yet he did see fear in the German's eyes. If the danger was in his imagination, it was real to him. He felt the anxiety in Fürst. He could smell the paranoia. It wasn't unfamiliar. He had seen enough of it in his time. At least in part, he shared a world with Otto Fürst that did fuck people up. He didn't know if Fürst had ever killed anyone in pursuit of his trade, but he would have been a part of the trade of killing that went with the job. His words, his suspicions, his need to protect himself would have seen people killed. And on any side you cared to mention. If you worked as a double or triple agent, you couldn't be too particular. Living with that could get inside you. The fear could get inside too, the ever-present threat of exposure. And where the stuff of your life was made up of lie upon lie upon lie, you could lose touch with who you really were. Some people couldn't leave that behind. It stayed inside, eating at your head, once you let it take hold. It looked like Otto Fürst had done just that.

'There'll be nobody in Germany to care what you did, Otto. Let alone what you did here. We don't matter. You don't matter, believe me. You are nothing.'

'Mr Gregory, please, I'm begging you to help me, sir.'

There were tears in the German's eyes, but he cried them silently.

Superintendent Gregory stood up. There was no more he could say.

'It's not my decision. Truth be told, it was made the day you decided to take the King's shilling. Never a wise choice in Ireland. Without that, maybe things would have been different. I don't know. I understand you'll be deported in a couple of days. You'll be allowed to collect your belongings, but under the circumstances, you'll be kept in Garda custody till then.' Gregory turned to Dessie MacMahon, who still stood by the door. 'Stay with him. I'll send in the Guards.'

Otto Fürst shook his head slowly. He was beaten.

'There will be no need, Mr Gregory. As you say, I am nothing now.'

The superintendent turned back to the German.

'I kept very little that they gave me when I was sent to Ireland. We got kits from the Abwehr. All very German. Most of it was useless, except as a means of identifying us as German spies when we were picked up. But I did hold on to this.'

Otto Fürst's hand was in his pocket. He took it out and put something in his mouth. It was only in that instant that Terry Gregory glimpsed the capsule and understood what it was. He flung himself at the German, knocking him to the floor, kneeling over him, trying to pull open his mouth. Fürst was already unconscious.

'Get a doctor here, Dessie! It's fucking cyanide!'

Even as Dessie MacMahon moved to the door, Gregory stood up.

'Leave it. There's no hurry now. He's dead.'

He moved to the table and took a cigarette, still looking at Otto Fürst.

'With a bit of luck, that should be my last dead body.'

He lit the cigarette. He left the packet on the table and walked out.

It was three days later that Otto Fürst was buried at Deans Grange Cemetery, close to Dún Laoghaire harbour where, had he not found another exit, he would have boarded the mailboat the same day to be deported. Superintendent Gregory attended the funeral in the usual way, to observe and record who was there. He was surprised to find as many as eight hundred people standing round the swastika-flag-draped coffin. Many of the mourners wore black armbands with swastikas; embroidered, painted, stuck on or otherwise homemade. He registered several members of Éamon de Valera's government, some TDs with small majorities in heavily Republican constituencies. They were there to polish their Republican credentials, in a gesture they believed was empty of meaning. Nevertheless, when Gregory met the glances of those who knew him, they looked away and left soon afterwards. Only Dan Breen, TD for Tipperary, once a member of Michael Collins' Squad with a British £10,000 price on his head, held Gregory's gaze. There was a look of contempt that said, 'What the fuck are you doing here?' There were not many of the newer IRA men. The few he saw gave him a nod of grudging recognition. The Boys were, by and large, ahead of politicians clutching what was left of the dead neutrality the world barely remembered. They were absent, happy to let the dead bury the dead. There were some dutiful members of the German community; a handful of forgotten pro-Nazis from big houses Fürst may have passed through on his Irish wanderings. But most who wept only knew the spy from newspaper reports. Gregory wondered what they were weeping for. His most charitable thought was that they had no idea. He knew there was no point in what he was doing. He would not write a report. He would not bother to list the names. He would not pull out their files to add Otto Fürst's funerary rights to the catalogue of these people's mostly venial sins of omission and commission. None of this meant anything any more. Those days had gone, as he would soon be gone himself.

He waited as someone spoke the indistinct words of a short eulogy. He couldn't hear. It struck him that he probably knew the dead German better than almost anyone in the crowd of mourners. There was a murmur of appreciation as the eulogy stopped abruptly and suddenly a voice called out, 'Sieg Heil!' Several hands shot up in the Nazi salute. Others followed, tentatively, awkwardly, till almost eight hundred arms were raised, but many only for a matter of seconds.

The throng started to break up. The crowd thinned and people moved away, most taking off their armbands as they went, not quite prepared to wear them on the buses and trams home. Gregory watched the gravediggers shovel earth into Otto Fürst's grave, smoking several cigarettes. Finally he walked to the grave and looked down at a large wreath. The flowers were white and orange; with the green leaves they were woven into, they made the colours of the Irish tricolour. The dedication read, 'With deepest sympathy and honour to a soldier of Germany who was faithful unto death.' That was for debate. Whatever the German spy's faith, it seemed doubtful honour came into it. 'Little faith and less honour.' That might have been better. It was an epitaph Terry Gregory almost felt he could have shared.

When the superintendent walked away from the grave, the picture of the phalanx of raised arms was still in his head.

There was probably nowhere else in Europe where eight hundred people could have gathered in public round a coffin draped in the Nazi flag, with swastika bands on their arms, to celebrate a Nazi funeral and raise arms in a Nazi salute. Ireland had few luxuries to offer its citizens after twenty-five years of independence, but for those who wanted it, there was the opportunity to participate in perhaps Europe's last Nazi funeral, played out that May morning, as much of Ireland's war had been, as a dark, insentient mirage.

NOTES AND ACKNOWLEDGEMENTS

Brothers-in-Arms

E mmet Warde and his brother Charles are based on Emmet and Charles Dalton. Emmet Dalton was a major-general in the Irish Free State Army. He was at Béal na mBláth when Michael Collins died. He had an unsuccessful career as a private detective. In an unlikely turn of events he founded Ardmore Studios (and the Irish film industry) in 1958. Charlie Dalton was in Collins' Squad as a young man. He participated in Bloody Sunday, in November 1920; my description follows his account. He suffered mental problems that may have been PTSD, including anxiety attacks about would-be killers. Gunmen of the War of Independence and Civil War were seen, variously, even simultaneously, as heroes and brutal killers. If these things were even discussed, it was in an atmosphere of denial or celebration; sometimes both.

The murder of Eamon Kilmartin and Brendan Davey echoes the killing of three teenagers by unknown Free State soldiers at the Red Cow, near Dublin, in 1922. In the real killings, the bodies were found at the time. A peremptory investigation discovered no one responsible; the killers were probably Free

State Intelligence. Charlie Dalton was a more senior Intelligence officer than I have made Charlie Warde; if he didn't pull the trigger he may have given the nod to 'lesson-teaching'. There can be little question that he was instrumental in the cover-up.

The kidnap and trial of IRA Chief-of-Staff, Stephen Hayes, by Northern Command, is accurate in outline. His trial wasn't in Northern Ireland, but he used the subterfuge of a confession, much of it fiction, writing it for weeks not days. He escaped in circumstances that still remain unclear. Even at the time this was fictionalised; a *Newsweek* report has Hayes leaping out of a speeding car while he was fired at.

Hayes was gaoled in the Republic for IRA activity and returned to a civil-service job in Wexford. Seán McCaughey was gaoled over the death of another man suspected of informing. He went on hunger strike for political status. The protest was ignored; he died in 1947. Outside the Republican movement his death received little notice. The IRA learnt that hunger strikes, powerful weapons in the War of Independence and later during Northern Ireland's Troubles, only worked against the British.

Otto Fürst is based on German spy Hermann Goertz. His relationship with the IRA pits incompetence against incompetence, but it can be asked if his death, which happened as Fürst's, suggests a more compromised role in the Intelligence war. The Mountjoy escape involved another spy, Günther Schütz. Using women's clothes supposedly bought to send to his sister in Germany, it is as odd in fact as fiction. The Dutchman, van Loon, participated in an earlier escape attempt. Goertz's funeral was very much as Fürst's; a bizarre postscript to Ireland's war. Goertz did stay with Iseult Stuart at Laragh Castle. She was on Abwehr lists of safe houses. It is strange that her husband, Francis Stuart, and one-time lover, Ezra Pound, broadcast Axis-radio propaganda; both writers of substance, and in Pound's case, greatness. Whatever is the opposite of serendipity, there it is. References to broadcasts by Stuart and Pound do use their own words; dates may be post-1941.

John Betjeman worked as British press attaché in Dublin from 1941. He did receive a letter from the IRA to explain the rescinding of a plan to kill him, partly because someone liked his poetry; although the letter was sent after the war ended.

Altered Dates

In writing of the Second World War, mixing real characters and events with fiction has meant some history getting out of kilter. The obvious example is the bombing of Dublin's North Strand; six months late, after the British Blitz was over. However, the story coincides with German bombing of northern English cities, including some on the Irish Sea. Garda Commissioner Eamon 'Ned' Broy retired in 1938. I have kept him on because his role in the Stefan Gillespie stories is useful. Concerning Dublin street names that changed after 1921, I use the new to avoid confusion. There have been questions about Éamon de Valera's head-of-government title, in previous novels and sometimes when referring to the past. Post 1937 constitution, he is Taoiseach or Prime Minister, but before 1937 he is President (for President of the Executive Council). I apologise for all the anachronisms I may have missed.

Acknowledgements

Books that particularly contributed to this story: Charles Dalton's account of time as an IRA gunman and Intelligence officer, *With the Dublin Brigade (1917–21)*; Tim Pat Coogan's *The IRA*, still the best broad IRA history; Sean O'Callaghan's account of German spies, *The Jackboot in Ireland*, a book that sometimes lets imagination fill gaps but contains information unavailable elsewhere. I must also mention Carol Reed's 1947 film *Odd Man Out*; there is no similarity in story, but in the bleak and shadowy circularity of the IRA he shows, there was inspiration.